African Girl
The Awakening

Kezia Dzifa Awadzi

Afram Publications (Ghana) Limited

Published by:
Afram Publications (Ghana) Limited
P.O. Box M18
Accra, Ghana

Tel:	+233 244 314 103, +233 302 412 561
Kumasi:	+233 501 266 698, +233 322 047 524/5
E-mail:	info@aframpubghana.com
	publishing@aframpubghana.com
Website:	www.aframpubghana.com

Cover photo and design by: Afram Publications

Cover Image: Rachel Abdulai

First Published, 2016

ISBN: 978 9964 70 570 1

Dedication

This book is dedicated to my father, the Late Dr. Kwablah Awadzi (Papa), who lived by the principles of the 4Hs: Honesty, Humility, Hard work & lending a Helping hand.

&

My mother, Mrs. Patricia Elizabeth Ann Awadzi, who insists that her children always "Reach for the Stars."

Acknowledgements

I would like to thank the following people who supported me in various ways through this journey: Mrs. Patricia Awadzi, the Late Mrs. Beatrice Lokko, my sister Korkoene Awadzi, and friends: Judy Gilmore, Laura Winefordner, Adejoke Shitta-Bey, Lilliana Bell and Dr. Swathy Sundaram.

I would also like to take this opportunity to acknowledge my parents and siblings, my friends: Grace Ampaw and Dr. Josephine Asmah, Edmund Adu-Danso, Neil Mortagbe; Step Publishers, the University of Ghana Christian Fellowship, Praise Valley Temple, (Ghana); Booker Warren and Dr. Eunice Warren, Dr. and Mrs. Jim Winefordner, Dr. and Mrs. James Okine, Philip & Joyce Dankyi, Michiyo Endo-Higgins and Atsuko Kitayama.

I cannot articulate enough the role my cousin, friend, writing and business partner, Dr. Christine Lokko-Richter (CNN Lokko) played in this journey from the inception to date. CNN and I embarked on a writing competition marathon and shared chapters of our works along the way. Sometimes, the only thing that kept me writing late at night was the fact that CNN expected the next installment by the time she woke up. She provided encouragement and critical feedback, and over the years, we have talked about the characters as if they were living, breathing people. Christine has been there with me throughout the various revisions of the book and helped me find a publisher. Thank you, Christine, for helping to make my dreams come true.

I am very grateful to Afram Publications for giving me this wonderful opportunity. Thank you to Editor Agatha Akornor-Mills for polishing African Girl to be a better product than I dreamed it.

Chapter One

"Hello, you are Dzigbordi, aren't you?" a masculine voice breathed so close to my left ear that I jumped. The thick paperback flew out of my hands and narrowly missed hitting his chin. I looked into his smiling dark eyes and felt my heart skip a beat.

"Yes… sorry… I mean…," I stuttered.

"I am sorry. I didn't mean to startle you. I just wanted to find out what book you were so absorbed in," he said.

He stooped and retrieved the book from the floor and straightened up. He took a look at the cover. "Wow! Stephen King! I haven't read this one. Is it good?"

My heart was still beating loudly at the idea of chatting with "Gorgeous Mickey" (my pet name for him). However, I loved reading and could talk about books to anyone, even a popular boy like Michael Mclean-Brown. Did he love reading or was he merely being polite?

"Yes, it is. I am enjoying it very much. Have you read any of his books?"

"Almost all of his books," Michael said without hesitation. "The last one I read was *Salem's Lot*. I liked it."

"I have read it, but it gave me nightmares – all those descriptions about vampires sucking blood…."

Michael threw his head back and laughed heartily. He sat on the table adjacent mine. I couldn't believe it— gorgeous, popular

Michael McLean-Brown and I discussing books together?

His voice brought me out of my reverie. "It isn't that bad. He is a graphic writer, isn't he? May I borrow this when you're done? I notice you are always holding a different book. We have some story books at home. Perhaps we can do some exchanges?"

"Definitely."

For a moment, we sat smiling at each other without speaking— two book lovers who had found a potential source of fresh reading material.

Then, one by one, students began to return. The bell rang, signalling the end of the break period. Michael jumped down from the desk. He turned to leave, stopped and looked back at me. "By the way, my name is Michael or Mike, if you like."

"I know."

He raised a quizzing brow, smiled, and strode away.

This incident took place a month after I had been in Achimota School (a.k.a. *Motown*). Unlike many students in the sixth form who had been boarders throughout their secondary school life, this was my first time away from home. I found everything bewildering, and it didn't help that I was shy and awkward. I weathered my first term by burying my head into my ubiquitous story books. It was my escape; it also made me appear busy. During the 15-minute morning breaks, I remained in class to read while other students rushed off to buy snacks, and that is why Michael had found me deeply absorbed in a Stephen King novel.

With the initial awkwardness out of the way, Michael and I frequently discussed and traded books, and over time, other book lovers got to know I had a collection of books at home.

They started chatting with me, and during break times, we ended up in impromptu group discussions on books.

Anytime Michael approached me, my heart would pound wildly. My stomach muscles would clench and my hands would feel shaky. I found it impossible to start up a conversation; he always had to initiate our interactions. After a few months, though, I grew more relaxed around him and my violent emotions metamorphosed into tenderness, affection, and respect. I liked the feeling of being in a "special clique", privileged to be friends with a popular guy. Mickey was a tall, attractive, fair-coloured boy with brilliant black eyes, and short, black, unusually curly hair, courtesy of his European ancestry. His eyes and hair made him stand out in a crowd in which males with brown eyes and kinky black hair were the norm. Mickey was an athlete who ran the 100-meter race, a cadet, and a prefect; he was also one of the brilliant students taking courses towards admission to medical school.

After two years of sixth form and one year of national service, I was going to the university and would have to adjust to a new environment all over again. I was very happy when both Mickey and I got admission into the University of Ghana— he to the Medical School and I to the Department of Agriculture and Home Science. The new university environment brought new dynamics in my relationship with Mickey, especially my involvement with his cousin, Maxwell.

Each time I think about the two of them, I wonder why my initial encounter with Michael played such havoc with my emotions, but not so with Maxwell, until a year into our friendship.

Chapter Two

On my first day in Physical Chemistry class, the Teaching Assistant (TA) paired us up for lab work; I with Maxwell Owusu. All first year students of the university were required to take two general courses in African Studies and I found myself with Mickey and Maxwell in one of the courses. After our first session, I noticed Mickey standing with my new lab partner, Max (as he was generally known). I went over to say hello and found out that they were cousins. As I stood chatting with the two young men, I could not help but notice how all the females passing by slowed down and feasted their eyes on Mickey and Max. They were almost the same height; Mickey around six feet and Max an inch or so taller, and both had broad chests that made their hips appear very narrow in their blue jeans. But while fair-coloured Mickey's face was long, Max's was more oval-shaped, his skin the colour of dark chocolate, and his eyes dark liquid brown.

As our friendship grew, I noticed more similarities and differences between the cousins. Mickey and Max were very articulate with excellent command of the English language, a quality I admired in men. Unlike Mickey however, Max was not a versatile reader; he mainly enjoyed biographies and spiritual books. Temperamentally, Mickey was sensitive and introspective; Max was much more pragmatic and laid-back. We became a threesome, working together on our assignments and sharing meals together. Surprisingly, Max was a good cook, and with occasional help from Mickey, I did not have to always prepare the meals.

Max and I became closer after Mickey started dating Frances Acolatse, a dentistry student. "Frannie" as she was generally called, was always immaculately dressed. She stood at five feet seven inches and had warm natural golden skin men swooned over. She was neither slender nor full figured and had a full bosom and small, curvy hips. Her long straightened hair fell in soft waves below her shoulders. By virtue of her father being a career-diplomat, the family spent most of their life abroad and she had been born a British citizen. Frannie was avidly courted by men of all ages, but it was Mickey who won her heart. They became known as "the Golden Couple." Thus our circle widened, and though Frannie was a few months younger than I and was nice to me, her poise and sophistication made me feel awkward in her presence.

Max and I often studied together and soon formed the habit of walking together to and from church on Sundays. One day as we conversed in my room, Max intimated that he wanted to date Sister Florence Osei-Britwum, a member of the University Christian Fellowship (UCF). Max and I were members of the UCF drama group. My first reaction was a sinking feeling. No, I did not begrudge Max's desire to be in a relationship with Florence, but this could change things between us, we would no longer spend as much time together as we did. First Mickey, now Max.

"Sister Flo is in the UCF choir, as you already know. She recently joined the prayer warriors. We have been having some lovely chats after meetings; she's quite intriguing!" Max's long fingers gestured excitedly as he spoke. He leaned back in the armchair and assumed his favourite sitting position, one bare foot on the cushion.

"Is she interested?" I hoped that my voice displayed adequate enthusiasm.

"I think so," he said, flashing a broad, dimpled smile. "She said she has to seek the face of the Lord. I think it is going to be a yes!"

"Congratulations."

Oblivious to my lack of excitement, Max went on, "But I wouldn't count my chickens before they're hatched. I have a strong feeling that she wanted to say yes, but felt she had to at least pray about it first to feel right in her spirit."

Max began to regularly walk Florence home from church. Almost every day, Max extolled Florence's virtues. "She is so prayerful, Dzigbordi. Do you know she spends a minimum of three hours a day in prayer? She also fasts at least once a week."

What a show off! I thought but had to admit that perhaps jealousy was preventing me from thinking highly of Florence. After all, my time spent in prayer and Bible reading averaged an hour a day, and except for special occasions, I seldom fasted.

Two months after professing his love for her, Florence asked Max to meet him at the University Botanical Gardens for an all-day prayer and fasting. It lasted from 8:00 a.m. until 4:30 p.m.

"We prayed about everything today: our current friendship,

potential relationship, the duration of study in university, our families and ancestors (to break the chain of generational curses), the church, the government, the elections in December, overseas missionaries, and crime rates in America." Max recounted unenthusiastically that evening as he wolfed down rice balls and groundnut soup.

"Did she come to a decision about the two of you?" I was trying very hard to stifle a giggle at the picture of Max praying about generational curses and crime rates in America, when all he wanted was a "yes" to his proposal.

"Not yet, needs more time," he said.

Our eyes met, and before I realised it, I was doubled up with laughter. Max's lips curved in a reluctant smile.

As time went by, I noticed that Max's wonder and delight with Florence was rapidly transforming into irritation and frustration. Eventually, he stopped talking about her or walking her back after church. One afternoon after service, Max began dropping hints about Rosemary Quaye, one of the ushers.

"She is a devout Christian, but so simple and natural: her hair, her way of dressing, the way she talks…"

Not again! I mentally rolled my eyes. Rosemary Quaye was the extreme opposite of Florence: subdued prettiness, so quiet and placid, with a low sweet voice which one had to strain to hear. If Max had to start another relationship, why couldn't he do so with someone more "normal"?

Most of my friends were dating, but I had not yet met anyone I thought I wanted to be with long term. Male friends eventually ended up as buddies who confided in me about their love lives.

Usually on weekends, they came over for supper in my room on the fifth floor at the John Mensah Sarbah Hall Annex, which I shared with Rachel Kotoka. Fortunately, Rachel preferred studying in the library and often went home on weekends to be with her husband and kids.

My brother Mawuli was then in his final year in the Business Administration programme. Times when he condescended to visit me were, unsurprisingly, when he was hungry, bringing in tow a couple of friends. I would serve them supper, or at least biscuits and soft drinks.

One of his friends, Nii Ayi Nartey (my Chemistry TA), began showing up at my room without Mawuli, under the pretext that he was just passing by to say hello. At first, I was very cordial towards him, until his crude hints at wanting a sexual relationship cooled my attitude. But it seemed my coolness rather whetted his lasciviousness. I had to tread carefully; I had to think of my Chemistry grade.

One evening toward the end of the second term, I was alone in my room poring over an English assignment. So absorbed was I in my task that I barely registered the knock on the door. A louder series of knocks made me jump. I unlocked the door and pulled it open; there stood Nii Ayi, grinning.

"Hi Dzigbordi!" he said, pushing past me to enter my room. He was clad in a snug pair of blue jeans and a white tee-shirt that accentuated his upper muscular body. I caught a whiff of his strong after shave or perfume. He carried a folder which he set on my desk.

"I was just passing by to see a friend and I decided to stop by your door," he gave his trade mark excuse.

"Oh, I see... err... unfortunately, I am trying to complete my English assignment for Language and Study Skills. It is due tomorrow," I said.

I picked up the book from the bed and moved over to the desk.

Nii Ayi sat down in the armchair and waved off my apprehension. "Oh, that's so easy! You don't have to worry about that subject; everyone passes it. You should be more worried about Chemistry. Your last assignment wasn't good. I brought your lab notebook to show you."

He opened the folder and took out my lab notebook.

"What's wrong?" I asked. Chemistry was the course I was most anxious about. On the first day in his class, the wizened, bearded lecturer had peered at us over his thick lenses and announced that none of us would be earning an A in his class. Dr. Charles Fosu was not known as "Prof Evil" for nothing. We heard that in the previous year, two students had fainted in the middle of his exam paper from sheer terror. Nii Ayi's voice broke into my musings, "Come over here and let me show you." He patted the side of the bed close to the armchair. I moved over and stood by the bed. "Your calculations were wrong. You must have used the wrong measurement of hydrochloric acid, which affected the weight of the compound after titration." His stubby, well-trimmed fingernail jabbed at the section.

"I see," I said, my eyes following the movement of his finger and trying to follow his explanations. "How does that affect my final grade?"

"I took three points off for that, so you have 70% for this

assignment which is still an A though. You just have to make sure you don't make any more careless mistakes. Feel free to come to me for help with the class work as well. Prof Evil's examinations are very, very tough."

"Thank you very much, Nii Ayi." For the first time in a long while, I was able to look into his face and give him a genuine smile. He smiled back at me. I was uncomfortably aware that our faces were only a few inches apart.

"You're welcome, Dzigbordi. Your brother Mawuli is my friend, and I would hate his little sister to fail Chemistry."

His hand came to rest casually on my right thigh, then his grip tightened, slid down my leg, and then up again until it was in contact with the warm flesh underneath my skirt. Shock at his audacity rendered me immobile as I gasped and stiffened. I gripped the hand underneath my skirt and tried to pry it off, but it now clutched the soft portion of my upper inner thigh. I felt myself struggling desperately for air.

"Come on, Dzigbordi! Relax, girl!" Nii Ayi said gruffly. He rose up from the armchair and stood before me. I was trembling with fear and as I opened my mouth to scream, he leaned forward and dragged me into a tight embrace. His mouth fell on mine in a tight wet kiss, and as I gasped for air, he shoved a thick tongue into my mouth. Nausea started to build from the middle of my stomach. After what seemed like eternity, he removed his tongue and started raining short passionate kisses on my face. I was so relieved that he was no longer kissing me mouth-to-mouth that his other kisses didn't seem to register. I was trying to recover my breath. His hands ran over me, and he murmured terms of endearment nonstop.

"Darling Dzigbordi! How I have longed to do this! You are so soft and so sweet! You feel so good. I promise I shall make it good for you too. Come on, girl, relax, don't fight it… go with the flow… Dzi… Dzigbordi!"

Behind my eyes, I saw white whirling specks flickering across a black screen and knew I was seconds away from fainting. I could scarcely breathe, let alone scream. In desperation, I dug my fingernails into his upper arms and then dragged them down sharply. Nii Ayi gave a ragged gasp and drew back. He shoved me away from him and I fell on the bed directly behind us, and narrowly missed hitting my head against the wall.

"What's the matter… with… you?" His dark brown eyes were bigger and darker than I had ever seen them. His left fist was clenched as if he was trying hard not to hit me. We were both panting. Nii Ayi clutched at his upper arms and inspected them. I could see traces of blood from the scratches on his skin. We glared at each other. I was struggling speak when I heard a knock on the door. I said, "Come in!"

Nii Ayi pulled down the sleeves of his tee shirt as he hurriedly plopped into the armchair. The door opened and in walked Max. I was now sitting on the bed, panting and sweating slightly. I didn't have to look in a mirror to know my elaborate hairstyle, done only that morning had become dishevelled. Nii Ayi was rubbing his arms as if he was trying to dispel goose bumps from his skin. Max looked from one to the other, his face registering a mix of suspicion and displeasure.

Nii Ayi asked, "Hey, Owusu, how be?"

"Fine," Max answered, still giving us a weird look.

11

"Sit down, Max. Would you like something to drink?" I asked hurriedly.

"I am okay," Max said. He walked over to my desk, moved the chair closer to Nii Ayi and sat down.

Nii Ayi said, "I was just in the vicinity and decided to drop in and say hello."

"That's nice of you," Max said. For the next twenty minutes, the three of us sat talking about the weather and politics. I kept shooting meaningful glances at Max, hoping he would discern my reluctance to be left alone with our TA.

Fortunately, Rachel returned from her outing. Nii Ayi said goodbye and left.

Soon after, Max also said his goodbyes.

"Let me see you off," I said.

As we descended the stairs, Max asked in as casual a tone as he could muster, "So…what is going on between you and our TA?"

"He was trying his dirty tricks on me! You don't know how glad I was when you arrived!"

My fear came rushing back and I felt my legs weaken. I stopped and held onto the scarred wooden banister. "He was interested in fooling around and didn't seem happy when I scratched him with my nails." I tried to sound lighthearted, so that I would not break down and weep.

"Dzigbordi, you need to take better care of yourself. What would you have done if no one had arrived?" Max asked.

I shrugged. "It is hard…I am not used to being rude to people…."

"Do you want to be harmed before you realise that the guy is an ass?"

I was shocked at Max's harsh, sarcastic tone. I felt hurt and then angry. "Why are you sounding as if I am to blame for what happened?"

I was still quivering with silent rage as we descended the last of the stairs that led to the Porters' Lodge.

He glared at me, "Dzigbordi, all I'm trying to tell you is that, in the long run, if you allow these things to go on, it would not matter who was at fault or whether you wanted to be a nice, well-behaved girl. Some things are irreversible! It is better to err on the side of caution and be rude than to allow things to slide until it is too late."

It was as if Max had poured oil on the blazing flames of rage that had been ignited ever since Nii Ayi laid hands on me. "So... you are saying that I was wrong for opening the door? Perhaps, I should have been a clairvoyant and realised that he was the one behind the door when he knocked, eh? Or I am to blame for inviting him in? Or you are saying that it is my fault because he jumped on me and forced his thick, slimy, repulsive tongue down my throat?"

All the pent up feelings of the past hour —stress, fear, anger, revulsion broke through the dam and the tears just poured down my cheeks.

In an instant, Max's anger vanished. "Dzigbordi, please don't cry, I am sorry." He whipped out a clean handkerchief from his breast pocket, then placing a hand on my shoulder, drew me closer, and began to gently wipe the tears off my face. "Please

13

stop it, I can't bear to see you cry." His voice shook ever so slightly, making me cry harder. What would have happened to me? Max gave up trying to stop my tears and rested my head on his shoulder. After a while, I moved away from him, clutching his wet and wrinkled handkerchief.

"I am sorry, Max, I don't know what came over me," I said. "I will wash it and return it tomorrow."

"The hankie doesn't matter, Dzigbordi. I didn't mean to blame you. It's just that I care so much about you that I don't want anyone to ever hurt you that way." Max's voice shook again. My heart did a somersault. In an instant, the atmosphere became charged. I didn't feel like crying anymore. Instead, there was a feeling of surprise and excitement. We looked at each other in silence. For the first time since we had become friends, I was taking a good, hard look at Max Owusu. I had been so used to him, so comfortable in his presence, that it was a long time before I really saw him. I gazed into his eyes and felt my heart pounding away. This was the man that women on campus wanted. He was not only very attractive and young but caring and protective. Now it seemed there was an emotional side to imperturbable Max. As the silence continued, I strongly suspected that things would no longer be the same between us. He opened his mouth to speak, but just then, a mutual friend, Jacob Mahama, who was passing by, stopped to chat, and Max eventually left with him.

That night, sleep fled from me. In the silence of the night, I kept interrogating what had transpired that evening between Max and I. What on earth had happened between us? Could

I be falling for him? My previous crushes on guys had been at first encounters. Now, I couldn't wait to see Max again, but I was also apprehensive. He was my buddy; I didn't want anything to ruin our relationship.

Much as I strongly suspected that things would no longer be the same between us, I was surprised when now we only worked together on assignments, but did nothing together outside course work. Our conversations were no longer spontaneous and our interactions turned slightly awkward. There was a feeling of anxious waiting, like waiting for a storm to break.

As for Nii Ayi, the next time we met in class, he barely gave me a glance. I became worried. Was he planning an academic reprisal against me? What to do? I didn't feel it expedient to involve Mawuli. My brother's temper was hard to stir but difficult to cool down when aroused. I asked Rachel for advice, feeling that she might offer a mature approach. Her suggestion was that I apologise to Nii Ayi. So one afternoon, after all the other students had dispersed, I offered Nii Ayi my apology. Surprisingly, he shrugged and said he had possibly "misread the signs." His rather flippant attitude made me mad. The cheek of the guy! It appeared I had no recourse to his impunity. Instead, I had to tiptoe around him so that he didn't ruin my grades. Why is life so unfair?!

Max and I eventually resumed our routine, but now I took extra care about my appearance. I even started putting on makeup. Sometimes when we were walking at night, Max would reach out and hold my hand for a few minutes. How long were we going to circle around the situation? What about Rosemary Quaye?

Max had stopped discussing his love interest with me after the Nii Ayi debacle.

"How is Rosemary Quaye doing?" I asked casually one evening just before we parted company.

"Rosemary... hmm... she's fine," he said in a low voice, avoiding my eyes. He led the way out of his room and locked the door behind him, pulling down the handle to ensure the door was secure. We began to walk toward the stairs in silence when he stopped, "Dzigbordi?"

"Hmm?" I stopped.

"I am no longer interested in Rosemary Quaye."

I felt my treacherous heart start a thump-thump beat.

"Oh?"

"Dzigbordi." He faced me, "I had wanted to wait until exams were over before we talked, but I feel we need to do so now to clear the air."

"Hmm...hmm...?"

"Will you come over to breakfast tomorrow morning? I'd like to ask you something," he said.

"Sure, thank you," I answered. "What time would you want me over?"

"How about nine o'clock?"

"Okay, see you then!"

Forgetting that he was about to see me off to my hall, I raced down the stairs. I could hear him chuckling as he stood on the landing.

Chapter Three

It was a few hours before my breakfast meeting with Max. I was still in bed, excited about the day before me, yet trying hard to focus on my quiet time.

"Lord, thanks for this great morning. You know what I am thinking, so I am not going to beat about the bush by praying for the poor and hungry and the cessation of wars across the world. I believe Max's going to talk about our relationship and where it is going, and I am not sure what to say. I like him a lot; I do love him as a friend. Honestly, I don't know whether this romantic feeling I am developing is just an aberration. I want him to kiss me, yet I am afraid that he would want to kiss me. Oops!" I gave a horrified giggle, "I am sorry Lord…that was unspiritual, although you created human beings, so in a way those feelings are from you. I am attracted to him, but I don't know whether I want to spend the rest of my life with him."

Most Christians I knew seemed to have the art of prayer down pat. Florence Osei-Britwum, Max's first love interest, was an expert in articulate praying. She always began with a hymn. In her introductory statements, Florence would rattle off a string of accolades and salutations such as "God Almighty, Most Merciful God, Lord of Hosts, King of Kings, Lord of Lords, Alpha and Omega, Jehovah, Yahweh, Omniscient God, Omnipresent

God, Omnipotent God…." She then used scriptural verses to support each prayer request. All throughout the prayer, we would chime in with "hallelujahs" and "amens". All Florence's prayers ended with "…in the matchless name of Jesus. Amen!" I on the other hand was more comfortable speaking simply as I stated my feelings, requests, and ambiguities. I wrapped up my prayer for the morning and hurried out of bed to take a quick shower. I dressed up in a knee length black skirt and my favourite flowery tee-shirt with large orange, green and white petals.

By 8:40am, I was ready. My permed hair was held in a ponytail by a hair band with a few curls left over my forehead. I looked at myself in the mirror and thought I looked quite nice. Finally, I picked up my handbag and key and locked the door, making sure that I switched my indicator on the door from "In" to "Away" before going downstairs to leave the room key at the Porters' Lodge and set off to Max's room.

****

Max was in Akuafo Annex B with Ali, a second year student majoring in Mathematics. Akuafo Annex B was directly across my annex, separated by a soccer field. At night, when standing on the corridor outside my room, it was possible to look across and see inside Max's room when the curtains were up and the room was lighted. It took me barely five minutes to walk to the annex, and another five to make it up the stairs to the second floor. I stood outside Max's door and took a deep breath. I knocked, and a few seconds later, the door swung open and Max was smiling at me.

"Come in, Dzigbordi, you look very lovely today," he grinned, reaching out a finger to touch one of the curls on my forehead.

"Thanks, how are you doing?" I asked as I dropped my bag on the bed and followed him to the verandah. Max was wearing khaki shorts and a tee-shirt and looked casual and totally relaxed.

"I am doing great. Breakfast is almost ready," he said as he turned over some French toast which smelled delicious.

"Anything I can do to help?" I asked looking around.

"Nope, all set! We are having cocoa and French toast. I also have rice water." He added, "Oh, the French toast is ready. You can put that on the table. I will be there in a jiffy."

Ten minutes later, we were seated across each other having a delicious breakfast. During breakfast, we talked about our first year university examinations, (FUEs) which were going to start in about six weeks. (Interestingly, freshmen were given the accolade FUEs). Already, students had started to curtail the nights of partying. Most of us were trying to recover notes taken in coursework from almost a year back. Professors were practically demigods, requesting absolute obedience from students. We weren't allowed to talk in class unless we raised a hand to answer a question. We didn't dare interrupt them when they were dictating lecture notes, so we frantically scribbled away and after class, borrowed notes from others who wrote faster and had better handwriting, to fill in the gaps.

Max and I discussed how we planned to study the various subjects; the final examination timetable was going to be on the bulletin board in a week's time. Our relaxed conversation during breakfast became rather sporadic as we cleared up and washed the dishes. Back in the room, Max sat on his bed and I took the armchair close to the bed. I wracked my brain for something to break the silence. "So, where is Ali? Did he go somewhere for the weekend?"

"No, he's around," Max said. I tried once more to break the silence.

"Did you narrow him?" I teased. "Narrowing" was a term used when a student bluntly or subtly got rid of the roommate so he or she could entertain his girlfriend or her boyfriend uninterrupted. Narrowing could extend overnight. Fortunately, my married roommate Rachel spent her weekends at home and did not have to "narrow" me.

"Kind of," said Max, laughing mischievously in response to my question. "I know it would have been more convenient to meet at your place, but I wanted to prepare breakfast and it just seemed easier to do it from here. Besides, Ali has narrowed me before and I have never done that to him, so I don't feel guilty."

"So Max, what do you want to talk to me about?" I had had enough dilly-dallying. He looked surprised, smiled and reached out for my hand. I smiled too at the warm tingly sensation and tightened my clasp.

"Dzigbordi, we've known each other since we started Legon. I still remember the first time I met you at chemistry practicals. You were wearing this plain navy blue tee shirt, with jeans and you looked so apprehensive! Then we ended up as lab partners and I found out from Mike you two had been classmates in Achimota," he said.

"Yes, Mickey was the first person who tried to get to know me," I said.

"I know, you told me that before. I already knew about you. I spent the long vacation with Mike years ago and when talking about the new sixth form students, he spoke about this new girl who always buried her head in story books. He said that although it was obvious you liked reading, he thought you did it because you were very shy. He decided to chat with you, knowing that other students would follow suit when they saw you were harmless," Max said with a grin.

"Oh…I thought he did so because he loved story books," I said, feeling a little bit let down.

"He did enjoy talking with you about books and exchanging books," Max assured me, "but he has always been good at going beneath the surface of things. He feels he has to step in and solve every problem. He is always reaching out and helping people, which is why he wants to be a doctor. I think it is because he is the oldest of his siblings and they lost their father when Mike was only twelve. He had to provide a lot of emotional support to his mother and siblings. But…my purpose of this meeting is not to talk about Mike."

"Why did you want us to meet?" I said, trying very hard to keep my voice steady.

"Well…over the last year, we have gotten to know each other very well. I have had girlfriends in the past, but you are the first girl I have felt so comfortable with. I thought of you as a sister and friend, but lately, I know I feel more than that." He looked down at our hands which were still joined.

"What do you feel?" I asked softly. Surprisingly, although I still felt the whirling excitement, I sounded calm and in control.

"I love you," he said, looking straight at me, "I want to know you also love me the same way, at least that there is a chance you would do so. I am hoping that this is the start of something that would end in marriage."

I smiled inwardly. The dramatist in me couldn't help but stand outside myself and watch what was going on. I opened my mouth, but before I could speak, he went on. "Dzigbordi, before you give me your answer, there are certain things you should know," he said.

My heart gave an unpleasant thump at the serious note.

"What is going on?" I said.

"I know we've talked a lot about ourselves. You've told me about your family and I have met Mawuli. My family is different," he said slowly. "You come from a very stable family. My father had two wives. I know I told you about my brother Alex, and a younger sister Adwoa Serwaa. However, I also have two half-brothers and a sister. My mother is the second wife. My father married Mummy five years after his first marriage. It was very stressful on both families. We lived in the same compound for years, and I won't even go into all the drama and fights that took place. One time, my brother Alex threatened our stepmother, Auntie Lydia, with a machete. The neighbours had to physically subdue him, or I am certain he would have injured her; he hated her so much! Another time, my mother and Auntie Lydia got into this huge wrestling match. It was bad; I will never forget that night. It was dark and stormy, with lightning and thunder, and here were two grown women rolling in the mud, scratching each other with their finger nails, and trying to pull each other's hair out. My father stood by unable to stop them. The neighbours had to step in once more.

"I used to feel like we were the local entertainment. Sometimes it took all the courage I had to hold my head up when walking through that neighbourhood. Fortunately, my dad built a second house and we got to leave the Mamprobi area. My stepmom stayed on at Mamprobi with her children."

Max stared in space as if he was lost in a different, darker universe. I had to bite my lip to prevent the torrent of questions from escaping. Perhaps this wasn't the right time to ask for more information. If I had known Max for this long and he hadn't mentioned his father's other nuclear family, it must be a situation that weighed heavily on his heart. I sat still, my hand in Max's, too afraid to move.

After about a minute of silence, he went on. "Anyway, my stepmother died two years ago and all her children have scattered. I don't get to meet them anymore."

"It must have been very hard for you," I said gently, "I am sorry you had to go through that, but I don't see why it should have an effect on our relationship. I know that it is only by the grace of God that I didn't end up in a similar situation."

Two-family set-ups were not an unusual occurrence , and created tension, especially for urban families. Limited space, insufficient financial resources for food, clothing, and school fees, made co-wives antagonists and turned half-siblings against one another. The horror stories I heard from friends made me appreciate Papa for not having a second wife.

Max broke into my thoughts, "I am happy this is not an issue for you, Dzigbordi."

"Why should it be an issue?" I hadn't heard of this being a criterion for selecting a marriage partner.

He hesitated.

"What is it?" I said.

"Well… it was an issue for Sister Florence," he said rather awkwardly.

"What!" I said, and then a light bulb went off in my head. "Oh… so that is why Florence went on praying for six months? I always thought that was a trifle bit excessive."

Max cracked a smile, "Yes. I also didn't think it was an issue at first. When I told her I was interested in her, she said she had to pray about it, which I expected from someone like Sister Flo. She asked a few questions, and when she got to know a friend of hers, Elizabeth Owusu, was my half-sister she was not happy. Apparently, over the years, Lizzie had given her own version of the two-family situation to Florence. She would have been happier if Mummy had been the first wife; then she could see her in the light of the 'wronged' woman.

"She said she and her prayer partner, Brother Samuel, had seen spiritual forces of darkness that were keeping my family in captivity because of my father having two wives. That is why we spent an entire day praying and fasting in the gardens to break the forces of darkness and chains of captivity over the Owusu family."

It was a serious situation, but I had to bite my lip to stop a smile. I could just picture Florence in prayer mode.

"Wow! And she did all that work and didn't forget to pray for crime rates in America! Did you break the forces of darkness?" I couldn't resist asking.

"I don't know," Max shrugged. "After several months, I felt she was stringing me along and decided to let go of the issue. I also think by then, deep down, I knew I was beginning to care about you," he said softly.

"Oh Max," I said, melting, "I hope I am not second best because Florence Osei-Britwum did not accept your proposal?"

He shot me a look of astonishment, "Of course not! I cannot believe you'd think that! Dzigbordi, in retrospect, I cannot say I was in love with Florence. In theory, she appeared perfect—beautiful, prayerful, committed to the Lord's work, evangelising and doing good deeds. Actually, I think she has the right motive, but she has some growing up to do. She would have driven me crazy in just a week! Perhaps, she would make an excellent minister's wife someday," Max continued, "I know you, Dzigbordi, and I love you for who you are. Perhaps, because we began as friends, we didn't have the opportunity to pretend with each other. My experiences with Sisters Flo and Rosie made me appreciate you all the more. I love your frankness, I love your sense of fun and the unique way you pray. I have enjoyed our time together so much. However, I didn't know just how much you meant to me until that night when I visited you and saw you and Nii Ayi looking as if you had been caught in flagrante delicto."

I tittered. Max occasionally loved to drop big words and phrases. He continued, "I am sorry I was so hard on you that night. I was just scared and angry that someone would do something to a woman who is so special and beautiful. I wanted to protect you, but I just didn't know how. I couldn't sleep that night. I wanted to go over to Nii Ayi's and beat him up for what he did to you, but I had no right to do that. I have barely looked at him in class ever since. I am praying I complete Chemistry without doing anything I would regret. The intensity of my feelings astounded me. I had to step back for a while."

I was so moved by his honesty that it was hard to know what to say.

"Dzigbordi, I have been going on about how I feel but have not given you the opportunity to respond."

"I don't know, Max…honestly," I said slowly as I tried to sort out my thoughts and feelings. "I like you a lot. You are the first guy I have been this close to apart from my brother. I have had so much fun. Lately, I have found myself thinking about you night and day and wanting to spend all my time with you. I have also been jealous of Rosemary when I thought you would start courting her. It must be love, right? At least, I am willing to go along on that premise."

"Oh Dzigbordi!" he exclaimed joyously, and then he was pulling me up. For a moment I had a flashback to when Nii Ayi pulled me toward him weeks ago, and then, I was no longer afraid. We were standing clasped in each other's arms. I raised my head and Max Owusu kissed me for the first time. It lasted less than a minute, and I was happy to note that my bad experience with Nii Ayi hadn't ruined my reactions to his kiss. His lips lingered on mine; firm, but not forceful. I found myself responding to his kiss. I felt excited, yet safe.

"Does that meet your expectation, Miss Dzigbordi?" Max teased, "I know you are a connoisseur of love scenes from all those books you have been reading!"

We laughed. I was giddy with excitement. We sat on his bed with our arms wound around each other's waists. We sat in relaxed silence, playing with each other's fingers.

"I don't know how I am going to mention it to my parents, or if I should do so for now," I said, thinking out loud. "We haven't talked about boyfriends before. I am not even sure whether Mawuli has introduced his girlfriend Gifty to them."

"I don't want to hide and sneak around," Max said, "but if you want to wait a while to tell your parents about me that is fine. I want you to visit me during the long vacation, and that means that it is inevitable that you will meet my mother, and probably my father. That reminds me, there is another issue I hate to raise, but must discuss with you."

"What is it?" I asked.

"It is my father…it is not personal, but he doesn't like Ewes much," Max said so quietly that I had to strain to hear him. His eyes wouldn't meet mine and he stared down at our linked hands. Papa was an Ewe and therefore by default I was one.

"What do you mean by 'doesn't like Ewes much'?" Without realising it, my voice rose. All the warm and gooey romantic thoughts fled.

"At work, an Ewe man got a promotion my dad was in line for just because the boss was from his tribe. This has happened to him more than once. I am sure he will get to like you once he knows you, but I mention it because he might be a bit difficult or standoffish at the beginning, and I don't want you to think that it is because he doesn't like you as a person."

Max lifted his head and looked into my eyes. His brown eyes were dark and pleading for understanding. I ignored their message. "But…that's not fair! Why should he hate all people from the Volta Region because of his experience? Why should a person's tribe be a basis for dislike?" I tried hard to control my voice which had begun to shake with anger and disappointment. I had heard stories in the past about some families who insisted that their children married within their ethnic group, but it was the first time I had heard of one tribe being written off because of a bad experience from one member.

"I am sorry. I shouldn't have mentioned it, at least not now. I have spoilt everything," Max said contritely.

"I cannot believe this!" I said, disentangling my fingers from his and sitting up. Although I was classified as Ewe, because of my father, my mother was a Ga from Accra. Perhaps, because we spent a greater portion of our lives in the Northern Region, Mawuli and I did not grow up selecting friends based on ethnicity. My parents had friends from different ethnic groups. So the possibility that Max's father would object to my ethnicity was a bitter pill to swallow.

"Why on earth did you make your father's second family an issue when this is more important?" I said.

Max said nothing.

"Pity it didn't work out with Sister Florence Osei-Britwum," I spat out. "She would have been the perfect partner for you, not only spiritually, but she would have met your family's expectation since she is Akan!"

I stopped my tirade at the stricken look on Max's face. "Oh Max!" I threw my arms around him and buried my face in his chest. "I am so sorry; it is not your fault."

He held me tight. "Dzigbordi, do you want to bail out? I will understand. I shouldn't have brought it up, at least, not today. I just wanted to cover all the bases so that you wouldn't find it weird if you visited me, met my dad, and he didn't act friendly."

"Of course, I don't want to bail out!" I said, guilty at the loss of my temper. "It was just unexpected. I appreciate that you told me about this. If you say things will work out, I am sure they will."

"True!" Max lightened up. "Besides, we do have to pass our first university examination! We have to make sure we survive that before making any further plans." He looked at his watch. "It is past noon. Ali is due back at twelve thirty. What do you want to do? I can come over to your place and we can study for a while, or if you want a break from me, I will see you off and we can meet later for supper."

"Why not come over to my place and we can study. I have some jollof rice we can have for lunch. We can do some more studying and then have supper."

"Give me a minute to change and then we can leave."

I moved onto the balcony and shut the door behind me. I saw some guys playing football on the field between our halls. It was a beautiful afternoon, but my emotions were far from beautiful. I leaned my chin against the wall; I felt drained from the seesaw of my emotions of the past three hours. I now had my first official boyfriend, but things were turning out to be

29

more complex than I had envisaged with stories of a depressing childhood and a tribalistic father. The door opened behind me. I turned. Max reached out his hand to me. Soon after, we were on our way downstairs to Sarbah Hall.

Chapter Four

The sound of a loud voice in the distance woke me up. It was the muezzin's call from the mosque five miles away. The night was still pitch-black outside my bedroom window. In about half an hour, the cocks would start crowing— first the lone innovative leader, then the rest would chime in and continue practically nonstop until daybreak. It was like that every day, two regular wakeup calls— the call to prayer, and then the crowing of the cocks between 5:00 and 6:00 a.m. If I wasn't out of bed by 6:30, Mama would be at my door, starting with a rapid fire of knocks, and finally thrusting the door open and poking a stern-looking face inside.

It was the first morning home after the end of year examinations. I was exhausted, the past six weeks had been a whirlwind of activities in my personal and academic life. The University of Ghana's end of year examination, fearfully known as "Mfodwo", named after a previous registrar, had taken over our lives the last weeks of the term. It was a very stressful time, heralded by sleepless nights, anxiety, weight loss, poor eating habits, and in some cases, poor hygiene. The university campus had been practically dead the last weeks of the term. Many students stayed away from their rooms, selecting places of study where they might be most productive. We went about carrying loads of books to and from the fully-packed libraries. Max and I studied together in our rooms, but at times, we would take a trip to the Balme Library. Despite the stressful period prior to Mfodwo, we had a wonderful time. We saw each other every day, sometimes for lunch, but almost always for supper which we usually bought from the night market on campus. It was around that time I started calling him "Maxi" and in return he settled on "DD" for me.

When we weren't studying, we were kissing, and making out. The exploratory respectful kisses we had exchanged on the day he professed his love had spiralled out of control into heavy petting sessions. The first time it happened on a Saturday night, I felt so guilty that I refused to go to church the following morning. We had discussions about the issue a number of times, and agreed to curtail those sessions, but the longest we went without that was three weeks.

The examinations had been a blurred nightmare. My finals were at different locations. My last exam for the year took place in the Great Hall, on the hill where the Registrar's office is located. It was an exhausting and sweaty 20-minute walk from my hall of residence. By this time, I was physically and mentally exhausted and more interested in getting Mfodwo over and done with than the outcome. I gladly turned in my paper 10 minutes before time and rapidly descended the hill in an effort to avoid postmortem sessions from my colleagues.

Maxi and Mawuli were scheduled to complete their last papers the following day after which I would leave for home (my parents didn't know my exam schedule). Mawuli was fervently hoping to make at least a Second Class Upper Division.

The following day, by the time Maxi's exam ended at noon, I was all packed up and ready for Papa to come pick me at 5:00 p.m. I said my goodbyes and went to share a lunch of kenkey, fish and pepper. I felt sad as Maxi and I emptied his drawers and boxed up books in cartons. Although I had gone home for the Christmas and Easter holidays, these rooms had been home the greater part of the past year. The emptying of the rooms was a realisation that we were going to be apart for three months… that seemed like such an eternity.

We sat side by side, our backs against the wall, on the bare mattress and shared a bar of Golden Tree chocolate he had discovered behind his bookcase. I rested my head on Maxi's shoulder, and he broke little squares of chocolate and held them to my lips to nibble on. Although we were alone, we spoke in low soft voices and kissed intermittently. It was very hard to contemplate that after living in each other's pocket for so long, we would have to change our routine. The only thing that made it partially bearable was planning how soon we could meet during the vacation. I wanted us to meet clandestinely, but Max insisted that it was best we did not hide our relationship from the parents. I knew that it was going to be difficult to broach that topic with my parents, but still promised to do so before Max's first visit.

We decided that I would break the news to my parents that for the first time I would be having a male visitor. If my parents were not amenable to that idea, I would send a message to him through his cousin Mickey. His home telephone had been out of order for a while, and his father was in no hurry to have the line restored because of the high bills.

Around 4:30 p.m., Maxi walked me to my room and left after an exchange of passionate goodbye kisses.

****

I was hovering between sleep and wakefulness when I heard the sound of one of the bedroom doors opening. I glanced at my bedside clock; it was a few minutes to 5:00 a.m. I stretched myself awake. The morning routine at home hardly differed; between 5:30-6:00 a.m., Mawuli, myself, and Naa Norkai (the young girl living with us) woke up and performed our assigned chores. My responsibility was to prepare my parents' breakfast tray and at the same time supervise Naa Norkai to sweep the corridors, the compound and take out the garbage. Mawuli swept and dusted the sitting room, and watered the plants. We all took turns scrubbing the bathtub and the toilet.

Today, I spent the first half hour washing my face, popping a piece of the fibrous yellow tree bark, *taa kotsa,* into my mouth and using the bathroom. I smiled as I chewed the sponge; even after the advent of the toothbrush and toothpaste introduced by the colonisers, Ghanaians, especially those along the coast, still had faith in the indigenous tooth-cleaning agent.

It was almost a quarter to six when I banged on Mawuli's door and proceeded to the kitchen. Eleven-year old Naa Norkai, looking as if she had just jumped out of a nap at the sound of my approach was assiduously examining a collection of brooms to select one for sweeping the compound. She was a distant relative of Mama's who had been living with us for the past year. She had come to stay with us so that in return for food and

34

board, she would help around the house since her parents did not have enough resources to take care of all their children. I would say Naa Norkai (and indeed all young relations who had stayed with us over the years) was lucky because my teacher-mother made sure that people who stayed with her learned how to read and write in English. Years before I went to boarding school, I was responsible for teaching these girls the alphabet. For a long time, I wanted to be a teacher because of the sense of pride and satisfaction I got when one of them could finally speak English.

"Good morning, Sister Dzigbordi," Naa greeted me in English, and with the respectful designation "sister" because I was older than her.

"Morning ,Naa, how are you doing?"

"Fine, thank you."

"Are you chewing your taa kotsa?" I asked. Mama was a firm believer in taa kotsa. Even though it had a bitter flavour and generated a lot of saliva, she believed that it was a better mouth cleanser. You used the toothbrush and toothpaste afterward for the flavor and soothing menthol effect.

Naa opened her mouth wide so I could see the yellow ball of mass in the middle of her tongue.

"Have you turned off the outside lights?" I went on with a mental checklist as I filled the kettle and set it on the stove.

"I am just about to do that and then sweep outside," she responded, picking up the palm frond broom.

"Okay, go ahead and do that now. No daydreaming on the job," I admonished. I started washing oranges to peel and

35

squeeze for my parents' breakfast. I could hear the theme song for BBC World News on the radio from their bedroom. Mawuli stumbled groggily into the kitchen as I was preparing to carry the tray. He selected a broom and duster; Mawuli was definitely not a morning person, and at 23 years, did not relish being dragged out of bed in the morning to do house chores.

But alas, Papa strongly believed that sleeping beyond 6:30 a.m. was a sign of laziness. "You cannot just stay in bed all day!" he ranted one day when he found that Mawuli and I were sleeping in late after we had stayed up watching a movie until 2:30 that morning. "You need to show interest in the house even if it is only watering a plant or two."

Now Mawuli was definitely being grouchy, "You could have waited for about half an hour before banging on my door."

"Oh… excuse me for being conscientious!" I retorted.

He mumbled some rude response and went out.

I heard the door of my parents' bedroom open and Mama's approaching footsteps.

"Good morning, Mama," I greeted.

"Good morning, Dzigbordi, how are you doing?"

"Fine, thank you. The tray is ready. Shall I bring it in?"

"In a minute; Papa is in the bathroom." She went on. "I think we will have some okro and garden egg stew today with yam. If we don't have all the ingredients, you'll have to go to the Kaneshie market, so make a list of grocery items we may need."

"Yes Mama," I responded, secretly delighted at the opportunity of getting out of the house.

"Where is Naa?" Mama asked.

"Still sweeping outside," I said, "Mama, I think she has improved tremendously with her English."

Mama smiled. "I am happy about that. You and Mawuli should practice more with her during the holidays. Oh, I hear Papa. Please take the tray to the bedroom." Mama moved toward the sitting room to talk with Mawuli.

I knocked on the door and Papa's deep voice bade me enter. He was clad in his favourite pink Chinese dragon dressing gown. I exchanged greetings with him and then set the tray by his bedside table and placed his cup of instant Nescafé and orange juice on coasters.

"So...what are you kids going to do during your vacation?" Papa said after he had taken the first sip of his coffee and nodded approval.

"Nothing much, just the usual... I will catch up on my reading and visit Grandma and the relatives," I said.

"Hmm!" he grunted. "I think we need to have a meeting with you and your brother and find out how the term went and what your plans are for the near future," he said.

Oh no! Papa's early morning meetings were something else—discussions about our school work, future plans, challenges, and successes. They usually took place before we returned to school from the holidays. He would meet us one-on-one, complete with a personalised folder.

"Okay, Papa." I said out loud. " When would you want us to have the meeting?"

"Why not today?" His response struck a note of terror in my heart.

I was counting on casually informing Mama that a male friend may pass by to visit one of these days. The meeting was going to upset my plans to gently introduce the Maxi topic to Mama.

Papa's meetings covered every aspect of our lives and there was no way I could avoid talking about Maxi. If Papa disapproved, that would be the end of it.

"Let Mawuli know. It is now 6:30, we can start at 7:00 GMT. I will begin with Mawuli."

Papa gave me an astute glance as if he could sense my apprehension. I stepped out of the bedroom and almost bumped into Mama.

"I checked the storeroom and I think we need some tomato puree and bathing soap. Make sure you add that to the list," she said. "I would like you back by one so that we can finish the cooking early."

"I will probably leave around nine thirty. Papa wants us to have a meeting." Mama usually did not attend these meetings, but Papa normally filled her in.

I went to the sitting room. Mawuli was vigorously beating out the dust from the cushions. The air about him was cloudy and I could hear him sniffling. "I have great news for you, Mawuli," I said mischievously.

"What news?" he asked suspiciously.

"Papa wants to have one of his meetings."

"Hell no!" he burst out, "When?"

"Today. And you're first as usual. Your time slot is 7:00GMT."
Mawuli groaned.

"Are you going to tell him about Gifty?" I asked.

"What about Gifty?"

"Papa asks about every aspect of our lives and you know that in the last few meetings, the final topic on the agenda has always been 'Relationships.' So what are you going to say when he asks you about that? Deny like you did the last time that you have a girlfriend?" I scoffed.

"Oh, so you plan telling him about Owusu?" he returned. "You want him to know that his precious daughter has a boyfriend? Let's just hope the relationship does not interfere with your Mfodwo results!"

Mawuli had almost caught Maxi and I once in our kissing sessions.

"You focus on your precious Gifty Marbell and I will take care of myself!" I retorted. I went to take a shower and dressed up in a pair of shorts and a tee shirt. By the time I returned to the kitchen, I could hear the drone of voices behind the closed sitting room next door. Mawuli's meeting was in progress. I started my shopping list, and was checking the refrigerator and freezer when Mawuli opened the door and stepped out of the sitting room.

"Your turn," he said. His expression gave nothing away. I walked into the sitting room, shutting the door behind me.

Papa was seated at the head of the dining table with some papers before him. He gave me a probing glance, and then asked me to sit down. He was silent for a minute or two as he flipped the leaves of his writing pad over to a fresh page.

"07:25 GMT hours," he said aloud as he scribbled something

39

down in his distinctive handwriting and underlined it twice. He leaned back and looked at me. I could feel my heartbeat increase.

"So... Dzigbordi," he began. "It is the end of your first year at the University of Ghana. You have spent a year away from home except for the Christmas and Easter holidays and your weekend trips. We haven't really had the opportunity to catch up, so I thought it best to do so now, so that you update me on your activities and inform me of your plans for the holidays and immediate future. Tell me once again about the classes you took this term."

Feeling relaxed now, I gave him a synopsis of the courses; the easy ones as well as the problematic ones. I also told him about the strategies I employed such as study groups, to successfully pass those courses.

"How did the first university examinations go? Do you think you did well?"

I informed him I did my best but wouldn't be sure about the outcome until the results were in.

"And how long do they take?"

I was sure he knew the answer. After all, this was Mawuli's last year of school and he had been through that process with him twice before.

I said, "It depends. I hear it can take up to two months. The results are placed on the bulletin board in front of the Balme Library. Students check periodically over the holidays and when the results come out, the news travels rapidly by word of mouth."

"We cannot wait for word of mouth, can we?" he said, "You better wait a month or so and then check once a week." He asked about the classes I would be taking the following year and the textbooks I would require. After school was out of the way, he wanted to know what else I had been doing. My parents already knew about my interest in literary works, and that semester, Maxi and I had co-written and directed a play that had been staged by the UCF drama group. I gave Papa a gist of what I had done in the Literary Club of the University Christian Fellowship. He nodded approvingly. "That is good as long as you don't allow it to interfere in your school work. You have to remember that school comes first. I know you love acting and writing, but that is more of a hobby," he reminded me. "So... now...other social activities; anything I should know about... boyfriends?" he asked, giving me a curious glance.

"Well..." I allowed my voice to trail off, but he just continued to look at me in silence.

"Well... I do... have a... friend... "

"A boyfriend?"

"Yes."

"Well, ... go on? Tell me who he is and how you got to know him."

"His name is Maxwell Owusu," I began slowly. "I met him... he is...was in my chemistry class and we were actually lab partners. He is a cousin of Michael McLean-Brown; the boy in Achimota...the one I told you and Mama about who was nice to me when I started sixth form."

"Was the Maxwell boy also in Achimota?"

"Yes…from form one to five, but he went to Accra Academy for sixth form."

A grunt, silence, then, "As I informed Mawuli when he told me about the Gifty girl, at your age, especially at Mawuli's, I have no problem with you having special friends. I met your mother in secondary school and we eventually got married. However—"

I sat up waiting for the other shoe to drop.

"Mawuli and you are at different stages. He has completed university and is looking forward to a year of national service and then hopefully a job. You on the other hand have only completed your first year. I have no idea what effect that Maxwell boy is going to have on your results."

At that statement, all the kissing episodes we had had during the last part of the term flooded my mind. I prayed that I passed all my subjects. Papa continued, "As I said, I have nothing against your having friends. Your mother and I would like you to introduce them to us if they come over. Also let us know in advance of any visits and whoever you go to see and where they live. You have to return home at a reasonable hour."

"Thank you very much, Papa. I was thinking of asking Maxwell to come over next week Saturday."

"Hmm! I don't think I have any problem with that, but be sure to discuss it with your mother first."

"Thank you," I heaved a silent sigh of relief.

"Anything else you want to talk about?" he asked

"No, thank you," I responded.

"Then please get me another cup of coffee."

He gathered his writing pad and files. His chair made a scraping sound as he pushed it back.

I could hardly wait to talk to Mawuli and compare notes, making a mental note to phone Mickey in the evening to inform Maxi that all systems were set to go for next Saturday.

Chapter Five

It was strange talking to Maxi after several days apart. His warm, but slightly husky voice sent a shiver of excitement down my spine. "Darlin' sweetheart, how are you doing?"

"Fine, Maxi! How are you?"

"Fine, thank you. So how did it go telling your old man about us?" he asked.

"It is a long story and I don't want you to run a huge bill," I replied.

"Maybe we can talk about it on Saturday. By the way, I didn't want to ruin the surprise, but I mailed a letter to you."

"You did?" My voice grew soft. I loved letters, and the fact that Maxi had sent me one made me feel as if he had bestowed a gift upon me. "What was in the letter?"

"What is the use of telling you? There will be nothing left to read if I do so," he said.

"Okay…I will wait impatiently!"

We laughed.

"What time do you want me to come on Saturday?"

"I don't know…late morning or early afternoon perhaps. It will give me time to complete my housework. I am on my best behavior at home, you know. The things we do for love!" I teased.

"Well…if our relationship is making you a better daughter, then it is for the best," he returned.

Later that day, my best friend JD telephoned and we planned to meet during the week. We hadn't met since the Christmas holidays and there was only so much one could write in letters. She had ended up at the medical school of the University of Science and Technology in Kumasi.

JD and I met in sixth form in Achimota Secondary School soon after I became friends with Mickey. She was one of the famous Tamakloe Triplets. Jemima was a school athlete and took part in all inter-house and interschool games; Kezia was always part of the dance troupe for formal school occasions, and sassy Karen was the outspoken prankster, feared by the boys for her sharp and witty tongue. The three operated as a unit, sometimes completing each other's sentences. Jemima and Kezia looked more like twins, and Karen more like their sister.

My friendship with "JD" Karen Tamakloe began during my second term in Motown. By then I had gotten used to the routine of bells for meals, break time, and bedtime. Partly due to Mickey McLean-Brown's influence, I had friends in my class, but most of them were in other houses and so we didn't associate much outside school time. The afternoon routine in school was that after lunch, students would retire to their respective houses for siesta. I usually spent rest hour reading, the only time I could get some privacy. One afternoon during rest hour, I was engrossed in a Sidney Sheldon on my corner bed by the dorm window. The blue wooden shutters were open and I lay with my face toward the window, totally lost to the world around me.

"You are always reading," said a voice very close to my ear. I jumped and the book flew out of my hand. It was déjà vu, but this time, instead of Mickey, it was Karen, one of the Tamakloe Triplets.

"I am sorry…I didn't mean to scare you." There was laughter in her eyes.

"That's okay. I was so lost in the story." I said. I didn't know what she wanted. All over the room, girls of all ages were sleeping; some of them snoring lightly.

"Please sit down," I gestured uncertainly, making way for her on the bed.

"What are you reading now?" Karen asked as I sat up and leaned against the window sill that jutted out slightly over my bed.

"*The Other Side of Midnight*," I responded, holding the book up so that she could see the cover.

"Is it good?"

"Quite good," I responded, in my element. "Sidney Sheldon is a great writer."

"I read one of his books a while ago. Mike lent it to me. I don't read fast though. It takes me a long time to finish a storybook."

"This one is also from Mickey," I said aloud, and opened the fly leaf which had, 'The McLean-Brown Family Library' stamped on it.

"Yeah, the stamp. Mickey says it helps them keep track of their books. Can you believe they have about 100 books on their shelves at home?"

"Actually I can," I responded. "At home, we have about 300 books."

Karen's eyes widened. "Wow! That's as big as some of the public libraries! It is even bigger than our school library. How did you get so many books?"

"Both my parents love reading and have collected books over the years. We even have books my father used in secondary school."

"Have you read all of them?"

"There are some books my mother would not allow me to read for years. I used to sneak out her Mills and Boon romance novels hidden on the back row of the topmost shelves of the book case."

"Maybe I can borrow some books from you sometime?"

"You are more than welcome to do so," I responded happily. "If you let me know what sort of books you like, I will get a couple from the library when I go home on exeat," I promised.

"Good. Thank you. You seem to be very good friends with Mike. He doesn't lend books to many people, only those he trusts to return them," she said.

"We exchange books. He is very nice," I said, feeling my face heat up.

"We are neighbours at the Airport Residential Area," Karen said, "We used to play together as children. He was so mischievous! He became much quieter after his father died."

"What happened to his father?" I asked.

"He was going to Koforidua for a funeral when he died in a car accident. We were in Form One then. We were in class when his family came to take him home. We cried and cried when we heard the news. We liked Dr. McLean-Brown. He loved playing with us. He would sometimes give us toffees and biscuits when we visited his home. Our parents went to his funeral. Michael gave the eulogy."

"That's so sad," I said, trying to imagine how Mickey felt. Was that why he was so sensitive and seemed older than the rest of us? I couldn't bear to think how I would feel if something happened to Papa. I changed the subject, "So…your parents named you after the daughters of Job?"

"Daughters of Job? Who is Job?" Karen asked.

My eyes fairly popped out. How could the Tamakloe sisters be unaware of where their names came from? I didn't think it was coincidence that all three girls were named after Job's daughters.

"You don't know Job in the Bible? He was the man God and Satan fought over. Satan dared God to visit misery on Job. He said Job would not love God if he had misfortunes. God agreed. Satan killed Job's animals, labourers, and all his children. Finally, he left Job with a lot of painful boils on his body. Even his wife told him to give up, but he did not. Eventually, God restored Job's blessings and gave him more than before. He also gave Job tens sons and three daughters."

"Jemima, Kezia, and Karen?" asked Karen looking enthralled.

"Correct!" I said in the tone of a teacher. "The Bible says that those three girls were the most beautiful women in the whole world!" I added. That made Karen very happy, and from that moment the two of us became friends. During the holidays, we would visit each other. My parents liked her. Karen was very polite, but also had a confidence and humour that shone through her conversations with older people. Papa always popped his head in to say hello to her. Karen wanted to be a medical doctor and was very focused in her studies. With my penchant for nicknames for people I was close to, I began calling her "Job's Daughter" and eventually, "JD".

***

"JD!"

"DziDzi!"

We flung ourselves into each other's arms laughing and dancing about in glee as we chatted in the mix of English and Ga we usually spoke when together.

"I can't believe it...finally!"

"Great to see you!"

"Don't know why you had to go to UST instead of Legon. Kumasi is too far away!"

"I wonder if doing medicine is worth it. I was away from my dearest friend and my sisters."

"I have so much..."

"...to tell me? Me too!"

Our words overlapped as we walked back indoors. Mawuli heard us and came out of his room and said hello to JD. They liked each other and usually teased each other whenever they met. Before Gifty came into the picture, I even hoped they would end up together. I slipped into the kitchen to get some drinks.

For the first two hours, we played catch up. JD had settled down at UST, she loved the programme despite the hard work involved. She had met a boy she liked very much, but unfortunately, he was already in a relationship. JD shrugged it off and said, "Tell me what has been happening with you. I know you have some news."

I didn't need further encouragement. I launched into the happenings of the last three months amidst constant interruptions, laughter and screams of apprehension from JD.

"I can't believe it! I leave you for a few months and you change so drastically! You now have a boyfriend and kissing and stuff!" JD said as she broke a piece of McVities' digestive biscuit and popped it into her mouth. "I knew you and Max were close, but I didn't think anything would come out of it. For some reason, I thought you were still in love with his cousin Michael. I used to wonder if part of the reason why you stayed close to Max was because he was Mike's cousin."

I was not amused. "I am… was not in love with Michael McLean-Brown. I like him, yes but that doesn't mean I love him! Besides, he has been with Frances Acolatse for months! He means a lot to me because he was so nice to me when I first came to Motown. Can't a person like someone of the opposite sex without it being misconstrued?"

"Ok! Ok!! I am sorry. I hope the meeting goes well with Max and your parents on Saturday. I wonder why Max is in a hurry to visit you at home. It would have been less stressful if the two of you had restricted your meetings to campus, or visited away from home. Then later you could have gradually informed your parents about it," JD said reflectively as she picked a thick slice of Mama's chocolate cake.

"I know," I concurred with a sigh. "I understand in a way that he wants our relationship to be above board, but it is surely going to complicate things."

"What is he going to do when it is your turn to visit? If his father feels that strongly about Ewes, how is he going to react when Max introduces you to him as a girlfriend? Do you think he is going to inform his father about it in advance or is he just going to spring it on him?"

"I don't have the answers to that. I am sure we are going to talk about that when Maxi comes on Saturday."

"I hope this tribal thing doesn't become a big issue."

We fell silent, both of us being aware that some Ghanaian couples did not survive long enough to marry if one or both families were against the union.

***

The rest of the week went by slowly. On Thursday, Mawuli and I went to visit my paternal grandmother who lived with her youngest son and his family. Grandma, though in her mid-70s, was still very feisty. She spent most of her time cooking or sitting in an armchair in the courtyard watching the traffic on the road, chatting with people as they passed by, and supervising her grandchildren. She was expecting us and had prepared the meal she always used to welcome us home for the holidays—*fetri detsi* (okro soup) with *akple* and *abolo*, both made from cornmeal. Grandma's okro soup was legendary —spicy, thick, with almost every kind of meat and seafood in it. After two helpings of the meal, Mawuli and I couldn't move for a while.

Before I knew it, it was Saturday. I was up very early to complete my household chores. Mawuli left home early to get a haircut from a roadside barber. I helped Mama to cook a lunch of light soup and cocoyam fufu. My parents did not comment about Maxi's pending visit. I wondered if they had forgotten about it or were just ignoring the event. At a quarter to twelve, while working with Mama in the kitchen I heard the rattle of the outside gate. My heart started skipping. The sound of hurrying steps and the opening of the backdoor reached my ears. Naa appeared a few seconds later to announce, "Sister Dzigbordi, you have a visitor."

"Who is it, Naa Norkai?" Mama asked, turning away from the stove and placing the ladle on a plate.

"I don't know, Mama," Naa responded.

"Why didn't you ask the person's name?" Mama demanded sternly. She had trained all of us that whenever we answered the telephone or the gate we needed to find out who the person wanted and the caller's name. Obviously, Naa had forgotten part of the procedure.

"Go back and ask the person's name and give him a seat on the balcony," Mama ordered. Naa flew out. I meticulously continued to cut the cocoyam into small chunks. Mama turned to me.

"Dzigbordi, it seems your friend has arrived. You may leave the rest of the cocoyam. I will finish it up. Remember to let Papa know of his arrival. I will come out later and say hello."

"Thank you."

I was drying my hands on a towel when Naa returned and said, "Please Mama he says his name is Maxwell Owusu."

"Good! Next time don't forget to ask."

I went to my parents' bedroom door and gave a series of taps.

"Yeeeees!" Papa yelled. I entered. He was seated behind his desk in the corner of the room, writing. He looked up. "Papa, I wanted to let you know that my friend is here. When you're ready, I would like to introduce you to him."

Papa grunted. "Hmm…might as well do it now and get it over with."

He pushed back his chair and followed me to the balcony. Maxi was sitting on one of the wooden armchairs on the balcony. He was dressed conservatively in a white long-sleeved shirt and black trousers, but his right shoe was off and his bare foot was on the same cushion he was seated on. He was in the process of examining his toes and scraping debris from under his toenails with his fingers. It wasn't the first time I had seen Maxi with his feet on cushions, but I flinched and bit hard on my lower lip.

Maxi had looked up with a smile on his face, obviously expecting to see me alone. At the sight of Papa behind me, he dropped his foot off the cushion and slowly rose to his feet.

"Good morning Sir," he said.

"Good morning, young man," Papa said after a long moment of silence.

"Good morning, Sir," Maxi said once more.

"Papa… this is… Maxwell Owusu, a friend from Legon. Maxwell, meet my father, Dr. Dzordzome."

"Pleased to meet you Sir," Maxi said, immediately sticking out his right hand.

"Hmm!" Papa looked at Maxi's outstretched hand for so long that I was afraid he would not touch it. Then he shook Maxi's hand briefly and let it go.

"Well…I will leave you two together, then."

We sat in silence until we could hear his footsteps fade away.

"Oh Dzigbordi, I am so sorry. I wasn't expecting your parents immediately. I couldn't find my comfortable shoes and I had to hurry so I wore these," he gestured to the formal-looking black shoes. "Unfortunately, these are very tight and I think there was a small stone in the right shoe. My toes felt very painful and I wanted to make sure I didn't have a cut. I couldn't see clearly with my leg on the floor so I lifted it briefly to enable me see well," he explained.

I understood what had happened, but would I get the opportunity to explain it to my parents for whom first impressions counted a lot? One of my friends, Fatima, had incurred their ire when on her first visit to my home, she had banged very loudly on the front door disturbing their siesta; from then on, they had never liked her.

"That's okay, Maxi." I did not want to make him feel bad. "Let me get you some water to drink."

"Later please," Maxi said, taking off his other shoe.

Please put your shoes on! I felt like admonishing him, but kept silent. I didn't want the visit to be more awkward than it already was, but I was afraid of Mama's reaction should she chance upon him with both shoes off. The harm was already done, though; Papa was going to inform her about what he had seen. How much worse could it get? I sat down gingerly in the chair next to Maxi and tried to relax.

In contrast, Maxi was quite unperturbed. He chatted about the last few days and asked if I received his letter.

"Not yet," I responded. "My mother checked the post office yesterday and there was nothing there for me."

"Well, I am sure it will arrive today or Monday. So you were going to tell me how it went with your old man?" he asked wriggling his bare toes carelessly.

Without warning, the sitting room door opened and Mama stepped out with an odd expression on her face. She gave me a sharp glance, and as Maxi rose up barefooted, I couldn't help wondering if she had heard Maxi call Papa "old man". I was sure she had. Would this dreadful day never end?

"Good afternoon, Mrs. Dzordzome," Maxi said in his most charming voice as he stuck out his hand. Mama hesitated, shook his hand for barely two seconds, and dropped it abruptly.

"Good afternoon." Turning to me she said, "Dzigbordi, I would like to see you for a moment."

I rose up and followed her.

"I am going to do my hair. Keep an eye on the light soup and turn the fire off in about 10 minutes."

"Yes Mama."

"Keep an eye on Naa. When she finishes with the weeding, give her some Math or English to work on till lunch time."

"Yes Mama."

"Around two-thirty, put the cocoyam on the fire and let Naa wash the mortar and pestle for the fufu."

"Yes Mama."

"Also remember to check on Papa every now and then."

"Yes Mama. Bye-bye." I returned to the balcony.

Maxi stayed for about three hours. Periodically, I would excuse myself and go inside to do some of the tasks Mama had assigned me.

"When do you want me to come over and visit?" I asked.

Maxi hesitated. "Can we give it a couple of weeks first? I was thinking that perhaps we can meet in town next week. You mentioned you wanted to go to the British Council Library, perhaps we could meet there and then go to Bus Stop Restaurant for some pies and ice cream."

That sounded like a good plan. I loved Bus Stop. They served excellent meat pies, mouthwatering ice cream and other types of food. That would be a real treat but, I became suspicious about the change of plan.

"Why don't you want me to come and see you at home? Is there a problem or something?"

"No," he said.

"Have you told your parents about me yet?" The idea that Maxi had bailed out on our agreement was not amusing at all.

"Well...I told my mum about you. I told her you will be visiting very soon."

"What about your father? I thought he was the problem?"

"I was going to do so... I will do that, but I want to wait for a few days. What difference does it make whether you visit now or later?" He paused, then continued, "Uhmm...you see...my father has been complaining since I got home for the holidays. He feels his Ewe boss has been treating him unfairly. If I tell him about you, he is going to ask your name and from your name it is obvious where you come from..." his voice tapered off.

I was furious. Why should I feel like a second class citizen because of my family background? Why should his father judge me before meeting me just because of my ethnicity? What is this about "Ewe bosses?" Was it only people from the Ewe tribe who were ever unfair to their subordinates? I was so angry I bit my lower lip to keep myself from screaming at him. If Papa ever heard that Maxi's dad was against me because of his tribe, the consequences would be irrevocable. I sat in silence, feeling the lump in my throat tighten up.

"Dzigbordi…." Maxi began.

"I'd rather not talk about it now. It is not the right place," I managed to spit out.

We lapsed into silence.

"Do you want me to leave?" he asked after a while.

"Perhaps you should. I will soon have to start pounding the fufu anyway."

He got up. "Dzigbordi…do you still want to meet at the library next week?" he asked, peering down at me.

"I don't know. Let me think about it. I will leave a message at Mickey's by the end of Monday. I plan to go on Wednesday." I also stood up.

"Dzigbordi, I am really sorry."

"That's okay."

In silence, I watched Maxi put on the offending shoes. I walked him to the gate and bid him goodbye. I brushed a tear off my left cheek as I walked back to the balcony. There was no time to go to my room and cry. Mama would soon be home and the fufu had to be ready by then. What an unmitigated disaster!

Chapter Six

Naa Norkai and I were preparing the fufu. She was pounding the boiled cocoyam in the mortar with the pestle while I gathered the pieces together in the mortar and directed it such that it was free from lumps, dipping my hand in water to prevent the starch from sticking to my fingers. I was dividing the smooth gelatinous mass into individual portions when we heard Mama's car horn at the gate. Naa hurried outside to open the gate.

Mama's beautiful hair was looking fresh and glossy, cascading down the middle of her back.

"Is everything alright?" she asked.

"Yes Mama. The fufu's ready, the soup has been heated and the table is laid. Your hair looks very nice. I think Sister Ruth did a very good job," I added.

"Thank you, Dzigbordi. Is Papa in his room?"

"Yes Mama."

"We should be out in a few minutes. You can start dishing out the food."

Five minutes later Mawuli arrived; his fresh haircut looked great, although his head seemed much smaller.

"So... did your friend come?" he asked, heading for the refrigerator for a drink of water.

"Yes…" I said curtly.

"That bad, huh?"

I concentrated on dishing the light soup into a Pyrex bowl. My parents soon came out and sat behind the table.

"Would you like anything to drink?" I asked.

"Hmm…I think I shall have a bottle of beer," Papa said after brief reflection.

"Star, ABC, or Gulder?" I asked as I had been trained to do.

"Star, of course!" Papa said as usual, although once in a while he would opt for another brand.

"How about you, Mama?"

"I think I shall stick with water."

I returned with the drinks. I spent time carefully pouring the beer, tilting the glass to control the amount of foam. My parents ate together in the sitting room, Naa in the kitchen and Mawuli and I in the "small sitting room." During holidays and birthdays, we all ate together at the dining table.

"So…what happened?" Mawuli asked in a low voice.

I gave him the gist of the drama, but left out the bit about Maxi's father's aversion to Ewe people. Mawuli listened with a horrified grin on his face. "That's bad. You see why I don't bring Gifty or certain friends here? Unless the person is very careful and aware of the situation, it can backfire. However, things may not be as bad as you think. Had it been as bad, I am sure the UG would have made a comment there and then."

"Oh yes, things are that bad. You know UG. They may not say anything for a long while. It doesn't mean they are not thinking it. It is sure to come up one day."

The "UG" was what we called my parents between ourselves when referring to them jointly; it stood for "upper gentry", a phrase we had coined from Catherine Cookson's novels set in 19th century England.

"Dzigbordi, I know it is a serious situation, but I really wish I had been there to see Max playing with his toes on the cushions when Papa came to meet him!" Mawuli laughed.

I couldn't help smiling myself. "You should have seen my face when Mama came out suddenly, just as Maxi was jiggling his toes and calling Papa 'your old man' in a loud voice. And you wouldn't believe it, but he seemed to have no idea how bad things were."

Mawuli did not seem surprised, "Yeah. His parents are probably different, and maybe he felt bad that he had been caught with his toes on the cushion. But I don't think he is aware the old man will hold it against him for a long time."

"I was a bit upset with Max," I admitted "But I am also upset with the UG. Papa practically grunted at him, and can you believe Mama would not allow me to serve him anything besides water? I felt so bad!"

My brother and I continued to eat, enjoying the feel of the smooth fufu as our fingers cut balls to desired sizes and dipped them into the soup and swallowed.

"Wuli," I said after some minutes. "What are Gifty's parents like? You have visited her at home before, haven't you?"

"A number of times," he responded. "They are pretty much okay. They are strict, but not as much as the UG. Her father works in a bank, and her mother is a business woman. Gifty is their only child, so they are very protective of her, but for some reason they like me and are very nice when I visit."

"Do you plan to marry her?" I felt like asking, but didn't want to push it. I hadn't seen my brother with a girl for that long and if he had been visiting her at home, bringing her to my room, and spending a lot of time with her on campus, it was a strong indication that he was serious about that relationship.

****

On Monday morning, my parents dropped me off at Grandma's on their way to work. I was going to spend the day there. They also gave me the post office box key to check the mailbox. I loved checking the mailbox; that feeling of anticipation, turning of the key in the lock and the excitement when I saw that the box was not empty. Most of the mails were for my parents, but sometimes, Mawuli and I received letters. Because most people did not have telephones and call charges were high, most of us preferred the post. After an hour at Grandma's, I walked with my cousin Gladys to the post office which was about 10 minutes away. Gladys was four years younger than I, but we were quite close. She wasn't my best friend, mainly because I felt she was too young for me to share everything with her, but I told her a lot, and she shared her school experiences with me. As we walked to the post office, I gave her a summary of the Maxi situation.

"I am sure it will turn out okay, Sis Dzi. I will put you on my prayer list."

Gladys had this ever-growing prayer list. She had shown me

her prayer list once (in a notebook). She placed checked marks by those that had been answered. Hers was an untarnished faith in the efficacy of prayer. I felt a modicum of comfort that something was being done about the problem with Maxi.

Mailbox #1082 was quite full. There were a couple of journals for Papa, a letter in a feminine script addressed to Mawuli, a bill from the telephone company, and….oh…there was Maxi's letter in his familiar cursive script.

"Did he write?" Gladys asked impatiently after watching me sort through the mail in silence.

"Yes!" I waved the letter triumphantly.

"Let me see!" She took it from me and spent a moment examining the handwriting and weighing it in her hand. "Looks like a long and juicy one," she added as she returned it to me. "When are you going to read it?"

"When I get home."

All the while as we chatted about other things, Maxi's letter was on my mind. I could hardly wait to get home and read it in private.

*****

Back in my room, I settled down on my bed and ripped open the envelope.

At Home
12.30pm
6/7/92

Darling DD,

It is so strange talking to you on paper instead of in our rooms at Legon. Sometimes, when I am alone, I turn my head, expecting to see you lying on my bed reading a story book instead of your lecture notes!

Seriously, DD; I've missed you terribly, and I feel absolutely despondent, but I will try not to go bananas over it. I never thought I'd miss you this much. DD, we have spent so much time together in the past few months that even though I am happy to be home and have delicious home-made meals three times a day, I can't help but feel as if there is a part of me missing (I think I left my heart with you for safe-keeping)! I can hardly wait until we meet again; hopefully in a week's time.

For the past hour, I have been sitting here at my desk thinking of the time we spent together this term as well as our time together yesterday. I cannot help but thank the Good Lord for letting us find each other. It is amazing that we spent so much time together without being aware of how much we meant to each other. I just want you to know that I cherish you, I love you…your humour, your smile, your loyalty…the way you make me feel as if I am the most important person to you. You are a very special lady, and I enjoy the times we spend together chatting, sharing, arguing and studying.

"Studying" brings something else to mind. I hope to God that our time together is not going to jeopardise your academic work. I can't help but feel guilty for all those

times we spent locked in a passionate embrace instead of being glued to our books. I know that if either of us or both do not pass Mfodwo completely, we are going to blame ourselves. When we return to school, I hope we shall be able to have a good balance of academics, spiritual endeavours and romance, and continue to work at cutting down our "sessions". I hope we will be able to encourage and support each other in our accomplishments. I would like to think that we will always influence each other positively in every sphere of our lives.

DD, I plan to talk to my parents about us as soon as possible; at least, Mummy. I know that when she knows just how much you mean to me, she will be eager to get to know you and to love you because I love you. Daddy is another issue. Yesterday, on my first night, he was still complaining about his boss Mr. Fordgor, who has been unfairly piling up his work and giving less work to his compatriot. Also, there was an opportunity to travel to London on a company-related trip, and Mr. Fordgor gave it to Mr. Dovi instead of him. I have every faith it would work out in the end, but I fear it may not be instant. I pray you will indulge me by being patient with me if it takes longer than we anticipated. A part of me wonders if I shouldn't have pushed you into telling your parents about us, but deep down, I feel I was right. From what you have told me of your home life, your parents require you to let them know of your whereabouts, meaning that you would have had to give excuses about visiting JD *or going to do your hair, or visit the library during the holidays for us to meet. I guess I couldn't contemplate not being near to you for three months. I hope you do not get into trouble over me.*

We have received a lot of visitors since I returned; with most of the young girls coming over to greet me. It is amazing how knowing that I have been away at varsity has made me a hot commodity! Even the parents look at me as someone important; I guess they are looking for potential grooms for their daughters, and someone on the path of higher education is a big catch. I hate to leave, but I shall have to end my missive at this point. I hear Mummy calling me to dinner. It is going to be fufu and palm nut soup with chicken. Don't you wish you were here?

See you soon, dear, and talk to you soon!

Love,

Maxi

I read the letter twice. I was a bundle of emotions; joy that he had written and reiterated his love, happiness that he had acknowledged the difficulties I was facing with my parents and the attitude of his father. Reading his letter made me feel the bond I felt was lost when he visited the previous day. I folded the letter, kissed it, placed it in the envelope and hid it in my secondary school trunk which now held my journals and letters.

Monday morning after my parents had left for work, I telephoned the McLean-Brown residence.

"May I please speak to Michael?"

"And who is this?" Mrs. McLean-Brown asked.

"Dzigbordi Dzordzome." I responded.

"Hi Dzigbordi, how are you doing?" I had met her on a number of occasions because JD lived close by the McLean-Browns and we had passed by Mickey's home to exchange books.

"I am fine, thank you, Auntie Mary," I answered.

"Good! Hold on, I will get Michael." There was a shout of, "Mike! Phone!"

"Hello! Who is this?"

"Hi Mickey, this is Dzigbordi!"

"Hi, DziDzi! How are you spending the holidays so far? We didn't have time to talk when Max called from here the last time."

"I am fine, Mickey. Doing mostly house stuff and visiting family. How about you, how are things?"

"About the same here. I am doing a lot of resting as well. I have been able to get a job and will be working in two weeks," he said.

"That sounds exciting," I said wistfully. I wished I could have a job that earned me a few cedis and also got me out of the house on a daily basis, but vacation employment a was not easy to come by.

"It is nothing exciting, just a clerical job. I shall be doing a lot of paper filing, but at least it is something. I hope the Mfodwo results come out soon. It is on my mind twenty-four hours a day."

"I feel the same way, but I think it can take up to two months or so," I returned.

"I don't want to add to your telephone bill. Do you have a message for Max? He said he was going to pass by later today," Mickey asked.

"Yes. Please tell him that I will see him at the library on Wednesday. I should be there around ten."

"Will do that. Have a good day, DziDzi. Don't forget to pass by when you come to visit the Tamakloes," he added. "Oh, and can you bring a PG Woodehouse when you come by? I loved *The Code of the Woosters*. I laughed out loud so much that my mother was afraid there was something wrong and came to find out what was going on. After I finished it, I lent it to her and now I hear her laughing in her bedroom late at night!"

"I will do so, Mickey. Okay I have to go now. Bye!"

****

For the next couple of days, apart from the usual housework, I worked with Naa on her reading. She was an intelligent girl who absorbed everything like a sponge, reading my old grade four primary school English textbook. I was also doing a lot of reading myself. Mawuli was out most of the time, but we chatted every now and then. He was anxious both about his Mfodwo results and the national service postings. He didn't want to be posted too far away from Accra for a whole year and from his girlfriend Gifty, who was slated to work in the same bank as her father. Papa had spoken to some friends who said they would be able to help, but nothing had been confirmed yet.

I had already informed the UG days ago that I would be visiting the library on Wednesday. Two hours after they left, I walked to the bus station. The morning crowd had lessened but there was the usual bustling cacophony out on the roads. There was a young driver's mate (conductor) shouting out the destination to attract passengers, "Odorkor! Odorkor! Odorkor, one more person!"

To get to the British Council I had to make two transfers, first to the Kwame Nkrumah Circle, a major intersection that connected other major roads in Accra and was perpetually bustling with vehicular movement as well as road side vendors selling all kinds of merchandise including music cassettes, books, dog chains, food and drinks. People jaywalked a lot, dashing across the busy road at the risk of their lives, while some drivers, especially the tro-tro drivers, ignored the lights that gave right of way to pedestrians. As I got down, I clutched my handbag under my arm in order not to fall victim to pickpockets. I traversed the sidewalks to board another tro-tro bus to central Accra, which would take me close to the library. About 15 minutes later, I got down at my bus stop. A five-minute walk saw me at the library. I loved the British Council Library. It had a good collection of books which a patron with a library card could freely borrow from. Immediately I entered the compound, I saw Maxi standing at the entrance. I felt my heart leap. As if he sensed my presence, he turned and looked directly at me. His face lit up and he began to move rapidly toward me. I smiled; of course, I loved him! There was nothing wrong with Maxi, sure, he had made a few faux pas during his first visit, but that was because we were from different homes and I hadn't thought to warn him how carefully he needed to act around my parents. He was now standing in front of me. We were gazing into each other's eyes. Our hands reached out of their own volition and clasped one another, and then hurriedly unclasped; very much aware we were in public. We turned and walked into the library.

Chapter Seven

Six weeks into the long vacation and my life had fallen into a steady routine of cooking, teaching Naa, and playing board games of Ludu and Snake and Ladders. Mawuli and I fell into the habit of meeting in our sitting room at night and chatting as we watched television. I formed the habit of sharing Mama's pot of tea late afternoons on weekends. I would tell her carefully edited stories about life on campus. Sometimes, Papa and Mawuli would join us, and everyone would try and tell a funny incident. It was particularly fun when Papa told us stories about work. He had a dry and witty sense of humour and could always make us laugh.

JD and I also took turns in visiting each other biweekly, as well as checking on the Mfodwo results. Sundays was for church. The UG and Mawuli generally did not attend church, but I had formed the habit of going every week after I joined the University Christian Fellowship.

Maxi had not been to my home since the first disastrous visit. We would meet at the British Council Library and go out to eat afterward. He joined me at church services on Sunday and we spent time chatting before he walked me to the bus station. Sometimes, he would accompany me on the tro-tro and then take another back home. We also wrote each other letters two or more times a week. I kept those letters locked in the old school trunk. Every other week, Maxi would mail a letter, but the other letters were sent through JD, or we exchanged them when we met at the library.

One of the most exciting things that happened during the holidays was Mawuli's clandestine birthday party. Mawuli turned 24 on August 1, on a Saturday and we had a family party for him, with relatives from both my father's and mother's sides — adults and children. My parents said Mawuli could invite his friends as well, but he replied that he wanted to make it a family affair. There were a variety of food and drinks. Mawuli went around paying attention to everyone and most of the adults asked about his plans after university, his national service posting, and whether he had a girlfriend. Some of them gave him some money which he refused seemingly vehemently at first, but eventually accepted reluctantly. The length of his vehement refusals was directly proportional to how close my parents were in the vicinity when the money was offered, but no one allowed him to refuse; everyone was proud of him for having completed university.

During the party, I also circulated a lot, making sure that everyone had enough to eat and drink; soft drinks (what we termed minerals) for the children, and beer, wine, and hard liquor for the adults. I also did something else; I surreptitiously put away some packets of biscuits, plantain chips, and bottles of soft drinks in the wardrobe in my bedroom. Later on, I transferred the booty into my old school trunk. During those trips to and from my bedroom, Mawuli and I would exchange conspiratorial smiles.

Three days earlier, we had just finished watching an episode of *Derrick* on the TV when Mawuli told me of his wish to have his own brand of a birthday party.

"But Mama is having a party for you on Saturday? You want two parties?"

"Yes… something like that. I know we are having a family party on Saturday, and the UG did say I could bring a few of my friends, but I think it would be more fun if we could have a party by ourselves without the pressure. I wouldn't want to worry that one of my friends would pick his toes on our pristine cushions," he joked.

"So when do you plan on having it?" I asked.

"I was thinking the Monday after my formal birthday party. Will you be able to help? You know, with the cooking, a few purchases, and helping to make sure the coast is clear during the party just in case of any contingencies," he said.

I nodded without reservation. It would be my birthday present to him. It seemed like something fun and adventurous—as long as we got away with it. If my parents found out about it, they would be very angry and hurt.

"How many friends are you thinking of inviting?" I asked.

"About ten people; I should say between ten and twelve."

"Try not to exceed 12; the more the people, the greater the possibility of discovery. If there are too many people flocking in and out of the house, some nosey neighbour is sure to spill the beans," I warned.

"You're right," Mawuli said. "I have to warn them not to arrive in droves. Luckily, only two of them have cars, so most of them are going to come by taxi or tro-tro."

"We need to make a list of things to buy. Some cookies, soft drinks, etc. I can cook some jollof rice and chicken. If I have the ingredients I can start immediately the UG leave for work. It should be ready by the time the guests arrive. What time would you tell them to arrive?"

"Between 10:30 and 11:00 a.m.; if everyone is here by noon we can party until 4:00pm. That should give us about one and half hours to clean up before the UG return. By the way, Gifty says she will be able to help with some food; you know, bring it from home. Perhaps the two of you can coordinate?"

I nodded and asked, "Do you have enough money for all this?"

"I have some money saved. Unlike you, I don't spend all my money on my hair," he teased. "I also have the birthday cash presents."

"As my birthday present to you, I will do the cooking, help with the organisation and pay for the ingredients for the jollof rice. Actually, it is your birthday and Christmas 'box' combined!"

It was just like in our younger days, when we got embroiled in all kinds of mischief. Papa was practicing in Tamale in the northern region. We lived a relatively isolated life, and apart from his school mates, I was Mawuli's main playmate. I was therefore heartbroken and lonely when he left for boarding school. When he came home for the holidays he was more distant in his manner toward me, and he seemed to have moved into a world I couldn't follow. As I got older, things changed for the better but we never recaptured the closeness we had in our childhood days. Mawuli's request for a birthday party made us collaborators once more.

***

The following morning, immediately after the UG left for work, Naa and I started the cooking. Mawuli arranged chairs in the sitting room and readied his music cassette tapes for dancing then he stepped out to buy more drinks and cookies.

Gifty Marbell arrived an hour later in a taxi with a big basket of fried fish, fried chicken, beef stew and a few balls of kenkey. Most of the guests were in by 11:00a.m. Altogether there were six men and four women, all third year students, so most of the conversation was about national service postings and Mfodwo results. Nii Ayi showed up with his latest girlfriend. Gifty and I served the food, Mawuli saw to the drinks, and Naa was at the gate keeping guard while enjoying a heaped plate of jollof and a coke. After everyone had finished eating, people started dancing to Western and Ghanaian highlife music. By four o'clock, everyone except Gifty had left. She offered to help clear up but I told her everything was under control and she and Mawuli had half an hour to themselves before he saw her off. Naa helped to finish cleaning up.

"Do you think all evidence of Operation Clandestine has been erased?" I asked Mawuli when the three of us met in the kitchen after double checking that everything was back to normal.

"I think so. We should be fine. Thank you very much, Naa Norkai and Dzigbordi. You guys were a great help."

"You're welcome," Naa said shyly. She was in awe of "Brother Mawuli".

"Remember…not a word to Mama and Papa!" Mawuli reiterated. It was the first time Naa had joined in any nefarious activities and he wasn't 100% sure of her ability to remain silent.

"Naa will not breathe a word. I hope you enjoyed your birthday party, Mawuli," I said.

"Yep I did. Seems like old times, doesn't it?" His smile made me feel sentimentally close to my brother that moment.

"Gifty did a very good job with the chicken," I commented. It was hard to figure out what Gifty was thinking most of the time. She wasn't one of those flashy extrovert girls I would have thought were more to Mawuli's taste. However, Mawuli was serious about her. Working with Gifty today had shown me that she had a sense of humour, and watching her with Mawuli made me realise that she cared for him a lot. Despite the fact that she was an only child and came from a wealthy home, she had an air of modesty that was appealing.

"Yes, she did a good job," Mawuli smiled softly, and then we were interrupted by a honk signalling the return of one of our parents.

The following day, my parents had just left for work when the telephone rang. Mawuli beat me to it. "Hello, this is the Dzordzome residence, Mawuli speaking, how may I help you?"

I hovered in the doorway just in case the call was for me.

"Yes?" silence.

"What? It is?" More silence and a strange look of apprehension.

"What about you... Do you know about mine?" The squawking of a voice rapidly speaking, "Thank you, I will check on it immediately. Bye!" Mawuli put down the telephone and looked at me with a mixture of excitement and apprehension.

"What is it?" I asked.

"The Mfodwo results are out! They came out yesterday!"

I felt weak. I prayed I had passed. What would I do if I failed?

"The apprehension's going to kill me. I am leaving for campus immediately. I will telephone Gifty so she meets me there. Don't worry, Dzigbordi. I'll look up your name and let you know about your results." He was already picking up the phone.

"You must be joking! Do you think I can be that patient? I am also going to check my own results!"

"What if Mama or Papa call and find out that we both left the house without informing them in advance?" Mawuli asked.

"They'll understand. I will leave a message with Naa in case they call. When you finish calling Gifty, I'll call JD so she informs Jemima and Kezia. I am sure Mickey McLean-Brown will tell Maxi."

"Why don't we share a taxi? If we combine our money we should be able to charter one to school," he suggested.

"Good idea. We can leave in about half an hour." An hour and half later the taxi dropped us off on the street closest to the Balme Library. Although it was only 10.30 a.m. and the university was on vacation, the notice boards on the left and right sides of the library were jammed with people. There was a buzz of excitement all around. I was able to shove my way to the second row and scrutinise the notice board closest to me. Results were arranged by departments and student names were in alphabetical order. There was a pass list, made up of several sheets, followed by a shorter list of students who did not pass, with the failed subject by their name.

I was frantically searching the Agricultural Science Department list. I finally found it, but it was difficult to get in front. People in the first few rows would not budge while they searched for their names, spending moments when they found it as if to make sure that it was not an illusion. I could hear a young man in front of me muttering aloud to himself, "Boateng, Ato, Boateng Kwabena, Boateng, Silas ... Britwum! Oh no! I can't find my name! Wait! Boateng, Yaw! Hallelujah! Praise the Lord!" he shouted, suddenly throwing up his hands in the air, then began to shove his way out of the crowd, beaming.

I hurriedly took his place. It was much easier for me because I went straight to the end of the names beginning with "Ds". I was moving my eyes down when I was rudely interrupted by a voice: "Congratulations, Dzigbordi, you passed!" I looked to my right side to see one of my course mates, Vera Addison, grinning at me as she pointed at my name. I stared at it for a minute. Yes! Yes! Yes! I shouted inwardly.

"How about you?" I asked politely, although I could already tell from her expression.

"I also passed, but can you believe that James Osei failed both physical and organic chemistry and Maggie Okine didn't pass Maths?" her hushed tone relished her role of gossip.

"How about Maxwell Owusu, did he pass?" I asked frantically.

"I don't know. I didn't notice his name on those who failed. By the way, congratulations to your brother also, he had a Second Class Upper."

I let out a little squeal. I knew our entire family would be very proud of Mawuli. Still, before I could relax I had to check on Maxi's results. I turned to push my way out of the crowd and ran smack into Maxi.

"Maxi! Did you make it?" I asked, staring into his face anxiously.

"Yes, thank God! You did too, right?"

"Yes, and Mawuli had a Second Upper."

"Yeah, I saw that. His girlfriend had a First Class! Can you believe it?"

"Oh that's so wonderful! I am so happy that we all made it." I feel weak with relief. "When I heard the results were out, I was so scared!" I blathered as we pushed our way out of the crowd.

"Rosemary Quaye has to repeat a course, I think Psychology," he said. "She was standing by the notice board crying."

"That's sad," I responded, but still too overwhelmed by my good news to invest further emotion into anyone who was not close to me. "I will look for Jemima and Kezia's names and then I am out of here."

"Would you like us to go somewhere for a meal and relax before you go home?" he asked hopefully.

"No… I can't stay for long. I still have cooking to do; this was an unplanned trip. But we can go to Circle together. Let me just find Mawuli and tell him I am leaving."

"Okay. I will just go over and say a few words of comfort to

Rosemary. I shall be waiting for you." Mawuli and Gifty were surrounded by their friends. I congratulated them and left with Maxi. While we walked to the station, I told Maxi all about Mawuli's clandestine birthday party.

"I wish I could have been there," he said wistfully.

"Sorry…it was just for Mawuli and his friends," I explained.

"DD, I would like it very much if you pay me a visit at home next week," he said as we stood by the roadside waiting for the tro-tro. I turned and looked at him in amazement. "What has changed?"

"Nothing, but before long the holidays will be over. You did your part of the bargain and introduced me to your parents, so I should do the same. I don't know whether my dad is ever going to recover from what Mr. Fordgor did to him."

Allegedly did to him, I corrected mentally.

"If my dad meets you, he is going to like you. It will help him remember that not all Ewes are like his boss," he explained his strategy.

"I hope it is not up to me to vindicate the entire Ewe tribe," I snapped.

Maxi looked sharply at me, a hurt expression on his face.

"You know I didn't mean it that way. I just think you two should meet. My mother has been asking when you are coming to visit," he said defensively.

"Okay…okay…truce! What day do you want me to come, weekday or weekend?

"Weekend will be better. You can come Saturday and spend the day, or Sunday after church."

"Saturday's better. Most of the time, Pastor preaches long sermons. I may not be able to spend the entire day on Saturday, but I will make sure we have some quality time."

He nodded. Just then, a tro-tro stopped by us. It was after we had taken off that I remembered that I had not checked the notice board to find out if Jemima and Kezia had passed.

****

I cannot describe the feelings of euphoria at home that night. When Mama heard the news, she threw herself in Mawuli's arms and gave him a big hug. Papa followed suit with a less exuberant, but heartfelt one. As if not to make me feel left out, both of them hugged me as well and congratulated me on passing my FUE. Papa of course, wanted to know about the grade distribution across Mawuli's programme: how many got first class? Four. How large was the class? Forty-eight. Mawuli went through the rest of the allocation of honours and people who just passed and those who failed.

As expected, Papa started discussing the next stage of Mawuli's life, which was his year of national service. Mawuli was still waiting for confirmation of his posting.

"You worked very hard for your degree, Mawuli," Mama said, gazing at him fondly. She turned me, "Dzigbordi, I hope you take a leaf out of Mawuli's book. He was very focused on his studies. It is good to have friends and I know you love writing and acting, but remember those are hobbies. You will always have time to play with friends and dabble in your hobby after you graduate," she said. I felt like cold water had been poured on me. "Your mother is right, balance is the key. We are not saying you should not relax sometimes, but from day one you need to work hard instead of studying at the last minute like you used to do when you were in secondary school," Papa added.

"I think we need to have another party for Mawuli soon," Mama suggested after we had been eating in silence for a few minutes. Mawuli and I shot glances at each other involuntarily. Another party? I adored parties, but three parties in one week was a bit much.

"Maybe we can do it when I formally graduate next year?" suggested Mawuli with a rather glazed look in his eyes.

Mama was resolute. "It is a good idea to have a big party next year after you receive your degree, but I was thinking of something on a smaller scale where you can invite your friends for a meal and some music. We can have it in a week or so. That will give you time to call and invite them or write or however you want to do it."

"Thank you Mama. I will work on that," Mawuli gave in gracefully.

"Perhaps 10 people?" Mama said, looking at Papa for confirmation.

"Yes, between 10 and 15 will be a good number," he replied.

Mawuli and I met in our sitting room after supper. "Wow! Three parties in one vacation! You are very lucky!" I opened the conversation.

Mawuli groaned. "I never thought it would get to a time that I will be sick of parties. What am I going to do? The people I want to celebrate with are the same ones who were here earlier this week!"

"Well…it is not as bad as you think. After all, they all knew it was a clandestine operation. All you have to do is to remind them to keep mum about their previous visit. I am sure none of them would mind coming here for another delicious meal," I said.

"Yes, you are right. At least, the one good thing is that all of them passed, even though Nii Ayi had a third class," Mawuli said.

"Poor guy!" I said.

"At least, he passed. There are three people in our year that did not make it at all. One of them was doing quite well, but he lost his mother just before the finals."

"That's hard luck," I said.

Something struck me, "You know, Mawuli, I think you should take this opportunity to bring Gifty Marbell home and introduce her to Papa and Mama. I was thinking today that she is the kind of person they would love—modest, polite, pretty, educated, well-brought up…and after that First Class, there is no way in the universe that Papa would have anything against her. He would probably be anxious to welcome her into the family so that some of her brains would be transferred onto the next generation of Dzordzomes," I giggled.

He was silent for a while. "Hmm, that might be a good idea. I don't know whether I will introduce her as my girlfriend yet, but at least, they will know who she is."

"Would Gifty be okay with that if you just introduced her as one of the crowd?"

"I will talk to her about it and we shall make the decision

together, but she understands what the UG are like and if I explain to her that we would have a better chance of success if we move slowly, she would understand as she has done for the past year and half," he explained.

"Lucky you," I sighed.

Mawuli rose from the couch, stretched and yawned loudly. "So you think Gifty is modest, pretty, educated, and well-brought up, eh?" he grinned like a cat that had taken a nibble at a mouse.

"I meant she appears that way!" I said, reluctant to make my brother's head swell with pride. "I mean she is the kind of person you like more as you get to know her." The fact that Gifty was a wonderful girl didn't mean that I was overly eager to embrace her as my brother's future wife.

Mawuli yawned once more. "I think I shall go to bed. I am just so exhausted. Remember to lock up, I think you are the last to go to bed."

I sat staring blankly at the TV long after he had left for bed, thinking of how I would inform the UG about my trip to Maxi's home next week.

Chapter Eight

I stood outside the gate of Maxi's home and gingerly mopped my face, hoping I was not wiping off all the face powder in the process. The walk from the bus stop to Maxi's home had taken me fifteen minutes and I felt hot and sweaty. I ran a hand over my hair to make sure the curls were still intact, and then knocked on the main gate. I heard running footsteps and the black gate clanged open. Maxi was standing there smiling. He wore a frayed pair of khaki shorts and a singlet. He was bare footed and looked rather dishevelled.

"Hi DD, come in. I hope you haven't been waiting for long. I was doing some cleaning." It was a large walled compound with pieces of coloured broken bottles embedded on top of the wall to prevent robbers from scaling over. There was an orange tree in front of the house with a rich crop of plump green oranges hanging on the branches. The compound had two separate houses; a bigger one in front, and a cottage at the back that Maxi had told me was used for guests.

"Mummy is in the kitchen, let's go there so that I introduce you two," he said, and led me to the kitchen at the back of the house. A brown slender woman was grinding fresh pepper in a black earthenware bowl. She looked up as we entered. I noticed that Maxi had inherited her eyes.

"Hello…" she began in a soft gentle voice.

"Mummy, this is Dzigbordi," Maxi said with a note of pride in his voice.

"Good afternoon, Mrs. Owusu," I said shyly moving toward her to shake her hand. She looked at her hand and laughed before wiping it on a napkin, and then enveloped my hand in a firm grip. "Good afternoon, Dzigbordi," she spoke to me in Akan. "Make yourself comfortable. Serwaa will soon bring you some water to drink. I will just finish up with the cooking. I hope you will be able to share in our meal?"

"Thank you." I could feel my nervousness ebb away. She was so welcoming and gentle. "Is there anything I can do to help in the kitchen?" I added politely.

"Not now. Serwaa's helping me. Seerwaaa!" Mrs. Owusu raised her voice suddenly, almost making me jump.

"Yes Muummy!" shouted a voice and moments later, Maxi's thirteen-year-old sister hurried in.

"Get Kofi's friend some water to drink, okay?"

"Yes, Mummy," Serwaa said with a sideways glance at me.

"Congratulations, Dzigbordi, Kofi said you also passed your examinations," Mrs. Owusu said.

"Yes, thank you," I responded.

"Come on, DD," Maxi said, and I followed him through the sitting room toward a room in the back.

"This is my bedroom. I used to share it with my older brother Alex, but it has been mine since he moved to Kumasi to work," he said. The cream-coloured room was bathed in bright sunlight streaming in through the window. The walls had posters of soccer stars. One poster had a big loaf of wheat bread and the Scripture, "I am the bread of life."

There was a dressing table with a mirror and a variety of combs, Vaseline petroleum jelly and powder. The bed was unmade and strewn with laundry.

"Oh, take a seat, DD," Maxi said, shoving the clothes to one side so that I could sit on the bed.

"Is it okay to be in your bedroom?" I asked nervously. He looked at me in surprise and smiled. "Of course it is okay. Mummy doesn't expect me to ravish you; at least not in broad daylight with everyone at home," he teased.

"Is your father at home?" I asked, unable to relax. I was hoping I could get the meeting over and done with as soon as possible. It was like getting an injection, the anticipation hurt more than the jab itself.

"Yes, he is in the cottage. He should be around any moment. Auntie Gertie, his sister, is visiting for a while. She is having problems with her husband," Maxi said casually as he began to fold the clothes on his bed. I felt myself holding back questions I so much wanted to ask him. Had he already told his father about my visit? If so, how had he reacted?

Maxi seemed rather nonchalant as he folded up his laundry. He looked up suddenly and caught me looking at him and smiled. "I wish I could give you a hug, DD, but I am smelly and sweaty, maybe later," he offered.

I choked back a startled giggle and took a closer look at him. Maxi was looking scrumptiously tempting in the singlet that left his broad chest practically bare, showing the rippling muscles and tufts of curly hair that usually had the ability to turn my thoughts to hugging and kissing. The khaki shorts showed off his glowing, black skin, narrow hips and long muscular legs, and his messy sweaty appearance made him appear even sexier. However, my nervousness had temporarily stifled my raging hormones.

"Thank you for the offer," I said primly, "Perhaps, later?" We laughed.

"Does your father know that I am coming?" I asked, unable to let go of that topic.

"No, I didn't tell him. I decided that it was best you just met. I have friends who pop in all the time and I don't give my parents any advanced warning. I told my mother because I wanted to make sure she finished cooking early enough for you to eat with us."

Just then, there was a low knock on the partially closed door. Maxi yanked it open. Serwaa stood there with a tray containing a glass of water, a bottle of chilled coke, a glass and an opener. She placed the tray on the desk after Maxi had moved some books aside and then carefully opened the bottle of coke.

"Thank you, Serwaa," I smiled at her. "Your brother has told me a lot about you. You are in form three in Motown, right?"

"Yes, Sister Dzigbordi," she glanced at me and lowered her eyes shyly.

"How do you find school?" I asked, feeling the burden as the older one to keep the conversation going.

"I like it," she responded.

"Serwaa is very good in school. Her report for last term was excellent," Maxi added.

"Well done, Serwaa!" I said, trying to resist the temptation of asking her what she wanted to specialise in—science, art, or business. That was too cliché.

"I have to go, excuse me," she said to my relief and left.

Maxi finished folding the clothes and arranged them in his wardrobe as we talked about the Mfodwo and news we had on who had passed or failed. I offered him some of my Coca-Cola. We took turns drinking from the same bottle.

"Do you mind if I leave you for a few minutes? I would like to take a quick shower," Maxi said when we were done drinking.

"Here?" I asked, wondering what his parents would think if they came to find me in his bedroom while he showered.

"Yes, it is fine, unless you'd rather wait in the sitting room or talk with Mummy in the kitchen," Maxi said. He was oblivious of the impact of his statement. I was not comfortable with either option. I wouldn't know what to talk about if I went to the kitchen. If I was in the sitting room when his father returned, I would have to meet him without Maxi. In my home it would have been a no-no for a guest to be in the bedroom. "I will wait here," I said. When he left I started reading a story book. I could hear the distant sound of splashing water. Then there was silence for a while. He must be towelling himself dry, I thought. I heard approaching footsteps and the door opened. "That was quick!" I said raising my head as I spoke, but it wasn't Maxi. It was an older version of Maxi; almost as tall as his son and with that unusually dark complexion. He had a small beard cropped close to his chin and slightly balding at the crown of his head with salt and pepper hair. He wore what was known in Ghana as a "political suit" which accentuated a growing pot belly.

I jumped to my feet, dropping the book to the ground in the process.

"Good afternoon Sir," I said. Oh no, I shouldn't be here. What was I thinking? I should have opted for staying in the sitting room. What would Maxi's parents think of me sitting in his bedroom on my first visit?

"Good afternoon, you must be a friend of Kofi's?" his father responded in English as he stepped fully into the bedroom and looked around.

"Yes Sir… Maxwell is taking his bath."

"What is your name, young lady?"

"Dzi… Dzigbordi Dzordzome," I responded nervously. What was going to be his reaction when he heard the Ewe name? Mr. Owusu remained silent for a moment, but I didn't see his expression change to one of unfriendliness.

"Where do you go to school?" he asked.

"I am Maxwell's classmate at Legon," I explained.

"Are you also reading science?"

"Agric Science, Sir," I answered. *Oh, when will Maxi come out of the bathroom and rescue me?*

"How did you do in the FUE?" Mr. Owusu inquired politely, but with a look of interest in his eyes.

"I passed, Sir."

"Good. Congratulations. Tell Kofi I came by looking for him," his father said before leaving. I sank back on the bed, feeling very weak. The long-awaited and dreaded meeting with Maxi's father had taken place. Nothing had turned out the way I had expected. I didn't know if he was angry with me,

89

but he had appeared friendly. Regardless of his feelings, I was impressed with the way he had spent some time chatting with me. I couldn't help feeling impressed with Mr. Owusu. If Papa had been in a similar situation, at best he would have grunted out a few words and disappeared.

I heard voices in the corridor. It was Maxi and his father. I couldn't make out what they were saying, and when Maxi returned moments later, he appeared unperturbed. He was only wearing the khaki shorts.

"Let me leave you to get dressed," I rose to my feet immediately.

"Nah…that's alright, you can turn your back to me; it will only take a moment."

"No, I will stand outside for a moment," I said, not wanting his family to come and find me sitting in the room while he got dressed.

He shrugged. "Whatever you feel comfortable with, DD," he said. "I see you met my Dad. How did that go?"

"Okay, I guess," I said hesitantly, "I don't know him well enough to figure out what he was thinking. Did he say anything to you?"

"No, not really, just that he met you." Maxi said picking out the clothes he was going to wear.

"I hope he didn't mind me being in your room?"

"Stop worrying so much, DD, I want you to enjoy your visit," he said. I stepped outside and shut the door behind me, hoping that no one would come and find me there and ask me to wait in the sitting room. A few minutes later, Maxi opened the door and I re-entered the bedroom. We spent a few minutes in silence while he finished dressing up. Finally, he stood in front of the mirror of his dresser and patted his hair down.

"All done! Now I feel much better and I am ready for my hug," he said, smiling at me. I was apprehensive about engaging in hugs in his home, but not he. Perhaps I should go with the flow. I moved into his arms and we hugged tightly. He smelt of my favourite Imperial Leather soap. His arms and chest felt thick and strong; they made me feel safe and cherished.

"Time to join the others, lunch is almost ready," he murmured into my hair and we pulled apart reluctantly. I picked the tray with the empty coke bottle and glass and followed him into the kitchen. The kitchen smelt delicious—freshly fried plantains and bean stew cooked in palm oil with smoked salmon.

The rest of the visit was pleasantly relaxed. Maxi and I, with Serwaa and his mother ate in the sitting room. A plate of food was kept covered for Mr. Owusu. We were in the middle of our meal when he stepped into the sitting room and sat in front of the television. Immediately, Serwaa stopped eating, went to the kitchen, and soon returned with a bowl of water and soap which she placed on the table in front of her dad. He washed his hands and dried them on a napkin. After taking the water back to the kitchen, she returned with his tray of food. He ate in silence. After the rest of us had eaten, Maxi and I carried the dishes to the kitchen sink, and I started washing them. Mrs. Owusu followed us not long afterward.

"Don't do that, Dzigbordi. Serwaa will do the washing up. Go and relax with Kofi." I returned to the sitting room with Maxi.

Maxi suggested a game of Scrabble. His father continued eating in silence and watching TV. Immediately he was done, his wife cleared the table. He sat for a few more minutes and then went into his bedroom, much to my relief. Maxi, Serwaa and I played Scrabble, which Maxi won. At the end of it, Serwaa seemed at ease with me. I said my goodbyes and left. Maxi accompanied me to Circle. When I got home, I went to my parents' room and greeted them. They responded cordially, but did not ask how the visit had gone.

****

The rest of the vacation was largely uneventful. The following weekend, we had the graduation party for Mawuli, with the same guests who had attended his clandestine birthday party. There was a variety of food; mounds of fufu with goat soup, jollof rice, stew, and goodies such as cake, jam tarts, doughnuts, pies, chips; all homemade by Mama, Naa and I. The UG were around throughout, but mostly kept in the background. Mawuli and his friends had a great time, and it was definitely an improvement on the clandestine party. Gifty Marbell was a big hit with the UG. Mawuli had introduced all his friends to the UG as they arrived. They shook hands with each friend and said a few words to them. Gifty arrived on time and looked very pretty. Her modest batik dress accentuated her tall slender frame. Mawuli did not introduce her as his girlfriend, but anyone who knew Mawuli could guess from his body language, the shyness and the pride in his voice as he made the introductions.

"Papa, Mama; this is Gifty Marbell. She is…was in my class. She is one of few who got a First Class honors."

Papa shook her hand heartily, beaming, and said "Well done, young lady! Your parents have done very well." He asked her a few questions, which Gifty answered shyly. Papa put a big emphasis on education, especially since he knew that females faced unique educational challenges, because some considered it a waste of resources to educate girls beyond a certain level. Most females who made it to secondary school branched into teacher training or vocational programmes. Others dropped out due to unplanned pregnancies or to get married. Gifty was one of the few ones who had not only made it but had done so with flying colours. Although the First Class was impressive enough for the UG, I think what won Mama over was the way Gifty made herself useful during the party. She collected used plates and debris and carried them to the kitchen, and my mother found the combination of high educational achievement, a modest demeanour, and the willingness to serve an irresistible combination. I had a strong feeling that Mawuli would not have much resistance should he and Gifty decide to get married.

A few days later, Mawuli and Gifty received their national service postings. Both of them were going to be in Accra; Gifty, in a bank and Mawuli teaching business courses at Accra Academy. The holidays were now coming to an end and it was time to prepare for school. I was busy with laundry, packing, cleaning, and preparing the hot black pepper sauce, shito— that indispensable staple for every Ghanaian student. During the last week, when I went round visiting family members, most of them pressed a few cedi notes into my palm.

JD and I spent time talking about how much we were going to miss each other and how we were going to try hard to write more frequently. "I wish we were in the same school. I like knowing that we can talk and meet frequently."

"I know, I know," JD soothed. "But things will be better this year. We will keep in touch more. I certainly would like to make sure that you don't spend the entire year locking lips with Maxwell Owusu!"

"Shush! I am not going to be perpetually lip-locked with Maxi …I'll only do a few lip-locking sessions."

We giggled, and then JD turned serious. "Be careful, DziDzi, it is very easy to get swept away. I know that you and Maxi intend to hold on to your Christian principles and not engage in premarital sex, but it is very easy to let go gradually, and before you realise it, you are doing things you never thought you'd do."

I looked sharply at JD. Was she speaking from experience? "You are taking a different approach from the crowd," I teased. "You know how the preachers and women leaders in the Christian fellowship stress that it is the women's duty to control the men and make sure that they do not get swept away by passion? I always felt that the men were the only ones who felt aroused and that the women are more restrained. I took that as a fact until Maxi and I began our relationship. Then I realised that women have just as strong emotions as men. It is very scary." I confessed.

"True," JD said. We moved the conversation into other arenas. An hour later, we were hugging goodbye. We wouldn't see each other for the next three months.

****

Early the following morning, I had the expected meeting with Papa at 6:30 a.m. at the dining table. Congratulating me on passing my first year examination he went on, "Don't rest on your oars just because you successfully passed the first year. The rest of the years in the university will be tougher as you specialise in your field of study. As your mother and I have told you several times, do not leave your work till the last minute; make your academic work a priority. Your brother made us proud and I hope you do same. I trust that from Gifty's experience you know that it is possible for a girl to come out with a First Class."

I liked Gifty Marbell, but was not amused that she had raised the bar that high. Still, my father's mention of Gifty as a standard was a definite confirmation that she was welcome in the family. I filed that away to tell Mawuli later, and continued listening to Papa. "I see from letters in the mail and the visits to his home that you are still with the Maxwell boy. I am happy that you did not spend the entire holidays glued to his side but visited him only twice and had him over once. There will be more time for boys after school. You did a good job keeping up with visits to your grandmother, aunties, and cousins. Your mother and I are also pleased that you helped around the house and spent time with Naa Norkai. I hope you keep that up."

I nodded in silence, but could feel a shy but pleased smile infuse my face. I was happy that my extra efforts to be pleasing to my parents during the holidays had been observed. I did feel a bit guilty because my father had no idea that Maxi and I exchanged more letters than what appeared in the postbox, and that we had had weekly clandestine outings at the library. "Your mother will give you your pocket money," my father ended.

I had to go to campus early next morning to register and then come back and take my stuff to school. The tiresome registration exercise started at the Registrar's office on top of the hill, then at our departments, and finally, at the halls of residence. At three o'clock, when it finally got to my turn to check in at the hall, I learnt that Rachel, my previous roommate had dropped out of school because of family-related issues. I had been assigned a new room on another floor and a new roommate. With great trepidation, I looked at the roster to find I'd been assigned a room with Florence Osei-Britwum of all people. *She is probably going to criticise everything I do and see demons in my cooking pots. And I wonder how she and Maxi are going to interact… after all wasn't he interested in her last year?* With these thoughts, my joy at being back to campus took a nosedive.

Back home, Naa helped me load my things in the UG's Land Rover. I took a shower and changed, and said my goodbyes to the UG when they returned from work just before 6:00p.m. My mother bustled around, making sure I had some homemade (home cooking) to take with me for the first few days. She also gave me my pocket money for the next two weeks.

After about an hour's drive through heavy traffic, we cruised into the parking lot. Immediately Mawuli stopped the car, three boys in raggedy shirts and khaki shorts rushed over shouting,

"Any work? Any work?"

"Sister, use me! I will only charge 50 Cedis!"

"No! Use me! I am very strong!"

"I will do the work chop-chop"

The young men known as any work boys patrolled the courtyard when school was in session. We used any work boys for all kinds of labour—to carry buckets of water when there was water shortage, to buy food for us, to do cleaning or sometimes dishes and laundry. Anytime we needed them, we would stick a head over the balcony and shout "Any work?"

Among them, Jacob had been my favourite errand boy. Dark, with spidery thin legs that belied his strength, he was usually chatty and had told me about how he was saving money for school. I didn't know how true that was, but it motivated me to pay him extra when he ran errands for me.

"Jacob and you," I pointed to another one. They dashed over to the car and began to drag things out. "Careful with the stove and the fridge," I warned. I went to the porters' lodge to collect my key from Mr. Amissah, the friendly porter on duty. I unlocked the door to Room 410 on the fourth floor and flipped the light switch. Apparently, my new roommate had not yet made an appearance. The dusty room could use a good sweep and mopping. The advantage of arriving first was that I could have the bed and wardrobe of my preference.

"Hmm, Dzigbordi, by the look of things, you do have work on your hands... " Mawuli had barely finished when Jacob said eagerly, "Sister Dzigbordi, I can help you clean."

"Okay, Jacob. Let's get all the things up first," I sighed. We got all the things up on the second trip and Mawuli left. Jacob and I made our way upstairs. He had already begun recounting how he was going to use his earning to take care of his sick mother. What a responsibility for his young shoulders! Before unlocking the door I walked to the corridor on the right side of the staircase and looked across to Akuafo Hall Annex B. The lights in Maxi's old room were on but the curtains were not drawn. I could see someone swiping the air with a broom, probably battling the cobwebs. I needed to finish cleaning before midnight so I could take a stroll over to Akuafo hall and invite Maxi over for some of my "homemade". The plans for my evening depended, of course, on the appearance of my new roommate.

Chapter Nine

Jacob stayed with me until almost 11:00 p.m. He fetched water, scrubbed, and together we mopped, dusted and arranged items around the room and balcony. Around 9:00 p.m., Maxi came over. We took a break and all of us enjoyed the food. Two hours later, I paid Jacob a generous sum, and gave him food to take home with him. Finally, Maxi and I were alone. It had been three long months since we had kissed. We had held hands discreetly whenever we met over the holidays, and we had hugged when I visited his home. Despite the influence of Western culture on students on campus, we still had to make do with assignations in dark empty classrooms or under trees at night. Maxi was wearing a very tight pair of black jeans and a multicoloured tie and dye shirt that had the first few top buttons undone showing glimpses of dark chest hair. We had been periodically brushing up against each other as we worked and I could see intense hunger in his eyes and felt my mouth go dry. It was like an elaborate dance of foreplay. By the time Jacob left, we had reached the limit of our endurance. Needless to say, our resolve at decreasing our romantic do's crumbled fast in the face of the abstinence imposed on us by the holidays. Florence Osei-Britwum was the only one who would have prevented anything from happening, and she did not show up. I pulled down the curtains, shut the door leading to the balcony, and turned the key in the lock of the main door. Maxi was sitting on my bed which we had made before Jacob left. We took one long look at each other and the next I knew, I flew into his open arms and we went tumbling onto the bed. Our lips met in one long, passionate, hungry kiss.

"Oh DD; darling Dzigbordi, I have missed you so much! I don't know how I survived this long vac!" Maxi whispered.

"I missed you too, Maxi," I said softly, pressing my cheek against his. "I can't forget how gorgeous you looked when I saw you in those shorts and singlet in your house."

He laughed. "Thank you. I shall save that outfit and always wear it especially for you." Still fully clothed, we pressed our bodies against each other. I placed my hand on his chest, slipping it through the opened buttons and began to stroke his bare chest. He pushed me down and unbuttoned my shirt and before I knew it, his hand was in my brassiere and his fingers were caressing a bare breast. I was in shock with pleasure. I heard a voice say loudly, "Oh God….Oh!" and realised it was me.

"Shhhhh!!!" Maxi said. I shut up, embarrassed, not only because of the moan that had escaped my lips involuntarily, but also because of the name of the Lord I had evoked under such clandestinely pleasurable circumstances. It felt so blasphemous. We did not undress any further, even though we continued making out for the next half hour or so.

Afterward, we lay on the bed talking. I mentioned some of my concerns about having Florence as a roommate, but Maxi didn't believe it was going to be as bad an experience as I envisaged. We spoke of our goals for extracurricular activities; more involvement in the Christian Fellowship and personal evangelism. Neither of us touched on the fact that we had reverted to make out sessions so early in the term. Before we knew it, it was almost two thirty in the morning.

"I should be leaving so that we both get some sleep. We can meet for breakfast late morning," Maxi suggested.

"It is rather late. If you leave now and someone meets you on the way downstairs or the porter sees you, he is going to think you were up here having sex," I argued. I didn't want anyone to have the impression that we were together late because of sexual activities.

"Well, we were doing something like that, weren't we?" Maxi teased.

"You know exactly what I mean!" I said. "The best thing would be for you to stay here till morning, and then go downstairs, and then no one would know that you were up here all night. We can have breakfast before you leave, so if anyone comes over, they would think you came here early to eat."

"How do I urinate then? Am I to hold it until after breakfast? I don't think I can do that. Also, what if Florence Osei-Britwum shows up early? That is going to be an embarrassing start to your relationship," he said firmly and left.

****

Florence showed up two days later just as I was about to leave for my first lecture. She was with an older man and a male in his mid-twenties. She greeted me cordially enough. "Hello, Dzigbordi."

"Hi Florence, I was wondering if everything was okay with you when you hadn't shown up," I said.

"We were out of town and the car broke down on the way. We had to stop in Kumasi and get it fixed. By the way, this is my father, and my brother James."

"Good morning, Mr. Osei-Britwum. Hello James," I said.

"The room looks great! I am sorry I left you to do all the cleaning," said Florence.

"That's okay; I got an errand boy to help out."

"Then please allow me to pay my share of his fee."

"No…don't worry about it. Now I need to hurry off to a lecture. I will see you when I get back."

For the first two weeks, I felt inundated— what with new information, new classes, a few new course mates, and a new roommate. Florence and I were polite but distant with each other. Most of my lectures were in the mornings and early afternoon from Monday to Thursday, and most of hers started late morning and went on until 5:00 p.m. Unlike other roommates who were friends and took turns with the cooking, we kept our food separate. She went to bed very early and would huddle under the blanket to keep out the light. The first time Maxi came over after Florence's return, despite my apprehension, I sensed no awkwardness. I got to know that she was in a relationship with the ex-head of the prayer warriors, Samuel Koomson. He had been her spiritual counsellor and prayer partner before she entered Legon and had prayed with her during the time she was considering Maxi's proposal. He was now in America. Two weeks after the term started, I returned from lectures to find

Florence lying on her bed with her face to the wall. I thought she was either sleeping or praying—two favourite occupations of hers, but as I sat on my bed and slipped off my canvas shoes, I realised that her shoulders were heaving slightly, and I could hear her sniffling.

"Florence! What's wrong?" I asked, all my uneasiness forgotten.

"Nothing," she responded in a husky, tearful voice.

I moved over to her bed and placed a hand on her shoulder. "Florence, don't tell me 'nothing,' I know that there is something wrong. Are you sick? Is anything wrong at home?"

She kept silent, and I was about to move away when she turned onto her back and looked at me. Her eyelids were swollen with weeping. I felt my heart sink with dread. "It is Sammy!" she wailed, dabbing at her eyes with a damp hanky.

"Sammy? What is wrong with Sammy? Is he ill? You haven't broken up, have you?"

"No!" then, "I don't think so…I am worried, I haven't heard from him for two weeks, since we got back to school! We promised we were going to write to each other at least twice every week and so far we have been able to do that. I know he planned travelling to Texas to visit an old friend and is probably busy, but at least, he should have had time for one letter! He didn't write me or call!"

A feeling of relief flooded me; relief that no one was ill, injured, or dead. Was I amazed! Florence Osei-Britwum, the apparently confident prayer warrior with abundant faith who could identify and slay demons was also simply a young woman in love. From that moment, she ceased to intimidate me.

"Florence, I am sure he will write. There must be a reason he hasn't done so yet. I am sure that the travelling is the reason for the delay in his letters. Perhaps it's taking a while before he can find a post office, or he might have given the letters to his friend to post it but the guy has not done so. As for calling you, you don't have a mobile phone, so how is he going to get hold of you here on campus? If there was something seriously wrong, you would have heard about it through his family."

She continued to sniffle and hiccup intermittently, but soon ceased crying. I wondered how to terminate our conversation and then I had a brainwave.

"I know what we should do, let's say a short prayer for Brother Sammy's safety, and then you need to eat. I have some beef jollof rice I made last night. We can eat together." I expected her to sit up and launch into one of her passionate sessions, binding every demon that was preventing Sammy's letters from getting to her, but to my amazement, she looked into my eyes and said, "Please pray for me, Sister Dzigbordi."

Oh no! How could I match up to the connoisseur of prayer? Florence, who spent at least two minutes singing and five minutes announcing the accolades of God before launching into main prayer topics? However, I couldn't refuse her request. She sat up, we held hands and then I began, "Dear Lord, your word says that when there are two or more people gathered in your name, you are there in their midst."

"Yes LORD!" Florence interjected.

"You said that if we call on your name, you hear and answer us," I went on.

"Yes JESUS!" Florence's voice quavered.

It was amazing how the interjections acted as encouragement and spurred me on.

"Again, your word asks us to bring our requests before you with prayer and supplication."

"OH YEHOWAH! Thank you Great Jesus!" Florence chanted.

"Lord Jesus, today I am here praying on the behalf of Florence and Samuel. You brought the two of them together. Your holy word says that unless the Lord builds a house, the labourers work in vain."

"AMEN, SISTER!"

"Sammy and Florence are building their home in your name. We are asking you to protect their 'home'. We are asking for travelling mercies for Sammy and your continual protection as he studies in America."

"Yes LORD!"

"We are asking that you give your daughter Florence the peace of mind she needs to study. We are praying that Sammy writes to her very soon. We bind any forces of darkness that are interfering with their communication while they are apart."

"AMEN! AMEN, SISTER!" Florence was in her element. I wished I could go on with more bindings, but I didn't know what else to add.

"We thank you for answering our prayer in the name of Jesus Christ our Lord and Saviour. Amen!"

"AMEN! Thank you so much, Dzigbordi, I needed someone to intercede on my behalf." Florence sounded much better in spite of her swollen eyes.

"You're welcome. Let me warm the food, okay?"

***

From that day, a friendship slowly took off. Florence never forgot that I had comforted and prayed with her when she was depressed. I, on the other hand, never forgot that despite her controlled demeanour, she had her fears and uncertainties. Two days after her 'breakdown', she got two letters and a birthday card from Sammy Koomson. He had been using her old room number as the address and the porter had taken a while to realise the error.

Lectures were more intense that year and a lot more was expected of us. I was particularly anxious about Human Physiology because Mrs. Sackey, the lecturer for the Physiology class had warned during the second week of class, "My class is not easy, and none of you is going to make a First Class." I had to work extra hard to ensure that at least I made second class honours, upper division.

Maxi and I still spent a lot of time together, but more at his place than in my room. We continued kissing and making out, and had several discussions on how far we could go. I felt guilty when we had a series of intense sessions so Maxi and I tried to find a compromise acceptable to both of us. Premarital sex was wrong, but what about the range of activities between total chastity and penetration?

Every two or three weeks, I visited home during the weekend, sometimes I spent the day. Strangely, I felt uncomfortable at home where the UG expected me to act a particular way and although I loved them, I was beginning to find their attitude chafing. These feelings were exacerbated by subsequent visits to Maxi's home, where I felt welcome. His father always took a few minutes to ask how I was doing in school and his mother always made me feel welcome. After the second visit, she allowed me to help her in the kitchen, and on subsequent visits I felt comfortable enough to cook for Maxi and myself if she wasn't in. I couldn't help comparing that atmosphere to that of my home. There was also a slight chilliness in Mama's attitude toward me midway in the first term of my second year at Legon. I couldn't fathom what was wrong; she had a look in her eyes that usually indicated that I had done something bad. I racked my brains but couldn't figure it out, and that did not make me eager to go home.

It was now the Harmattan season, when the monsoon trade winds swept across the Sahara Desert to the Gulf of Guinea. The weather turned hot, dry and dusty, and the nights were sharp and chilly. Our lips and skin became very dry and cracked and we kept them constantly coated with Vaseline or shea butter. Sometimes, during the day, we could see a haze of dust in the air. The trees were shedding their leaves which had turned brown. Indoor furniture got their fair share of the pervasive dust and we had to dust twice daily. Despite the discomfort, I had an anticipated joy since I always associated the season with Christmas.

After a series of class tests, we left for a month-long holiday. Maxi and I decided we would limit our interactions to a few telephone calls and a lot of letters. I was relieved about that decision; I didn't want to go through the hassle of asking for permission to visit him, or devising excuses for assignations.

****

At home, Mama appeared more cordial toward me. She was busy with a lot of shopping and cooking. During Christmas, she prepared a lot of food packages that she distributed to family, friends, co-workers, and her pupils. Her preparation and distribution began very early. By the second week in November, she mailed out Christmas cards to friends and family who lived abroad, and by the second week in December, to people within the country.

I helped with the baking, frying, and cooking. Mama believed that cakes tasted better when made at home, so Naa and I spent hours creaming sugar and flour, and beating eggs. Although it was a laborious process, there was a tremendous feeling of satisfaction when the mixture turned smooth and creamy.

When it drew closer to Christmas, we limited our trips downtown because the streets were choked with pedestrians and drivers, who had descended on the city to shop and celebrate with friends and family. JD and I went shopping in the city together and we had a hard time finding transportation. We spent hours in the city, buying Christmas cards and presents for our family. We pushed our way through the crowds, taking extra precaution with our handbags, because the pickpockets were even more unscrupulous during that time of the year.

A few days to Christmas, we all helped put up the Christmas decorations around the house and Papa began playing Christmas carols piped through the speakers in the sitting room and on the balcony. As per tradition, we all sat at table for a Christmas dinner and then Mawuli, Naa, and I watched Ben-Hur. Throughout the evening, we were constantly interrupted by children who came carolling and we in turn gave them food or money. On New Year's Eve, we stayed up late engaging in different pursuits around the house and around 11:30 p.m., we all gathered in the sitting room to pray; thanking God for His mercies during the year and to usher in the New Year. At the stroke of midnight, we hugged each other and wished ourselves a happy New Year and then said another short prayer for the New Year. After that, we shared a meal before going to bed.

Everything seemed anticlimactic after New Year's Day. In the second week of January, I was back to the routine at school. We had a very short break for the Easter holidays. I stayed to study and hang out with my friends, so I only went home on Easter Friday and returned early Tuesday morning, which did not please the UG much. More weeks went by, and soon it was time for the Mfodwo frenzy. The Christian Fellowship organised prayer and fasting sessions during the examination period. Every evening, we would meet in the Akuafo Hall chapel and pray. Sometimes, students gave testimonies of how God had helped them overcome adverse circumstances during examinations. Maxi and I took up the Mfodwo routines we had used the previous year, but this time we had only one subject in common, so we were in different study groups.

One evening, we had dinner together in my room and sat on my bed with books on our laps, but talking about other things half the time. Florence came in from the library while Maxi was there and greeted us. She had her dinner while reading a textbook. She soon started gathering her bathroom kit, at which sign Maxi decided to leave. I went to "throw him" (to see him off) and returned to find Florence still sitting on the bed gazing into space. She looked up as I shut the door behind me and said, "Dzigbordi, may I speak with you?"

The rather solemn tone gave me a feeling I was in for bad news.

"Yes, Florence, what is it? Is anything wrong?"

"Not exactly… please don't take it the wrong way. It is about you and Brother Maxwell."

"What about us?"

"The two of you are spending a lot of time together, and I fear that is interfering with your studies. Our parents have put a lot into getting us this far, and it is important that we honour their hard work and not disgrace them," she paused and then went on, "Also, it is not good to encourage men. They are weaker than us when it comes to matters of the flesh. It is the duty and responsibility of the women to place limitations on how far they go with us. The more time you spend in their company, as much as you and Brother Maxwell have done this past year, the greater the chance that you two would fall in the way of the flesh."

I still didn't say anything.

"I am sorry, Dzigbordi, I didn't mean to annoy you; I just wanted to speak to you as a fellow Christian sister. Please do not be angry with me."

Without thinking of how I really felt, I began to reassure her.

Although I said I was not angry, my resentment grew as the days went by. What right did Florence have to lecture me on my relationship with Maxi? The cordiality we had developed as roommates soured. Now I felt uncomfortable whenever Maxi visited me. Then, Mfodwo was over and we were back at home for the long vacation before our final year.

****

About two weeks after school closed, it was time for Legon graduation ceremony. Family— immediate and extended and friends of Mawuli's, sat for hours in the courtyard of the Great Hall as the Chancellor and other invited guests gave long speeches. We were happy and extremely vocal when Mawuli, then Gifty went up the dais to shake hands with the Chancellor, the Pro-Vice Chancellor and members of the University Council seated in the front row, and to receive their degrees. At Gifty's turn, this august group, as per tradition, stood up for her— for having obtained a first class and (in her case) being a female to boot. After a lot of picture taking, we met back home in the evening and had a huge party for Mawuli, of course with Gifty present.

As the holidays went by, I had a lot of assignations with Maxi. We sometimes ended up in his home after my trips to the British Council Library, or he sometimes attended my church and we went out to lunch afterward.

The holidays seemed long and endless, and although I tried to be helpful about the house as usual, the UG must have noticed my restlessness, which did not enhance our relationship.

Mawuli spent most of his free time with Gifty and other friends. Gifty was welcome in our home, but Mawuli was very smart enough not to exploit that and instead visited her on her turf.

On three occasions, Papa had to go on work-related trips and Mama went along with him. During that time, Mawuli spent more hours away from home and I clandestinely brought Maxi home. We spent time in the sitting room, but on a couple of occasions, when Naa was the only person home, we sneaked into my bedroom and made out. One time he stayed till 6:00 p.m. and the watchman saw him leave, however I didn't think he would report that to the UG. I also felt comfortable about Naa Norkai. After all, hadn't she earned my trust with her silence about Mawuli's secret birthday party?

A few days after the UG's return from the last trip, rumour had it that the Mfodwo results were out and so I went back to campus. With a sense of déjà vu, I pushed my way through the crowd in front of the bulletin board for my department and started scanning toward the end of the "Ds" for the pass list. This time, I did not see my name. I couldn't believe my eyes; however I remembered the experience of the student from last year, who had been so anxious that he had not seen his name the first time he read the list. Smiling, but feeling my heart beat erratically, I carefully went through the list, starting from the very beginning of surnames under "D". However, "Dzordzome, Dzigbordi, A." was nowhere to be found.

Chapter Ten

I stood at the bulletin board and went through the list of names over and over. I had not passed my second year examination. How was I going to tell my parents? I blindly pushed my way through the crowd. Some people glanced at my face and turned away. Facial expressions could easily tell who had passed and who had not. Maxi was waiting for me at the edge of the crowd and for a few seconds, we looked at each other without speaking.

"Did you pass?" I asked him.

"I passed," he responded simply.

"Hmm…congratulations, then," I returned dully.

"DD, you did not fail the exam, you have a conditional pass," Maxi said gently, "You failed Crop Science practical and you have to retake it, but you don't have to repeat the year."

I was relieved that I would not have to repeat the entire year, but why couldn't I have passed outright?

"Did you see my name on the conditional pass list?" I asked.

"Yes… Doris Quansah told me your name was there, so I went to check. DD, I know it is a disappointment, but the good news is that you passed."

I shrugged, and began to walk out of campus. He fell in step with me.

"I feel so bad as if I am somewhat responsible. I am so sorry," Maxi said.

I wasn't in the mood to deal with his guilt trip so I kept mum. As my bus pulled away, Maxi shouted, "I will call you tomorrow!"

Mechanically, I paid for my fare and received change from the mate, failure on my mind. I could imagine my parents ascribing blame to Maxi, Mawuli being disappointed and Florence silently gloating, "I told you so."

I had just gotten home when I heard the telephone ringing. I picked up the sitting room extension and said, "Hello?"

Mama was at the other end. "I called earlier, and Naa Norkai told me you had gone to school to check on the examination results. Are the results out yet?"

"Yes, the results are out," I said quietly.

"And...?" Mama asked, "Did you pass?"

"Yes." I said and stopped. Shouldn't I be adding that I had a conditional pass?

"Well... congratulations. You should be sounding more excited." There was a modicum of relief in her voice. "How time flies! One more year to go and you will be all done. Anyway, I was just checking on things."

What had I just done? I should have told her right away about the conditional pass. Now it was going to be even more difficult to do so. But... did I have to tell the UG about it? I would retake the exam, and pass it, and everything would be okay. I would inform Mawuli about it; I could trust him not to spill the beans to the UG, and he may be even helpful in suggesting ways I could successfully handle the situation.

I did have moments of uneasiness when Papa came home

114

and asked me about the examinations. He gave me one of his probing looks, and I felt as if he could see through me, but it could just be my guilty conscience. Mawuli came to my room when the UG had gone to bed because he sensed there was something wrong. After I told him what had happened, he assured me that if I passed the retake it would not affect my chances of getting a second upper. "I had a few Cs in my second year and I still made it. It will be great to have a first class or second upper, but I think as long as you don't have a third class or pass without honours you should be okay."

****

Maxi telephoned me from the post office late one morning. He told me that the date for Crop Science practical was exactly four weeks away.

"It is a pity that you can't stay on campus. A lot of people retaking the examination are doing so. I met Kojo Bensa and he also has to retake the examination. He says there are eight others affected and they are all studying together. The TA has arranged a revision session before the exam day to go over everything."

I spent the following day with JD. Although Jemima and Kezia usually said hello to me when I visited and went on with their pursuits, on this visit, they spent 15 minutes with me to reassure me that it was not the end of the world and that I would pass the Crop Science practical exam retake.

"The main thing is that you passed Biochemistry and Human Physiology; those were the tough ones. With the practical exam, from what I hear, you have to make sure you know all about the botanical names of weeds and plants and be able to identify them and also have a notebook with samples of weeds, isn't that so?" Jemima inquired.

"Yes…I suppose I shouldn't be too surprised I failed it. I didn't spend much time on it and it was hard for me to remember the differences between one blade of grass and another."

"This time will be different," Kezia encouraged me. "You can ask the teaching assistant to help you. I know Kenneth Asafo, he's a pretty nice guy."

I explained that I was keeping the conditional pass from my parents and would find it hard to make it to the review sessions.

"Don't worry about that," Kezia said firmly. "Jemmy and I will talk to Kenneth and if you cannot make the group session, I am quite certain he will meet you another time and tutor you." When JD and I were left alone to talk, I told her of my ambivalent feelings about Maxi successfully passing Mfodwo.

"Does a part of you blame him for your conditional pass?" JD asked.

"I don't know," I responded, "I don't think he is responsible for what happened; I think it is because my parents, Mawuli, you, and Florence Osei-Britwum went on about how I needed to be careful that our relationship did not result in examination failure."

"I didn't mean to make you feel that way, Dzigbordi," JD said. "Not all failures are attributable to a relationship. Perhaps, it would have felt that way if you had failed one of your main courses or had had to repeat a year, but it is Crop Science practical, for goodness sake! You shouldn't feel bad about it, and you shouldn't allow anyone to make you feel ashamed."

I felt much better; JD was the kind of person who found it hard to lie, even if it would make a person feel better. We went to buy waakye a few doors away. This mix of rice and beans, gari, stew, pepper and fried fish, always made us so full we simply lazed around on the couch. Later, I helped JD with dinner preparation and only realised how late it was when Mrs. Tamakloe returned from work.

"Oh no, it is after five already! It will take me almost two hours to get home!"

"You did cook before leaving home, didn't you?" JD asked.

"Yes I did, but you know my parents want me home by six!" I scrambled to gather my belongings.

"Why not call and leave a message with Naa that you are running late?" JD suggested.

"Brilliant suggestion. Mind if I use your phone for a minute?"

"Of course not, go ahead!"

I telephoned home but for some reason, Naa wouldn't pick up the phone, which was rather unusual. Eventually I gave up. JD saw me off to the bus terminal.

****

By the time I got home, dusk had fallen and the watchman was there to open the gate for me.

"Good evening, Baba Idrisu," I greeted, breathless from my rapid walk. He always greeted me with a grandfatherly smile, but tonight, he wouldn't make eye contact. The garage was slightly open and I could see my mother's car parked but there was no sign of my father's. I went to the back door and knocked. Naa

117

opened it immediately. Her small round face looked solemn and I could see streaks of dry tears on her cheeks.

"What is wrong, Naa, and where were you? I called home around five to let you know I was running late but you didn't pick up the phone." Curiously, like Baba Idrisu, her eyes slid away from mine. She bent her head and her shoulders shook with the force of her silent tears.

"Naa! What is the matter? Did you get into trouble?" I asked in a sibilant whisper. She didn't answer, and I was about to coax her further when Mama shouted from the bedroom "DZIGBORDI!!!!"

Uh oh! TROUBLE! There is something very wrong and I am a part of it. Could she have found out that I failed Crop Science?

"Yes Ma!" I began to move along the corridor toward the bedroom door, my heart thumping and butterflies fluttering in my tummy. I knocked three times on the UG's door.

"Come in!"

I took a deep breath, twisted the door knob and stepped into the bedroom. She was sitting on her side of the bed and had her reading glasses on the bedside table. She gave me an accusatory look in silence for several moments.

"Good evening, Mama. I am sorry I am late. Karen and I got talking and I forgot about the time. I did try calling home around five so that I could leave a message to let you know, but I couldn't get through."

Mama continued looking at me, her expression unchanged. I stood there feeling my stomach churning in discomfort, wondering when, if ever, she was going to speak.

"Dzigbordi," she began very calmly, "Did you, or did you not have that boy over to this house several times when your father and I travelled out of town?"

I felt my stomach heave violently and for a moment was scared that I was going to vomit all over her bedroom floor. This explained why Baba Idrisu had looked uncomfortable and Naa had been crying. Mama launched into full mode.

"That boy is a bad influence on you; you have changed ever since you started seeing him. You have spent the last few holidays sulking around the house. You have become duplicitous and conniving. Do you think we do not know that you spend all your time with that boy? You lie to us that you are going to the library or visiting Karen and then sneak over to see him. You think that pretending you visit him once or twice a month is pulling wool over our eyes, don't you?"

I stood there, aghast. How did she know so much? My feet were trembling like a tree trunk being uprooted, but I still couldn't move a step.

"I have read his letter encouraging you to sneak around and be deceitful with your parents. What kind of person would do that? What kind of home was he brought up in?"

All of a sudden I was gripped with an intense wave of rage. My nervousness dissipated, and before I knew it the words were pouring out of my mouth. "So, you've been sneaking about reading my letters? I cannot believe that I have no privacy in this house. Did you break the lock of my old trunk to get to the letters?" I knew there would be a huge price to pay for my insolence but I was too angry to care. Mama was also staring at

119

me with shock and rage. "I did not go through your letters! I never go through your materials!" she threw back.

LIAR! I screamed silently. There were a few charged, silent minutes and then she resumed speaking calmly.

"Dzigbordi, your father and I are very disappointed in you. We've worked hard to make sure you have everything you need, and in return, we expected you to obey our rules. Based on my knowledge of you and the information I have on him, I can only conclude that you did this based on his persistence."

"Maxi...Maxwell wasn't the one who made the decisions to sneak around; I did. At first, I wanted everything to be open and above board, but you and Papa treated Maxi as if he was below your notice. It was just too much trouble getting him here so we...I decided it was best I saw him at his place instead."

"Then why didn't you just tell us that you were going to see him? Why did you have to make up all those trips?" Mama's voice was scornful.

Needled by her tone, I retorted, "I didn't lie! I did not make up those trips. I did go to the library! I didn't tell you I was passing his home because you would have made a fuss over it!"

"Yes, so you brought him here to our house; you made Naa, an impressionable young girl in our care, a girl who looks up to you to set a good example, an accomplice in your duplicitous behaviour. When you were left with her alone in the house you brought that boy into our home and took him to your bedroom where you remained with him for hours and did goodness knows what with him. Is this the way we brought you up? Is that what you learn in that church you go to every Sunday, or in the Christian fellowship group you are always bragging about?"

She touched a raw nerve. She made me feel guilty for making Naa Norkai an accomplice. Had I contributed to the corruption of an innocent young girl? Still, did my behaviour excuse my mother's act of snooping through my things in my absence?

"You are twisting things around," I said in a shaky voice, "I did not do anything wrong with Maxwell Owusu and I still don't think it is right that you went through my things. He did not encourage me to hide anything from you; in fact, he was the one who insisted that he visit me at home so that it wouldn't be as if I was hiding things. The mistake was trying to be open about our relationship."

"Well, let me tell you that he is not welcome in this house any longer. You are free to do whatever you want to do while you are on your university campus, just do not bring it to the house!"

Blinded by the tears, I opened the door and rushed onto the corridor almost colliding into Papa and Mawuli who had obviously just returned from work. I ran to my room, slammed the door behind me, turned the key in the lock and threw myself on the bed, sobbing bitterly.

I lay in the dark for hours, long after I had finished crying. I followed the sounds in the house. The UG remained in the room for a while and I could hear the murmur of their voices. Mawuli unobtrusively tried the handle of my door and went away softly when he found it locked. Hours later, I heard the sound of the windows being shut, someone was locking up. By midnight, I was feeling pangs of hunger but didn't dare go to the kitchen in case I met anyone. At 1:00 a.m. when I was certain that everyone was asleep I turned on the light in my bedroom and carefully examined my old school trunk. It was still securely locked with the key still hidden in one of my old shoes in my wardrobe. I opened the trunk and found Maxi's letters there bound together with the green hair ribbon. I knew it was unlikely that Mama had read those letters, so how had she found out so much and why did she say that from what she had read she attributed my rebellious behavior to Maxi? At 5.00 a.m., I started on my chores. Naa still wouldn't look at me. When Mama came out at 5.30 a.m., the breakfast tray was ready.

"Good morning, Mama." Her only response was to stare right through me.

I finished my chores and remained in my room until the UG and Mawuli left for work.

I went to the kitchen and made myself some breakfast. Naa was still unable to face me. "Naa, I am not blaming you for what happened, I know you did not deliberately tell Mama about Maxi's visit. What happened?"

The poor girl poured out her tale interspersed with sobbing gulps. Mama had returned home from school unexpectedly early and had called her to the sitting room to interrogate her. She told Naa that she was already aware that I had brought a boy to the house on more than one occasion when she and Papa were away. She warned Naa that if she lied she would be sent packing. Then she questioned her on the times Maxi and I had been in the house together—how long he had stayed, what we had done, whether we had been in my bedroom together, and whether Mawuli was present.

"Sister Dzigbordi, I didn't want to betray you, but what could I do? She already knew about it and I was afraid to lie to her!" Naa renewed her sobs.

"I am not blaming you, Naa, it is okay."

****

For the next few days, the UG neither spoke to me nor responded when I greeted them. I did not go out of the house that week, not even to church on Sunday. The following week, having obtained the schedule for the study group for Crop Science via Jemima Tamakloe, I went to campus twice without telling the UG. On the second occasion, the session ended later than I had anticipated and I arrived home just after Mama. Then on the evening of the eighth day after the fight, Papa asked Naa Norkai to summon me to the sitting room. This time, there were no files, pens, or papers. Mama was also present.

"I waited all this while before talking to you because I wanted to give you the opportunity to address the events that occurred in this house a week ago. Your mother told me what happened, some of which I have been aware of for some time. During the course of a conversation with our neighbour, Mrs. Obeng she asked how many sons we have beside Mawuli and your mother informed her that she had only one. Mrs. Obeng said she was puzzled, because she had seen another boy who looked like Mawuli's younger brother frequently entering and leaving our home. Your mother questioned Naa Norkai and found out that any time we left town, you brought that boy to our home and even spent time with him alone in your bedroom.

She questioned Baba Idrisu, and he also confirmed he had met that boy here in our absence."

My mother broke in, "Dzigbordi, you accused me of breaking into your trunk and reading your letters. Let me make it clear that I have not, and I repeat, NOT done anything of that sort. This is how I got to know about what you and that boy were up to: a few months ago, you lent me that novel on Queen Elizabeth I and I found a letter from that boy in it. I had no idea what it was before I read it and that is when I found out what was going on."

Papa took over the session once more. "Dzigbordi, we are extremely disappointed in you. Let me also state that that boy is no longer accepted in this house. Your mother and I have seen that he is a bad influence on you. I must say that from the moment I saw him, I knew he did not come from a good home. He has also demonstrated by subsequent actions that he is rude and presumptuous. Such behaviour is not permitted in our culture. You tell him that I do not want to see him in this house and that he is not welcome in this family. Also, you live in our home and we expect courtesy from you, and as long as you live under this roof, you will obey our rules. Do you have anything to say?"

"No." They probably expected me to apologise but I just couldn't bring myself to do so.

"Then you are excused," Papa said.

JD telephoned the following day while my parents were out. I gave her a synopsis about what had occurred in the past week and she was appalled. I told her to let Maxi know what was going on.

****

For three more weeks, my only outing was to campus to study for the examination. I felt so depressed, as if my life was at an end, with nowhere to go. I was able to have a private tutoring session with Kenneth Asafo, thanks to the Tamakloes. By exam day, I felt confident I was going to pass. It was easy for me to identify the crops and weeds, and I wondered why on earth I had thought it so difficult previously.

The first Sunday I went back to church, Maxi was there. After the service, I spent about an hour with him telling him about the confrontation with my parents. Maxi was dismayed but he commiserated, "Don't give up, DD. A few more weeks, and we will be back in school. I am sorry you had to go through that time on your own. I wish I could have been there for you." He went on, "I don't understand your parents. Don't they know how unhappy they are making you? You have lost so much weight and you look so sad! But don't worry. We just have to be patient, trust in the Lord, and intensify our prayers; God will work a miracle for us. We shall have a testimony to give on our wedding day, just you wait and see!"

I couldn't wait to return campus. I started crossing off dates in my pocket calendar. University spelt freedom from tyranny and depression. As if in answer to my prayer, the days seemed to go faster. On the day that I was leaving for school, there was no early morning meeting at the dining table with my father. Other than that, the routine was the same as the previous year. Mawuli dropped me off in the evening. I was still assigned to the same room and roommate. Once more, Florence didn't arrive on the first night. Jacob, the errand boy, helped me clean up and unpack some of my things. He had grown a few inches since I last saw him, and he told me all about his family members and how each one of them was faring.

As we worked together I could hear the arrival of vehicles in the courtyard and students welcoming each other back to school. These sounds made me feel relaxed for the first time in a very long time. For the next three months or so, I wouldn't have to walk around on egg shells. I was home.

Chapter Eleven

I was just leaving the room when I heard shouts of "410! 410!" from the courtyard below. It was Maxi's voice. I rushed to the balcony and peered down.

He said, "Hi! I wanted to be sure you were in before climbing all those flight of stairs!"

I waved back, excited, "I was just on my way to check on you. Come on up!"

Nervously, I checked myself in the mirror, unlocked the door and stood in the doorway waiting. Soon I could hear his footsteps thumping laboriously up the stairs, then the running sounds as he ascended the final flight. We went inside and locked the door behind us. We both sat down on my bed with our backs against the wall and held hands. We spend minutes catching up on what had happened in the past week. Maxi kept caressing my fingers every so often. I moved until I was resting my head against his chest and under his chin. Before long, we were kissing; gently at first, then fervently. I felt passion melt away the feeling of isolation and confusion I had been carrying around for so long. I couldn't fathom how I was going to survive living at home after I graduated. I was an adult, yet the UG still treated me like a child, but I had neither the emotional nor financial independence to break away; I felt bereft. The emotional charge from being with Maxi helped me feel more alive than I had in months, and now all the discussion we had had about our "sessions" did not seem in the least important. Even as I clung to him with my arms wound tightly around his neck, the tears fell, flowing silently down my cheeks, and then before long, I was shaking with sobs and weeping bitterly. Maxi seemed to understand without explanation what I was going through, and the sensations that wracked my body ignited the sparks of passion into a roaring fire. He was kissing my tears, his lips traversing my face, his voice unsteady as he murmured endearing words to me— he loved me, he would never leave me, things would work out, he didn't want me to be sad. His words made me cry harder, but despite the tears, I couldn't stop touching his face and returning his kisses. I didn't want him to stop. For the first time, I wasn't sure I would be able to put a brake on my feelings that were spiralling out of control, but I did. Exhausted, I lay against his back, his hands clasping me. My puffy eyes felt gritty and I sniffed periodically. Feeling emotionally drained, I soon dozed off. After about an hour, I woke up feeling hungry. We ate ravenously and then went back to sleep in each other's arms. Once during the night, I sneaked him into the bathroom so that he could urinate. Fortunately, no one saw us. In the morning we had a breakfast of tea, bread, scrambled eggs and some doughnuts. He was gone before Florence arrived in the afternoon.

****

Our final year at the university was packed with activities and we were bent on enjoying everything. One significant event at the beginning of my final year was my budding friendship with Lilliana Forson. She was a friend to Florence Osei-Britwum and used to visit occasionally. Lilly was full figured and almost Maxi's height, unshod. She had dark brown skin and long hair that cascaded down her lower back, usually confined in tight braids. Her big, light brown but sad-looking eyes were her most distinctive features. One afternoon early in the first term, Lilliana and some friends visited Florence. Soon after, Maxi, Mickey and a few other friends came to visit me. Eventually, the two groups started conversing freely as Florence and I passed around plates of biscuits and glasses of Ribena drink. In the process, Florence's friends, who were mostly speaking Akan, started teasing Lilliana because although she was Akan, she didn't speak the language fluently.

"You are a disgrace Lilly, a disgrace! You don't speak your parents' language properly!" shouted Nagtoma Yakubu. I saw Lilly flinch slightly, although she smiled quietly. Her big brown eyes looked sadder than usual.

"Ha! She is not the only one! Look at Dzigbordi! With a typical Ewe name like that, one would expect that she would speak Ewe properly, but she does so with such a terrible accent!" Paul Kpodo laughed. I shot him an angry look.

"It is just so sad how the white man has destroyed our culture," Kenneth Agyeman said mournfully. "They forced us to speak English in our public schools and now the younger generations are losing touch with their culture and feel it is a disgrace to speak their own mother tongue!"

"I doubt if that was the objective of the teachers," I interrupted. "We have so many different languages in Ghana and using English as a common language makes for easy communication. And as you know, English is important to advance to higher education."

"Ha! That excuse doesn't wash! I think it is high time things changed. It is high time we returned to our roots and learned once more to be proud of who we are and where we come from!" Paul said.

"Well... things are changing," Florence came in. "Who knows, maybe ten years from now, primary school teachers would be using Ghanaian languages to teach."

"I hope not, to begin with, do you think we are going to come out with a consensus as to which universal language we are going to use to teach in our schools?" I asked.

"Well... Akans make up the largest ethnic group in Ghana, and already most regions use that language for trading and communicating, even in the far north," Kenneth began tentatively. Instantly, a babble broke out in the room, with the non-Akans vehemently opposing the idea. "Why should we Gas be forced to raise our children to speak and write Akan?" Nii Quarshie Quartey protested, his loud voice overriding everyone else's. Nii Quarshie was a hunk of about six feet four inches tall. He had a high forehead, bushy hair and thick black lips which interestingly added an aura of dangerous charisma. I had known him in Achimota, but we had only become friendly in Legon.

"I think English should be the primary language taught in the primary and secondary schools. It will be very difficult for us to agree on which Ghanaian language to use and also being able to speak English gives Ghanaians a great advantage when we travel outside to further our education," Maxi contributed. Most people in the room nodded in agreement, but a cultural fanatic like Kenny wasn't about to let go without a fight.

"I don't see people leaving Ghana to seek greener pastures outside as something positive," he broke in. "Look at the brain drain that is taking place now! Instead of staying and rebuilding our economy, most of us are escaping to countries like Germany, Britain and America, and enriching their economy! We spend time in other countries doing menial jobs such as scrubbing toilets and picking up garbage for money. Instead of seeing the grass as being greener on the other side, we should stay and focus on making Ghana our motherland great once more!" His brown face was contorted with emotion as he hit the air with a bunched fist to emphasise his point.

"There goes our future politician!" Mickey said, and we all laughed.

"It is obvious why you are joking about this, Mike. After all, your father wasn't really Ghanaian, was he?" At this snide remark from Kenneth, the room went so quiet that one could hear a pin drop. It was just like Kenneth to make such a crass remark. His abrasive personality always put me off. He always found any means possible to add a political twist to any conversation. I opened my mouth to speak, but Mickey beat me to it. His voice was low and calm but I knew him well enough to realise he was extremely furious.

"I am as Ghanaian as you are." His voice began to rise. "I was born and raised in this country. I am a Ghanaian citizen, and my father was Ghanaian. The fact that he was of mixed race doesn't make him or me less so. I have the same rights as all other people. Isn't it rather ironic that the current president has a white father and an Ewe mother?"

Paul Kpodo broke in rather nervously, "Come on, Mike, Kenny didn't mean it that way; we were just having a friendly intellectual discussion. No need to get worked up over this, man!" he said rather hastily and the others began to murmur platitudes. It wasn't often that one saw Michael McLean-Brown shed his easy-going, dignified exterior and I found that rather riveting. The group soon broke up and the guests began to trickle out; the get-together had ended.

***

The following Thursday, I met Lilliana on my way to lectures. We fell into step and began to walk in the same direction. "Dzigbordi, there's something I want to discuss with you. Can we meet some time?"

My curiosity was aroused but I was running late. "Sure. When would you like us to meet?"

We arranged to meet on Saturday afternoon. Throughout the week, I wondered what Lilliana wanted to talk about; it was like a tantalising mystery. At exactly 1:00 p.m. on Saturday, there was a knock on the door, Lilliana entered and after about fifteen minutes of chit-chat, she revealed her purpose of wanting to see me.

"I wanted to talk to you because of the conversation in your room last week," she began. "You remember Paul was teasing us about not speaking our mother tongues properly," she paused.

"Yeah…I get a lot of such comments, it used to upset me a lot but now, I don't let it bother me."

"I know it shouldn't but it bothers me a lot." Lilly confessed in her gentle voice as she ran a hand through her braids. "I find it stressful talking to people in Twi; I get very self-conscious."

"I understand what you are talking about," I mused, biting into a biscuit. "I also used to feel self-conscious, but in the end I had to put on an 'I don't care' demeanour." I ran my tongue over my teeth chasing biscuit remnants. "So…what did you want us to do about it?"

"Well…well…" Lilly began, clutching her glass of drink. "I thought we could talk about strategies to deal with people like Paul Kpodo and Kenneth Agyeman and also pray about the issue."

What is there to pray about? I gazed at Lilliana, unsure how to respond to her suggestion. She continued in a firmer tone, "Not to change their attitude, but how we can handle the situation."

"Sure," I concurred. I still found it a rather puzzling approach to take but felt there was no harm in praying. We decided we would meet the following week on Tuesday at 7:00 p.m. on the Mensah Sarbah field, where people met to pray in the early hours of the morning or late at night. Lilly's prayer style was similar to mine, conversational and chatty. The first meeting went so well that we became prayer partners, and then friends. I told her about the difficulties Maxi and I were having with my parents. She confided to me her heartache, "I am six feet tall and even though I am always in flat shoes, I still tower over most men and of course they don't like it. In secondary school it was always difficult to get someone to dance with me during entertainment nights."

"But you are so beautiful and graceful!" I protested. "I wish I were at least above 5ft 3. You stand out, you are unique and everyone notices you. You could have been a model."

"But that's just it; I don't want to stand out. When I was in primary school, I used to slouch in an attempt to disguise my height. Maybe God will find someone who will accept me for myself," she philosophised.

"Where did you get your height from, your mother or father?"

"Both! Although now my younger brothers and I are taller than my mother."

"Lia" as I started calling her, was a hybrid of Florence Osei-Britwum and me. She had the habit of looking for spiritual undertones in everything, but unlike Florence, she was quite talkative and humorous when she wanted to be. Our friendship grew after Nii Quarshie Quartey revealed that he had fallen in love with her. All he did was sigh intermittently and talk about Lia. "She is so gorgeous! She is the tallest girl I have ever met; she must be over six feet!"

I smiled inwardly as I listened to Nii Quarshie rhapsodise over Lia's appearance. It looked like her long-awaited prayer was being answered. Lia had also noticed Nii Quarshie that day in my room. Why wouldn't she? He was charismatic, eloquent, popular, athletic, and above all, he was taller than her.

"He likes you a lot," I hinted baldly.

"Yeah…" she said, trying to sound nonchalant. "I like him too…I have noticed him around for some time now. However, I don't know whether I like him-like him, or whether I just like him because he is taller than I am."

"Does it have to be one or the other? Perhaps, he is the answer your prayer. He is popular, a Christian, a man of integrity, and tall!"

Lia laughed but was still hesitant. "I know…I just need to be sure he is the one. I will pray about it for a while before making my decision. After all, it is a lifelong commitment."

After three weeks of prayer and a day of fasting, Lia was convinced that Nii Quarshie was the answer.

Chapter Twelve

My years at the University of Ghana were perpetually interrupted by one aluta or the other. Aluta was short for "aluta continua," the description for demonstrations or strike actions against the administration or government for whatever students were dissatisfied with, like the paucity of student loans given by the government. When we went on aluta, we refused to attend lectures. This state of affairs could last from one day to months. Initially, I enjoyed alutas— they were opportunities to avoid classes and relax. I enjoyed watching the colourful procession from the comfort of my room. However, after the first few alutas, I began to find them a nuisance; aluta over, we still had to catch up with school work. One time, soldiers came to campus to quell the demonstrations, resulting in gun shots. I had gone visiting home that day and missed not only the spectacle but a bullet that had made a hole in the wall of my room! The campus was closed down and we had to stay home for weeks afterwards. In the final year, that was an unwelcome additional pressure on students. We were so anxious to do very well in our class tests and final examinations so as to merit a good degree.

Maxi thought we could get married immediately after we completed our national service, but I knew my parents would not agree to my marrying Maxi just yet. I was also reluctant to move from my parents' home straight into my husband's.

"But you can still achieve your dreams!" Maxi said. "We support each other! Didn't we write plays together? Haven't we got ideas to open up a business?"

"It is not the same. You know when a woman gets married, her husband ends up calling the shots. In addition, Christian men are always using the Bible to demand obedience from their wives."

"Come on, DD! I am not going to act like your parents and tell you what to do and when to do it. We are friends, lovers, and equal partners. The apostle Paul didn't mean that women were unequal in a marriage, just that if there is a conflict of interest the man should make the final decision."

"Don't tell me Paul didn't think women were unequal! You know his position about what role women should play in the church, and how at church they should keep silent and ask their husbands questions later at home; how they should dress, wear their hair, and…"

Maxi suddenly leaned forward and planted his lips on mine, cutting me off. He had been in the armchair and I had been sitting on his bed, with my legs tucked underneath my thighs. I tumbled backward, dragging him along. Books and papers scattered everywhere. "Why…why…" I began in a shaky voice, trying to ask him what elicited that sudden kiss.

He seemed to understand as he said, "Because while you were lambasting St. Paul, it hit me all over again just how much I love you." My heart melted. I was the one who always initiated the conversation about love and our feelings for each other. My eyes filled up and I couldn't speak for a moment.

"I wish I knew why you love me, Maxi. You could have anyone—someone more beautiful, someone with a less complicated life…" my voice was shaking slightly.

"I want you. Who says you are not beautiful?"

"Well…I know I am okay, maybe pretty, but I am not tall like Lia, not fair like Frannie or spiritual like Florence. Sometimes, I wish I had a unique characteristic that made me stand out," I bemoaned my lack.

Maxi reached out a finger and gently traced my jaw line from behind my ear to my chin.

"DD, you are unique. You are you, and you are beautiful. That has nothing to do with height or outward piety. You have something that makes you special that I find hard to describe. Perhaps it is your lack of artifice, your humour and… I am the one who is lucky to have you; you're everything I want in a woman."

I laughed to stop myself from crying. "Oh Maxi, you are a hot commodity among the young girls on campus. Now that you are a TA, it is even worse; all of a sudden, none of them understand their lab assignments and need to see you outside class."

Maxi smiled and shook his head. "You know that none of them matter— you do."

"Yes, I know. But I can't help doing the 'why me?' thing."

He started picking up some of the scattered papers on the bed and looked studiously at them as if he was embarrassed about what he was going to say.

"I can't explain it, except to say that you are the first person I imagined spending my life with. Whatever the reason is, I see beyond now into the future. I think of us living together, with children, building our dreams together… I actually see it and it feels just right. You give my world meaning."

I was awed and humbled. No one had ever made me feel so important. I believed that marriage was the end point of our current relationship, but before we did that, I wanted to do other things. Was I being an idiot and too over-analytical about what I wanted from life?

A week later, the final of all Mfodwos was over. On the night prior to our departure, Maxi and I spent the evening with some friends who had thrown an impromptu party. I laughed and joked but my heart was laden with the thought of the changes that were going to take place in my life. Just after midnight, Maxi walked me back to my room and helped me pack till two in the morning.

"Stay." I said when he spoke of returning to his room. I wanted to prolong our farewells. He shook his head. "I can't. I still have a bit of packing to complete. As I told you, Daddy will be coming for my things around six in the morning I have to be ready by then. I have barely done anything."

"So…it is goodbye, then," I said bleakly.

"Don't say it like that DD," he admonished softly. He pulled me toward him, sat on the bed and held me on his lap with his arms about me. I wrapped my arms around his neck and pressed him against me. I planted kisses on his neck, half-hoping it would help change his mind.

"I know what you are doing, DD," Maxi groaned.

"What am I doing?" I said in mock innocence, lifting up my head so that we could kiss. We tumbled onto the bed. Maxi looked into my face. "I cannot believe that after looking forward to finishing school for so long, a part of me wishes we still had another term to go. I am going to miss you so much, DD! How are we going to cope with your home situation?"

His words made us realise the enormity of the looming change in our relationship. I could see the dark despair in his eyes and before I was aware of it, the tears were trickling down my cheeks.

"Shush! Don't do that, DD. Let us not ruin this night," Maxi said gently.

I did my best to quell my weeping.

"I don't want to go," he said.

"You have to finish packing, remember?"

"Will you come back with me? I know I was the one who wanted to end the evening, but I want to spend every minute I can with you. You can take a nap while I pack."

I didn't need further coaxing. We locked up and went over to his place. We were done by 5:30a.m. and then he walked me back because I did not want his father to find me in his room.

Two hours later as Mawuli drove me home, my mind was inundated with fears and questions and I barely noticed the passing scenery. What did the my future hold? I didn't know. Only time would tell.

Chapter Thirteen

After the hustle and bustle of campus, life was bland at home and I tried to occupy myself with various activities. I spent time with my cousin Gladys who had completed her national service and was waiting to gain admission into the University of Ghana. I got actively involved in the new literary wing of my church, His Eternal Praises Tabernacle (HEPT). The founder, Sylvester Quainoo (Pastor Sly), had been a student at the University of Ghana when he received "the call." Lia and I were in charge of the literary wing; Maxi, was now member of the church, and part of the prayer warriors group. Nii Quarshie was in the choir, playing the drums. The UG were very skeptical of the HEPT and saw it as one of the many "mushroom churches" that were formed for the purpose of making money out of naïve persons.

"What kind of church is named 'His Eternal Praises Tabernacle'?" Papa huffed. It was true that in the last few years, there seemed to be churches springing up all over Accra but HEPT mostly comprised of poor young individuals and there was no way Pastor Sly was making enough money from the weekly collection bowl to enrich his pockets.

Sometimes, Maxi voiced his impatience with the UG's stance. The latest argument started because he had been telling me about how some of the young girls in his neighbourhood had come over to his home the previous week to visit. I had noticed very early in our relationship that Maxi loved mentoring young adults, especially the ladies. They looked up to him with awe-filled puppy eyes, hanging on his every word because he was tall, good looking, and a university student. Maxi enjoyed the hero worship. On my last visit to his home, some of these ladies had been present and had stayed for a long time, giving Maxi and I barely 30 minutes to ourselves before I had to leave.

"What's the matter, DD?" Maxi asked one afternoon after church. He had been regaling me with news about his ladies the week before.

I had been silent all the while.

"Nothing," I said and lapsed into silence. "Dzigbordi, surely you are not upset because Lizzie, Maggie, Jenny, Roseanne, Gertie, Esi and Yaayaa visited me? These are my neighbours, and they like coming to visit to share their adventures with me and ask for advice. I like talking to them and inspiring them to focus on school and make educational achievement a priority."

I couldn't help noticing the hint of self-importance.

"Sure, just neighbours! As if you haven't bragged about how all the neighbourhood girls and their parents are eager to ensnare you into their family!"

"Bragged? I didn't brag! I was just telling you about what was going on in my life," he shot back.

"I am well-informed about what is going on in your life, thank you!" I felt the prickle of tears.

We were now almost at the bus station. We both hated to part on bad terms, especially as it would probably take us another week before we could resolve our quarrel. I tried to think of a way for us to settle our argument in the shortest time possible so that I wouldn't be late returning home, but by then, Maxi was also aggravated.

"So, what is wrong with you? Are you telling me that you don't want the ladies to be visiting me at home?"

My candid response should have been a resounding yes, but instead I mumbled, "I am sorry... I am just sad and upset that these girls can freely come over to your house and spend time with you while I can't."

We joined the line of people waiting for the bus.

"That is not my fault, is it?" he snapped back. "You are more than welcome to visit my home anytime you want to do so. You have been to my place on a number of occasions and both my parents have made you feel at home. My dad even put aside his prejudices because he knew you are important to me. My mother cannot help but wonder why you don't come around anymore during vacation. She keeps asking if there is something wrong."

"You haven't told her anything?"

"Of course I haven't told her, not yet. What can I say? That your parents do not think I am good enough for you? That although every other family thinks I am a big catch, I am not up to the Dzordzome standard?"

It was the first time Maxi had shown just how irate he was about the situation. I sometimes forgot to put myself in his shoes. It was natural that when he saw how other females flocked over to his home and how their parents welcomed him he would feel even more upset about his strained relationship with my parents.

Maxi continued. "Tell me what you want from me, Dzigbordi. Do you want me to edit what I tell you about my life so that you would not be upset about girls who visit me at home? Or do you want me to tell the neighbours that visitors are not allowed?"

A large tro-tro bus entered the station and was moving toward us. *Please, please don't let this be my bus. I don't want to end things this way!* The mate slid the door open and jumped out of the bus. Slowly, the queue snaked its way towards the bus. Fortunately, I was toward the end and had some moments before I had to take my seat.

"Do you want us to end this relationship?" I asked.

"No." Our eyes met. "I am sorry, DD. I know you are going through a lot, and I am trying to be as supportive as possible. You talk about how you feel when other girls visit me. On my part, anytime I talk with them I always think of you and ask myself why it isn't you who is freely visiting my home, chatting with my parents… I think that is what affected me and made me say all those things, especially as you seem to have the impression that I am just having fun," he said.

Reluctantly, I boarded the bus. He waited for the bus to move before he started walking away.

I spent the night thinking the worst, and feeling that it was probably best to end things; but the following morning, Maxi phoned while the UG were at work, expressing his love as well as his willingness to hang on till things got better.

****

The Mfodwo results were out the following week. Kezia Tamakloe telephoned to inform me that both Maxi and I had been awarded Second Class, Lower Division. I accepted the news with equanimity especially as it wouldn't hinder me from going to graduate school.

My parents and Mawuli congratulated me seemingly without reservation. Lia had a Second Upper and Nii Quarshie a Second Class Lower Division. The next news I was awaiting with apprehension was where I would be doing my year of national service. I was hoping to get a position in Accra. Meanwhile, at HEPT it was decided that we needed a newsletter that could be published every two months. Pastor Sly asked the literary wing to do research on the feasibility of the project. I decided to visit a Christian publishing and printing company that the University Christian Fellowship (UCF) had worked with in the past—Visionaries Inc. I met with the editor-in-chief, Mr. Harry Koomson, a man in his late 50s who had been an employee of Visionaries for the past 30 years. I candidly informed him of HEPT's position. We didn't have a lot of money and wanted something simple yet attractive, perhaps 2-4 pages that would contain news and tidbits, jokes, a poem and a profile on a church member in every issue. Mr. Koomson listened with interest. He informed me that a chunk of the cost would come from typesetting and the printing. He summoned his graphic designer, Mark Oklu, and for the next ten minutes, they conferred together and punched numbers into a huge calculator on Mr. Koomson's desk. The total sum made me shake my head. There was no way HEPT could afford to spare such funds on a newsletter which was more of a luxury than a necessity. I thanked Mr. Koomson and Mark for their time and started to rise up to leave.

"Wait!" barked Mr. Koomson, making me jump. "I have an idea…if your church can find someone who knows how to type and is not totally unfamiliar with a computer, someone who is prepared to come and do that here, then Mark may be able to help with the designing. That would cut down typesetting costs. We can use inexpensive paper like newsprint."

I felt a wave of pure elation rush through me. "Oh, Mr. Koomson, that is very wonderful of you! Thank you so much. That would work for us." I beamed at him and Mark who was smiling quietly at my excitement.

"Wait!" Mr. Koomson cautioned. "You will have to find someone who can type and do the job well. We will be able to help with the designing but Mark and Judy will not have time to help with any typing."

"That is no problem," I responded confidently. "I had typing lessons when I was 14, and I am a fast typist. In addition, my parents have had a computer at home for the past five years. I know a little bit of designing because my brother Mawuli taught me how to design calendars and birthday cards," I said trying hard to convince Mr. Koomson that the plan was feasible. At my words, Mr. Koomson sat bolt upright and both he and Mark looked at me with interest.

"That is very impressive!" Mark finally said. "I type, but use two fingers and I have to look down at the keyboard."

"What kind of computer does your father have?" Mr. Koomson interrogated.

"A Toshiba," I replied.

"We have a Mac computer. It is different from the PC but it is not hard to learn how to use it." Mr. Koomson said. "Okay, we are going to try you out. You can come in twice a week in the afternoons and get started."

I was happy not only because I had been able to cut down the cost for publishing the HEPT newsletter, but because I would have the opportunity to work at Visionaries Inc., even if it was just for a few days a week. I loved their magazine, and one of my ambitions was to have something similar in the future that catered to teenagers. I started to thank Mr. Koomson and Mark, when yet another idea came to mind. "Mr. Koomson, when you are satisfied that I am a good typist, I would like to suggest something that would be of great benefit to both of us," I said tentatively. Mr. Koomson looked at me with surprise and then his stern, age-lined face softened with amusement.

"Yes, Miss Dzigbordi?"

"In return for typing manuscripts for Visionaries, you will not charge HEPT anything for designing the newsletter and will give us a discount on the printing," I said boldly.

He laughed. "Let's take it one day at a time, Dzigbordi! It does sound like a good idea. I don't know about the printing costs though; we cannot pay for the paper but I am sure we can work something out."

"If it is okay with you, can I come in next week and learn the basics about the Mac computer? I don't mind doing some typing for you. I can use it to learn about graphic design so that when it is time for the HEPT newsletter, I will be able to design it myself," I suggested, hopefully.

He laughed, raising his hands up in mock surrender. "That's alright as long as you work out the details with Mark so that you come at a time that there is a computer available." I thanked him fervently and left his office with Mark in tow. He showed me around the small suite. "It would be great if you can help out. There are lots of typesetting jobs, and Fatima, our typist, cannot handle everything on her own. It is worse now because she is going to have a baby soon."

I started going to the publishing company Mondays, Wednesdays and Fridays. Alice, the assistant editor gave me a pile of manuscripts to type. All the manuscripts were handwritten, some of them barely legible. I enjoyed reading the manuscripts as I typed them and would sometimes laugh out loud. My job was to type them out but I saw no reason why I should not correct mistakes of spelling and grammar.

****

One afternoon, Mark informed me that Mr. Koomson wanted to have a word with me before I left for the day. I couldn't help a flutter of apprehension. Mr. Koomson and I didn't talk much and I felt as if I was under constant observation. When I went over to his office, I was even more apprehensive to find that Alice was present.

"Sit down, Dzigbordi," Mr. Koomson gestured unsmiling, to the second chair in front of his desk which was piled with manuscripts and back copies of Vision, the magazine of Visionaries Inc.

"How are things?" he asked.

"Fine, thank you," I responded.

"Alice and I have been looking at the manuscripts you have been typing for us. We noticed that you made some changes to them," he spoke in a deadpan voice.

Uh oh! Am I in trouble? Perhaps I should have typed them as they were written. At least, I should have asked Alice for permission before making changes?

"I am sorry…" I said to both of them. "I should have asked your permission. I read as I type and I automatically correct the grammar. It wouldn't happen again."

Mr. Koomson looked at me without a change of expression, but I caught a slight smile on Alice's face. She said gently, "No… Dzigbordi. We are not angry with you. It took initiative on your part to edit the manuscripts as well as type them."

"What are your plans?" Mr. Koomson broke in abruptly.

"My plans?" I asked in confusion. What did he mean? Plans for my life? Plans for the long vacation? "Ehmm…I will probably go to graduate school after I do my national service."

"Are the national service postings out yet?" Alice inquired.

"No…they should be out any moment," I said.

Then once again, Mr. Koomson took over the conversation.

"Dzigbordi, we have been watching you for the past few weeks. We see that you are very eager to learn and are interested in writing. We wanted to find out whether you would be interested in spending your national service year with us. In addition to what you are doing now, we will expose you to all aspects of publishing: soliciting stories, selecting stories, editing, interviewing, organising writers' workshops and competitions, as well as marketing. Visionaries Inc. is not just a publishing company. We believe in spreading the word of God through writing. We believe that the Bible is not just something to read but it should transform every facet of our daily lives. If you accept this position, it would involve hard work, commitment and passion. Are you interested in the position?"

They stared at me as I sat in stunned silence. By Mr. Koomson's speech, I had an assured position in Accra for national service, and I was going to be in my dream job in a Christian publishing company. Visionaries Inc., the second largest Christian magazine publisher in the country.

"Dzigbordi? What is your answer?" Mr. Koomson's voice dragged me out of dreamland.

"Oh! Sorry! I would love to work at Visionaries! It's a miracle to be given this opportunity. I promise to do my best," I gushed.

Mr. Koomson almost smiled, "We will discuss the details next week."

The job at Visionaries changed my life in more ways than one. I was on a perpetual high, very eager to face each day. At work, I got on well with the staff, although I was still a bit scared of Mr. Koomson. I was one of the first people to arrive at work and usually the last to leave. The UG didn't complain because I called home whenever I was going to be late and they had the work telephone number and could reach me anytime. They didn't know that Maxi sometimes came to my workplace after his day at work (he was teaching science courses in a junior secondary school in Accra). He also mailed most of his letters to the Visionaries Inc. post office box.

Mr. Koomson and Alice assigned me stories to write and I began seeing my name in print. I would open the magazines and read my stories with the byline Dzigbordi A. Dzordzome and smile. It was even more exciting when readers responded with letters about a story I wrote.

Before long, the national service year was almost over.

Brother Henry, as everyone in the office called Mr. Koomson, called me to his office for another "talk". He wanted to know if I was interested in extending my time with them, which I agreed to. I now had a job. I began to think that I would just stay on and work there instead of going back to school like I had planned, but although Maxi was happy that I had found my niche, he wasn't satisfied with the status quo. One of our dreams was the opportunity to be able to go to graduate school in the States and Maxi began to outline what we could do, which was mainly saving up for the Graduate Record Examination (GRE) and researching universities we could apply to for admission. Alternatively, he suggested we put aside graduate school and get married as I was now in a relatively stable job.

Although I wasn't ready, someone in my family was eager to tie the knot. Mawuli and Gifty began speaking seriously of marriage. After his national service, Mawuli had been able to secure a good job with an international financial company. Gifty also had a great job. Both of them were saving and making plans to get married.

Almost a year after our last Mfodwo, it was time for the graduation ceremony. A few days to the ceremony, the UG gave me permission to have about ten of my friends over for a get together. It was a difficult moment for me; I felt like saying "no thank you," but that was their moment of triumph as well. I didn't want to ruin the occasion as we had gotten on well for so many months. However, I felt very bad and sad because I was unable to add Maxi to the invitation list because of my parents' previous mandate. I invited Lia, Nii Quarshie, four other friends in my cohort, and my cousin Gladys. One of the hardest things of my life was explaining to Maxi why I could neither invite him nor refuse the UG's offer to hold a party for me. He looked at me but didn't make any comment. All he said was that he would spend the day with his family who were holding a party for him.

Mama had two outfits made for me and paid for my first manicure, pedicure and eyebrow wax. I felt all grown up and beautiful when I left the house with my family to the graduation ceremony. When the UG dropped me at the designated spot for graduates, I immediately began searching for Maxi. I found him among a group of our friends. We spent the next half hour having pictures taken in our graduation regalia by a professional photographer. The UG joined the crowd after parking the car and we took some more pictures.

Although Maxi was in the group, neither Mama nor Papa acknowledged him. The ceremony dragged on in the courtyard of the Great Hall. The after party was a bitter-sweet occasion. The UG were very nice to my friends and there were lots of food and drinks. There was music and dancing. Gifty and Mawuli spent a few hours at the party. People kept asking of Maxi. I felt guilty that I hadn't at least asked the UG if he could come to my party. I now felt Maxi would feel betrayed. I also wondered how his party was going. How did he explain my absence? I never got to know the answers to those questions, because neither of us asked about the other's party. It was that reticence on both our parts that emphasised the thorniness of the issue.

Toward the end of my second year with Visionaries Inc. Papa summoned Mawuli and I for one of his early morning conferences. Mawuli had the first time slot, which lasted almost an hour. He came out smiling, so I knew that everything had gone well. When I took my turn, Papa had my file before him. There was a sheet of paper with the day's date and time written on it. In his usual format, he recapitulated events concerning my academic and professional life. He asked me about my future plans, specifically, whether I wanted to keep working at my current job. I informed him I was interested in a master's in a writing-related profession preferably abroad.

"How do you intend to do that?"

"I am going to look into scholarships. I am also saving toward the GRE," I responded.

"My educational plan for my children is to help all of you get to the master's level if you want to. Studying abroad is a good idea because of the constant interruptions in the Ghanaian universities because of strikes. I cannot promise to fund your entire master's education, but I should be able to help for the first semester or two. Hopefully you will be able to get funding from the school."

I stared at him, breathless with joy. I would never have thought that my parents would approve, much less help financially to make my dream of studying abroad come true.

"Thank you!" I said.

"Your brother Mawuli is also interested in an MBA abroad. However, he says he wants to marry Gifty in the next year or so. She is also interested in furthering her education, so they will both apply for schools abroad. She should be able to get one without any difficulty; she is a hardworking, focused, and clever young lady."

Wow! A wedding! Mama would be thrilled. "When do they plan getting married?"

"They haven't set a date yet, but by the end of next year. They are saving for a flat at the Sakumono Estates. There are some very nice houses there." He said with enthusiasm and then went back to the previous topic. "Do the research on the schools you want to apply to and get information on the GRE examination and the date you can take it. Work on that as soon as possible. All the schools have deadlines."

****

I could hardly wait to see Maxi's reaction when I told him my news that weekend. He said he was happy for me, and also suggested that we get married before I left.

"I will also take the GRE and apply to schools, but it may be more difficult for me because I am helping to support my mother as well as contribute toward Serwaa's school fees with my income from teaching. It may also be more difficult for me to get a full scholarship from the start. However, if we get married, we can go together to America as a couple and I can get into school a semester or so later."

I was still reluctant to take that step toward asking the UG for permission to marry Maxi. I knew they had not relented toward Maxi, and as much as I loved him, the last thing I wanted to do was to complicate issues by demanding a wedding before I left the country. If I postponed graduate school, how were the two of us going to live on our incomes? It would take a couple of years before we could save enough to rent a room in Accra. "I don't know whether now is the right time," I began slowly, feeling selfish. "I don't know how to tell my parents that I am getting married now, especially as I am not yet in a position to support myself. Mawuli and Gifty have been in a relationship for quite a while and are still saving to get decent quarters before getting married."

Maxi gave me a look and shook his head sadly, "Sometimes I wonder if you are interested in getting married to me!"

"Maxi, that's not fair! I don't think we should quarrel over this. I would like to get married eventually but I don't think it would work out if I ask my parents now, and we do want to get married with our families' approval, don't we?"

"We have prayed and prayed and fasted about this issue. Perhaps it is time to take a step of faith," he insisted. I shook my head. The following week, Maxi accompanied me to the United States Information Services (USIS) which had a library with materials on schools in America. I researched schools with vibrant Mass Communication departments. Although I found several schools that met my criteria, I could not apply to all of them because of the application fees. I finally settled on four.

Papa helped me buy a GRE study guide. Every day after work, I would spend at least an hour studying and working on the practice examinations. I took the exam two months later. I wasn't sure how well I did, but it would take six weeks before I knew my results. The day following the GRE was a Sunday, and as usual, Maxi and I walked to the bus station after church. We were chatting about our plans for the following week when all of a sudden, he cut into the middle of my sentence.

"DD, there's something I want to tell you. I wanted to keep it as a secret but I think I can now tell you."

"What? What is the secret?" I asked excitedly.

"Well…I wrote to your father a week ago…" he started.

"WHAAAAAAT?" I shouted so loudly that people around me stopped and stared.

"I said, I wrote to your father," he repeated.

"Why? What for? Why did you write him?" This couldn't be good!

"Well…" he hesitated and then went on firmly. "I know that things are better for you at home and I felt it was time to test the waters and have some faith that God would answer our cries. We have prayed about this…fasted twice a month for the past two years. You, Lia, the prayer warriors, and your cousin Gladys have supported us in prayer. Must we continue to pray without taking action?"

"What did you write in the letter?" I was deaf to his reasoning.

"Nothing to worry about…I just said I was writing to

apologise if I had done anything wrong, that you mean a lot to me and I know that the rift between us has weighed heavily on you."

We looked at each other, and it was as if we were standing on opposite sides of a river bank. Maxi obviously didn't understand how the UG operated. Papa would see his letter as an intrusion, and instead of assuaging the anger it was going to exacerbate it. If Maxi mailed the letter last week, my father should have received it by now. Why hadn't he said anything to me?

Maxi was waiting for me to say something. "Well... it is already done. The Lord's will be done," I said quietly. But I had the feeling that the peaceful time at the Dzordzome residence was over and that trouble was once more on the horizon.

Chapter Fourteen

My feet felt like heavy cement blocks and my heart thumped hard, as I approached our gate.

"Where are Mama and Papa?" I asked Naa after she had taken my handbag and Bible out of my hands.

"They are in the bedroom." She walked ahead of me and it struck me how much she had changed in the past year. After staying short and plump for a long while, Naa had suddenly shot up in height. In addition, she had developed curves, slimmed at the waist and now displayed a modest bosom. Her thick hair, which had been kept short for years under the aegis of a roadside barber, was now plaited in neat cornrows. Naa could now read and write fluently in English and was an excellent cook. She had been taking sewing classes for three years and was a seamstress. All her savings were deposited into her post office savings account book which she guarded jealously. Naa's mother was now clamouring for her daughter's return home. At almost 16, she felt Naa should start thinking of marriage, with her skills, she would be a prime catch in the village. Mama was heartbroken to lose Naa, but Naa's younger cousin, Dede, was going to live with us and undergo the same training. I followed her indoors and knocked on my parents' bedroom door.

"YEEESSSS!" Papa shouted. I opened the door and entered

the room. They were lying in bed watching television, and both turned to look at me. Their facial expression did not give anything away.

"Good afternoon," I tried to sound as normal as possible.

"Afternoon," Mama responded, while Papa gave his usual grunt.

They know…I know they do! I thought as I went into my room and sat on the bed. Or…do they?

That evening while we were having dinner, I informed Mawuli about what Maxi had done. He was horrified.

"Dzigbordi, you have to control that boy. The right way to manage the UG is not to keep barging in where one is not wanted. Maxi has done everything wrong from the beginning, and now he is sending Papa letters! Honestly, why did you let him do such a thing?"

"I didn't let him do it! I had no idea that he was going to write to Papa!"

"Well, then you have a bigger problem on your hands than you think. If he's not going to work with you but would keep taking such steps without your knowledge, I can see worse times coming ahead of you two. Regardless of what you say, there is no way the UG would believe that he did it without your consent, and even if they did, it is going to put him in a worse light," Mawuli warned.

"Well…it is hard for Maxi to understand; it is the difference in our upbringing. He says after doing so much praying and waiting, it is time to take some action, that the only way we can see any miracle out of this situation is to take steps of faith like people did in the Bible."

159

"Hmm! The people in Bible times hadn't met the UG!" Mawuli joked darkly. "Just be prepared for any eventuality! And no matter what, don't lose your temper. They will be putting a lot of money in your graduate education in America and you don't want to show yourself to be ungrateful. The best thing probably would be to apologise." Mawuli picked up his empty plate and got up. At the door he turned, "It just hit me, are you sure Maxwell didn't send that letter because he wants to mess up your chances of leaving the country?"

"Don't be ridiculous!" I retorted. "I don't know why you are so suspicious of him!"

"Alright, alright! Just checking!" Mawuli said, slightly contrite.

"Big brothers always feel they know everything!" I muttered.

****

It was a busy time at Visionaries the following week. Although Vision was a monthly magazine, we sometimes missed deadlines because of electricity outages that made it impossible to do any computer work and delayed our work at the printers. We were also brainstorming on the cover titles for the next two issues, which was an activity I especially enjoyed.

On Sunday, I arrived at church later than usual and did not have time to talk to Maxi. As soon as the service was over I extricated Maxi from our group of friends and we started walking toward the bus terminal.

"So...how are you doing?" Maxi inquired with unusual concern as we began our stroll.

"Fine... and you…?"

"Okay."

"By the way, I don't think your letter arrived," I said.

"Why do you say that?" he asked curiously.

"Because my parents haven't said anything to me about it," I responded, hoping he didn't sense my relief.

"I don't know why they haven't said anything because it did arrive," he said quietly without any discernible facial expression.

"How do you know it has arrived?" We were now standing under a tree where a boy was turning sizzling sticks of beef kebabs over a hot charcoal grill. It was a place where we sometimes rendezvoused if church service closed on time. We would sit on the bench under the tree and snack on kebab and a bottle of soft drink. This time, because we were not purchasing any food, we didn't use the bench. The kebab boy greeted us politely and threw a few hopeful glances in our direction.

"Do you want some kebab?" Maxi offered. I responded with a glare. How can he be talking about food in such a situation?

"Okay… okay! I got a letter from your dad on Monday. Someone delivered it to my home."

"What did it say?" I asked in a shaky voice, unable to fathom why neither of my parents had commented on the fact that Maxi's letter had arrived. Maxi pulled out the Bible he was carrying from under his armpit, opened it to the center, took out a folded sheet of paper and handed it to me. I opened it with trembling fingers and a photograph of Maxi and I in our graduation regalia fluttered to the ground. Maxi picked up the picture as I began to read the letter.

161

Mr. Maxwell Owusu
P.O. Box 333
Adabraka, Accra
19th May 1996
Sunday
13:25GMT Hours

Dear Mr. Owusu,
Despite my clearly stated wishes, you keep trying to ingratiate yourself into my family. You obviously do not have any respect for your elders, otherwise I would not have had to repeat this; but let me make it clear once and for all:

(i)   I have no wish to have you visit my home with or without my knowledge,

(ii)   I definitely do not wish for you to send me unsolicited letters.

I think it is very impertinent of you to write and inform me about my daughter's feelings. Whatever she has discussed with you is her business. I cannot make it clearer as to how I feel. Please do not invade my privacy anymore.

I trust that you will respect my wishes and leave me alone. This is my final word on the subject.

Dr. N.E. Dzordzome

I must have read the letter three times before lifting my head. Maxi's reason for writing the letter in the first place was because he wanted to "test the waters" after years of prayer. Well, now he had his answer. Papa's letter did not in the least surprise me, but why hadn't he summoned me and yelled at me for what had happened? I folded the letter and handed it back to Maxi.

"At least, I tried," he said quietly as he shut his Bible.

"What do you want to do next?" I inquired.

He shrugged. "Nothing for now; just take it a day at a time. We will continue praying about it. Nothing is too impossible for God. He has handled problems a thousand times more monumental than this. To our Lord, this is smaller than an ant on an elephant's back."

I felt the tension in my stomach ebb slightly. We continued to lean against the tree trunk, lost in our individual thoughts. Although Maxi had spoken pragmatically about the situation, I knew he must be hurt and disappointed. Papa's letter had been quite emphatic. For the first time since he had told me about the arrival of Papa's letter I felt overwhelmed with guilt.

"I am sorry you didn't get a better response," I said gently. I had been so focused on my feelings and my family's reaction and the fact that I disagreed with what he had done. I took a deep breath and made a declaration that I knew would be hard for me to fulfill, but which I meant to keep. "Maxi, I promise to try again sometime soon. Give it time to settle and I will talk with my parents. I don't want to do it now because it will make matters worse. We would have a better outcome if we wait for things to calm down first."

For the first time that day, a genuine smile lit up his face. "Thank you, DD. I know how difficult it is for you," he said softly. I smiled back, and then added firmly. "Maxi, in the future, please do not take any action with my parents without our discussing it first."

He looked startled at the decisiveness in my voice and then smiled. "That's fair. I should have done that previously, but I was so afraid you'd say no. It won't happen again."

****

That night, after I said goodnight to Papa, who was reading in the big sitting room, he looked up and said, "We need to have a meeting. Tomorrow morning after my coffee would be a good idea."

"Okay Papa." I responded, my heart sinking. At last, he was going to speak about Maxi's letter. The following morning, the two of us convened around the dining room table. I sat there trying to appear as calm as possible as I waited for Papa to speak. "I wanted to know where you are with the process of applying to school in America," Papa started. For a few seconds, I felt slightly dizzy. I had been so convinced that he was going to talk about Maxi that it took me a while to switch mental channels.

"The GRE results should arrive in a week or so," I replied.

"How about the application materials?" Papa asked.

"I received the packets for University of Florida, University of Chicago, and Wheaton College."

"Any other schools?"

"There are many more good journalism schools, but I

selected these because of the application timelines that would allow me to get in early next year. They are all due around July."

"Well, it means you need to work on them now. I know it takes about two weeks for mail to get to the US but you need to make allowance for delays. We can send them by expedited mail to be on the safe side."

At the end of the week, the mail with my GRE scores arrived. I had met the requirements for graduate school. My verbal and math scores added to 1200. I had listed the names of the schools for my results to be automatically sent when taking the GRE. The schools also required TOEFL, but I had a letter from the University of Ghana stating that I had passed Language and Study Skills, which demonstrated that I was an effective communicator of the English language.

Mawuli and Gifty's wedding was set for December 28 at the Aggrey Chapel in Achimota School. Gifty's mother wanted a lavish wedding for her only child, while Mama believed in simple, modest affairs. Finally, they compromised on 60 guests. Gifty and Mawuli meanwhile were busy furnishing their flat at Sakumono Estates and attending marriage counselling sessions in the evening at the AME Zion Church. I was going to be the bridesmaid and would also write and perform a poem at the wedding. The fabric for our dresses was already bought and designs discussed with the seamstress. Gifty's wedding dress was going to be a gorgeous, creamy affair, with short sleeves and a long train. The entire gown would be embroidered with patterns of kente, making the gown look as if a host of small brightly coloured butterflies was nestling on the material.

Meanwhile, Naa's younger sister, Dede, had joined the family so that Naa could help train her before leaving. Dede was a mischievous 10-year old who spoke only Ga. She did her best to dodge work, and on most mornings ,I would catch her sleeping in the store room. When she heard footsteps approaching she would jump up from the stool and pretend to be working hard, but I would see a streak of saliva drooling at the corners of her mouth. We were trying hard to help her learn English as soon as possible and settle into the routine of the house but she seemed more interested in chasing birds around the compound than sweeping.

***

Soon thoughts of the wedding and Dede receded to the back of my mind when a thick admissions packet arrived from the University of Florida. They had accepted me for Spring 1997! There was a thick form of several pages including materials from the College of Journalism and Mass Communication on the courses I would take, the name of my advisor and information from the International Students' Center on housing, banking, immunisation and visa requirements. However, I hoped that Wheaton College would send their packet soon. That was my first choice because it was a Christian school and I felt that in a way, it would be like working at Visionaries. I was nervous about Florida. Anytime I mentioned that I applied to University of Florida, people's usual response was either "Florida is very expensive! Only the rich people live there," or "Florida has a high crime rate." The crime rate scared me the most. I put the

University of Florida packet away. Then in November, I heard that Wheaton had rejected me, and not long afterward on November 19, there was a letter in the mail from University of Florida requesting a formal letter of acceptance which I mailed off the following day. I hadn't realised that there was so much to do before I could leave for America. I needed to see a doctor to get the necessary shots for mumps, hepatitis A and rubella, obtain yellow fever and tetanus shots for my Ministry of Health card, and take a physical with a signed medical form to indicate I was in good health. I also had to get an X-ray done and a screening to indicate absence of tuberculosis. The most important hurdle to overcome was getting an American visa.

I didn't know much about the American visa except for the green card lottery which was done every year. You had to mail in a letter with details of your name, age, address, educational status and other pertinent information. If you won the green card lottery, you would be able to live and work in America. I may have been unaware about the visa procedure, but almost everyone I knew had a story or tidbit to tell me about the scary process. Apparently, obtaining the visa depended on the mood of the interviewer, scarier still, the clothes you wore could determine the outcome. Most important of all, you had to do everything possible to make sure your visa application was not denied because if they stamped the back of your passport to indicate that you had been denied the visa, it was very difficult to get it the second time.

The night before my trip to the embassy, Papa met with me to make sure that I had all the required documents, money for the application fee, the passport photographs, and my passport. It was a first come, first served procedure, and although the embassy gates opened at 8:00 a.m., I had to be there very early to stand in line. Mama woke me up at 2.30 a.m. to get ready. Papa and I left home an hour later. The streets of Accra were silent and the roads still littered with rubbish from the previous day. It took less than half an hour for Papa to get to the embassy at Osu. Although it was just after four, there was already a line in front of the embassy gates with about 15 people before me. Papa wished me luck and left. More people started arriving soon afterward. I noticed that some of the newcomers were replacing others in front of me. It appeared that some applicants paid to have people wait in line for them.

After dawn broke, a young man in a pair of black trousers and a white long-sleeved shirt began walking up and down the long line. He was clutching a Bible in hand and singing a hymn. Then in a loud voice, he informed us that he wanted to pray with us and thank God for the day. He bowed his head and began to sing once more. Some people bowed along and others ignored him. The man read a passage from the Bible and prayed that God would grant us grace and favour before our interviewers. After he finished praying, he went up and down the line singing and receiving donations. For all those who donated, he would say "Thank you, may God bless you!" I could sense a slight release of the tension among some of us in the crowd, particularly those who had donated money. Soon after the young preacher left, the embassy gates opened. First, those who had won the green card lottery were summoned, and we watched with envy as they were allowed in. After a while, the first fifty of us were allowed in. The first step was filling the application forms we were handed and paying the application fee. There was a lot of waiting and moving from one area to the other. However, I didn't remain there as long as I thought I would. One of the personnel looked at my form and asked me if I had had an interview with Mrs. Nancy Keteku at the US Information Services and I responded in the negative. He told me that I had to leave and meet Nancy for an interview. As I got up to leave he took my passport and stamped the back of it. Oh no, just what I had been warned against! I had been denied the visa and there was a record of it. *Well, don't worry about it. If I don't get the visa, it means that God doesn't mean for me to leave the country at the moment. I will continue to work at Visionaries and put my efforts toward marrying Maxi and settling down.*

The following day, I went to the USIS to meet with Nancy Keteku. She was a white woman, but was dressed in a traditional Ghanaian outfit. I sat outside her office eavesdropping as she talked to a young woman who was before me. It didn't seem as if that interview was going very well. Mrs. Keteku was making it clear to the lady that the school in the US that had granted her an I-20 was dubious and there was no way that she would be granted a visa. The young lady left in tears, and it was my turn. Mrs. Keteku was very friendly. She was impressed that I had been admitted to the University of Florida. She asked me a few questions about myself and then told me what I needed for the interview. I had to show that I had ties back home so that the person interviewing me would have relative confidence that

I was going to return to Ghana after completing my studies. She suggested that a letter from a fiancé or business would be adequate. I also had to show that I had financial means to complete my education in the United States. When I informed Papa at home about the outcome of my interview with Mrs. Keteku, he said he would provide documents that showed he had adequate funds to support me for the first year. Then we discussed how I was going to establish that I had ties at home.

"How are they going to know you are going to come back?"

"Well… they know that I have family here. I can also get letters from my pastor at HEPT to show that I am actively involved in the church," I responded, and then added, "Perhaps, Visionaries will also give me a letter."

"Hmm… Hmm…," said Papa pacing thoughtfully, "That is okay, but stronger ties would be more helpful. Like a fiancé."

I stared at him in total shock. For a moment, I thought I was hallucinating. Papa looked at me. Perhaps this is my cue? Then I spoke aloud, "Maxi and I plan on getting married one day. I can ask him to write the letter."

I held my breath while waiting for him to speak. Was he going to jump on me for mentioning Maxi's name?

"Well, if you decide you want to get married when you return we will not stand in your way," he responded and with that, concluded the meeting.

****

That night I prayed a long prayer of thanksgiving. Our miracle after so many months, even years, had finally arrived and in such an unexpected way. Late at night I slipped into Mawuli's room and told him the news. He congratulated me, but also put a fly in the ointment, "The UG are smart. I am sure they are hoping that by the time you return from America, you would have found someone else or broken up with Owusu. Two years is a long time for a long distance relationship." I thought there might be some truth in his deduction of the UG's thought processes, but there was no way that Maxi and I were not going to survive our relationship after all that we had been through.

The next day, I left work an hour early and showed up at Maxi's school unannounced. I peeked into his empty classroom. He was so absorbed in the stack of exercise books before him that he didn't see me in the doorway. I was happy that for once I would be able to tell him something positive about the situation with my parents. As if he felt the intensity of my gaze he looked up suddenly. He stood up abruptly, pushing back the wooden chair so that it made a loud unpleasant grating sound against the cement floor before toppling over.

"DD! What are you doing here? Is everything okay?" he asked.

"My father said if we wanted to marry after I finished school he wasn't going to stand in our way," I blurted out.

"What? How did that happen? What did he say?"

We sat on two adjacent desks and I gave him an incoherent version of what had occurred the night before.

"Indeed, it is the work of the Lord! Didn't I say that nothing is too difficult for Him? I shall write the letter for the embassy tonight and you can pick it up tomorrow. When do you plan going for the next interview?"

"Friday, by then I should have put everything together. I shall see Mrs. Keteku on Thursday to show her everything. If I don't get the visa at least I know I did everything I could."

"Oh you are going to get it, and then when you finish your degree two years from now, we can get married. I will work on getting admission to your school and join you and we can marry either here or in America." We smiled at each other in glee.

On Thursday, I went once more to the USIS. Mrs. Keteku went through my materials and nodded in approval. She gave me a sealed envelope for the embassy that I presumed indicated that I had met with her. I thanked her for all her help and she gave me her business card so that I could contact her in future.

On Friday, I went through the same routine as the first time, but this time, I went further in the process. There was a lot of waiting and while I did so, I observed what was going on. There was an eclectic crowd there, students, people joining their families in America, others seeking visitors' visas, and pastors going for conferences. Most of the interviews were pretty quick and people were either rejected, or told to come later in the afternoon for their passport. I could tell from facial expressions, those who received the visa and those who were rejected. Soon it was my turn. A man in his early 30s was my interviewer. After all the time I had taken in gathering the information he didn't ask me much; he was mainly interested in the packet Nancy Keteku had given me. He looked at the documents from the school, asked for my passport and pictures and then told me to come after 3.00 p.m. for my passport. Was that it? I stepped out of the room with a relieved grin on my face. I felt people glance at my face. An old woman murmured "Congratulations" to me.

Mawuli took me to the embassy to pick up the visa in the afternoon. This time, the process didn't take long. I was soon handed back my passport as well as a sealed envelope containing my I-20. I returned to the car and we took off for home. I scrutinised my passport. *Oh! So that's what the almighty American visa looks like!* My visa picture was a digital image. There was name of the school, the date the visa was issued—13 December 1996, and the date of expiration, 13 December 2001. I had been granted a five year visa even though I was positive that I would be back after two years. Two thousand and one seemed so far away; it was in another decade, in another millennium. I had more than enough time to do whatever I needed to do in America.

I had my foot on the path to my destiny. Maxi would join me soon; we would perform the traditional wedding by proxy before he left Ghana. He would also obtain a master's degree while we enjoyed ourselves, and afterward, we would return home and live happily ever after. Yes, God was good, despite the difficulties with my parents concerning Maxi, and with the visa process, everything had worked out perfectly.

As Mawuli circumvented cars and pedestrians around the Circle area, I stared at the scenery in a daze. The sun was bright and I could feel a slight breeze through my half-opened window. The world was beautiful, and a feeling of exhilaration came over me. I felt like rolling down the car window and shouting out my version of Eddie Murphy's movie: "I am coming to America!"

Chapter Fifteen

It was the Christmas Eve of 1996. In three days, I was leaving for America. I sat on my bed with two half-filled suitcases open before me. I kept vacillating about what to take along with me. Of course, I needed all my letters from Maxi, photographs, books, enough to take me on the long trip and clothes. How many clothes could I stuff into two suitcases? In addition, after wanting for so long to travel abroad to study, I was now flooded with fear as the fulfillment of my dreams loomed before me.

Mawuli and Gifty were getting married on December 28, and although it had been planned for ages that I was going to be the bridesmaid, I had to resign myself to the fact that I would not be present at my brother's wedding. It was after I was granted the visa that we paid close attention to the documents that had accompanied my acceptance package. The school expected international students to arrive several days before classes began. The orientation was on December 30. I also had to find accommodation, report at the students' infirmary, meet with my advisor, and register for classes. The list of activities to accomplish by myself was daunting

"It is not the end of the world," Mawuli comforted me when I sobbed the news out to him and Gifty in our sitting room one evening.

"Don't cry, Dzigbordi," Gifty said, patting me on the shoulder as she pressed a clean white handkerchief in my hand. "I do wish you could have been there and we are going to miss your presence, but we also know that it is an opportunity in a lifetime and you have to leave. We will send you lots of pictures and a copy of the wedding video." I leaned against the shoulder of my future sister-in-law and gulped back my tears. I had become very fond of Gifty in the last couple of years. I felt that she had brought out the best in Mawuli. Since they began their relationship, he appeared more mature and still had that mix of charm, humour and politeness that our older relatives loved so much about him.

"What are you going to do about the second bridesmaid?" I asked. Maame Yaa, Gifty's best friend was the first bridesmaid.

"I haven't thought of that," she responded thoughtfully.

Then, an idea hit me. "What about our cousin Gladys? With a bit of adjustment, my dress would fit her. She will also be able to recite the poem on my behalf."

"Hmm…that's a thought!" Mawuli said reflectively, "Do you think she will do it?"

"Yes…I know she'd love to. I will phone her and find out." The thought of my favourite cousin representing me at the wedding made me feel as if I would still be a part of it.

"Are you okay with that, Gifty?" Mawuli asked his bride-to-be.

"Yes. I would love that if it is fine with your cousin," she responded, smiling back at him.

Most of my time was spent packing for the trip, shopping,

helping with the wedding preparation and bidding relatives and friends farewell. Relatives invited me to luncheons and dinners. It was difficult accommodating everyone's wishes, but I tried hard not to disappoint anybody. In spite of all the upheaval, I was able to spend a lot of time with Maxi. Now that I was leaving and the UG were occupied with the wedding, they didn't even try to monitor my movements anymore. Maxi and I met several times a week in his home. On two occasions, we had long prayer and fasting sessions— for my safe arrival in America, success in my studies, and the strength for both of us to hold on to our relationship.

We were excited at the thought of living together abroad before settling down in Ghana. "I would like at least two years together where we can get used to each other and enjoy life as a couple before children come along." I said.

"Why? We know each other pretty well already. Better to get childbearing out of the way. We are now 26. If we get married at 28 (latest) and have Max Jr. when you're 30, you will be still bearing children in your mid-thirties and get Trixie-Ann. You know they say it is best to have the first kid before 30 years."

"Easy for you to say, you're not the one who is going to go through nine months of pregnancy and goodness knows how many hours of labour!" I retorted.

He opened his mouth to argue then stopped. We looked at each other and burst out laughing. "Oh Maxi…Isn't it funny that we are about to launch into an argument about exactly when we should have children? And by the way, how did you decide on those names? I can understand Max Jr., but Trixie

Ann? Where did that come from?"

"I like 'Trixie'. It means 'the blessed one', and Ann was my grandmother's name!" Maxi said defensively even as his lips curved in a somewhat reluctant smile.

"Maxi….perhaps we should save our fight over baby names until later?" I suggested sweetly, vowing silently that no kid of mine was going to be given the name Trixie. I already had a selection of possible names for a girl—Elizabeth, Katherine, Patricia, or Justina.

"That's a good idea, DD, let's save naming our children for later," Maxi agreed, caressing my fingers as we sat in the sitting room. The home was empty because his father was at work and his mother and Serwaa had gone to the market. I saw his lips tremble, and then he cleared his throat and spoke.

"DD…Oh DD…" he began and then stopped.

"Oh Maxi!" I threw myself into his arms, feeling quite overwhelmed by the conflicting emotions that had wracked my mind ever since the date of my departure was set. I raised my face to press my lips against his, but he gently pushed my head aside.

"I want to talk to you DD, I want you to promise me something."

"What is it?" I asked, shaken by the desperate note in his voice.

"I want you to promise me that you will never change; you wouldn't let the life and temptations in America change who you are. I want you to promise that you will come back home to me."

My life had been so intertwined with Maxi for the past five years; we had gone through so much together that I couldn't conceive how he would have the slightest doubt that I would forget him when I got to America. I was usually the insecure one in the relationship.

"For the past few weeks, I have been wondering why on earth I wanted to leave home and go and study aboard, and if my parents hadn't sacrificed I would have cancelled the trip. You are the one who will have all those gorgeous young ladies making sheep's eyes at you in adoration. You are so gorgeously handsome, confident, loving, exciting that a part of me is worried for leaving you."

He smiled sadly at me. "DD, you should know that no other woman matters to me. You are so amazing, beautiful, intelligent, creative, loving, and so incredibly passionate."

My body threatened to break down and cry.

"Have you booked the hotel yet?" Maxi continued, and I could tell he was trying very hard to make the conversation more pragmatic. I was arriving in America on December 28 and would use the first few days to find a place to stay. Originally, the plan was that I would stay in a hotel for a few days while I went apartment hunting. Papa and I had one of our early morning meetings a few days back, and I hadn't been surprised that he had a printed out an itinerary of what I was going to do during the first few days of my arrival in America. "I will not be staying in a hotel after all," I explained. "It is one of those miracles. I was talking to Mickey two days ago when I went to visit the Tamakloes. He said the University of Florida is associated with a teaching hospital…I have forgotten what it is called. He was interested because he is thinking of coming to America after completing his housemanship. He has an aunt called Esther Benjamin who lives about two hours away from there."

"I don't think I have heard of her," Maxi said after a reflective pause.

"She hasn't lived in Ghana for over 35 years. She is married to an American. Anyway, he was worried because I was going to land in Gainesville not knowing anyone. Isn't it just like Mickey? He contacted Mrs. Benjamin and she says I can stay with them! They will even drive me to Gainesville and help me find a flat…I mean, an apartment!"

"Hallelujah! Thank God for His mercies! Our prayers are being answered! I was so worried about you having to navigate your way through the system."

"So was I! Anyway, I wasn't sure my parents would let me impose on strangers, but they spoke with Mrs. McLean-Brown and also to Mrs. Benjamin via telephone. It turns out that Mrs. Benjamin was in Achimota the same time as my parents! She and my mother were in the same dorm and they used to be friends, but Auntie Esther left the country immediately after sixth form and they lost touch. She lives in a city called Tallahassee, so my father changed the final destination on my ticket so that I end up there."

"I feel much better that you have Ghanaians living not too far away. I am sure they are going to keep an eye on you and make sure you are okay. Hopefully, they will be God-fearing people. We have to make sure we include them on the list for our last prayer meeting," Maxi assured, then added, "I guess we wouldn't meet tomorrow right? You and your family will be getting ready for Christmas and the wedding?"

I continued to nestle in his arms. "Yeah, I will be helping my mother and aunties with the baking. It's going to be very busy because they are having the traditional ceremony and the wedding on the same day." I had felt guilty because I hadn't invited Maxi to the wedding and I had a feeling that he would have felt more secure in the UG's decision to accept him in the family when I returned from America, if I had wangled a wedding invitation for him. We sat in silence holding hands and kissing every now and then. For the past few weeks, every kiss had increased in intensity and there was a note of desperation in the caresses we exchanged. That day, we tried very hard not to let passion sweep away common sense. We knew his mother and sister would return from the market any moment. Still, by the time we heard his mother and sister at the gate, I was lying on the settee with Maxi's body urgently pressed against mine. The first three buttons of my blouse were undone. We had barely enough time to straighten our dishevelled clothes before Maxi went to let them in.

****

The days seemed to fly by. I cried inwardly, *slow down! I want to savour what is left!* The praise and worship session in my last HEPT church service was extra stupendous. By remarkable coincidence, most of my favourite worship songs were sung that day and I felt tears ran down my face as I felt the love of God enfold me. During the prayer session, I was summoned in front of the congregation, anointed with extra virgin olive oil and prayed over by the prayer warrior group. Pastor Sly gave a speech about how I would be missed. After the service, I was surrounded by people who stopped to have a few words of farewell with me. I felt touched and loved by the demonstration of affection.

"I want you and Maxi to come over to my place on Boxing Day for a farewell luncheon," Lia invited as Maxi, Nii Quarshie and I lingered on after most of the congregation had dispersed.

"Will you be able to make it?" Maxi asked. I wished Maxi and I could have talked over Lia's invitation in private. I would rather have spent my last day alone with Maxi. However, the look in Lia's expectant face made me hesitate. For the last months between preparing for the visa interview, the wedding plans and spending time with Maxi, I had neglected Lia. I would have to make it to her luncheon.

"I don't think I will have trouble getting out," I told them. That night, I informed Mama about the luncheon at Lia's and she barely blinked before nodding casually. It felt so weird! How different life would have been if the UG had had that attitude all along!

Christmas was a quiet time. I wondered how our parents felt; this was the last Christmas Mawuli was going to spend as a single man, and my last Christmas at home for a while. JD came over to visit in the evening. The two of us spent hours on the veranda giggling over old times, sharing secrets and promising eternal friendship. She was going to come over to the airport to see me off, but we still cried as we said goodnight. The following day was the farewell luncheon at Lia's. She had prepared a lot of food: jollof rice, palm nut soup and fufu, and spicy kelewele with chilled bottles of Fanta and Coca-Cola. "Let's have a short prayer session together," Nii Quarshie suggested some time after lunch. We all nodded in agreement and then joined hands. After a short hymn of worship, Nii launched straight into prayer mode: "Heavenly Father, we come before you today with thanksgiving in our hearts and with praise on our lips. We thank you for all the miracles and wonders you have worked in our lives all these years. We thank you for giving us the opportunity to come together once more before your daughter Dzigbordi leaves this country for America. Oh Lord, you have been good to her and have given her this magnificent opportunity to go out there and study so that she can return and make a difference. You have also given her the golden opportunity to be your ambassador in that land of turmoil and temptation. We know you are going to be there with her every step of the way and bring her back successfully. We thank you for the miracle you have worked with her parents regarding our brother Maxwell. Indeed, you make a way for us where there seems to be no way. We bind any demons and principalities that would interfere in their lives in the name of Jesus! We also thank you for our sister Lia who has provided this wonderful feast for us. We pray that you will bless her exceedingly, abundantly above all that she put into the luncheon. We thank you in the matchless name of Jesus, Amen."

"Amen!" the three of us echoed.

Nii Quarshie and Lia revealed that they were planning on getting engaged around June 1997 and marrying in early 1998.

"I wish you were around to be a part of it, Dzigbordi," Lia said sadly.

"I cannot believe I am going to miss your wedding as well!" I was disappointed not to be there for Lia's wedding, but happy that their relationship which began in my room at the University of Ghana was going to culminate in marriage.

We were so full and relaxed that no one wanted to make the first move to break up the party. We were at a secluded corner spot and I moved my chair close to Maxi so that I could discreetly hold his hand. I felt a strong zap of electricity between us. My thoughts wandered about feverishly. *Just a few hours... less than 24 hours to go... I wish I could kiss him...spend time with him alone...hold him one more time.*

"Are you taking all your gospel tapes with you?" Maxi asked after a few minutes silence.

"No, I can't take everything. I only have two suitcases. I am leaving a lot of the tapes, my picture albums and a lot of other things I wish I could have with me."

"I would like the tapes and also a copy of the last play we wrote, 'Any man's woman.' May I pass by your place in the morning and pick them up?"

I hesitated. Maxi was coming to see me off at the airport with JD and I wanted to suggest bringing the stuff there. I felt a little bit uncomfortable because he hadn't been in my home since the fiasco with the UG. Even though Papa had given his consent for our marriage, I didn't know how he would act if

Maxi showed up. However, there was no way I was going to make Maxi feel uncomfortable or rejected. "Sure…but please come before 11:00 a.m. My father will take me to the airport to check in at noon."

I took a look at my watch. "Oh no, it is almost seven. I have to leave now. I don't want to arrive home too late."

"I will see you off," Maxi said, and we all stood up. Nii Quarshie accompanied us until we got to the tro-tro stop. Maxi and I were finally alone. We stood underneath a streetlight and looked at each other for several minutes. I could not move. Even though we didn't exchange a word, I felt as if we were talking to each other. *I want you so much; I want you so much that I can barely stand. This is my last night with you for a while, and I wish there was somewhere we could go and spend some time alone together.* I felt my hands tremble as I looked into his face. We continued standing by the tro-tros without speaking.

"Let's take a taxi instead," Maxi said aloud so sharply that he snapped me out of my trance, "The bus would take too long and we don't want you to be late."

He flagged a passing taxi and within minutes, we were seated in the cool darkness of the back seat. Maxi told the driver to drop us at the station close to my home. I leaned against Maxi and we clasped hands, then his fingers began moving all over me. I began shaking and when he dipped a hand down my blouse I groaned audibly.

"Shhh!" Maxi warned in my ear as he gave it a flicker with his tongue. Even with the music in the cab, the outside sounds filtered into the vehicle; tro-tro mates shouting out for passengers, hawkers yelling out their wares, and rude sharp sounds of impatient drivers honking loudly, everything was one big blur. Maxi and I stumbled out of the backseat and paid the fare. The driver had a knowing smirk on his face as he drove away. Without discussing it, we began to walk away in the opposite direction from my home. The road was dark and unpaved with several potholes. Whenever a vehicle approached, the road would light up and the car would speed by leaving us choking in the cloud of dust in its wake. We passed houses on either side of the street which had families sitting outside chatting. We passed children playing late at night by gutters at the roadside. We passed traders carrying wares on their heads and cyclists pedalling furiously by. We walked further and further into the darkness, but each time we thought we had found isolation, we met someone. We walked and walked. I knew it was getting later and later and the time we had bought by taking a taxi was running out but it was our last night together for a long time and I couldn't bring myself to turn back.

"Oh DD!" Maxi exclaimed hoarsely as he finally stopped abruptly at the side of the road. "I am so sorry...I wish I had planned things better. I had thought of booking a room in a hotel for a few hours just so that we could have time together without any interruption, but I was afraid."

"Afraid?" I asked in wonder.

"Yes... I was afraid that you would see it as a sign of coercion. I didn't want you to feel that you had to sleep with me because we were in a hotel room. Also, what if someone we knew saw us come out of a hotel together?"

"Oh!" I said longingly.   A hotel would have been much safer, more productive, and definitely more enjoyable than our current situation.

Maxi and I kissed feverishly, recklessly. There was nothing but the sound of an owl overhead… the buzzing of mosquitoes… the quiet moans that escaped our lips… the sound of our hearts beating… our bodies pressed against each other. The growing brightness of an approaching vehicle made us spring apart. By the time the car passed us, we had begun walking back where we came from.

The walk back seemed long and exhausting. Maxi walked me to the gate of my home and said goodbye. When I reported to the UG, they did not seem in the least upset about my late return.

"Did you have a good time?" Mama inquired.

"Yes!"

"Good. Well, try and get some sleep. Tomorrow will be a long day," Mama said.

"And we should meet in the morning and make sure you have all your documents," Papa added. "I will take you for early check-in and then Mawuli and your mother can take you in the evening. I hate final goodbyes."

As I shut the door, I realised I hadn't mentioned anything about Maxi's impending visit. There's no way I am going back to let them know. I shall just leave things be. I doubt if there would be any trouble on the last day of departure.

****

Early the following morning, Mama gave me items to put in my hand luggage: gari, dried anchovies popularly known as "Keta school boys" and shito—familiar food items to tide me over for my first few days and enable me to gradually adjust to new culinary experiences. She added a box of Golden Tree chocolates and a bottle of whiskey for Auntie Esther and her husband.

My meeting with Papa took place after his morning coffee. We went over documents, passports, tickets, itinerary, and he gave me $200 in various denominations (including coins) to use for the first few days. It seemed like so much money to me. I calculated its value into cedis and I felt quite rich. I made sure I packed all the documents and my passports into the front pocket of my hand luggage. I lay out my going-away outfit: black skirt and matching jacket, green sleeveless top and black pumps. Mama tapped on my door and pushed it open.

"It is very cold at this time of the year in the states, so I brought you a pair of stockings." I spread out the stockings. It was my first time of seeing a pair outside the movies. I decided I would wait till I reached America before putting them on. Mawuli came to my room and spent some time chatting. I made him promise he would write frequently. He informed me that his office had an internet account with email access and he gave me his email address so that I could write to him. I didn't know too much about emails but thought it seemed like a very fast way of communicating judging from what he had said.

Hmm… something Maxi and I can do instead of waiting every two to three weeks for letters. Soon after Mawuli left the room,

I heard a loud knock on the gate outside and the sound of the gate being opened and not long afterward, Dede was at my door.

"Please ,Sister Dzigbordi, you have a visitor!" piped Dede.

"What is his name?"

"Maxwell!" she responded.

"Thank you." I said. I picked up the box of items I planned to leave with Maxi. I walked into the sitting room and opened the door to the balcony. "Hi, DD! Did you get some sleep last night?" Maxi greeted.

"Not much, but I can sleep on the plane. Would you like some water to drink?" I asked.

"Yes, that would be so nice. It is so hot and dusty today… the crazy Harmattan weather playing its tricks as usual!"

I placed the box down and went to the kitchen. I grabbed a bottle of cold water from the fridge and a glass from the tray and fled.

For the next 10 minutes or so, Maxi and I chatted. Every now and then, I glanced surreptitiously at my watch. He had arrived at ten forty five and I had more than an hour before leaving for the airport. If Maxi stayed for the next 30-45 minutes, everything should be on track. Maxi was in the middle of a funny story about his sister when the door opened and Mama stuck her head out. Her eyes zoned straight onto mine.

"Dzigbordi, your father is ready to take you to the airport," she said abruptly, and shut the door decisively behind her. I felt shaken and embarrassed. She hadn't acknowledged the presence of Maxi in any way. Also, according to our itinerary, we had 45 minutes before leaving for the airport. I looked at Maxi and he looked back at me.

"You better go get your things together, Dzigbordi, and I should be leaving," he said sadly and stood up. I didn't know what to say. I wished I had dissuaded him from coming to the house in the first place.

"I will see you this evening," I said in a loving voice. "Thank you for coming." I watched him carry the box out of the compound. I hadn't thought the box was heavy when I packed it, but it appeared heavy as he carried it.

I returned indoors, my chest thumping with a mix of emotions— hurt on Maxi's behalf, anger at myself for not making sure he would be welcome and fury at the UG for the way they treated him. About five minutes later, Papa asked if I was ready. By then the suitcases had been loaded into the car. I sat beside him in silence as Dede opened the gate for us. The car went slowly up the street, bumping into potholes every now and then. My heart was still pounding with shock and distress. Had Maxi had enough time to reach the bus station?

A minute later, I could see him in the distance, trudging along with the box in both hands, his shoulders slightly hunched as he tramped under the blazing afternoon sun. Papa made no comment, but stared straight ahead, but I knew there was no way he had missed seeing Maxi. I turned my head slightly as we passed him. He was looking at the car with a blank look on his face. I wondered what he was thinking. I wondered what would have happened if I asked my father to stop and give him a ride.

As we passed by Maxi, a gust of Harmattan wind blew by, raising a whirl of dust. Papa and I continued the trip in silence. I didn't see the scenery we were passing. My mind was still on my beloved, walking in the hot sun with a load in his hand as he watched his girlfriend and her father pass by him in a whirl of dust without offering him a lift that would have taken him closer to his home. I could have died.

Chapter Sixteen

We left for the airport around 7:00p.m., after I exchanged a tight goodbye hug with Papa; my annoyance dissipating when I realised I would not be seeing him for two years. Mawuli drove us to the airport. Mama was in front and Gifty and I in the backseat. Every now and then, Mama would turn and ask a question: "Dzigbordi, do you have your passport and tickets?" or "Did you remember to pack some storybooks for the trip?" All I did was answer, "Yes, Mama."

When we arrived at the Kotoka International Airport, Mawuli dropped us at the entrance and then went to park the car. As we stood facing the parking lot, I turned to look toward the entrance and saw a group looking in my direction. My heart leapt; a tall, dark man in a black and blue batik shirt that accentuated his broad shoulders with my favourite tight black jeans —Maxi! With him were JD and Mickey.

"Karen and some friends have come to see me off," I murmured as Mawuli approached us from the other direction.

"Good evening, Mrs. Dzordzome!" JD said.

"Hello, Karen. It is very nice of you to see Dzigbordi off. How are you doing?" Mama returned warmly.

"Fine… although I am sure I will be crying in a few minutes. I am going to miss DziDzi very much!"

191

"Oh… this is Michael McLean-Brown, Mrs. Benjamin's nephew," I gestured in his direction.

Mama beamed at Mickey. "Thank you so much for helping Dzigbordi find a place to stay, and for reuniting me with my old friend." Mickey shook Mama's hand and smiled at her in that charming way of his.

"And you already know Maxwell," I added. Maxi murmured a "good evening" in a very low voice and I wasn't sure whether Mama heard him. I felt embarrassed for Maxi after Mama's enthusiastic response to Mickey's introduction, but fortunately the awkward moment was lost as Mawuli and Gifty exchanged greetings with my friends.

"Hey, Dzigbordi, let me carry your hand luggage so that you rest your shoulders for a while," Mawuli suggested solicitously, "You are going to be stuck with it for the next 24 hours or so." I passed it on to him thankfully.

"Well, let's go indoors. I think I hear some mosquitoes buzzing about, you don't want to spend the first weeks with malaria," Mama said walking into the airport. I dropped behind so that I could walk with JD and Maxi. The path to the entrance was strewn with porters who were offering to help travellers transport their luggage for a fee. There was a long line outside that led to the check-in counter. I was so glad that I had checked in early. We hung around for a while but soon moved to the section that led to the departure area. Mama and JD had brought along cameras and took several group pictures. After chatting for a while, the conversation began to dwindle; even JD who could be animated under the most strenuous conditions was now silent. I wished that my family would leave so that I could have some time alone with Maxi, but I also knew that would not happen.

All of a sudden, I felt very enervated. I wanted to get the goodbyes over and done with and focus on what was ahead. "Perhaps you should be getting ready to leave for the waiting area?" Mawuli suggested. I smiled gratefully at him. "Good idea," Mama echoed and then looked slightly uncertain. It was as if it had now hit her that I was leaving. "Well…" she opened her arms and I rushed into them and we hugged very tightly. "I love you, sweetheart" she said to me softly, her voice quivering.

"I love you too. Thank you for everything, Mama," I murmured. Mickey gave me a chaste hug; the kind where the sides of the bodies touched but there was no contact at the breast or groin areas. Then, it was the turn of JD, who was already crying. We pressed against each other, holding tight for more than a minute. It was surprising that after weeks of crying on command I couldn't really turn on the waterworks on the night of my departure. Then I threw my arms around Mawuli and Gifty simultaneously. Gifty had tears in her eyes and oh… goodness gracious me… were those tears trembling in Mawuli's eyes? My brother gave me the tightest hug I had ever received from him and that made me start crying. "Shh!! Don't start… you were doing so well," Mawuli murmured playfully making us both laugh.

"I love you. All the best with the traditional ceremony and the wedding. I shall be with you in spirit!" I said. Maxi had taken part in the general conversation, but I noticed that he had also kept in the background; as if he was trying to make sure he didn't intrude. He looked at me seriously and then gave me a smile that didn't reach his eyes.

"Have a safe trip, DD," he said softly, then reached into his pocket and passed me an envelope which I discretely placed in the pocket of my jacket. Feeling slightly defiant, I moved closer and hugged him. "I love you, Maxi. I am sorry," I said. Mawuli handed me the carry-on bag. The first few steps were the hardest I have ever taken in my life. I looked back and saw them standing still, frozen, staring after me. They all waved at me and I waved back, feeling overwhelmed.

"Bye, Dzigbordi!" yelled JD, making me smile.

"Byeeee!" they all cried out like little children echoing their teacher. Mama was waving with a fixed expression of uncertainty on her face. JD was vigorously flourishing a big white handkerchief. Mickey was smiling broadly. Mawuli and Gifty were holding hands as they gesticulated, and there was my handsome Maxi, taller than all of them with that sad look in his eyes. I wanted to run back to them and throw my arms around them for one last goodbye, but that would just prolong the inevitable. Just as I entered the long corridor that would take me to the customs and departure area, I turned back to wave goodbye for the last time. That picture would remain in my mind for the rest of my life, for at that time there was no way I could have known that for one of the people in the group, it was to be our final farewell.

****

The flight had been uneventful. The most stressful part was the take-off. It was the first time I had flown and all those instructions about what to do in time of emergency made me apprehensive. Can I remember what to do about correctly placing an oxygen mask over my face? I carefully perused the brochure which had diagrams demonstrating emergency evacuations, but it didn't make me feel better. I had always been bad at following directions when it came to assembling equipment, and all that talk about how the oxygen may be flowing through the mask even if we didn't feel it flowing didn't help. What if I thought it was flowing but it wasn't? To my surprise, I noticed that most of the passengers were not even listening to the instructions but were reading or talking to one another. I was very fortunate to have a window seat and was able to watch the lights of Accra fade into the distance.

After dinner, which I couldn't eat, I covered myself with the thin blue blanket I had been offered and soon fell asleep. We arrived in Amsterdam at 5.30a.m. It was my first time experiencing differences in time zones; for my watch registered 4.30a.m. Ghana was one hour behind. It was freezing in the Schiphol Airport, and I had about five hours of layover time before taking the next plane to Atlanta, GA. Although I was wearing a jacket, I was still barelegged in my short skirt. Every now and then, I would tuck one of my legs under the other in an attempt to warm up, but then it would become numb and I would have to bring it down to restart circulation. I was not wearing the stockings because I had ripped them in my disastrous attempt to get them on at Schiphol Airport restroom.

I pulled out Maxi's letter from the front pocket of carry-on bag and unfolded it for the third time:

At Home
27th December, 1996
3.33p.m.

Dear DD,
After all the plans we've made for our future over the years to the extent of even planning and naming our children I didn't think I would ever write these words to you. I tell myself that maybe it is just because I am hurt and emotional and that I should wait until I feel calmer and re-evaluate the situation, but I don't think I can hold what I feel inside me. I don't know whether we have a chance. I don't think there is really a future for us to be together. I just returned from the tro-tro station carrying the stuff you gave me. Mummy and Serwaa were in the sitting room eating when I arrived. They were both interested in finding out how you are doing. I don't know how I kept my cool as I told them that you are fine and were on your way to the airport to check in. I am not going to beat about the bush any longer: I feel hurt and betrayed by what happened in your home this afternoon. I feel as if I have been used, abused and discarded. When you needed help with a letter to the U.S. Embassy for your visa, your parents had no problem encouraging you to use me, but afterward, from what happened today, I can

see that they have resumed their habit of treating me as if I am an invisible object.

Unfortunately, unlike some other countries where marriage is between individuals, in our culture, marriage is also between families. I can't help wondering if that attitude from your family is ever going to change. Are they going to keep their word that they would put no impediments to our marriage? And if we do get married, are they going to continue to treat me like a piece of filthy rubbish in an overflowing gutter by the roadside? For all these years I have been with you, I have been made to feel as if I am not good enough; as if my family is not as important as your family. I am proud of my family and believe my family is equal to yours, but because I love you, I have put my pride aside and swallowed whatever insults your parents have dished out to me. I must confess that I blame you for what happened today. I can't help but think that when it comes to your parents, you find it difficult to stand up for me. You are so afraid of incurring their displeasure that you don't take a proactive stance, you don't take any risks, and you don't defend me when they attack me. With all my father's so-called prejudices, he has been very cordial to you and has made you feel welcome in his home. If he hadn't done so, I would have protected you and defended you. I still cannot believe that you sat in the car with your father and drove by me without even offering me a lift. I felt like a second class citizen, a charity case as I walked down your street

197

with your discarded belongings. What I do know from personal experience and from the Word of God is that we have to be prepared to stand up for what we believe in. All the great people of old had to do it—Noah, Moses, Esther, Deborah, Paul, Jesus, just to mention a few.

Maybe, I should give you the benefit of the doubt—maybe you did ask your dad to give me a lift and he said no. I don't know. I must admit, I feel hurt and angry towards your parents. I am praying that this spirit of bitterness I have toward them will abate soon. I really don't want to come to the airport to see you off. The thought of meeting your family and experiencing a similar kind of treatment has quenched any enthusiasm to make the time and effort to see you off. However, I did promise, and I don't want to make your moment of departure more stressful than it would already be. I hope you learn to take a stance and make an attempt to correct wrongs that are done to those you love. Remember to continue to hold onto the Lord and He shall direct your path.

Love,

Maxi.

4.45p.m.

PS: My mother just left my room. She wanted to find out if it was okay for her to come along with me to the airport and see you off, but I tactfully (I hope), found a way of dissuading her without arousing her suspicions. If she had come and your family had treated her disrespectfully, I know I wouldn't have been able to

stand by and let that happen; definitely NOT!
Maxi.

5.27p.m.
PS (again!): I re-read what I wrote and felt I may have been a bit too harsh and perhaps more candid than I should have been, especially as you are embarking on a new life and have several other important things on your mind. I was tempted to tear up, or at least, rewrite this, but have decided to leave things as they are. I do love you, DD, but please try and see my side on this issue.
Maxi.

I rubbed my eyes tiredly. Was this a break up, and if it wasn't was it fair for me to ask him to trust me and hang on? I had bought some aerogram from the airport post office. I wrote a letter to Maxi apologising for what had happened and accepting responsibility in the matter. The flight to Atlanta took about four hours. Once again, I was assigned a window seat. This time, I wasn't sleepy and I did some reading. Most of the time, I looked at my watch which was still on Ghana time and imagined what was going on at Mawuli and Gifty's wedding.

Soon, the person seated next to me engaged me in conversation. She was in her early 50s, attired in traditional Ghanaian outfit with an elaborate matching headgear. By the end of the trip, she had told me a lot about herself. Her name was Doreen Ofori and was visiting her family in Atlanta. She made the trip to America four times a year. Her oldest son was a rich and successful businessman in the city, with three children ranging from two to 14 years. What made her stick in my mind years after the trip was the way she whipped away the headphones KLM had given us to listen to movies or music and stashed it into her handbag. When we were served a meal, she did the same with the unused silver ware.

"Do you need yours?" she asked me, pointing to the clean silverware on my tray.

"No," I replied. She picked them up and placed them in her handbag as well.

"I want to give them to the children as presents," she explained unabashed.

Atlanta International Airport was astir with fast-paced activities and buzzing with a cacophony of sounds. After going through customs and immigration, my main headache was finding the departure gate for Tallahassee. I felt lost and out of place.

"Good afternoon, Sir, please, how do I get to Gate B 34?" I asked a man in uniform who looked like he might be an airport employee.

"Go down the escalator and take the train to Concourse B."

"Thank you very much." Train in the airport? What was a concourse? I trudged along. The carry-on was heavy; the strap was cutting into my shoulder. Getting my foot on the moving escalator for the first time was a nightmare. By the time I finally got onto the last plane, I was sick of being in the air, tired of the unappetising meals and snacks, fed up with drinking cups of coke, and I was nursing a migraine. The novelty of flying had also worn off and I was no longer apprehensive when the emergency procedure was read. All I wanted was a warm shower, a change of clothes, good food, and hours of uninterrupted sleep.

****

I had been sitting on an uncomfortable seat in the baggage claim area of the Tallahassee International Airport about 30 minutes, waiting for Auntie Esther to pick me up. I was tired, apprehensive, cold, and in need of visiting the bathroom, but I had two suitcases and my hand luggage at my feet and couldn't manage to convey all the items to the restroom. Besides, what if they arrived while I was away? We had spoken with the Benjamins the day before I left Ghana and had given them my flight itinerary. After I got hold of the bags, I sat in the front row at the baggage area looking out for a black female whose appearance suggested Ghanaian origins. Whenever I saw a black woman around my mother's age, I would try to catch her eye, but for the most part, the person would look through me and move on. There was a time when I thought I had found her; a medium-tall, dark brown woman, with shoulder-length braids and grey hair around her hairline who was approaching me. She wore blue jeans, a red cashmere sweater and had a warm smile curved around her lips. I jumped up to my feet and began to smile in return. However, before I could move, a black teenage girl ran past me into her arms and began to shriek "Nana!" I sunk back into my seat in embarrassment.

The few women in skirts wore long boots and stockings. I must have been an odd sight; short shirt in winter with bare unshaven legs in black pumps. I tried leaning in the chair to rest my weary neck, but the back was low and barely reached my shoulders. I shut my eyes to rest them for a moment, yawned, and then opened my eyes as I covered my mouth with a hand.

201

I caught sight of a black couple hurrying through the sliding doors. The woman was about five feet two inches, with short graying dreadlocks. She wore a sweatshirt, jacket, and brown corduroy pants which emphasized her curvy hips. She wore large hoop silver earrings and comfortable brown shoes which I later on got to know were Hush Puppies. The man with her appeared to be in his 50s. He was tall—a little over 6 feet. His salt and pepper hair was cut very short, and he had the same golden complexion reminiscent of Mickey McLean-Brown. However, I had already noticed that while in Ghana people with that kind of complexion stood out, in America among a crowd of whites, it wasn't as outstanding. He was more conventionally dressed in a white shirt, black leather jacket and pants. They stood still and began to scan the area.

"This must be Esther and Phillip Benjamin," I thought, rising to my feet and trying to catch their eye. They took a look at me and began to move in my direction.

"Dzigbordi?" the woman inquired, my name sounding strange with her American cadence.

"Auntie Esther?" I returned. Before I could say anymore, she had reached out and clasped me in her arms, her head resting on my shoulder as we hugged. Looking down at her, I could see gold studs in the two additional holes in each ear.

"Sorry to keep you waiting for so long! The traffic was horrendous! All that construction on Capital Circle! I hope you didn't think we had abandoned you. Hmm…you look very much like Julia, except for around the eyes which are your dad's. Pip, take Dzigbordi's suitcases, okay? Do you have all your bags?

We parked right in front of the entrance, so we can't leave the car there for too long!"

"Hi Auntie Esther," I said when she had finally stopped talking. "Thank you for picking me up and giving me a place to stay."

"Nonsense, Julia knows I will do anything for her, although we haven't met in years. We used to be naughty girls in Achimota, always up to mischief! It is a pity we lost touch over the years. I haven't been good at keeping up with all those old student association meetings." She grabbed the handle of one of the suitcases and began to drag it away.

"Hey, Esther, you haven't introduced me to your niece yet!" her husband wailed plaintively as he picked up the bigger suitcase and dragged it after her.

"We can do that outside, we left the car out there for too long," his wife responded, already halfway out of the sliding door. I lifted the carry-on bag onto my shoulder and followed them. By the time I got out, they were stowing the suitcases in the boot of their Mazda minivan.

"Well…since your Auntie Esther refuses to introduce us, I am your Uncle Pip. According to Ghanaian tradition, I am a sort of honorary uncle, aren't I?" Mr. Benjamin said, sticking out his hand with a humorous look in his dark brown eyes. *I think I am going to like him… very much.* "Pleased to meet you, Uncle Pip," I said out loud, shaking his hand. We settled in the car, with him and Auntie Esther in the front.

"How was the trip? Long and tiring, I suppose? You must be hungry, right? There is no food cooked at home, so Pip will stop at a restaurant so that we get something to eat. Is that okay? Pip, where do you think we should go—somewhere away from the construction zones?" Auntie Esther shot out another volley of questions. I was a little disconcerted, not knowing whether she was expecting a response to the questions she had asked me about the journey and my state of hunger. I decided to keep quiet, as the last question had been addressed to Uncle Pip.

"Yes…good idea. I will find somewhere close to home," he responded. I leaned back in the seat and shut my eyes, allowing their voices to wash over me as they discussed restaurant options. I wished we could have gone straight to their home. I was so exhausted that I didn't mind foregoing food for sleep. I opened my eyes as the car came to a halt in a parking area. The smell of the food from the restaurant hit me immediately I descended from the van, and I felt my empty stomach give a lurch as a wave of nausea hit me. The odor was unfamiliar to me but smelt like oil mixed with some unknown foods. Later on, I would associate it with hot oily melted cheese over pasta. The place, which was an Italian restaurant, was not fully occupied and we were quickly seated. The waiter placed menus and glasses of cold water with ice floating in them before us.

"What would you like to eat, Dzigbordi? Pizza? Pasta? I think I will have a salad because I had a heavy lunch. What are you going to have, Pip? The last time we came here you loved the veggie pizza."

"Hmm…perhaps some lasagna for me. Find anything appetising, Dzigbordi?" Uncle Pip asked looking at me across the booth. I desperately scanned the menu. Most of the foods were unfamiliar to me and had fancy names like rotini, rigatoni, fettuccine, ziti, pene, and, alfredo…cheeses such as feta cheese, spinach cheese and goat cheese, cottage cheese and brie, with descriptions of ingredients such as creams and wines; all which I wasn't used to in main dishes. I finally settled on a spaghetti dish which seemed relatively simple, which was the familiar name I could identify. After we ordered, I took the opportunity to use the restroom. My new uncle and auntie kept the conversation rolling as we waited for the food.

When the food was delivered to the table, a huge mass of spaghetti in a white sauce literally covered with gooey melted cheese was placed before me. The smell of the food hit me strongly and I felt like vomiting. Exercising great self-control, I picked up my fork and tried to follow the example of my hosts who were digging into their meals with gusto. I pulled out strands of pasta from the bottom of the heap, trying to get some that was uncontaminated by the cheese but even then it was like sawdust in my mouth. I knew I wouldn't be able to eat the food. Soon, Auntie Esther and Uncle Pip had cleared their plates and I was the one left still attempting to eat.

"I am sorry… I am full," I finally said, knowing there was no way I could finish the meal.

"That is okay, you must be very tired, anyway. We will get a take away box so that you can take the food home with you. You can have it for lunch tomorrow," Auntie Esther said as she signalled to the passing waiter. I stifled a groan. The waiter returned with the bill and a box for me to pack the food in.

"Tallahassee is a great place to live; as you may already know, it is the capital city of the state of Florida. We also have two universities here— FSU (Florida State University) and FAMU (Florida Agricultural & Mechanical University). Too bad we didn't know you were coming earlier; you could have applied to one of those schools and you would have been much closer to us." Auntie Esther said.

"The…University of Florida is our rival in football. In fact, do you know that FSU and UF are playing in the Sugar Bowl in New Orleans on January 2? Of course, FSU is going to win!" Uncle Pip teased. I didn't know Uncle Pip well enough to tease him back, and I hadn't yet developed loyalty to UF to care whether they won the game or not. Besides, I had no idea what on earth Sugar Bowl was. Uncle Pip was obviously trying hard to make me feel welcome, but it was hard for me to respond to his repartee. I smiled back at him but the car was dark and there was no way he could have seen it. Fortunately, Auntie Esther kept talking. "I know Dzigbordi must be exhausted, but perhaps we can drive around a bit so that she has a look at the town?" she asked her husband.

"Hmm… great idea, we can show her the university campuses so that she sees what she is missing. Perhaps after FSU beats UF in the Sugar Bowl, she would want to transfer to Tallahassee!" he quipped, and I tried to make a laughing sound, while crying inside, *I want to go home… I want a bed and a bath and sleep. I don't care about university campuses!* But of course, I kept silent. The next 15 minutes went by in a blur as my host and hostess pointed out several building that all seemed to be made of the same muddy brick colour and gave me names and some of the histories. I sat at the edge of my seat and craned my head toward the window as they droned on. Then Uncle Pip suggested that we postpone further sightseeing to daylight hours and drove us to their home.

The Benjamins lived about a 10-minute drive away from FSU in a three-bedroom, two and half bathroom house. They had two daughters who were no longer living home— the eldest, Cecilia was in Harvard pursuing a doctorate in Anthropology, and the youngest, Emily, was already married with two children and lived in Tallahassee. The home felt lived in and cozy and was decorated with old furniture and family photographs that captured the children at different stages of their lives. However, the house was freezing. I followed their example and took off my shoes immediately I got into the house and as I was without socks on my feet, the initial contact with the hardwood floor was a shock. Auntie Esther showed me to the room I would be using during my stay there. She had already laid the bed with fresh sheets and it looked very inviting. She also pointed out the bathroom, which had fresh towels awaiting my pleasure. I was touched by the efforts she had made to get ready for my visit and didn't hesitate to tell her so.

"Rubbish! That's the least I can do for Julia's daughter! I am so glad that I have been able to get in touch with her again. How is Michael doing, by the way? I haven't seen him in years since his last visit. He promises to come over when he completes his housemanship. He is also looking for schools over here," Auntie Esther said. I wasn't sure whether she was waiting for an answer on Mickey's status. As I hesitated, Uncle Pip came into the bedroom carrying both suitcases.

"Well…we will leave you to settle down and get some rest. Feel free to take a bath if you want to. Pip and I have our own bathroom in the master bedroom. If you need anything, do not hesitate to knock on our door. And sleep in as long as you want to. I am sure it will take you a couple of days to recover from the jet lag," Auntie Esther said kindly. "When you wake up we can give your parents a call so that they know you have arrived safely."

"Thank you…thank you very much, Auntie Esther." I was dizzy with sleep and hurriedly unpacked the suitcase containing my toiletries. Ten minutes under a hot shower, brushing of my teeth and a change of clothing made me feel slightly better. Without much ado, I turned off the bedroom light, climbed into bed and huddled under the heavy comforter. I tried to stay awake for a few minutes, to reflect over what had happened in the last few hours, but felt my body gradually sinking into the softness of the mattress and my mind take flight and begin to drift out of my control. *What is a Sugar Bowl?… I am so sleepy! Let me at least say the Lord's Prayer… Our Father, Who art in Heaven…* That was the last thing I remembered until the following morning.

Chapter Seventeen

"**D**zigbordi? Dzigbordi, are you awake?" The loud tapping sound accompanying the sound of my name dragged me out of the realms of deep sleep. Who was the owner of that strange voice calling out to me? "Yeessss?" I called out in a croaky voice. I groped for my spectacles on the night stand and put them on. Esther Benjamin stepped into the room, looking all sprightly, dressed in a grey tee shirt and matching sweatpants. Her grey locks were tied back with a red scarf.

"Hi! I apologise for waking you up. Your mother called about half an hour ago and I told her you were still asleep. She said she would call again in an hour so I thought I'd wake you up so that you can have a cup of tea before she calls again. Did you sleep well? I hope we didn't disturb you this morning." Auntie Esther had managed to disconcert me with the questions she asked in quick succession. I attempted to answer one. "I slept well, thank you. I didn't mean to sleep for so long."

"Don't worry about it. It is only 10:30 a.m. I am an early bird; usually up before 6:00 a.m. What would you like? We have Lipton, green tea, mint tea, ginger tea, peach-flavoured tea, chamomile tea, herbal tea and earl grey. I also have decaffeinated green tea. I drink a lot of that as I like to cut down my caffeine intake." The choices boggled my mind. I was familiar with only Lipton and Earl Grey.

"Lipton tea, please."

"What do you want with it? Milk, sugar, sweet 'n low, honey, lemon (fresh or packet)...? I only have honey with my tea; it is healthier, but I have some sugar." Esther Benjamin pressed on.

"Milk and sugar please, thank you." Moments later, I was rushing into the bathroom, and 20 minutes later I had dressed and remade the bed.

****

I remembered that I hadn't given the Benjamins the gifts my mother had given me for them.

"Auntie Esther, I forgot to give this to you yesterday. It is from my mother."

"Oh... chocolates, Ghana chocolates and pebbles!" she exclaimed with delight. "I love pebbles," she added holding the bag of different coloured balls of chocolate which had a covering of a hard crunchy shell and a peanut in the center. "I could never decide whether to take my time and suck the pebble slowly until all the colour disappeared before focusing on the chocolate portion, or whether to just crunch through the hard shell immediately and get to the chocolate and peanut. Pip is going to enjoy the whisky. I should remember to thank Julia when she calls." She placed the gifts on the marble countertop and returned to the stove where she had been stirring scrambled eggs. "I think I will make some peanut butter soup for dinner. Emily will come by this evening with the children to say hello to you. Her two-year old son Jonathan loves peanut butter soup. Alexander (Lexi), the five year old is unfortunately allergic to a lot of foods including peanuts, shrimp, and eggs. We are hoping he grows out of it. He is going to miss a lot of good food if he doesn't."

I felt relieved. It looked like I would have some home cooking this evening. "May I help you with anything?" I volunteered.

"No, everything is under control, don't worry. Oh, I almost forgot, there's your tea," she gestured in the direction of the counter area opposite the stove. There was a cup of tea brewing on the kitchen counter, with a jar of milk and a container of granulated sugar by it. "Thank you for the tea," I said again.

"You're welcome. There is toast and I am making eggs as well." I added two teaspoons of sugar and poured in enough milk to give the tea a dark brown colour. The tea was not as sweet as I preferred it, but on the whole, drinkable. I looked around the kitchen. I found the location of the kitchen strange. Back home, I was used to kitchens being located at the back of the house, away from the dining room areas, with a door separating it from other rooms in the house. Auntie Esther's kitchen had no separation area from the dining area; no doors and no windows. People in the dining and sitting area could watch the cook in the kitchen. I also noticed something else, there were few doors in the house as a whole and no corridors. There were doors leading to bathrooms and bedrooms but everywhere else was open.

Auntie Esther handed me a plate half-filled with eggs, accompanied with toast and butter. I went to place them on the dining room table. "Wait!" she said, rushing after me with a mat and coaster. "Put the plate on the mat and the tea on coaster. The table is antique, and I don't want stains on it." I did as she asked and looked at the table with new eyes. So, this is antique, stuff I had read about in books and seen in movies. There was nothing unusual about it to me. It looked like an old table. Hmm, then Ghana was full of antiques! The eggs were good, except that they needed a little salt. I saw salt and pepper shakers in the middle of the table and reached out for the salt as Esther Benjamin returned to the dining area from the kitchen with her mug of tea. "I don't put a lot of salt in my cooking. Too much salt is not good for you," she remarked sitting across from me. I withdrew my hand. Mama usually complained whenever she saw me add salt to her cooking.

"The food is very delicious, thank you," I said politely, after swallowing my first mouthful of eggs. That moment, the telephone rang. "It must be Julia," Auntie Esther said, and went to get the phone.

"Hello? Oh, hi Julia! Yes, yes, thanks for the presents, especially the pebbles. Remember how we used to buy them in Achimota during break time? I am going to hide them from everyone and enjoy them very slowly… Hahahahah! Yes, oh stop it! No thanks necessary. Give my love to Nick. Let me pass you to Dzigbordi."

I started to rise from the table, but she brought over the cordless phone. "Hello? Mama! Yes, I am fine, thank you. The flight was fine. Yes Mama. Everything is okay. How did the wedding go? That is good! I am sure Gladys did a very good job. Yes, I will hold . Please give my regards to everyone. I'd appreciate it if you call Karen and let her know I arrived safely. 223512 Yes, that's the number. I love you too!

"Good afternoon Papa. Yes, it is still morning here. I am having breakfast. Yes, Papa… Auntie and Uncle will drive me to Gainesville tomorrow or Tuesday. I will let you have the account number after we go to the bank. Yes, and the budget. Thank you. Bye!"

Soon after the call ended, there was the sound of a key turning in the lock and the front door opened. Pip Benjamin entered carrying bags of groceries. I got up and rushed to help.

"No, Dzigbordi! Stay and finish your meal!" Auntie Esther commanded. I felt a bit uncomfortable as I was not used to sitting and eating while people of my parents' generation worked.

"Hi, Dzigbordi, I see you are finally up! How was your night?" Uncle Pip asked, smiling broadly at me as he followed his wife to the kitchen.

"Fine thank you, Uncle Pip."

"She just finished talking to her family. Julia sends her regards. Look what she sent us… Whisky for you, and chocolate for me! No… (Auntie Esther smacks his hand) you can't have any of my chocolate."

"By the way, when do we drive down to Gainesville?" Uncle Pip asked.

"Hmm… tomorrow is probably best."

"We can leave around 8-8.30. It takes a little over two hours. All being well we should be back by early evening," he said.

I picked my plates and mug and went over to the kitchen sink. "Dzigbordi, you don't need to wash the dishes. Just leave them in the sink, I will put a load in the dishwasher," Auntie

Esther said. "Go and relax in the living room and watch some TV. Pip, show Dzigbordi where the remote is and she can select the channel she wants to watch." I tried hard to relax as Auntie Esther worked away in the kitchen. Uncle Pip was in the study, adjacent the dining area doing some work on the computer. Every now and then, Auntie Esther would call him to help with a chore—take out the trash, help her open the fresh jar of peanut butter, and empty the dishwasher. I found it rather odd to have a man helping with the household chores. However, Uncle Pip seemed at home in the kitchen and didn't appear to mind the constant interruptions when he was working in his study, and once as I looked at them surreptitiously, I saw him standing behind her with his arms casually around her waist as she stood at the stove stirring an open pot. I felt a bit uncomfortable at the display of affection I wasn't used to seeing among couples in public. Soon, the smell of the cooking permeated the house. Just after noon, Auntie Esther approached me once more, "Are you hungry, Dzigbordi? I can warm up your pasta for lunch." I almost flinched at that suggestion.

"Thank you, Auntie Esther, but I am still full from the late breakfast. I think I shall be fine for quite a while," I said, although the aroma from the cooking was beginning to generate hunger pangs.

"Well, let me know when you feel like eating," she reiterated, and then returned to the kitchen area. I just hoped that I wouldn't be forced to eat spaghetti for supper. Two hours later, Uncle Pip caught me dozing off and shooed me off to my bedroom for a nap. "We'll wake you up when Emily and the kiddies arrive. You are still tuckered out from the trip and remember you are in a different time zone. You need to get as much rest as possible so that you recover before school starts." I gave in and stumbled into "my" bedroom. The blinds were drawn, shutting out the sunlight. I gratefully snuggled under the comforter. The sounds of a screaming child woke me up abruptly two hours later. After I joined the family, I was introduced to Emily. "Hi! You must be Dzi... body! I am Emily," she said, smiling as she extended a hand from under her son's bottom. "I would give you a hug, but as you can see, my hands are full. I hope we didn't wake you up from your nap."

"Hi, Emily," I returned, shaking her proffered hand. "No, I had had enough sleep. Hi, Jonathan," I reached out to shake one of his hands, but he shrunk back and buried his head in his mother's neck.

Emily was tall, with her father's physical appearance (especially his eyes), but her mother's chocolate brown skin colour. Like Esther Benjamin, she was quite talkative and friendly. She introduced me to her other son, Alexander, a chubby five year old who was quite tall for his age. "This is Dzigbordi... Do you mind if the children call you "Gi" for now? It would take them a while to wrap their tongues around your name. Now, Lexi shake hands with Gi...Wait...Mum always told us when we were growing up that in Ghana older women are called 'Sister' or 'Auntie'. Perhaps, they can call you 'Auntie Gi'?

"Sure," I responded. For supper, Lexi had some macaroni and cheese because of his allergies, and the rest of us soon settled with steaming bowls of groundnut soup and rice. The soup was delicious; I would have added a bit more salt and pepper if I had been at home, but it was such a comfort to eat Ghanaian food that I enjoyed every bit of it. The portions were small; I wouldn't have minded a second or even third helping, but no one else went for more, so I didn't either. Emily continued chatting with me as we ate, asking questions about Ghana and telling me a bit about her work as a salesperson in one of the department stores. Auntie Esther fed Jonathan little spoonfuls of rice and soup from her bowl and joined us in the conversation every now and then. I wondered where Emily's husband was, but no one mentioned him. From the talk during supper, I got to know that Auntie Esther was a pharmacist with a company named Eckerd's, and that Uncle Pip was a professor of history at FSU.

"Daddy's their 'African expert,'" Emily said proudly.

African expert. Is it because he is married to an African woman?

"Yes," Uncle Pip smiled. "I enjoy teaching African History to both undergraduate and graduate students. I have been to Nigeria; I was there for two weeks five years ago. I also went to Ghana ten years ago. We plan to visit Ghana again sometime soon. I liked Ghana, the people there are so friendly. Of course, I may be biased because I am married to a wonderful Ghanaian woman!" he laughed. I smiled, thinking that after my two years in America, I would return home to be the "American expert".

Presently, the meal was over and we all settled down in front of the television to watch the news. After half an hour, Emily began to bundle the children up for the trip back. Not long after that, Auntie Esther declared that she was going to bed.

"Let's plan to leave for Gainesville by 8.00a.m. That should give us time to get some things done before the university staff go on lunch break," she advised. I followed suit and went into my room. I changed into sleepwear and was soon dead to the world, with my Bible on my chest and my glasses halfway down my nose.

****

The trip down to Gainesville was my first outing in daylight. Throughout the journey, I couldn't help but compare the scenery with that of my hometown in Ghana. The main thing that struck me as very strange was the differences in colour. It was a crisp and chilly day with bright sunlight, which I found quite bizarre; I was used to cold days accompanied by wet and dull weather or haze due to Harmattan but not cold with sunny days. After the hustle and bustle of driving in the streets of Accra, this journey was pretty tame on broad, practically empty roads with no potholes. There were also road signs periodically informing drivers about distances to various destinations, and warnings to drivers about the consequences of littering. Barely two hours after we set out, we turned off the Gainesville exit and began following signs to the University of Florida. As we travelled through the city, I looked around with eagerness. It doesn't seem like a big place, it looks small and very quiet compared to Accra, I thought. We were now traveling on University Avenue. As we went along, I noticed a building with a sign that said "Apartment Hunters."

"We should come by Apartment Hunters before we leave to look at Dzigbordi's options," Uncle Pip mused. "They may be able to show us some places today."

"Yes, and we also have to go to the bank first so that she can have an account opened," Auntie Esther added. "Dzigbordi, you will need to do that so that you can send your father the routing number to transfer you some money." I murmured my assent and said a silent prayer of thanksgiving for their help. Soon we turned off 13th Street, into the main entrance of the UF campus. "I think we can park here," Auntie Esther gestured to a parking lot immediately to our right. "School is not in session, so there should be no parking restrictions." Uncle Pip obediently turned to the right and found a parking spot immediately. I opened the door and stepped out, feeling my stomach jump about nervously. I was carrying a folder with information the school had sent me as well as the itinerary my father had printed out for me.

"What do we do first?" Uncle Pip asked both of us.

"Let's go to the International Center and check out the orientation, and then see about the bank and the apartment. I know there are other things you need to do, Dzigbordi, such as the rest of your immunisations and registration, but those are things you can do when you return," Auntie Esther suggested.

"Where is the International Center?" Uncle Pip asked.

"Tigert Hall," I responded, having read several times the

material that had been mailed to me. We wandered around the campus for the next 15 minutes. It looked huge and very tidy. The buildings were mostly brick coloured with small blue sign boards and white lettering identifying the name of the halls. Criser Hall, Grinter Hall, Tigert Hall. The International Center was on the ground floor. The reception area was large, with a seating space for visitors and smiling faces behind high counters on which stacks of documents were tidily displayed. In the right corner of the room was a display of small flags of different countries around the world. Above the display, high up, were five wall clocks with the hour hand at different positions. Below the clocks there were labels designating the times of the cities the clock depicted: New York, Hong Kong, London, Paris and Rome. My eyes scanned the flags to see if I could identify the red, gold, and green colours of the Ghana flag which was distinguished by the black star of Africa, however I couldn't find it. When it was our turn with the receptionist, we were welcomed by a buxom white woman with a warm smile. She had short dark spiky hair with sprinkles of gray. Her face was weather-beaten and creased with laugh lines. She spoke with a Russian accent I identified from watching *Dr. Zhivago*.

"Hello! I am Maria. I am a programme assistant at the International Student Center. Are you one of our new international students?"

"Yes, I am," I responded, feeling a little shy. I wondered what her last name was. I was used to older women introducing themselves as "missus" or "miss" instead of merely their first name. I wondered whether it would be polite for me to address her as "Maria."

"My name is Dzigbordi Dzordzome. These are my Uncle and my Aunt, Dr. and Mrs. Benjamin." Maria shook their hands briefly and they exchanged greetings before she returned to me. "Wow! That is an unusual name. I will learn to pronounce it correctly over time. You are going to see a lot of me in your years at UF. This is the place to come when you have questions such as the minimum number of course credits you need to take each semester and other immigration requirements. You will bring proof of health insurance here each semester before you are allowed to register for classes. You will also come here to sign your I-20 form whenever you are going to travel out of the country."

I nodded, feeling overwhelmed. She smiled and went on speaking. It was as if she could sense how I felt. "But enough about that; we will show you the ropes during orientation. For now, I will say, welcome to the US and welcome to UF!"

"Thank you," I murmured.

"Which country are you from?" Maria asked.

"Ghana."

"We have a lot of people from Africa here; in fact, I think one of the Ghanaian students left his address here with us. He said that we could contact him when new Ghanaian students arrive so that he will be able to help them settle in. I'll need to check on that before you return for orientation."

"That is very generous of him," Uncle Pip commented, suitably impressed.

"Yes," echoed Maria. "You will find that international students help each other a lot here."

"When is the orientation taking place?" Auntie Esther broke in just as Maria was finishing her sentence.

"We had one this morning. The second orientation for new international students is Friday, January 3 at 8:30a.m. Do you live in Gainesville?" she asked.

"No, we are in Tallahassee; we drove down to Gainesville for the day. We shall look for an apartment for Dzigbordi today. Hopefully, we can find something. We will return her to school on Thursday." Auntie Esther explained.

Maria nodded, "It is a good idea to get accommodation as soon as possible. You should try Apartment Hunters on University Avenue. Also, there is a bulletin board in front of the Division of Housing office where students put notices for subleases."

"Is there anything available on campus?" Uncle Pip asked suddenly. Maria's expression turned regretful. "Most likely not. Your niece qualifies for graduate housing, however campus apartments are in great demand. There is a long waiting list, which can take up to a year. You can pass the housing office and check. It is advisable to put your name down on the list even if you get an apartment off campus. That gives you the option to live on campus when it is time to renew your lease. The housing office is on 13th Street, just after Museum Road. It will be easier to drive there. Here is a campus map."

Maria unfolded a light green map. I noticed it was printed on high quality bond paper with a glossy finish. She indicated where the housing office was located.

"Thank you, Maria for being so helpful. We will pass by the

housing office today," Uncle Pip smiled genially as he picked up the map. We said our goodbyes. Auntie Esther also asked for directions to Barnett Bank, the bank recommended by UF.

"Maria seems like a very nice woman. She was very friendly," Auntie Esther commented as she walked briskly.

"Yes. You will soon be a part of the Gator family. However, I still think you would have had a warmer welcome at FSU," Uncle Pip said solemnly, with a twinkle in his eyes. I smiled back.

"Hmm, I wonder how long she has lived in the United States. She has a very strong Russian accent, but her English is quite good," Auntie Esther mused as we got walked to the car.

Auntie Esther studied the map and directed Uncle Pip as he drove. Soon, we were parked in front of the one-storey brick building. Ten minutes later, a receptionist in the main area took us to a suite where "Graduate and Family Housing" was printed in the glass wall. We were directed to an office where an older white woman was seated behind a desk with some files spread out before her. There was a computer on the desk as well. She looked up as we entered. She had light blue eyes and long grey hair which she wore in a single plait. She stood to her feet; she was almost as tall as Uncle Pip.

"Hi, I am Celeste Buchanan, Assistant Director for Graduate and Family Housing. Please have a seat." She smiled briefly, and then gestured to two chairs in front of her desk. Auntie Esther settled on the one closest to the wall. Uncle Pip remained standing, gesturing for me to take the other seat. I hesitated. I felt it was impolite for me to sit while Uncle Pip remained standing.

"Sit down, Dzigbordi," Auntie Esther said. Celeste Buchanan murmured something indiscernible and hurried out of the office. She returned a minute later dragging a chair with wheels. Uncle Pip thanked her and sat on my left hand side and then made the introductions.

"Welcome to UF. Are you a new international student?" Celeste focused sharp blue eyes on me.

"Yes."

"What is your name again?"

"Dzigbordi Dzordzome," I said.

"Hmm… Di… Ji… Do you have your passport and I-20?" she asked briskly. I scrambled in my bag and handed them to her. She perused them for a moment and then placed them on the desk.

"So you want to apply for graduate housing?" she asked.

"Yes Madam," I responded.

"That is a good idea. The waiting list is quite long. Some students apply as soon as they get admission. The average wait is about six months," she paused, got up and went to a desk close to the door. The table was covered with small stacks of different coloured sheets of paper. She picked up a few of them and returned to her chair. "Here is the application form and some information about family housing and residential areas. There is a $50 deposit fee. You can fill the forms and return them later with the check." She slid the papers in my direction.

"Is there anything available at all?" Uncle Pip asked after a moment's silence. "It is my niece's first time in the United States, and she doesn't know anyone in Gainesville. It would help a lot if she stays on campus at least for the first semester. By that time she would have settled and can find something else."

Celeste Buchanan was silent for a moment. "Not in graduate student housing, but there may be something available in the dorms. I can check into that if you like." The three of us nodded simultaneously. She went to one of the several file cabinets lining the back walls and pulled out some files. "Looks like there is a single room available in Thomas Hall." I felt hope rising.

She turned to the computer and asked, "What is your social security number?"

I gave her a blank look. "I don't think I have one."

"Every student is assigned an identification number. I can look it up…let me have your passport once more." I slid it back to her. She carefully typed in my last name. "Ah! There we are, 988-98-2573. You better write it down and memorise it. You'll need it wherever you go on campus." I took out my address book and wrote down the number carefully. The next fifteen minutes were spent finalising arrangements about my move to the dorm. Celeste Buchanan said I should report to the housing office when I returned to Gainesville to get the paperwork done and pay the rent of $840 for the semester. We thanked her profusely for her help and left.

"We can scratch the Apartment Hunters off our list," Uncle Pip said happily as we drove toward the bank which was also on 13th Street. "I am happy you will be staying on campus. It is much more convenient."

"And safer, and cheaper," Auntie Esther piped in.

"Thank you for asking about housing availability on

campus. I thought there was no hope from what the lady at the International Center said," I told them. Auntie Esther twisted her neck so that she was looking at me directly in the eye. "Dzigbordi, one of the things you will have to learn quickly is not to be afraid to ask for what you need no matter how futile you are told it would be. In America you have to be very tenacious to get what you want. Most people do not have all the facts on an issue, so you cannot assume that they are telling you the truth." I wasn't sure whether she was reprimanding me or giving me advice.

"Thank you, I will keep that in mind," I said. We spent the next hour at Barnett Bank. At the end of the visit, I had opened an account and ordered check books. By that time it was almost 2:00 p.m. and we were all hungry.

"We have done enough for the day. Let's find somewhere to have lunch and then hit the road once more," Auntie Esther suggested.

"Where should we have lunch? Dzigbordi, do you have any preferences?" Uncle Pip asked.

"Anything is fine with me," I returned, hoping that we were not going to end up in a restaurant similar to the Italian one they had taken me on my first night in America.

They pitched restaurant names for a few minutes, and then came to a decision. "Why don't we go to the mall and lunch at Ruby Tuesdays? It has a lot of variety for Dzigbordi to choose from," Uncle Pip suggested. Uncle Pip was right, Ruby Tuesday had a buffet session. I gave a silent sigh of relief when I saw food I was comfortable with such as black eyed peas, rice, corn, mashed potatoes, and chicken. I enjoyed my meal which I had with a cup of Coca-Cola with a lot of ice cubes. I fell asleep halfway on the journey back and woke up just as Uncle Pip turned into the driveway of his home.

"Wake up, Dzigbordi, we are home!" Auntie Esther said. "You are still suffering from jet lag. Why don't you go and rest for an hour or so? There is nothing to do. If you are not sleepy, you can watch TV for a while."

I went to my room for my journal, a pen and some paper and returned to the dining table. I carefully placed a mat on the antique table before putting my stuff down. I nibbled the end of my pen. So much had happened to me in the past few days. I wanted to share every single one of my experiences since I last saw Maxi at the Kotoka International Airport in Accra.

29th December, 1996.
My Darlingest Maxi, ….

Chapter Eighteen

It was New Year's Eve. Auntie Esther handed me a sheet of paper after I had finished breakfast that morning, "We should get our errands out of the way early so that we bypass the shopping crowd. It is going to be congested because of New Year's Eve." She went on, "I have a list of items you will need for your room in the dorm. If you think of anything I have left out you may include it."

The list included a refrigerator, bed sheets, cooking items, cutlery, plates, a telephone, an answering machine, an iron etc. I hoped the money I had on me would cover all those purchases. Uncle Pip stumbled in dressed in a rumpled grey tee-shirt and brown baggy pants and still looking groggy. However, there was already a broad smile on his face. He touched my shoulder lightly and looked into my face. "Hi Dzigbordi, did you sleep well?"

"Yes, thank you, Uncle Pip. Good morning."

He moved over to his wife and clasped her from behind. "Hi there, dear, what are our plans for the day?"

"Shopping for Dzigbordi," she responded promptly. She gestured to me to give him the list. He glanced through it, murmuring as he did so, "Wal-Mart for the kitchen stuff, iron, and bed sheets, and perhaps Lowes for the fridge?" They began to discuss the best routes to take to avoid traffic and the order in which they wanted to make those errands.

"I will check my email and then take a shower," Uncle Pip said.

When the phone rang ten minutes later, Auntie Esther asked me to answer it.

I picked up the receiver. "Good morning."

I heard a series of clicks on the phone and then a faint familiar voice.

"Good afternoon, is that you, Dzigbordi?"

"Yes Mama!"

"How are you doing?"

"Fine, thank you."

"Papa wants to know if you have been to the bank yet so that he gets the money wired before the bank closes today."

"Yes, we went to Gainesville yesterday. I will get the bank details. Please hold on."

"How is everyone?" I asked when I had returned and provided Mama with the needed information.

"Everything is alright here. Mawuli and Gifty are at Akosombo on their honeymoon. They phoned yesterday to let us know they arrived safely. Everyone misses you."

After the call, I asked the Benjamins if there was a post office nearby so that I could mail my letters.

"There's one close by, where we have our postbox. It is no problem; I have to check the mailbox, anyway," Auntie Esther assured me. The day was sunny, with a cool crisp breeze. It was warmer than the previous two days, but I was still getting used to the contrast between the brightness of the sun and the cold weather. The post office was the first stop. There were already people standing in queues. Some people were using the main area where to my surprised interest, I saw they could weigh their items, purchase stamps and mail off packages without help from the clerks. Uncle Pip demonstrated to me how to use the self-service, and about ten minutes later, five letters were in the beginning stage of their trip to Ghana. The next stop was Wal-Mart. Moving around the store was an impressive experience. Wal-Mart seemed to have everything, perhaps except for raw food products—electronics, medicines, clothes, toys, kitchen ware, and school supplies. The Benjamins knew their way round; they would consult the list and dash off to a specific aisle. I followed them pushing the cart.

"Wal-Mart products are generally cheaper," Uncle Pip said, "However, personally, I don't like the corporation because it has driven most of the mom and pop stores out of business."

"That's sad," I commiserated. However, from my perspective as a customer, I thought that cheaper was definitely better. Just like how I couldn't stop thinking about what time it was in Ghana, I couldn't help converting everything into cedis. The going rate of the cedi to dollar was about ¢1,700 to $1 and so everything was expensive to me. I also wondered why most of the prices were not rounded up to a whole number but ended in 99 cents. It was so bizarre to me! Quickly, the cart became full of items on the list. Every time an item was placed in it, I would mentally add up the cost. The Benjamins also tossed in some stuff they needed for their home. About an hour later, we were at the checkout counter. Auntie Esther placed all the items on the conveyor belt regardless of whether they were on my list or not. The checkout lady, a young black girl with short permed hair greeted us with a smile and began to scan the items.

"I have money to pay for my things," I told Auntie Esther as she pulled out her check book and began writing. I took out the envelope in my purse where I had placed the money my father had given me.

"Put your money away, Dzigbordi," Esther Benjamin responded. "These things are a gift from your uncle and me."

"No, Auntie. Please let me pay for them!" My horror was not an act. How could I let the Benjamins welcome and shelter me, and then pay for my school materials when I hadn't known them for long nor was I related to them? The UG would kill me!

"Nonsense, Dzigbordi! These are a few things…just the cooking pots, a bed sheet, an iron and an answering machine. You still have the refrigerator and other things to buy. You also need to hold on to some money until Nicholas wires you the rest."

"Let it go, Dzigbordi," Uncle Pip said, smiling at my look of consternation. "It won't take you long to learn that there are times you just can't win some arguments with my wife. You have to give in gracefully."

I stammered my thanks. Auntie Esther handed a check and her driver's license to the checkout girl. I wheeled the cart out and we loaded the things in the boot of the car (the Benjamins called it "the trunk"). Lowe's was another huge store, but didn't have as much variety as Wal-Mart. Uncle Pip led the way to the household section where we inspected their selection of refrigerators and finally settled on a small table top fridge which cost $109.99. It was the least expensive one there and I tried not to convert the price into cedis. I liked the idea of having a fridge of my own, though. At the checkout counter, an older white man scanned the item and gave us the final price. I took out the envelope and handed over two hundred dollar bills. He gave me back a handful of notes and some coins. Next, we went to Albertson's for some groceries, by which time I was exhausted and ready to return home.

****

Auntie Esther prepared ham and cheese sandwiches for lunch, which were quite tasty. We had just finished the meal when the telephone rang. Uncle Pip got up from the table to answer it.

"Hello? Hello!!!" I heard him shout. There was a pause. "Hi Mike! How are you doing?" Silence and then, "Wait, let me pass you to your auntie so that you don't use up all your money." My heart began to thump. Esther Benjamin took the phone from her husband.

"Hi Michael! Good of you to call. Is everything okay? How is your mother doing? You did? That's wonderful! Yes, she is fine. She got here in one piece. Give my love and Happy New Year wishes to everyone. Oh, hold for Dzigbordi!" I half-run to the telephone instead of waiting for her to bring it over. Auntie Esther and Uncle Pip left the room. I saw my fingers trembling and clutched the receiver tightly.

"Hello?"

Silence.

"Hello? Hello?" Had the line been cut? "Mickey, are you there?"

"Dzigbordi?" No one in the whole wide world had that voice. That voice was like a dark, rich, potent drink and made me feel like I had swallowed an elixir. The surprise took my breath away. I couldn't speak.

"DD? Dzigbordi? Are you still there?" His voice now sounded harsh with urgency, with desperation.

"Maxi? Oh Max…" my voice broke.

"DD, I cannot talk for long. Mike just got international direct dial at home and he called so that I could surprise you. It is expensive… I just want to tell you that I love you and I miss you. Oh, I miss you so much, DD! I shall write as soon as I get your address, okay?"

I was weeping by then. "I love you too Maxi. Maxi, I am so sorry for what happened the day I left. I…"

He cut in. "DD, I can't stay on the line… I wanted to wish you a Happy New Year and let you know we are still okay, okay?"

"Okay, Maxi. Goodbye and Happy New Year." I was about to put the phone down when I heard another voice. "Hello? DziDzi, are you still there?"

"Hello, Mickey! Thank you so much…thank you."

"That is my Christmas box to the two of you. We'll keep in touch, okay?"

"Yes, we will. Thank y…" The line went off before I could complete my sentence. I placed the receiver down very carefully.

I could still hear the murmur of voices in the kitchen. I kept my back to the dining room area and quickly wiped away the tears from my face with the sleeves of my sweater. I carried the plates into the kitchen.

"Nice of Mike to check up on you," Auntie Esther said.

"Yes. It was nice hearing from home," I tried sounding as casual as possible. My mind went over the conversation with Maxi. He loved me…he hadn't given up on us…he missed me! I felt strong and energised. I felt like skipping and dancing. When Uncle Pip encouraged me to take a siesta afterward, I didn't argue. I hugged a pillow. "Oh Maxi, I miss you so, so, so much!" I fell asleep still clutching the pillow in my arms.

****

Emily visited with Lexi and Jon late afternoon. I spent time playing with the children. Uncle Pip prepared dinner while Emily and her mother chatted, and from their conversation, I gleaned that her husband, Alexander, was on contract with a company in Connecticut for the next six months. I also had an impression that Emily and her husband were on a trial separation. Just before we sat down to dinner, Emily's sister telephoned from Vancouver. She said she would be in Tallahassee for spring break and would meet me then.

Dinner was great. Uncle Pip had prepared a dish which was a combination of pasta, fish and eggs in a sauce I couldn't identify, which tasted very good. It was served up with warm whole wheat bread rolls and salad. Unlike the salads at home, which had mayonnaise, eggs, vegetable salad, baked beans, this was a plain salad accompanied by bottles of Ranch and low fat Thousand Island salad dressing. I dished as much of the pasta as I dared to do without appearing like a glutton. To my delight, Auntie Esther included a side dish of hot chili pepper (Ghanaian style). It was absolutely delicious and I rhapsodised over it. Auntie Esther seemed thrilled that I liked her pepper as most of her family had low tolerance for spicy food.

After dinner, I helped Emily carry the dishes to the kitchen and upload the dishwasher. It was the first day Auntie Esther allowed me to help around the house. After the table had been cleared, we settled down in front of the television. Auntie Esther and her daughter played with the children while continuing to chat. Uncle Pip changed the channel to the Sci-Fi channel where the Twilight Zone marathon was taking place. However, as the time got closer to 7:00p.m, my attention began to wander, and I felt more homesick than I had ever felt since leaving Ghana. What a very strange way to usher in the New Year! My body was present in America, but my mind was now in Ghana. I was remembering the traditional New Year Eve celebration we had as a family—praying to usher in the coming year; watching the clock as midnight rolled close; counting down the seconds, as if something momentous changed between 11:59 p.m. and 12:00a.m. Perhaps, it was just our perception; that feeling of hope; of seizing control of our lives and achieving great and wondrous things in the coming year, but it made those minutes extremely significant. This year was undoubtedly different for my family— Mawuli was on his one week honeymoon and I was in America. The Benjamins had given no indication that they would mark the incoming year in any special way. The time was 6:59 p.m. and it was now a minute to midnight in Ghana. What were the UG doing? Were they feeling lonely spending their first New Year's Eve without either of their children? What about Maxi, what was he up to? As far as I knew, he would follow his usual tradition of attending the all-night service at HEPT. On New Year's Eve, church had a service that started at 7:00 p.m. with intense prayer, and then erupted into praise and worship frenzy between 11.30 p.m. till 12.30a.m. Although I enjoyed my family's New Year's Eve tradition, I always wished I could have been part of that service. I leaned back in the chair, gazed at the television and averted my face from the Benjamins as I whispered, "Happy New Year Mama, Papa, Mawuli, Gifty, Maxi, Gladys, Grandma, Lia…"

At 8:00p.m., Emma was ready to take Jon and Lexi home.

"Will you come by tomorrow?" her mom asked.

"Nope. I will be doing some house cleaning during the day, and in the evening, we will attend Sonia's kid's first birthday party. I promised to help her supervise the children and maintain her sanity," Emily said. "I wish that the 1st fell on a Friday. It is just so depressing returning to work knowing that the holidays are over. Are you doing anything special?"

"No, we will just have a quiet day. Perhaps, we will drive Dzigbordi around town to see the Christmas lights before they are taken down," her mother returned.

"We will be dropping Dzigbordi off in Gainesville on Thursday, so remember to call or pass by to say goodbye," Uncle Pip added.

Emily turned and smiled at me as I stood holding Jon in my arms. "Of course, I am gonna remember to see my new cousin off! Here Jon, come to Mom. It is time to go!" The little boy opened up his arms and reached for his mother.

"Give Auntie Gi a good night kiss!" his mother encouraged. Immediately, Jon turned back to me and planted a smack close to my lips. He was so warm, bright, and lovable, and smelt of innocence and Johnson baby powder. His affectionate manner made me feel less sad. He turned toward his mother, lifting his arms and jumping up and down in an attempt to get back to her. The children exchanged hugs and kisses with their grandparents and then we all went outside to see them off.

I spent the rest of the evening watching television. Uncle Pip read through magazines and newspapers, while Auntie Esther appeared absorbed in the show, but periodically chatted with us. By quarter to midnight, they were both asleep—Uncle Pip in the rocking chair with his mouth half open and his wife reclining on the couch with her face buried into the fabric of the couch. I flipped though channels with the remote and eventually settled on CNN, where a crowd of people were waiting to ring in the New Year at Times Square. Everyone was bundled up, and from what the commentators were saying, it was very cold over there. However, the crowd appeared excited and full of anticipation. I watched on until the countdown ball began to drop, and everyone was chanting "Ten! Nine! Eight! Seven! Six! Five! Four! Three! Two! One... Happy New Year!" There was commotion, streamers, confetti, excitement, singing the Christmas carol "Should auld acquaintance be forgot, and never brought to mind, Should auld acquaintance be forgot, And days o' lang syne!... "

I felt a tear trickle down my right cheek and hurriedly brushed it off. I gave myself a hard mental shake. *What is the matter with you, Dzigbordi? You have so much to be thankful for. You got the U.S. visa, the UG have agreed that Maxi and you can get married, you arrived safely, and it was a miracle that a few days before leaving, you got in touch with the Benjamins who have treated you like family. Mickey cares about you and Maxi loves you. This is the beginning of your dream. You left your family, your friends, and Maxi because it was that important to you. Things are going to get better, and in about a year, Maxi will join you. Just think how much fun the two of you are going to have together!*

I sat up straight in the chair, and just then Auntie Esther stirred, turned her head, and opened her eyes. She stared sleepily at the television and sat up. "Oh no, Pip, we missed the dropping of the ball...it is past midnight!" Her husband opened his eyes and also looked at the television for a moment.

"Yep, looks like we missed it again this year. Happy New Year Love!" he said to her, and then looked at me. "Happy New Year, Dzigbordi!"

"Happy New Year, Uncle Pip, Auntie Esther." I smiled back at them with a heart full of thanksgiving for the year that had gone before, and with anticipation, and hope for the New Year.

****

It was strange that just after six days with them, I felt as if I had known the Benjamins for a long time. Even Auntie Esther's scrutiny of my salt and sugar consumption was reminiscent of my mother. As for Uncle Pip, I had grown to like him a lot in those days. He seemed so comfortable in his own skin. I asked him for his pasta recipe, but he didn't give it to me.

"Not just yet, Dzigbordi, we want to make sure that there is something that would bring you back to us. I will prepare that dish for you whenever you visit."

"Yes, don't be a stranger, Dzigbordi. This is your home. Gainesville is not far from Tallahassee, and we will be expecting you for all the holidays. We can drive down and pick you up or you can come by Greyhound bus." Auntie Esther reiterated, after they had driven me to Gainesville and were ready to say goodbye. "You have our telephone number, email address, and postal address, so keep in touch, okay?"

"Yes, Auntie. Thank you so much for everything. I don't know what I would have done without you," I said with heartfelt thanks.

"Nonsense, Dzigbordi," she responded briskly. "No one is indispensable; you will soon learn that there is always a way out…always an alternative in every situation. If we hadn't been in Tallahassee ,you would have still survived."

I usually didn't argue with her, but this time, I couldn't keep silent. "It is true that I would have survived, but it wouldn't have been the same. You picked me up from the airport, gave me a place to stay, and helped me get accommodation on campus, you…"

The laughter of this dear couple interrupted my litany. Esther Benjamin lifted up her arms in mock surrender. "Okay, okay, Dzigbordi, your point is well-taken. By the way, keep in mind that the third Monday in January is a holiday in honor of Dr. Martin Luther King Jr. I hope you will be able to spend that weekend with us. We will call you when we arrive in Tallahassee."

As we exited the room, I locked the door behind me. We went through three more doors before emerging into the courtyard.

"This place is very secure, I like that." Uncle Pip murmured as he stood looking at the three storey building.

"Yes, it is," I echoed. I liked the idea of having to use a key to access various sections of the hall. The size of my room was 9.5 by 10.5 feet and the floor was covered with green tiles. It contained a twin bed on one side of the wall with a very firm mattress. A few inches from the bed was a vent. I soon found out that the heat in the room was controlled from elsewhere and that the temperature was turned up in the early hours of the morning. The radiator would make clanking sounds as the heat came up. The room also contained a desk and a chair. I ended up keeping my refrigerator on top of the desk, which left very little room to spread out my books while I studied, so that semester I would do most of my reading on the bed. Other furniture included a dresser and an in-built closet. There was also a surprise addition, a porcelain sink in a corner close to the door. Although it was primarily for ablutions, as time went on, I also used it to wash my dishes instead of carrying them to the communal kitchen. My bedroom was the last one on the floor and overlooked the courtyard. The large trees a few feet away provided shade from the sun. It had a large window I could crank open to let in fresh air. I spent the rest of the day unpacking my clothes and skimming through the tons of materials I had been bombarded with during the check-in process. Campus maps, campus directory, information on telephone features such as call waiting and call forwarding, information on the campus long-distance carrier (Campus MCI, which I later found out stood for Microwave Communications Inc.), laundry room usage, hall security, sexual harassment, and various campus activities. I was especially excited about the telephone. Very few people I knew of in Ghana had landline telephones they didn't share. Most people made their calls at work or at the post offices. Now, not only did I have my own phone line, but local calls were free, apart from paying a basic rate each month, and for students living on campus, the basic fee was already incorporated in the rent, so I didn't have to pay anything extra. I was also thrilled with my answering machine. It was a novelty to me. I wished I could talk to someone from home, and then I realised I could. With Campus MCI, all I needed to make a long distance call was to use my PIN. I could call home and speak to the UG for some minutes, give them my telephone number, and get news about Mawuli and Gifty. I dashed back to the desk and began scrambling for the sheet of paper with the information on how to make long distance calls... then it hit me. Calls to Ghana were about $2.54 per minute. Even if I spoke for only five minutes, that was more than $10! My heart ached with disappointment.

A few minutes later, I heard the sound of my phone ringing. My first call! It was the Benjamins, calling to check on me and to let me know that they had arrived back in Tallahassee. I felt better after talking with the Benjamins. I scrutinised the information UF had sent to me in Ghana once more, reviewing what had to be accomplished in the next few days. Orientation for international students was at 8:00a.m. the following day. I also had to meet with my advisor, pay health insurance, register for classes, complete my immunisation requirements, get my student ID card, buy textbooks, and complete the budget.

As I worked away at the desk, I could hear voices on the corridor, the opening and slamming of doors and the excited squeals of friends welcoming each other. Darkness began to fall just after 5:30p.m. The noise level on my floor intensified. I remained in my room, only sneaking out once to use the bathroom. After 7:00p.m., I felt emptiness in my stomach. Fortunately, I still had the gari, shito and fried fish. I sat behind the desk and propped up a storybook and read while eating. The shito set my tongue aflame, and that was when I realised I didn't have a source of drinking water except for the sink. When the hot, tingling sensation on my tongue become unbearable, I rushed to the sink, filled a cup with water and took one large sip. Instantly, I spat it back into the sink. Eww! The taste was disgusting! As fiery as my tongue felt I couldn't swallow the water. In the end, I broke a piece of Golden Tree chocolate and sucked on it. After a few minutes, the burning sensation on my tongue began to subside. I definitely would have to find a good source of tasty drinking water.

By the time I settled in bed, it was still noisy on the floor. I listened to students talk loudly about their dinner plans. I found myself surveying my room; the clothes hanging in the closet, a picture of Maxi and me on top of the fridge, the pile of books on the desk, the telephone and its answering machine. Before long, the sounds outside the room subsided, and long periods of silence followed. I felt apprehensive about what lay before me the following day. I missed Maxi, my family in Ghana, and my new family in Tallahassee. It was my first night alone in a foreign land, and I had a small room in the corner of a dormitory. However, looking around the space and seeing my belongings gave me a feeling of comfort. This place, this little room for however long, was going to be my home and sanctuary.

Chapter Nineteen

217 Thomas Hall
University of Florida
Gainesville, FL 32601
4th January, 1997
Saturday
5:47p.m.

Dear Papa and Mama,
It was very lovely talking to both of you yesterday. Mama, I am happy you love my voice message on the answering machine. Uncle Pip helped me set it up. Thank you so much for the money. I checked with the bank yesterday and the money had come through. I have enough to pay the school fees for this semester and do other things. I will let you have the budget as soon as possible. I hope to set up an email account on Monday. That would make communicating much faster! The ordinary mail takes about two weeks to get through. The good news is that the post office is about five minutes' walk from my room. I wasn't able to tell you a lot about the orientation on the phone. It went well. There were 14

new students apart from me, from Japan, China, India, France, and Ireland. There was a young girl from Nigeria, Folasade Onyilogu, and we talked a bit during the break. I found that there are Ghanaians living in Gainesville. Some of them are in school, and others have been here for several years and are married with children. One family, the Odonkors, left their telephone number at the International Students' Center so that if any new Ghanaian students arrive, they can help out if necessary. Mrs. Stella Odonkor came to meet me at the center. She said that when her family arrived in Gainesville, they had such a hard time settling in because they didn't know anyone, and because of that, she and her husband decided not to let that happen to other Ghanaians. Mrs. Odonkor has been living in the United States for eight years. She came here with her husband who now has a Ph.D., and she is studying towards a Masters in Occupational Therapy. Her husband returned to Ghana two years ago and visits once a year. They have a 3-year old daughter named Helena Katherina, and an older son Simon Peter, who is in Ghana attending Accra Academy.

Mrs. Odonkor took me home with her that first afternoon. She lives in a UF apartment complex called "Diamond Village". The villages are residential housing for single graduate or married students. Most of the houses here seem to be made of mainly wood, which according to Auntie Esther, can actually be carried and moved to another location. Strange, isn't it? In Ghana, *only the very poor live in wooden houses!*

The alligator is the mascot for the University of Florida sports team, so UF students are called "Gators". I hear that alligators inhabit lakes on campus and when there is heavy rain, they sometimes crawl onto the roads. Very scary! Makes me remember 'Return to Eden' where Tara was chewed by an alligator and needed plastic surgery, and 'Alligator' in which an alligator terrorised residents of Chicago. However, Mrs. Odonkor says the alligators are usually harmless unless they are provoked and that we are not allowed to feed them. We had spinach stew with egushi and boiled eggs and yam for lunch. It was so delicious I felt I was back at home! I enquired how she came by the ingredients and was told that she usually got Ghanaian foodstuffs from the big cities such as Atlanta and Washington D.C. that have Ghanaian stores.

This morning, Mrs. Odonkor picked me up and took me shopping at a grocery store called Publix. I bought some bread, canned milk, sugar, cereal and bottled water. We went back to her apartment where I spent the afternoon. Some Ghanaians came round to welcome me. Not much other news. I have done the necessary inoculations at the students' infirmary, met my adviser, have had a picture taken for my student ID card, paid my health insurance for the semester, and registered for classes. Tomorrow, I will be going with Mrs. Odonkor to church.

I will end here for now. Please give my love to Papa,

Grandma, Mawuli and Gifty, Gladys, and anyone else I should remember. Also, please let them have my address and let them know that I will write to them all soon.

Love,

Dzigbordi.

****

217 Thomas Hall
University of Florida
Gainesville, FL 32601
5th January, 1997
Saturday
10:18 p.m.

My Dearest, Darlingest Maxi,

Although I have already written you three letters since I left home, there is still so much to tell you. It is as if I need to share every little detail of my experiences with you, no matter how mundane they appear. I now pause from my writing and look at you. You remember that picture we took together after church the Sunday after Brother Asiedu's wedding? It is sitting right on top of the refrigerator, so any time I turn my head, there you are. I wish I had brought more photographs. I will really love the one of you in that infamous pair of jeans. Please mail me another picture of you so that I put it up in my room;

preferably one of you bare-chested or in a singlet with the black jeans!

How is everything? I know you are looking for other jobs, and I guess because of the holidays, it is much too soon for you to have any news on the applications you sent out before I left. If the teaching is bearable, perhaps you can continue with it for a while? After all, you said your priority this year would be saving for the GRE so that you can make the admission for the fall semester or latest spring 1998. I know it is tough on you because you are contributing to the household expenses and also paying Serwaa's school fees. I will see what I can do to help with the GRE application fee as well as the fees for applying to UF. I should be able to do so once I get a job on campus. Are you still interested in chemistry or do you have some other courses you would like to consider? I met a Ghanaian who is in the chemistry department and he says that all their graduate students are given graduate assistantship positions that come with stipends. The graduate assistantship also covers tuition. When I settle down, I will pay a visit to the chemistry department and pick up an application packet.

Student orientation was interesting. We were informed on everything—from immigration law, UF requirements, housing, socialising with Americans, physical and mental health. We were each given a handbook with all that information—the correct way to address Americans, the best time of the day to call Americans at home, what to do when you are invited to someone's home. And you wouldn't believe it… how important it is to bathe because Americans prize hygiene! Hmm… I don't think they have met Ghanaians, who are brought up to take two baths a day! There is so much information to absorb and digest and my room is already cluttered with papers. The song "Count your blessings name them one by one" has been ringing through my head for the past few days. By a remarkable coincidence, it was one of the songs that we sang in church today. I felt as if God was giving me a special message. Look at all the miracles that have taken place in the past few weeks! I am going to hold onto this as a testimony and remind myself when times get tough that there is, indeed, a God who is concerned about our day-to-day existence as well as the big picture. Glory be to His name!

Aren't I beginning to sound like your Florence Osei-Britwum? Last time, we heard she was in Texas. If I get her address, I will drop her line or two. It is funny how being in this country makes anyone from Ghana a welcome sight. Perhaps, I shouldn't say "anyone." There are a couple of Ghanaians who are already getting on my nerves. But before I branch into that topic, let me tell you a bit about my first church service in America!

Stella Odonkor took me to church today. She is a member of First Assemblies of God Church. The church is huge. It is somewhat similar in structure to Calvary Baptist Church in Accra. The congregation is primarily white, but there are a quite a few black faces as well. They have two services every Sunday and we attended the second service. A lot of the rituals were similar to orthodox churches in Ghana. Praise and worship wasn't bad. I knew most of the songs, but for those I didn't know, I could sing along because the words were put up on a screen in front of the church. They had the welcoming session where visitors had to stand up. They gave me a card to provide contact information. The collection bowl was passed round on the bench while the choir ministered. I missed the dancing we used to do during first and second collection. I dropped in a dollar note in the basket. I have no idea what is the acceptable amount to put in the collection bowl! In my calculation a dollar is about 1,700 cedis, which is about 10 times what I would have put in the basket at HEPT! The preaching was okay. The pastor (who was white) preached on forgiveness and the power of evangelism. On the whole, the church seems okay; they talk about evangelism and have home cell meetings and all that, but I don't have the feel that it is my spiritual home.

Before my fingers give up on me, let me tell you about my first meeting with my advisor Dr. Tanaka. I found my way to Weimer Hall, which is the name of the College of Journalism and Mass Communication. When I write "found my way," I mean it took me over an hour to walk to the building which is about 10 minutes away from my dorm! All new students were given a colourful glossy *campus map, but I tell you, the map confuses me even more! By the time I got there, it was almost 5:00p.m. I wandered about the building, clutching the piece of paper with Dr. Emil Tanaka's information and wondering how on earth I was going to find him. I was on the staircase about to climb to next floor when a white young man accosted me. He was around 5 feet 7 inches, with vivid blue eyes, short curly blond hair and had a welcoming smile.*

"Hi, are you lost?" he drawled.

"Yes, I am trying to find Dr. Tanaka's office," I said.

"Oh! Dr. Tanaka! He is on the fourth floor; the third and fourth floors are where the faculty offices are located. I will walk you there."

"Thank you!" We proceeded to mount the stairs.

"I am Brad," he offered.

"My name is Dzigbordi," I returned.

"What an unusual name! It will take me a while to get the hang of it. You have an accent. Where you from?" he asked.

"I am from Ghana."

"You're new," he stated.

"Yes."

"What are you specialising in?"

"Print journalism."

"That is what I am doing! I am in my second year and plan to graduate this fall. Is Dr. Tanaka your adviser?"

"Yes, he is." I said.

"He's cool!" his voice was alive with enthusiasm. "He is also my adviser." He hurried ahead and opened the door

250

that led out of the stairwell onto the fourth floor. I was panting slightly and tried to steady my breathing. The corridor was carpeted, dark, and cool. There were offices on either side of the hall. All of them had their doors shut and the lights off. Most of the offices had strawboards on which faculty had put pictures, information on office hours, newspaper clippings and cartoons.

"It looks like the professors have left for the day. Anyway, most of them have been out this week, but I know Tanaka is around. Oh… he has left." He stopped by a closed door with a darkened office. "DR. EMIL TANAKA" was inscribed in white font on the black nameplate. "I am sure he will be in tomorrow," he suggested.

"Yes, I will come back tomorrow morning," I concurred. We turned and walked back to the stairwell and down the stairs. A few minutes later, we were standing in the courtyard.

"Thank you so much for all your help," I said fervently.

"It is a pleasure. Wait; let me give you my number. Call me if you have any questions or want to get together," he said. "Do you have a pen and paper?" I dug into my handbag and took out my pocket diary and opened the first page.

"It is 376-5412," he said. I wrote it down and scribbled his name by the number.

"Thank you, Brad." I reiterated.

"Take care!" he said and strode away.

---To Be Continued---

****

Monday
6th January, 1997
8:00p.m.

My Darlin' Maxi,

I met Dr. Tanaka Friday around noon. He was in his office when I arrived, seated at his desk and shuffling a stack of papers. I expected him to look totally Japanese, but he didn't; he was tall and bulky with receding grey hair. He looked like he was in his late 50s. The only thing that looked slightly Japanese was his small dark eyes. He looked up when I knocked and gazed at me enquiringly.

"Good afternoon, Sir," I said.

"Come in…have a seat," he gestured to the chair in the corner by his desk. I sat down. He looked at me without speaking.

"My name is Dzigbordi Dzordzome," I began.

He continued looking at me. I didn't know why he wasn't speaking. His silence made me jabber.

"I am from Ghana in West Africa," I went on desperately. His expression was as if he wanted to say "So where are you going with this?"

"You are my adviser. I wanted to greet you and find out what classes to take," I ended with a gulp. He gave me a friendly nod. He picked up a pink sheet from his cluttered desk, which was the plan of study for print

journalism students. For the next 10 minutes, he told me which classes were being offered this semester and what I needed to take. Based on my timetable this semester, I have classes every day except Fridays.

This afternoon, I went for the first reporting lab class. It was in a computer lab. There are about 20 of us in the class. Most of them look much younger than I am, very talkative, confident, and happy. There is only one other black (male) in the class. Dr. Tanaka gave us a gist of what the class entailed, which is mainly writing news stories. He stressed on the importance of grammar (when we turn in assignments, points will be taken off per error). He also emphasised the importance of keeping up with the news and asked that each of us subscribe to 'The Gainesville Sun', which is the city's newspaper. In the class, he will give us an assignment to type out on the computers which do not have any spell checks or print functions. The assignment is timed and electronically submitted. During the class, we also had to select news stories and interview at least three people for the story. The first story is due next week Monday. Right away, he passed the newspapers around. I was hanging back a bit, not quite ready to take my turn searching for a story and feeling quite nervous at the thought of conducting interviews on my first week when Dr. Tanaka called me to the front (or, I should say, he caught my eye and gestured). I don't think he knows how to pronounce my name yet!

"Do you have any ideas for a story yet?"

"No Sir." Was I supposed to have thought up a story before the first day of class?

"I have a suggestion. You know that the newly appointed United Nations Secretary-General is from Ghana, right?"

"Yes, Kofi Annan," I contributed.

"Yes, Coffee Annon," he repeated. "I think for your first story, you can do something on Coffee Annon. Give us the perspective of Ghanaians on his appointment. If there are Ghanaians in Gainesville, you can interview them and come up with a good piece."

"Thank you!" Ah, such a relief. After class I telephoned Stella and she agreed to help. She also gave me telephone numbers of other Ghanaians I could interview. My other piece of news before I stop is that I have set up my email account! Each student is given an account and a home page where you can put up a bio and picture. The service is free for graduate students. Undergraduate students have to pay $20 a semester. I had to choose a user name. I figured that there was no other Dzordzome on campus so I used that. My email address is: dzordzome@grove.ufl.edu. We can start designing a strategy on communicating via email on a more frequent basis, and save the letters for more private information.

My Beloved, I cannot end this missive without letting you know for the umpteenth time just how much you mean to me, how much I miss you and pine for you, and

how much I am looking forward to our being together.
God bless you for being that special, wonderful, and
unique partner who lights up my life.
    All my love,
      DD.

****

Date: Tue, January 7, 97 13:01:26 +0000

From: dzordzome@grove.ufl.edu <Dzigbordi Dzordzome>
To: Mdzordzome@bc.gn.apc.org
Subject: E-mail…At Last!

Dear Mawuli,

How are you and the missus? I hope you are both
fine and enjoying married life! What about the new
flat? As you can see, I have an email account. I set it up
yesterday and you're the first person I am writing to.
This is exciting! Please give this email address to the
UG and JD. I have been to three of the four classes I am
taking this semester. I think the most challenging one
is going to be Reporting (lab). It entails interviewing
people and my stomach churns at the thought of it.
There are so many things to get used to that I didn't
envisage. One of them is memorising passwords or
what they call pin numbers for my bank account and
school records. I keep messing it up because we are told
not to write it down. For my first pin number I decided

to use Maxwell's birthday. However, the Americans have a different way of writing the birthday. We do day/month/year and they do it by month/day/year. So when I was trying to remember the pin, I didn't know whether I had done it the American way or the Ghanaian way! In the end, I think the numerous attempts froze my account and I had to call and have it reset. At least, I have memorised my school ID number. Everywhere I go on campus to talk to someone, the first thing they ask me for is that number.

This is a test run! I shall write more when I get a response from you. Hope all's well at work. Give my love to Gifty.

Love,

Dzigbordi

****

Date: Thurs. 9 January 97 08:01:26 +0000
From: Ndzordzome@ghana.com
To: Dzordzome@grove.ufl.edu <Dzigbordi Dzordzome>

E-mail address received from your brother. We hope your classes are manageable. Awaiting budget for the spring semester. Please send ASAP. Everybody is fine.

Papa

Date: Thurs. 9 January 97 11:01:26 +0000
From: Nii Quarshie Quartey
Physics Department
University of Ghana
Balme@ug.gn.apc.org
To: Dzigbordi Dzordzome
Dzordzome@grove.ufl.edu
Subject: Keeping in touch!
Hello Dzigbordi!

Lilly and I are happy that we have your email address and will be able to keep in touch with you. How are you doing? I trust that by the grace of the Lord who neither slumbers nor sleeps, you are doing fine. We are fine. We miss you though; we miss your presence at HEPT, especially in the drama department. My sweetheart looked so lost without you when we attended church service the first Sunday after your departure. Pastor Sly remembered you in prayers during the New Year Eve all night service. We bound all demons and principalities in your path and released the spirit of peace, love, and sound mind.

Oh, as you may have guessed from the email address I used, Balme Library has an email account. We are able to receive and send emails for a small fee. It is cheaper if you can type out the message on a floppy disk. It costs more if they have to do the typing as well. You may use this address to send information to Maxwell or Lilliana; just use me as c/o. I will check periodically to see if there are any messages. I promise not to read anything you write them! I nearly forgot; I have a message for you. Call the telephone number 0272315 (Accra) this week sometime between the hours of 7:00-10:30p.m. (Ghana time).

Dzigbordi, I will stop here for now. The typing is killing me. Next time, I shall tell you all about the earthquake we had. I hope you have a great week and please continue to stay in touch. Lilly sends her love.

God bless,

Nii Q.

****

Date: Fri, January 9, 97 19:01:26
From: Dzordzome@grove.ufl.edu <Dzigbordi Dzordzome>
To: Nii Quarshie Quartey
Physics Department
University of Ghana
Balme@ug.gn.apc.org
Subject: Message for Maxi

My Dear Maxi,

I am sure your ears are still ringing from the shrieks of amazing and unadulterated joy when I heard your voice. That is the nicest surprise EVER!!!!

I got Nii Q's email yesterday afternoon. He asked me to call 0272315 for a message. I had no clue what that meant. Yesterday evening after I finished my mundane supper (they call it dinner here), I dialed the number and listened to the rings that sounded so different from the harsh-sounding American longer tones. After five rings, I was about to put the phone down when it was picked up and it was YOU! That is when I started screaming. I am surprised my neighbours did not come and check on me. I know you tried to speak, but I kept on asking you questions like "where are you?", "whose number is this?" and so on. When you could finally get me to calm down a bit, that was when you revealed the surprise you had been keeping to yourself for the past two and half months. I cannot believe that you saved for a mobile phone when it became clear that I would be leaving the country. I can still hear your voice when you said, "I wanted to make sure that I am there for you anytime you need to get a hold of me for any reason." Maxi, I started crying at that point. We've always laughed at people who go about carrying big mobile phones and talking all over town. I guess you are now one of them! The good thing is that you don't have to pay to receive calls, so I will be able to call you without incurring costs for you. Thank you so much! We have to device a way that you can let me know if you need me to call you immediately.

I miss you so much, Maxi. I wish I could describe just how much, but for the sake of propriety and the safety of the email system in Balme Library, I shall desist. Sometimes, a year seems such a long time! I can't wait till you join me. I passed by the housing office today to check on my status. I am #54 on the list for Diamond Village, #43 for Maguire, #22 for Tanglewood, #20 for Schultz, and #18 for Corry (those are the names of housing complexes on campus). When I was talking to one of the staff, she asked me whether I am expecting a child or husband to join me. I told her I was expecting my fiancé later this year. She asked for your name and information and added it to my file. It felt so good and so real! I am actually making plans for us to live together here in the near future. Oh Maxi, I can't wait!

I can just picture us in a one-bedroom apartment on campus. Maybe we can even have a Trixie-Ann before leaving (haha!). I will say goodbye for now. I hope you enjoy the rest of the week. My warm regards to your mom, dad, Serwaa, and everyone at HEPT.

    Love, DD

Chapter Twenty

It was when I stood on Stella Odonkor's bathroom scale that I realised how much weight I had lost. "Four point five kilos— wait; that's four point five times two point two…10 pounds in six weeks?" It looked like the stress I was undergoing was effortlessly stripping the meat off my bones. Down the corridor, I could hear a cacophony of voices and the blaring of television from the sitting room. Throughout the afternoon, Ghanaians had trickled into Stella Odonkor's apartment. In Ghanaian tradition, she served everyone with drinks and food. I sat quietly in one of the armchairs answering questions when asked, smiling continually, and nodding at appropriate places.

Eventually, I excused myself and went to use the bathroom. That was when I noticed the scale under the sink. The scale was a manual one and had both kilograms and pounds units of weight, which pleased me no end. One of the many confusing things I was trying to get used to was the unit of measurements in the US. Unlike most countries, the US. had refused to go metric. Why do Americans have to be so contrary? However, I had to admit that I was gradually adjusting. It was peculiar how several little things had exasperated me about my new temporary home in the early days—the conversion of Fahrenheit into Celsius and the unique way of spelling certain English words (particularly detrimental to me because I lost points in the Reporting class anytime I used non-American spelling or phrase). Back in Ghana, I had been considered well-educated, well-read, and considerably fluent in English. However, in America, people assumed that because my accent was un-American, I was automatically incompetent in the usage of the English language. If I have to hear once more about how they cannot understand my accent I am going to scream. Another pet peeve was my "alien" classification. Before coming to the US, I was familiar with usage of "alien" in movies as a depiction of something not very positive; creatures from other planets that had to be hunted, subdued or mistrusted. No matter how often I told myself that "alien" was just a synonym for "foreign", I still flinched inwardly whenever it was used to depict my status in this country.

Everything seemed fair game as grounds for attacking the American way of life during those first weeks of homesickness. It didn't matter that I knew I was going through the stages of acclimatising to the new environment, and that no one had forced me to come to this country; that I had yearned to come over and experience American culture and be independent and free. It didn't help that my feelings were a normal part of the transition process.

****

I re-entered the crowded sitting room from the bathroom, everyone looked up at me, and it struck me how strange it now was to see so many black faces in a room. The guests were discussing the murder of Bill Cosby's son Ennis Cosby that had occurred about three weeks before. The conversation among the group of Ghanaians continued in Akan and English. "This is shocking! It is in America that such a thing would happen. To be murdered while changing a car tire!" Daniel Commey said. I felt I had heard him say the same sentence verbatim on the two other occasions the topic had come up. Daniel was one of the few single Ghanaian males I had met in Gainesville. He was of a stocky build, about five inches taller than I and dark brown in complexion. He was the one who had questioned me the most so far—my marital status, immigration status, how long I was going to be in the United States and if I ever intended returning to Ghana. In return, he informed me that he was studying towards a master's in engineering and was going to graduate in August.

"Bad things also happen back in Ghana," William Richter broke in, sounding almost defensive. "What about all those stories we hear about the robberies and kidnappings and desecration of graveyards?" Dr. Richter and his family had been living Gainesville for the past 18 years, and all his four children had been born in the US. He lectured physics at UF and his wife Wilhelmina (whom I already called "Sister Mina") taught Akan at the Center for African Studies. I liked the Richters; they were both friendly and full of advice for me as a first timer in America, but they were not as pushy and inquisitive as some of the other compatriots I had met.

"I think it is a conspiracy! The more I listen to the news reports, the fishier the story sounds. Why would someone shoot

Ennis Cosby and not take his money? What was that so-called girlfriend of his doing while all this was going on?" Daniel Commey asked. "It goes to show that riches cannot protect you from tragedy," added Rashida Ibrahim, her voice smacking of faint satisfaction. "These Hollywood people think they own the world and eventually they realise that bad things happen to both the rich and poor." Rashida was the spouse of Idrisu Ibrahim who had lived in Gainesville for the past 20 years and was a mechanic with his own business. I found her loud and brash, and I had a feeling we were never going to be friends. She was one of those who had interrogated me when she met me for the first time—what kind of visa did I have? How was I sponsoring my study in the States? She told me more than I needed to know about her family and how they won the green card years ago and were now U.S. citizens; and how her husband had his own car repair business and was very successful. "You will soon need a car to get around in Gainesville. The buses don't run after 5:00p.m. and on Sundays. When you are ready, come to Idrisu, he knows a lot about second-hand cars, and at times he helps his customers sell junk cars. He will make you a good deal."

Why would I want to own a junk car? If I ever buy a car I would want something that is reliable. Buying a car wasn't something I had considered doing. Back home, owning a car was a privilege not a right. It is in America that children expected a car when they hit sixteen years. Mawuli was still saving for one and was hoping to get a loan from his job to help out. He was still commuting to work by tro-tro, even though he had been working for almost four years. I smiled as I wondered what the

UG would say if I added a (junk) car on my budget because it was a necessity. Rashida Ibrahim was staring at me, and her next statement made me wonder if she were a mind-reader. "I know your family is helping you out with your schooling, but there is no reason why you cannot get a job to buy certain things. You can get a job on campus. Sure there is a lot of competition there because international students are allowed to work only on campus; however, there are ways around that. There are so many things you need here that people can do without back home like a car, a computer, a TV…" It was funny how people who lived abroad for a while started to feel that certain things which were once luxuries back home were now "necessities." I conceded that having transportation may make my life easier, especially as I was still unfamiliar with the bus routes. One of my priorities these first weeks was to familiarise myself with the different bus routes so that I could find my way about the city by myself. So far, the Ghanaian community had rallied round and made sure that there was someone who would telephone me when they are going grocery shopping to find out whether I needed a ride on the weekends. Stella Odonkor gave me a lift to church on Sundays.

The discussion of the Cosby tragedy continued. It epitomised the senseless violence in America I had heard about before leaving Ghana. The stories about the Gainesville Ripper, Danny Rollings, who cut a swathe of terror through the city of Gainesville in the early nineties leaving five dead students in his wake left me horrified and frightened seven years later. Ghanaians showed me the apartment complexes where the killer crept through French windows and attacked unsuspecting students, and the woods in which he hid in-between expeditions, and those reminiscences made the event so real to me. In fact, the 34th Street Wall, a 1,120 feet concrete wall that ran along a side of one the major streets in the city, still had a portion that was a memorial to the four UF students and one Santa Fe Community College student who lost their lives to Rollings in 1990. Since 1979 the 34th Street Wall had been the one public place residents were permitted to use graffiti. The wall usually had artwork and messages inscribed on it such as declarations of love, birthday wishes, lamentations, and graduation congratulatory messages. Although people painted over messages after an appropriate interval had lapsed, the remembrance message for the five students; a black boarder with their names in black and white could always be seen and was reproduced if painted over by error. It reminded me that the feeling of safety was only an illusion. Nothing is certain in life. Disaster can strike in a split second.

"Most of the crimes that happen in this country are crimes of opportunity, that is why you have to be careful in whatever you do," Dr. Saul Tagoe said, looking directly at me. He was doing his post doctorate in nutrition at UF, and his wife Millicent was a certified nursing assistant. She had two jobs and was always at work during the day and at night. The Tagoes had a set of young and active twin sons, and I wondered how she got any time to sleep.

"You're scaring Dzigbordi!" Esi Ansah said to Saul. "Like Uncle William said bad things happen everywhere, even in

Ghana, so you have to be careful no matter where you are. Gainesville is relatively safe, especially on campus. My advice is that you stick to well-lit areas at night and use the services of SNAP (the Student Night Auxiliary Patrol) whenever you can," she said reassuringly. Although Esi had lived in Gainesville for a shorter time than most of the Ghanaians in the room, she was the one whose accent sounded most American. Esi had come from Ghana for a master's in education five years ago and had stayed on to continue in a doctorate programme. She and her husband Mark had been in a relationship in Ghana when she received admission to UF. He was unable to come with her at that time so they had a long-distance relationship for two years. The summer before she enrolled in the PhD programme, she returned to Ghana and married Mark, and then he joined her. Their long-distance relationship that had successfully segued into matrimony had buttressed my hope in my relationship with Maxi.

While the group continued chatting, I took a surreptitious glance at my wrist watch which was still on Ghana time. For weeks, I had refused to write dates the American way (month/day/year), persisting in using the British style. However, I had to stop because it caused problems when I put dates on school work or dated checks. The two things I still persisted in doing were keeping my watch on Ghana time, and wearing Ghanaian clothes on weekends. The time was 9:15p.m. now in Ghana. I wanted to leave within the next fifteen minutes so that I arrive in time for my rendezvous in 45 minutes.

I waited until I saw Stella go to the kitchen and then followed her. She smiled. "Oh, time for you to be returning to your room. You call home on Sunday afternoons, don't you?" It was the same thing every week. Stella took me home for lunch after church service. If the food wasn't cooked, I would help her do so, or entertain Helena Katherina while Stella worked in the kitchen. Sometimes, Ghanaians would visit and discuss American news and Ghanaian sports and politics. I left anytime between 4:00 and 4:30p.m. It took me about 20 minutes to make the trip on foot. I returned to the sitting room and started saying my goodbyes.

"Are you ready to leave yet? I can give you a ride," William Richter offered. Moments later, we were on Museum Road, going towards University Avenue.

"You forgot your seatbelt," he reminded me a minute or so after we had commenced the journey.

"Oh, thank you," I said, reaching out to grasp the seatbelt behind me. I was not used to automatically putting on my seatbelt when I sat in a vehicle, but I had been informed by more than one person that not only have seatbelts been proven to save lives, one could be given a traffic citation for not wearing one.

"How are your classes going?" Dr. Richter asked me.

"They are okay."

"What are you taking again?" he asked as he swiftly changed lanes and overtook a white Nissan van that had been crawling in front of us.

"Reporting, Introduction to Statistics, Communication Proseminar and Mass Communication History," I practically chanted.

"The reporting class is the one you interviewed us for some weeks ago, right?" he drawled. His accent was still predominantly Ghanaian, but there was a slight difference in the way he enunciated his words.

"Yes, the Kofi Annan story," I said.

"So, how did you do? I am sure you got a good grade. Did you submit it to *The Alligator*? It is a very important story with global implications."

"I didn't get a good grade. I actually got a D. The professor said the story was interesting, but he took out a lot of points for grammar," I confessed.

The traffic light in front of the main campus entrance turned red. William Richter looked at me. "That's surprising; I have heard you speak and I wouldn't have thought you were the kind of person who would have problems with English grammar. On the contrary, I would have bet that your grammar is quite good."

I sighed, "I thought the same myself. I have always been good in English at both the primary and secondary school level. I also worked with a publishing company for two years before coming here, so I thought I wouldn't have much trouble with reporting. However, Dr. Tanaka says that my style and grammar are more British than American. He suggested I spend time at the English tutoring lab to improve my English."

"But that lab is for people who have no background in English at all!" Dr. Richter was indignant. I moved my hands in a helpless gesture. "I did take my second story there and spent half an hour with a tutor. I don't think it was of much benefit. My grade improved a bit, but not by much."

Apart from the grammar issue, I also felt stressed on a weekly basis because we had to turn in stories, which were either hard news or human interest. Either way, it involved interviews, which were the bane of my existence. I felt so shy and nervous and stressed. While most of my colleagues chased after current stories and conducted several interviews in the hope of publishing the story in the college newspaper, *The Independent Alligator*, I did my best to select stories that wouldn't require a lot of interviews, and I made no effort to submit my stories to the newspaper.

"Don't worry about it. Things will get better. Are the other classes going well?" Dr. Richter asked.

"Yes…I will have to work harder at Statistics, but it should be okay. Proseminar has a few assignments, but we are mostly taught how to use email, how to find library resources, and use Lexis-Nexis. It has helped a lot with my other classes. Mass Communication History is also not bad. It is just that I have problems speaking in class, and I know that participation is part of the grade," I said.

We were now at the last traffic light, ready to make a left turn into Thomas Hall parking entrance. He stopped in the middle of the parking lot and let the engine idle for a while. "About speaking up in class…that's a problem most Ghanaians have when they come here initially. The system back home is different; we are expected to be quiet and attentive, raise our hands when we want to speak, and most of the time, shut up until the teacher solicits contribution. In this country, when you are silent in class, you are portrayed as disinterested, unintelligent, uninformed, or all of the above. It is especially hard for foreigners because you already come with a set of preconceptions. But as I had to do, you will soon learn to speak up in class. It is amazing what motivation you get when you realise that 5-15% of your final grade is based on speaking up in class."

His feedback did not make me feel any better. How was I going to survive school in America? As if I had asked that question out loud, he went on.

"Dzigbordi, I know things seem difficult and strange at the moment, but they will get better soon. Before long, you would have settled down and made friends. Meanwhile, know that you can call me and Mina anytime you have questions or need help."

"Thank you, Dr. Richter."

"'Dr. Richter' sounds like one of my students," he observed.

I smiled. I had problems with men who were not old enough to be my father and not young enough to be a colleague. Most people called him Uncle Will, but he didn't feel like an uncle yet. I wouldn't feel comfortable addressing him as William. On the way to the room, I stopped by the vending machine outside for a can of coke and a small pack of Lays Potato Chips for supper. It was my staple food during the week. Although the floor lounge had a kitchen section with a stove, the other students seldom cooked and seemed to find it weird that I did. I also noticed that some of them found the aroma of the foods I prepared such as rice and beans, fish balls and so on, strong and strange. I cooked on Friday nights when most of the students went out to party.

After six weeks away from home, my communication with my family and Maxi was becoming routine. Now, I wrote to Maxi twice a week, one by email, and the other letter via post. Mawuli and I exchanged short emails about twice a week. My letters to the UG were twice a week via email, and Mama usually wrote me by post as well every two weeks. Every other week, I called the UG, and every other week they telephoned me, so that we spoke every Saturday.

Sunday was the day on which I made my weekly calls to Maxi, and we both looked forward to them. Although I tried to keep them short, sometimes we forgot about the time. Two Sundays ago, the format of conversation changed abruptly. We had been chatting for about 10 minutes when Maxi said, "DD, I sent the picture you requested in the mail last week. You should get it soon."

"The one of you in my favourite jeans?" I asked, even though I knew what the answer was going to be.

"Yep!" he chuckled. "I meant to keep it as a surprise, but couldn't resist telling you. I have four copies for you! Two of them are five by seven inches and the other two are 10 by 14 inches. There is a set of each size with me in a singlet, and in the other one I am bare-chested. Charity took the pictures with her camera. I must say myself that they are pretty good." The image of Maxi bare-chested or in a singlet made me all warm and tingly in the lower part of my body, and I also had a sharp pang of jealousy at the thought of his neighbour feasting her eyes on his gorgeous body as she snapped the pictures.

"I am so looking forward to receiving those pictures."

"I really miss you, DD. I wish I could hold you once more," Maxi said, and the raw yearning in his voice was like a spark in a dry forest. I began to feel hot, as if I was running a low grade fever.

"I miss you too," I said in a low voice.

"Do you remember Boxing Day?" he asked suddenly.

"Of course, I do! How can I forget it? That was the day we went to Lia's for lunch," I responded. "Why are you asking about Boxing Day?"

"I am remembering what happened after we left Lilly's place," he replied.

"Hmm…" I said.

"What are you thinking?"

"Well, I was thinking about what happened before we left Lia's," I returned.

"Eh? What happened before we left her house? I thought we had lunch, talked, prayed, and then left?" Maxi asked with a puzzled note in his voice.

"Nope, not only that!" I said mischievously.

"I can't think of anything else."

"I don't believe you've forgotten!" I added with mock indignation.

"Tell me, DD! Help me remember!" he pleaded.

"It all started there. We were sitting outside holding hands. There was this strong and powerful electric current that ignited our linked hands and travelled up our arms to other parts of our bodies…"

"Go on… tell me more…" Maxi said. The passion in his voice excited me all the more and made me feel naughty, and more alive than I had felt since leaving home.

"And we knew what we were both thinking. We didn't need words. I knew you wanted me, and you knew I wanted you, and we both knew that we knew," I said.

"DD, PLEASE go on!" Maxi begged. So I did, making sure that I spoke in a lower voice so that he would have to strain to hear, and that anytime I used naughty words or innuendos, I rolled the words slowly and seductively on my lips. I tasted the words on my tongue and savoured them the way I imagined a wine connoisseur would savour vintage wine. The process of doing all that was driving me crazy.

"We walked down to the station cursing ourselves for not spending the day by ourselves. I know we imagined the wonderful passionate things we would have done together if we had had a room for a couple of hours…how I would have allowed you to slowly unzip my skirt, unbutton my blouse, unhook my brassiere, and then, finally roll down my panties very slowly until I was standing in the middle of the room with the panties tangled up about my ankles. You know, I had on this new matching flowery pair of underwear that fits me so well. The brassiere in particular accentuates my boobs and outlines my…" I paused and as I whispered the word, I heard him groan out very loudly. That only encouraged me more.

"We then…" I stopped abruptly. I could hear a voice… someone talking to Maxi in the background in Twi.

"Kofi, is everything okay? I was passing by and I heard a strange noise."

Oh no! It was his mother! Those strange noises must have been Maxi groaning and moaning as I talked filthy to him! Had she understood what was going on? The voices were now slightly more distant. Maxi must have taken the receiver off his ear when his mother came into the room.

I remained silent as I waited to hear Maxi's response. I could hear him cough twice and clear his throat before he answered her in Twi.

"I am fine, Mummy," he said rather huskily.

"Oh, are you sure it isn't your stomach bothering you? I know that Serwaa put too much pepper in the light soup today," she went on. There was a moment's pause, and then, "Hmm…you seem slightly feverish. I hope you are not coming down with malaria. Have you been spraying your room with mosquito spray like I asked you? Those devious mosquitoes always find a way in."

"Mummy, I am not sick!"

I stifled a giggle at Maxi's irritation.

"Oh, alright. Oh, were you on the phone?"

"Yes, I was just finishing up a call," he responded evasively.

"I will leave you to it. But let me know if you feel any worse. Perhaps it might be wise to start a regimen of Chloroquine before you begin to feel worse." she advised.

"Hello?" Maxi asked, sounding embarrassed. I couldn't answer immediately, for I was laughing almost hysterically.

"DD! Stop laughing!" Maxi said sternly. "I am sorry for the interruption. I left the door ajar and Mummy heard me."

"That's okay. I have to go now. I stayed on the telephone

longer than I meant to do. We will talk next week, okay?"

"Alright, I love you, Dzigbordi Dzordzome."

"I love you too, Maxwell Kofi Owusu."

On Thursday, my long distance phone bill from Campus MCI arrived in the mail; to my horror, I was due to pay $213.31. It was obvious that I could not continue on that trend. When I called Maxi last Sunday, I made it clear that I wouldn't be staying on the line for more than 10 minutes.

"Oh…" his voice trailed off.

"I am sorry, Maxi, the phone bill just arrived and it is quite high."

"How high?"

"About $230."

"Two hundred and thirty dollars?" he yelled after a pause. I had a feeling he had converted the amount into cedis.

"Yes, and that is about my phone budget for the entire semester," I said forlornly.

"So, what are you going to do?" he asked anxiously. "Does it mean we can't talk?"

"I will take a look at the budget and see if I can cut from some other places. I will call every week, but we can't talk for very long. I think 10 minutes is reasonable, especially as we are writing letters and emails on a weekly basis."

"Good," he sighed, "I do understand about the money issue, but DD, I really need to hear your voice. It is a pity you don't have enough time to complete last week's story."

"Well, let me see…we have six minutes left. I will tell you as much as I can for the next five minutes and then we use the last minute to say our goodbyes, agreed?" I asked.

"Yes! I am ready. I have told everyone I am on the phone; I have locked my door. I am all yours!" His excitement made me smile, and even though I was not as worked up as I had been the previous week, I did my best.

"Can we do this next week, I mean, if we have nothing important to talk about? Like you said, we do email and write to each other. We could use our calls to...."

"Good idea," I cut in briskly. "I have to go, Maxi. Love you."

"Thank you, DD. I love you!"

Two days later, I lay on my bed with the two large photos, tracing my fingers over Maxi's larger than life physique that seemed to leap out of the picture. In one of the pictures, he was in his singlet and jeans under a tree in his compound with a soccer ball at his feet. He was smiling into the camera to me. In the second picture, he was bare-chested, lying on his bed on his side, with his right cheek cupped in his hand and supported by an elbow. In that picture, he was also smiling into the camera. Maxi looked so gorgeously handsome and sensual. I had to get picture frames the next time I went to Wal-Mart. Throughout the week, I thought up a nice hot scenario for our love making session or what I have come to know as "phone sex" in America.

Chapter Twenty-One

A week later, I was thinking about the precedent we had set for our weekly calls. The way things were going, it seemed like our calls were to be used mainly for phone sex. I didn't want the situation where Maxi would automatically be expecting me to go into seduction mode the moment I telephoned him. Perhaps, this was a subject I needed to raise when I wrote to him next week. I also wanted to suggest that we speak every fortnight instead of every week, that way, we could talk for a longer time instead of having very short conversations. I was worried about the telephone bills. I couldn't help feeling guilty. By my own desire to travel abroad, I had created the situation where we were now in a long distance relationship. Now, he was all alone back home. Was it too much to make Maxi happy by having sex over the phone for 10 measly minutes every week? That was something I needed to consider before writing to him, and as the days went by, I found myself postponing that conversation with Maxi.

****

It was Saturday, February 15, and my 27th birthday. The first birthday I had spent outside Ghana, and I was feeling depressed for a number of reasons. My mother had always made each birthday special. On the week prior to the day, birthday cards trickled in via post from the UG, Mawuli and Gifty, Lia and Nii Q, and Gladys. I had a surprise; a card signed from all employees of Visionaries and an encouraging letter from Brother Henry commending me for having been an asset to his company, and urging me to apply the same approach toward my studies in America. As each card arrived, I put it up on display in my room. By Saturday, the only close friends I hadn't received birthday wishes from were JD and Maxi. On Saturday morning I was awakened at 6:20a.m. by a call.

"Hello?" I called out groggily. The clicking sound informed me it was an international call.

"Happy birthday to you….happy birthday to you…!" a male voice sang off key.

"Please, 'Wuli! It is too early in the morning for your singing! I shall pay you to cease." I pretended to grumble.

"Humph! Don't tell me you are still in bed! I should think that you will be up watering a few plants?"

"Hahahaha very funny," I said, laughing at our old joke. "Thanks for calling. You are the first one to call. I also got the card from the two of you on Tuesday. I suspect that Gifty reminded you to send it off on time. I was the one who used to keep you on track with birthdays and anniversaries!"

"Yep! How well you know me. In fact, all I had to do was to sign the card and she did the rest," he said without shame.

"Good thing you are married. You definitely need a wife to keep you organised! You are calling from your flat, right?"

"Of course, I told you we got IDD a week ago. Seems like a

good idea to be able to keep an eye on my little sister around the clock without having to go through the UG."

"Pshaw! I am sure you had other reasons for getting IDD," I retorted. "Is Gifty around?"

"Yes, we are about to leave for the market. Hold on."

"Hi Dzigbordi. Happy birthday! How are you doing?" Gifty asked.

"I am fine, thank you. How are you doing? Is my brother treating you well?"

"Of course he is; he can't do otherwise. He knows I will 'show him hot pepper' if he misbehaves!" she chuckled.

"That's the spirit! Thank you so much for the lovely card. Mawuli said you were the one who selected it."

"Don't mind your brother! We went to Placito together three weeks ago after our trip to the market.

"I love Placito...they have a good selection of cards."

"Yes, they do. Your brother asked me to select a card for you because he thought I'd be better at it. He kept finding one fault or another with the cards I chose."

I was giggling helplessly. "So, what did you do next?"

"I handed him the third card and informed him that this was IT! If he was dissatisfied with my choice, he could very well go and choose a card himself. And why on earth did I have to select the card in the first place when he was in the shop with me?"

"And what did he have to say about that?" I asked, curious to catch a glimpse of how they interacted in their marriage.

"As if he cared. He looked it over, then took his sweet time to peruse the text inside. He told me that was an appropriate one for you, and then added 'I don't know why you are so upset about this, Gifty. Isn't it too early for the hormones to take over?' Ooops!" Gifty stopped abruptly.

"What?" I asked, not knowing what the matter was. What had he said? Something about Gifty being hormonal?

"Oh my God, I mean…Goodness gracious me! Gifty!! Oh! Wow! You are pregnant?" I screamed.

"Shhhh!" she hissed. "Everyone will hear!"

"Hahaha…! Who would care in America? Gifty, there is nothing to be ashamed of. You are honorably and respectably married; wedlocked through holy matrimony, remember?" I teased.

"I know! Traditionally you are supposed to wait till around three months before you inform people so we wanted to do that," she explained.

"Oh…I am sure everything will be fine with my little niece or nephew. So the UG don't know yet?" I asked.

"Not yet, although my mom guessed when I visited her last week. She took one look at me and said 'Daughter, you have something to tell me, don't you?"

I laughed. "Poor you, I have heard that there are some women who have a sixth sense for identifying pregnant women. It looks like your mother is one of them!"

"Yes. So, we will soon have to mention it to your parents as well," she said.

"How far gone are you?" I asked.

"Six weeks, I…"

I heard Mawuli's voice in the background reminding her that she was on an international call.

"Ooops! I have to go. My lord and master is right. We'll talk another time, okay? I will email you this week."

"Okay. Thank you so much, and congratulations. I shall keep mum with the UG until you break the news," I promised.

I had just finished my morning devotion when the telephone shrilled again.

"Good morning? Hello?"

"Happy birthday to you… happy birthday to youuuu! Happy birthday dear Dzigbordi…. Happy birthday to you! Hip Hip hip!"

"Hooray!"

"Hip hip hip?"

"Hooray!" I responded laughing. I knew Mama wouldn't cease until she had gotten in three sets of the hips and hoorays.

"Hip…hip... hip...!"

"Hooray!" I ended.

"So, what are you doing today? Are you cooking anything?"

"I was thinking of some jollof rice with corned beef."

"No chicken?"

"No...." I responded. After some two months in America, I was sick of chicken; I had eaten it fried, boiled, baked, and grilled.

"I hope you are able to get together with some friends and have a good day. Don't sit in your room all day," she urged.

"I won't," I promised, although I didn't have friends except for people I knew in the Ghanaian community. Stella Odonkor was going to give me a ride to the grocery store later in the afternoon, but I hadn't told her it was my birthday.

Papa wished me a happy birthday next and asked how classes were going. By then, it was after 8:30a.m. I had a quick shower, hoping that I wouldn't miss any calls while I was away. I breakfasted on a bowl of cornflakes. Afterwards, I got my ingredients and went to the kitchen to prepare the jollof. There was no one there and I worked very quickly; chopping red onions, bell peppers and carrots, and opening up cans of tomato sauce. Periodically, I hurried to my room to check if anyone had telephoned in my absence. There were no new messages. I returned to the kitchen with a book. When the meal was ready, I carried it to my room, cranked open the windows for some fresh air and curled up in bed with another storybook.

Around 12:15p.m. the telephone rang once more. "Hello? Good afternoon!"

"Hi! This is Danny…Daniel Commey," a male voice intoned.

"Oh, hi, Danny."

"I am downstairs. I came over to Library West to pick up an interlibrary loan. I thought I'd stop by and see how you are doing. May I come up?" he asked. I hesitated. I hoped he wasn't going to stay for long. I wanted to be alone when Maxi telephoned. I glanced around the room. Although my bed was ruffled and had books on it, the room was relatively tidy. Still, I felt a bit awkward. "Sure, I will be down in a minute to let you in," I hurried downstairs. Daniel was standing in the courtyard.

"Hi Dzigbordi, how are you doing?"

"I am fine. Thank you for passing by. Do you mind if I check my mailbox before we go upstairs?"

"Of course not," he answered. "Expecting something, are you?"

"Just mail from home."

I slid my key into box 217, grabbed the letters and locked up. We began to walk back toward my dorm section.

"So, how are things? I haven't seen you since early January, which is why I decided to pass by. I know I should have given you notice instead of just showing up. I called a couple of hours ago before leaving home, but your line was engaged," he said.

"That's okay. I was on the phone earlier."

"Wow! Something smells very, very good in here!" exclaimed Danny as he stepped into the room. "What have you been cooking?"

"Jollof rice," I responded. "Please have a seat," I gestured to the chair behind the desk. He ignored it and went to sit on the bed. I deposited the mail on the desk and pulled out the chair and sat down. I felt a bit uncomfortable watching him on my untidy bed. He looked around the room.

"So many cards! What is the occasion?"

"My birthday," I responded.

"When?" he asked as he opened one of the cards.

"Today," I said.

He looked up at me. "You should have said something. I would have gotten you a present or taken you out to lunch or dinner. We could have had a small party for you. It is not good for you to spend your first birthday all alone," he said. I smiled, touched by the dismay in his voice.

"I am fine. I have had a good day so far. My family called from Ghana, and I have also received cards and letters from friends as well. It is a bit different from my previous birthdays, but not as bad as I had expected."

"Hmm…" He finished looking through the cards by the window and moved to the desk. I watched him in silence as he read the cards on the table and on top of the refrigerator. He picked up the picture of Maxi and myself and focused on it for a few seconds.

"So, where is the boyfriend's card?" he inquired.

"It is not up here. It may have arrived in today's mail," I responded, not sure how to take his question.

"Don't you want to check?" he persisted. I scanned through the mail on my desk. There was an envelope which felt like it contained a card, but the handwriting was JD's. There was also a lighter envelope in Maxi's writing and another envelope, but I couldn't ascertain who it was from.

"There's a letter from him," I said, not knowing why I needed to defend Maxi.

"Hmm," he said noncommittally and then sashayed back to the bed. He wore tight light blue jeans that molded his hips, a UF tee-shirt, and a black leather jacket with sneakers. Before he sat down, he shrugged off the jacket and dropped it on the bed. I observed that the shirt seemed a size too small. His chest seemed to strain against the somewhat flimsy fabric, and his thick bulging upper arms were barely concealed by the short sleeves. I glanced at Daniel Commey surreptitiously. On the few other occasions we had met, it had been in a crowd of

285

other Ghanaians. I now noticed that although he was shorter and stockier than Maxi, he was attractive in his own way. That realisation made me feel even more uncomfortable. I wanted him out of my room before Maxi called. However, Ghanaian tradition demanded that at least I offered him a drink of water, and as he had commented on the aroma of my cooking, there was no reason why I shouldn't offer him lunch as well.

"Would you like some water to drink?" I asked.

"No, thank you. I just had a cup of coffee. Perhaps, later," he said. Later? Just how long does he intend staying?

"Would you like some of the jollof? It is still nice and hot."

He smiled eagerly. "Yes, I'd love that. The aroma is driving my stomach crazy."

I laughed. "Let me warn you that there is no meat. I used corned beef, vegetables, and boiled eggs."

"That is fine with me," he said. I got out a plate and kept filling it with food until he signalled it was enough. I added a boiled egg and a fork and handed him the plate. I brought out the black pepper sauce so that he could add some to his food if he wanted to. He put a teaspoon of pepper on his plate, sat up on the bed with his back against the wall and began munching away, moaning with pleasure as he swallowed the first few mouthfuls. I prepared a plate for myself and placed it on the desk. We ate in silence for a while.

"This is so delicious, Dzigbordi."

"Thank you," I said.

"Your boyfriend is lucky. You are a great cook."

"Thank you."

Danny chatted about his experiences in America and asked me questions about school. The conversation was much more pleasant that I had anticipated. About half an hour later, we had both finished eating. I put our plates in the sink and offered him a tangerine for desert. Twenty minutes later Danny stretched and yawned. "I should be leaving now," he said reluctantly. "I have to study for a test on Monday."

"Thank you for visiting," I said.

"We should do this more often. Perhaps next time you can come over to my place for dinner and we can play games. Do you like Scrabble?"

"Yes! I love Scrabble," I said, forgetting my reluctance to be alone with him.

"Good! I have some friends who play with me. I can get two of them to join us. It is more exciting when there are many players," he suggested. I gave him a genuine smile. I definitely felt more comfortable with a foursome than a twosome.

"I will see you off. Did you drive here?" I asked as I reached into the closet for my jacket.

"I parked at Library West. I knew it would be difficult getting a parking spot here during the weekend," he said. He moved away from the bed and toward me. "Birthday hug?" he added with a grin as he opened out his arms.

I was flabbergasted. "Ermm... no thank you."

He was standing close to me now. "Come on Dzigbordi, I don't have any evil intentions. It is your birthday and you have been good to me. I just want to give you a hug and wish you a happy birthday."

I hesitated. It seemed rather unnecessary, but perhaps, I was being overcautious. "Fine, just one hug," I warned. He moved forward and pulled me into his arms. It was not the careful hug that I was used to exchanging with Ghanaians of the opposite sex. In this one, he held me tight so that my bosom pressed into his hard chest. I could catch a whiff of Old Spice, an aftershave I was very familiar with, thanks to my father and Mawuli. I pulled away, but he tightened his arms about me and pressed his lips into my neck. I pushed back in earnest, and a feeling of desperation began to overwhelm me.

"Please, let me go," I said as firmly as I could.

"Relax, Dzigbordi, it is just a hug. You know you like it," he said.

I felt angry. Why did guys assume that women wanted "it" anytime they felt like it?

"No, I do not want it! Besides I do have a boyfriend!" I retorted.

"And what has that got to do with the price of eggs in China?" he shot back.

"What do you mean by that?" I asked, frankly bewildered.

"I mean...you are over here and he is over there. Surely, you've heard of the saying that 'What the eye does not see, the heart doesn't grieve over?' You surely don't think that your boyfriend is going to remain chaste all the time you are away, do you?"

"The point of this discussion is that I am not interested!" I said, pushing hard at his chest as I wondered whether it was going to end up in a struggle like it had with Nii Ayi all those years ago. Danny let go of me with a quizzical look.

"No hard feelings, right?"

I didn't answer. The audacity of his actions had left me speechless.

"Come on, Dzigbordi. You can't hold it against me for trying. You are practically the only unmarried Ghanaian woman in Gainesville and that makes you irresistible. You are not going to hold that against me forever, are you?"

I remained silent, struggling with conflicting emotions. I was very upset at the liberties he had taken with me, and furious that he could dismiss the importance of my relationship with Maxi. Thankfully, he didn't persist.

I said, "Fine. Let's forget about it."

"So are we on for Scrabble sometime?" he asked.

"Only if we are in a group."

I could still hear him laughing loudly in the corridor after I locked the door behind him.

****

After Daniel Commey left, I eagerly ripped opened Maxi's letter. To my disappointment it was his regular weekly letter. The letter with the strange handwriting was from Mickey. He mentioned he was thinking of visiting America in the next year or so. He concluded by wishing me a happy birthday. I did not want to leave the room in case Maxi phoned. Not having a mobile phone was definitely restricting, but I couldn't afford one yet. It made it imperative that I got a job as soon as possible. I had talked to Dr. Tanaka about the possibility of getting an assistantship, and he made it clear that such positions were highly competitive and that course grades played a big part in gaining and retaining graduate assistantship positions.

"There are no vacancies this semester, perhaps next semester or next year," he said. "I think you should use the time to settle down and get accustomed to expressing yourself in American English. You will have a better chance if you apply next year when the faculty knows you better," he advised. I had looked for on-campus jobs and made some calls, but people found it hard understanding what I was saying, besides, most of the positions were already filled. There were several library positions but those were for students on financial aid.

Should I telephone Maxi and find out what was going on? But…why did I have to call him on my birthday? The more I thought about it, the angrier I got. I couldn't help contrasting this situation with his birthday which had been on January 27, about three weeks ago. I had planned it so carefully! I made sure I mailed him a card 15 days to the time. In addition, I had bought a blank cassette tape and recorded a message especially for him. On the tape, I reminisced over the past, talked about the present, and dreamed about our future. I was spiritual, I was romantic, and I was passionate. It is amazing how long 30 minutes of talking can be. In the end, I was only able to fill side A of the cassette and a few minutes of side B. I included $10 as a present mainly because I knew he was going to call me on my birthday and wanted to make it easier for him to do so. In addition, I had telephoned him early in the morning and talked with him for five minutes.

I didn't sleep properly Saturday night. Apart from thinking

about all the possible reasons why Maxi hadn't phoned, I debated with myself about whether I should mention Danny's behaviour. I fell into a deep and tired sleep just as dawn was breaking. When I woke up, it was after 8:00a.m. and I had about 30 minutes to get ready before Stella arrived. I wanted to call Maxi, but if he was in church, he wouldn't be able to pick up, and that would make me even more worried. It would be best to call him after I returned from church service. I cannot remember what happened in church. I stood up and sat down when I saw the congregation do so. I suppose I must have joined in the praise and worship and overall shown some semblance of normality.

I checked my messages when I got home and there was still none from Maxi. I couldn't wait any longer. I dialed my code for long distance calls and punched in the international code, the country code, and then Maxi's mobile number. I waited, listening to the silence, and then the long rings that went on and on. Just when I thought I was going to have to call later, I heard a click as the call was answered.

"Hello? Hello?"

"DD? DD!" his voice was warm and surprised. "I was expecting to hear from you hours later... happy birthday!" He certainly sounded alive and well. What on earth was going on?

"The birthday was yesterday," I said.

He laughed again. "I know that! I mean...happy belated birthday, or is it belated happy birthday?" he tittered. I felt a new surge of rage. To use Danny Commey's expression, what had 'belated happy birthday' or 'happy belated birthday' got to do with the price of eggs in China?

"Why didn't you call me yesterday?" I asked baldly.

He paused. "Erm…" Then I heard a voice, a female voice that did not sound like it belonged to his mother or sister break in. The female was speaking Twi. "Brother Maxwell, let me leave you to your call. I will go to the sitting room and chat with Auntie," it said. My heartbeat changed its rhythm to a skip-skip-skip…beat-beat…skip.

"Who is there?" I demanded abruptly.

"Charity…" he raised his tone. "Charity, wait! …eh…DD, please do me a favour and call me later, please, okay? Call at the usual time and we'll be able to talk."

"WHAT?" I shouted. He was abandoning me for Charity?

"Please, DD," he entreated, and then added very softly, "I will explain later." And just as I was spluttering incoherent words, trying to string together some words I heard a click; he had cut the line!

Chapter Twenty-Two

I could feel the prickling at the back of my eyes as my right fingers tapped restlessly on the window pane and I stared with unseeing eyes at the courtyard. What acceptable reason could he have for not calling me yesterday and why the dismissive behaviour today? Wait a minute! He had said she was going to the sitting room to talk with "Charity." My mind flashed to those bold and provocative poses she had taken of Maxi with her camera, especially, the one where he was bare-chested in bed. Even if their relationship was asexual, I didn't like the thought of how close they had become. I knew only too well how seemingly platonic interactions could be transformed overnight into sizzling passionate relationships.

I did not want to call him back that evening. I had already wasted $10 for the five-minute call. Besides, wasn't he taking me for granted by flippantly asking me to call back "at the usual time"? I had no inclination to read or go to the library to research for my project. I had to resolve this issue before my schoolwork suffered. At five o'clock, I found my fingers shaking as I redialed his number. He picked up on the second ring. "Hello DD. Sorry for my behaviour early on. I wanted time to relax and talk with you and I thought it was best for us to talk after Charity had left."

I just hoped "relax and talk" wasn't a euphemism for phone sex. It was the last thing on my mind at that moment.

"I see," I said.

"Before I forget… how was Valentine's Day? I got your card in the mail. I liked it," he said.

"It was okay." That reminded me that he hadn't sent me Valentine's Day wishes. "Did you hear that we had another earthquake on that day? It is the third this year! People are saying that it is a sign that God is angry with the nation because of its evil doings— pouring libations and the lack of moral values. I even heard that the origin of Valentine's Day is suspect," he offered eagerly.

"Hmm…"

"How was your birthday?" he pressed on.

"Fine!"

There was a moment's silence. "You are angry with me, aren't you, DD?"

"Do you think I have a reason to be?"

"Perhaps you do. Is it because of Charity?"

I exploded. "Everything doesn't have to be about Charity. You didn't even bother to call and wish me happy birthday, neither did you email or write. I sat at home most of the day because I didn't want to miss your call and when I didn't hear from you, I thought something bad must have happened. I call you the following day and all you tell me is to call at the proper time and then you slam the phone down on me!"

"I did not slam the phone down on you!" he shot back.

"Yes you did!"

"I couldn't have slammed the phone. It is a mobile phone!"

"Don't be so facetious! You know what I mean. You cut me off in mid-sentence because you didn't want to abandon your precious Charity!"

The harshness of my voice jerked me out of my tirade. Things had disintegrated very rapidly and now we were both angry. I could hear my watch ticking away as the money for the call silently mounted.

"Dzigbordi, you are being unfair to me. You didn't even ask why I requested that you call back. You just attacked me without cause," he said coolly. He had this habit of switching into icy cold mode when we were in a heated argument. It aggravated my anger, because it made him seem logical and in control, while I appeared irrational and erratic even when I felt I was in the right.

"Without cause, really?"

"Have I given you any reason to believe that my relationship with Charity isn't above reproach?"

I took a deep breath and tried to calm down. "Why didn't you call me yesterday?" I decided that it was best our problems were tackled in a chronological fashion.

"I did mean to call you. I thought I would go to Mike's place and use their phone for a few minutes. I knew his mother wouldn't mind. So I got up early and went to his home. However, when I got there, they told me that their phone lines were down," he began.

"Hmmm…" *What about the post office?*

He began to speak more calmly and confidently, assuming

that we were over the worse.

"I thought the best thing would be to call you collect. I knew it was important to you that you heard from me on your special day. I tried that, but the operator said the number wouldn't go through," he went on.

Maxi, you wanted to call me collect on my birthday?

"Then I thought the practical thing would be to go to the post office and phone you. However, the trotro I boarded ran out of petrol and we had to wait for refueling; by the time I got to the post office, it was closed—you know they close early on Saturdays."

I kept quiet. He seemed to have left everything to chance.

"Are you still on the line?" he asked.

"Yes," I croaked. I used two of my left fingers to pinch my right arm in case I was dreaming. His explanations were beyond belief.

"That is really what happened. It was like everything I wanted to do in order to hear your voice did not work. It was as if the devil was trying to create havoc for us. You left Ghana not too long ago and we are already facing these misunderstandings. We need to stand strong and resist the wiles of the enemy. Dzigbordi, I know how important birthdays are to you, and I know you went out of your way to make mine special. Even though I suspected that you might be a little bit upset about what happened, I thought you would understand when I explained things."

I shook my head, but of course, he couldn't see that. It was hard for me to understand. I couldn't even bring myself to ask him about the birthday card. He went on, "I did send you a birthday card, but I mailed it out a few days later than I should have done. I was a bit broke because Serwaa wasn't too well two weeks ago and I had to buy her medicine. That is what I used the money you gave me for. It was like an answer to prayer. I didn't mention her illness because I didn't want you to worry."

"How is she doing now?" I asked mechanically; I still wasn't satisfied with his rationalisations, but I knew how close he was to his sister, who I was fond of myself.

"Much better; she was able to return to school last week," he said.

"And today? Why couldn't you talk?" I pressed.

"Well, Charity came here after church to talk to me. She is very depressed because her parents want her to marry this businessman from Kumasi after she finishes secondary school. She wants to go to university. I have been helping her with Chemistry and Biology and I would be surprised if she doesn't get A's in her 'A' level exams. I think she deserves higher education. Besides, Mr. Sawyer is about 40 years old, and already has a pot belly. His first wife died three years ago and left him with two boys who are now 12 and 15 years. I have met him before. So disgraceful! However, her father owes the man a lot of money and he told Charity that Mr. Sawyer was the one who had been paying her school fees all these years. He was even the one who bought the camera for her. She had always thought of him as a family friend, not knowing he was just lying in wait for her, like a spider waiting for a fly to be fattened for consumption." I could sense his indignation. I tried unsuccessfully to dredge up some sympathy for Charity. Perhaps, later on I would be able to share Maxi's horror over her possible fate, but although her father could be putting pressure upon her to marry Mr. Potbelly Sawyer, she couldn't be forced to do so against her will. "She doesn't have to marry him if she doesn't want to," I voiced my thoughts.

"Dzigbordi, it is not as simple as that. Mr. Sawyer has promised to help the rest of her siblings complete secondary school if she marries him. One of her concerns is also that as a Christian, she is required to honour her parents, and thus, she has to accept the marriage," Maxi said earnestly.

"That's rubbish! If we all did everything our parents told us to do just because of the Ten Commandments, where would we be?"

"It is not rubbish! Charity is a young Christian, and while these things come instinctively to you, who is much older and more experienced, she needs guidance and encouragement," he returned gravely.

I rolled my eyes. My opinion was that the girl liked Maxi and knew that going to him about that issue would engage his full attention for a few weeks, perhaps even months. I had met Charity on a few occasions and my perception of her was someone who appeared soft and helpless but had a strong spine of steel underneath her external demeanour. In the long run, Charity would do what Charity wanted to do. Our discussion on her possible marriage was taking me away from the conversation I wanted to have with him regarding their relationship.

"Were the two of you alone in your bedroom when I called?" I asked.

"Why do you want to know?" he returned.

"Were you?" my voice rose in both pitch and volume.

"Yes, we were. I took her there because there were several visitors in the house and I wanted a quiet place where she could feel comfortable to talk. I could tell at once that she was depressed and emotional," he explained. *My word! Maxi, always solicitous to young ladies, especially, those who hero-worship him, asks what is wrong about taking her to his bedroom and shutting the door. She sits down… where… on the bed? Does he sit by her side? Does he hold her hand? Do they…?*

"Did she cry?" I asked sharply.

"Yes."

"Did you hold her?"

"Dzigbordi!" he yelled.

"Well, did you?" I yelled back.

"For a few moments, yes, but there was nothing…it was just a brotherly… there is nothing going on between us!"

I imagined him holding her as they sat together on his bed, Charity sobbing with her head on his chest.

"Did you wipe away her tears?" I asked.

"No! I just offered her a handkerchief." He sounded tired and bemused.

Maxi had this absolutely sexy way of dealing with my tears. He would place a hand under my chin and tip it up ever so slightly. With the pristine handkerchief he always had on him in the other hand, he would gently wipe under my eyes, down my cheeks, beneath my nose (sometimes making me blow), and then would end by planting a sweet, firm kiss on my lips.

Afterwards, he would cradle my head against his chest and let me relax against him. It is so caring, so intimate, and always made me feel loved and safe. I had one more question. "Did you kiss her?"

"NO!"

I didn't know what to say next.

"So…apart from what I did, how was your birthday?" he asked in a more upbeat tone; he wanted us to put our quarrel aside and get back to normal. I wasn't ready. I was on the verge of expressing those feelings when I thought of something and stopped.

"It wasn't bad." I said simply and then went on to tell him about the people who had called from home and the letters and cards I had received. To his credit, Maxi seemed dampened that everyone else had gotten in touch with me one way or the other. "I am sorry, Dzigbordi, I should have planned better," he said.

Now I felt slightly better. "That's life, I guess," I shrugged, and then went on. "It wasn't a bad day. One Ghanaian friend visited me. I had finished preparing lunch so I invited him to eat with me," I said. I noticed a change after I mentioned the word "him." It was so slight that I would have missed it if I hadn't been watching out for it. Was it a sound he made or a change in his breathing pattern?

"Oh… that's nice. Who was it?"

"One of the single guys here. I think I mentioned him before—Danny—Daniel Commey," I returned airily.

"Commey… Isn't he the one who you said annoys you?" he asked with a slight note of relief in his voice.

"Yes, he is the one. But I was pleasantly surprised that he wasn't that bad after all. We had a great time. He said if I had told him earlier about my birthday, he would have taken me out or bought me a present or even thrown a party for me," I giggled slightly, and then went on. "He enjoyed my cooking and promised to have me over to his apartment for dinner and a game of Scrabble sometime."

"I see!" I could tell Maxi was not amused at my narration. I smiled grimly.

"So, were you alone with him in your room?" Now he was turning the tables on me, just like when I interrogated him about Charity's visit.

"Yes," I responded.

"Did he hold you?" he asked with a note of humour in his voice. Of course, he was confident that Danny hadn't held me. Maxi thought I was so enthralled with him that I never allow another man to lay a finger on me no matter the distance between us. His tone irritated me.

"Yes," I responded bluntly.

"He did?" he sounded taken aback.

"Yes, he did," I responded emphatically and without further elaborations. He was quiet. I knew the last question he was going to ask. Part of me wanted him to stop. Was my desire for him to suffer like I had worth what would follow? I should cease before things went too far. Hadn't it already gone out of control once I had confirmed that Danny had held me in his arms? There was no turning back now...

"Did he kiss you?" he asked in a low, heavy menacing tone.

He practically hissed out the word "kiss". I felt a slight thrill of fear. I hadn't heard that note in his voice before in all the years I had known him. I wanted to lie. I wanted to explain the circumstances surrounding Danny's actions, but when I opened my mouth, what came out was a bald, "Yes."

Silence! I could hear the sound of Maxi's heavy irregular breathing.

"And you have the audacity to complain about Charity?" he bellowed, making me jump up in a fright and drop the telephone receiver onto the bed. I grabbed it back with trembling fingers. I was about to speak although I had no idea what I was going to utter, but for the second time that day, Maxi, hung up on me.

I paced around the room, too restless to settle down. What had I just done? I had been so furious with Maxi that I deliberately set out to make him jealous, giving him tit for tat. Now things had spiralled out of my control. I was usually the dramatically emotional partner in our relationship. Once, during a quarrel with Maxi in my room at the university, I had been so furious that I had hurled a mug across the room smashing against the wall and shattering into smithereens. Although it had whizzed by Maxi's head during its journey, he had barely flinched. He had merely given me an indomitable look, asked me to clean up the mess, and walked out of the room, shutting the door quietly as he left. It was amazing just how little we knew about the people closest to us. Why had I allowed my temper to overcome my common sense?

The following morning, after sleeping better than I had anticipated, I left home very early for the computer lab to finish up my story before class. I signed into my email account to check my email. There was one from Balme Library, from Maxi. With a beating heart, I moved the down arrow without focusing on any of the green glowing words. The email appeared to be a very long missive and I printed it out on the dot matrix printer. After five minutes of screeching and grinding sounds, four single-spaced sheets later, I tore off the email and deposited it in my bag. I set off for the reporting lab at Weimer Hall, taking off my jacket. The day was bright and warm, not so my feelings. The afternoon went by fast. We turned in our stories and picked up assignments for the following week. Dr. Tanaka handed back the previous week's assignment. I had made a B minus, my highest grade so far.

I had two hours before my last class of the day and went downstairs to the Journalism library and started reading Maxi's letter. It was long and somewhat disjointed, and he repeated himself several times. "I knew when you left for America that we were going to face a lot of trials, tribulations, and temptations. I knew we would have to stand fast and strong in order to make it, but I didn't know that we would hit a rock so soon." Somewhere down the first page he said, "I wouldn't have thought that not quite two months after we parted you would be kissing or allowing another man to put his arms around you and make love to you. How long did we know each other before we first kissed, Dzigbordi? Did you sleep with him, Dzigbordi?"

He repeated why he hadn't called me on my birthday, and then segued back into Danny Commey. "Look how long it took us before we kissed and this Commey boy has been able to get you to do so in six weeks? I don't know what to think; I cannot believe that you were so upset about my making a mistake on your birthday that you decided to punish me by flirting with another man. Dzigbordi, is this how it's going to be? Are you going to hit at me in a way that would hurt me irrevocably anytime I do something to disappoint you?" On and on he went in that vein until the end of the fourth page where he stopped abruptly in mid-sentence.

I hadn't realised that resolving misunderstandings in long distance relationships would be so complicated. Writing via mail would take too long, calling was expensive, and writing back would be expensive for him to retrieve. I resolved to call him after classes and worry about how I would pay the bill later on. It was a quarter to midnight in Ghana when I dialed his number.

"Hello?" Maxi sounded alert but no hint of friendliness. But I was heartened that he picked up my call. If Maxi hadn't been interested in making up, he would have ignored my phone calls until hell froze over.

"Good evening, Maxi," I responded, trying to be lighthearted.

"Hello Dzigbordi."

"I got your email. I just wanted to let you know that nothing happened the way I inferred it did."

Silence.

"Danny did come to visit me on my birthday and we had lunch together. He hugged me and I rejected him, and that was it. Are you still there?"

"Yes," he responded.

"You heard what I said?"

"Yes."

"Do you have anything to say? You are quiet. I don't know whether I am wasting your time with explanations and should leave you to go to sleep, or if you want to talk about it."

"We can talk."

"So that's what happened. You are right in that I was upset that you didn't call and you kicked me off the telephone when I called the following day. I get it that Charity was upset because of the possibility of a forced marriage to her father's friend. However, I thought that I should have gotten priority when I phoned you. You took me for granted. When I tried to express my disappointment, you seemed to take it lightly and I got upset and said something that I knew would upset you."

Finally he opened up. "I didn't kick you off...I asked that you call at a time when we could be alone to talk. I went off the telephone in a hurry because I knew it was costing you money. I wasn't putting Charity before you; I just wanted to make sure we had a relaxed time to talk without the pressure of someone waiting for me. Also, people come to visit us after church and so even if Charity were not around, I may have had to interrupt the conversation to greet visitors. That was my reason for wanting you to call later."

The way he presented things now made the sequence of events sound logical and above board.

"So, are you okay now?" I asked.

"I want to know what happened with that guy and why you kissed him," he said.

"I didn't kiss him; he kissed me. And he didn't kiss me on the lips. It was on my neck," I said.

305

"Your neck!?"

I went ahead and gave him a succinct recapitulation of events. He was in no way mollified. "Why did you agree to see him again after what he did?" he demanded.

"I agreed to see him in the company of others," I corrected.

"I think you shouldn't have told him that, else he would think he still has a chance with you."

"He knows he doesn't have a chance with me."

"Dzigbordi, why do you find it hard to just tell the guy to leave you alone? I am a man and I know how men think. After the liberties he took, I think you shouldn't interact with him. I think you should make it clear that you do not want any association with him. I would feel more comfortable that way."

"I understand how you feel," I said at last. "As you brought it up first, let me also state that I feel uncomfortable with your relationship with Charity, and would also prefer it if you curtailed, or at least, modified your interaction with her."

"Charity? What has she done? I told you that she is like a sister to me! There is nothing, absolutely nothing going on between the two of us!" he bridled.

"Hmm…"

"What do you mean by 'hmm'? Dzigbordi, are you trying to blackmail me? Are you saying that unless I break off my friendship with Charity, you are still going to keep interacting with Commey? I am not going to allow myself to be blackmailed in this relationship!"

"I am not blackmailing you. I am letting you know that I am also uncomfortable with Charity."

"Well, my relationship with Charity is different..." he began.

"Maxwell, please do not tell me once more about how she is like your sister," I broke in.

"But that's the point!"

"You are close to her both emotionally and in proximity. You tutor her. She visits you at least once a week. She relies on you to provide her with emotional support. Her parents welcome you to their home..."

"But it is not my fault that your parents do not welcome me!" he interjected.

"That is neither here nor there. I am just giving you the big picture. She visits you in your bedroom, takes sexy pictures of you..."

His indignation was high, "But you wanted those pictures! I asked her to take them of me because you asked me for them!"

"But I didn't ask you to make her the designated photographer!" I shot back.

"Dzigbordi, what is the point of all this?"

"The point of all this is that we are apart in two different countries and we will have to interact with people. Perhaps, we should acknowledge that we both do not feel comfortable with the other having close friendships with people of the opposite sex."

"I didn't say you shouldn't make friends with men, I just don't want you to put yourself in the position where they end up kissing you!" he snapped at me.

"And...I also do not want you to put yourself in the position where girls, apart from your biological sisters, have the opportunity to cry in your arms!" I shot back.

"Is there any point to this conversation?"

"Yes. If you are willing to cut off all association with Charity, I would do the same with Danny. Wait, I am not done!" I said firmly when he tried to break in once more. "When you are able to admit that it might be difficult for me as well as you to carry out that strategy, we can think of compromises that would satisfy both of us."

He remained silent. I continued. "We can both think over what we talked about for a day or two and then talk some more, okay?" I cut the call without waiting for his response.

It took two and half weeks and a total of five additional emails, three letters by snail mail, and three telephone calls to resolve that issue. Eventually we were able to work out a solution satisfactory to both parties. I accepted that I couldn't ask him not to see Charity and all those girls who seem to hang on him for spiritual, moral, and academic assistance. However, he concurred to not entertaining girls in bedrooms, his or theirs. I also promised that I wouldn't entertain single guys in my room. I don't think either of us was totally satisfied with the outcome, but we promised to adjust our decision to meet situations as they arose.

As I had expected, the phone bill was astronomical, and I was still wracking my brain for an ingenious way of paying it off. But in the next few days, there was a lot to cheer me up. The fight between Maxi and I was finally over, my grades in Reporting kept improving, and the weather was getting warmer outside. Spring was round the corner.

Chapter Twenty-Three

"Hello-o?" I heard a breathless Caucasian male voice a few yards behind me. The courtyard in Weimer Hall was bustling with students pouring out of classrooms.

"Hi there!" The voice sounded closer, right behind me. I turned sharply and almost bumped into the medium height blond student who was gazing expectantly into my eyes. He had smiling, bright blue eyes and short curly blond hair. I put on my warmest, friendliest smile, and waited for cues to his identity. My greatest challenge had always been identifying faces, unless the individual had a very distinct feature, it was hard to remember the person after an initial meeting. Fortunately, I had an excellent memory for names and conversations.

"I was sure it was you. I have been looking out for you for months, but this is the first time I have seen you in Weimer," the guy went on.

Wait, it had to be…"Brad! It is great to see you," I felt my lips stretch out from cheek to cheek. I had very fond memories of Brad and how he had rescued me on my first day in the college.

"What's up?" he asked me. I still hadn't figured out the correct response to that common campus greeting.

"I am fine. The spring semester was tough at the beginning, but I think things are better now," I moved out of the way of the crowd that surged about us.

"I wondered how you were doing. I had forgotten your name, or let's say I didn't know how to pronounce or spell it out. I thought about asking Tanaka about you each time I had a meeting with him, but always forgot about it until I was out of the meeting!" He heaved his heavy backpack off his shoulders and deposited it on a bench in the courtyard and sat down. "Do you have class now?" he asked.

"No, I just had a meeting with Dr. Tanaka."

I followed his example and took off my backpack and sat beside him. I shrugged off my black jacket in response to the now hot weather. I was wearing a pink tee shirt from Ghana, blue jeans and sneakers, with my newly braided hair held back in a pony with a pink hair band. I noticed Brad looking at me with a rather thoughtful expression.

"You never called me," he said. I felt guilty and flustered. I had experienced a feeling of panic anytime I thought of phoning him during my first few days in Gainesville. After that I kept debating whether he had meant me to call, or if giving me his number had been merely a polite gesture. I had worried for weeks that I would pass by him without recognising him. Looking back into his eyes, I wondered how on earth I could have forgotten what he looked like. Those blue eyes were so stunning, like those of Paul Newman in *Cat on a Hot Tin Roof.*

"I am so sorry, Brad. I meant to call you the day after you helped me, but I wasn't sure whether you really meant for me to call or not. Then I read in the International Student Handbook that it was polite to call within the first 48 hours and thought I had left it off too late," I explained. I watched his face crinkle up with a smile with a flash of those brilliant white teeth. *Some of these white guys are really hot.* Apart from some movie stars, my attraction had always been toward Ghanaian men.

"I wouldn't have given you my number if I hadn't wanted you to call. I thought you had forgotten about me. I'm surprised you remembered my name," he said.

"No, I haven't forgotten you. You were very kind to me. I am bad with faces, but I don't forget names."

"Would you want to grab some coffee or a sandwich from the Reitz Union?" Brad asked.

I looked at my watch which was now finally adjusted from Ghana time to Eastern Standard Time. It was just after 1:00p.m. I hesitated. From what I had read, having coffee together was casual. Lunch really didn't have any romantic connotations either. It was dinner that was probably unwise. "I'd like that. I haven't had lunch yet," I said. As we walked along the sidewalk to the Reitz Union, I looked at the lawn where students sat or lay sunbathing. Some were reading or chatting, and a few were actually lying on the grass. As usual, I surreptitiously examined the half-clad bodies basking in the sunshine. After the first cold months, the weather had warmed up and all of a sudden everyone flung off heavy sweaters, jackets and pants and walking through campus was such an eye opener! My eyes feasted on the shorts and skimpy tops, topless sturdy males running along the pavements in the evening, and bodies gaining golden tans. The girl on a skateboard with skimpy shorts and a green exercise brassiere held my eye for a while as did the students kissing on the grass, because I could not imagine a woman in Ghana wearing such attire in public or being kissed in public.

311

Some weeks ago when I wrote to Maxi about the change in weather, clothing and people kissing, he wrote back admonishing me to continue holding steadfast my principles, and praying. He also asked me to remember the mission of evangelism. "You have to find a way of reaching these people, DD. God had a purpose for bringing you to America besides your studies. Who knows, perhaps, there is a soul waiting for you to save?" Maxi may have had a point but so far, I had not been able to bring myself to stop by one of students on the lawn and preach the gospel of salvation to them.

Now, Brad and I were on the second floor of the Reitz Union. We stopped at Wendy's and joined the queue of students waiting to order their lunches.

"What are you having? I think I will have a cheeseburger," Brad said.

"I will have the chicken nuggets and chips," I said without hesitation. That was what I always selected at Wendy's or McDonalds.

"Chips? I don't think Wendy's sells chips. You can get some from the vending machine, though," Brad said.

"Oh, I meant fries. I still get that mixed up. We call them chips in Ghana," I explained.

"Interesting… I have a friend, Jack, who visited London and he says they call them chips as well," he said.

I ordered my meal with Coke, making sure that I asked for it without ice. The food court was very crowded, but Brad managed to find us a spot which had been recently vacated. We deposited our trays of food and began eating.

"So, tell me your name once more," he said as he removed the foil wrapping around his burger.

"Dzi-gbor-di" I responded slowly.

"Gi…. Write down the phonetic transcription." He shoved a paper napkin toward me and searched the outer pocket of his backpack for a pen.

"Ji-bor-di" I wrote.

"Jibordi… that's easy! Write it down as it is supposed to be," he requested.

I wrote down my first name and added my surname as well. As I guessed would happen, he looked somewhat bemused. We spent the first 10 minutes or so discussing my name, why it looked odd with all those 'dzis' and the meaning of my name. Then we started talking about school. He told me a little about which professor was teaching what course and what to expect. I found it very enlightening.

"Do you still plan graduating in the fall?" I asked. It was sad that my newly-found friend would be leaving at the end of next semester.

"Yes. I have already begun looking for a job. I have my second interview next week. It is with CNN," he said.

"That's great! I do hope you get it. Are you doing the thesis or non-thesis option?" I hadn't made up my mind whether I wanted to write a thesis or just take an examination and have it over and done with. Either option was intimidating.

"Non-thesis option, of course! I do not have the time and patience to deal with a thesis. You have to go through the defense, do a lot of writing and revisions… I hate writing."

"Then you are in the wrong profession, aren't you?" I teased.

"Writing stories is different from writing a thesis."

We finished our meal, but kept on talking. He asked me about Ghana, about my family and about my experiences in the US. He told me about his landscape artist mother, and his music professor father at the university. He spoke of his two older sisters—Janice, who was married with four children, and Esmie, who had recently taken a trip to Rome with her fiancé. They sounded fascinating and very bohemian.

"You should come over to meet my parents sometime soon. They have several international friends, and I am sure my mother would love to meet you."

"Yes, that would be nice," I said in a noncommittal tone. I wasn't sure whether his parents would mind issuing an invitation to some foreign girl they had never met.

"I am serious! They'd love it if you come over. We have get-togethers most Friday nights and we all bring friends. We play games and talk about serious stuff such as politics and the economy."

"Sounds like fun," I offered. Games sounded like fun, but I didn't know much about American politics except for what we studied in class. As Dr. Tanaka had mandated, I subscribed to the Gainesville Sun. However, I found it difficult keeping up with reading the newspaper daily.

"So, what do you do for fun?" he asked me.

"Hmm...mostly reading and writing letters home," I responded reflectively. That sounded boring when I said it out loud.

"Would you like to go to a movie sometime? We can go this week; there's one I want to see," he said. Was it a date or was he just being friendly? "You do watch movies in Ghana, don't you?" he added, after I had been silent for a few seconds.

"Yes we do!" I responded. "What's the title of the movie?"

"*My Best Friend's Wedding*, it just came out a week or so ago. Julia Roberts is in it. She is so-o hot!"

"I love Julia Roberts!" I exclaimed.

"Have you seen any of her movies?" he asked curiously.

"Yes… a few. I have seen *Pretty Woman* and *Sleeping with the Enemy*."

"So… how about this weekend, perhaps a matinee on Saturday? It is cheaper then," he explained.

"Sure…" I responded. I was getting excited. It was at least five years since I had seen a film in a cinema. My film watching had been mostly through videos and television. He said he would check the movie times and get back to me. I looked at my watch and found that we had been talking for over two hours.

"I am sorry… I have to leave now. I have an appointment to babysit in forty minutes," I explained hurriedly. We disposed of our trash and left in opposite directions after descending the steps of the Reitz Union.

"Ji… bordy!" I heard him yell after I had taken about 20 steps in the direction of home. I swivelled about to find that he was hurrying back.

"Yes?" I asked, wondering what on earth the matter was.

"You still haven't given me your phone number! No more disappearing acts, okay?"

As I walked toward my apartment, I reminisced over the several changes that had occurred in the previous months since my big fight with Maxi. I experienced my first spring break, which I thoroughly enjoyed with the Benjamins. Daylight Savings Time occurred on the first Sunday in April and took me unawares. I noticed that as the seasons changed and the weather became warmer, my optimism increased and school work improved. Soon it was the end of the semester and time to take finals and submit projects. Fortunately, it wasn't like Mfodwo where I had to wait for months before receiving my grades. All I had to do the Monday evening after the semester ended was to dial 37-Gator (UF's on-line information and registration system), and hear the introductory message, "Welcome to Telegator. You have fifteen minutes to complete your call." I walked through the menu on Telegator, and five minutes later, I got to know I had received a "Satisfactory" for Proseminar, a B for Reporting, B+ for Introduction to Statistics, and A for Mass Communication History. After consultation with Dr. Tanaka, I signed up for Mass Communication Theory in Summer A and Individual Work for Summer B.

Another significant change in my life was that two weeks before the spring semester ended, I got a call from the housing office that there was an apartment available in Diamond Village. If I was agreeable, I would have a week to sign the contract and move in. An hour after the call, I had signed the paperwork. My apartment was upstairs in Building 303, which was the building directly opposite Stella Odonkor's. Her family helped move my belongings to my new place. It was so bare! I didn't have any furniture or bed. The Richters gave me an air mattress to use for the meantime.

"Don't rush to buy furniture just yet," advised Stella. "Many students graduate at the end of spring and leave their furniture behind because it is more expensive to transport furniture."

"How would I be able to get the furniture they leave behind?"

"What you do is to check the dumpster every morning and every evening," Mina Richter chipped in. I didn't want to spend money on furniture, especially as I had already spent most of my budget for the spring and was still trying to find a way of paying some bills before my father sent the next financial installment. However, the idea of pawing my way through the trash for useful furniture was a bit distasteful.

"You don't need to go into the dumpster," William Richter clarified. "Students leave serviceable furniture by the dumpster and other people take what they need."

"My husband and I got our computer desk from there," mused Stella. "We have used it for three years." My eyes widened. That was a good solid piece of furniture.

Three days after I moved in, I got a couch for my apartment. It was about six feet long, and had a pink background with green and yellow flowers. It looked intact, and relatively clean. Stella helped me carry it up. I was so excited. The following day, I found a chair and a standing fan still in working order. Stella also gave me a small foldable table she was not using. The apartment was gradually taking a semblance of home. I was very excited each time I locked or unlocked the front door. It was the first time I had a home—bedroom, bathroom, kitchen, and sitting room all to myself.

Barely a week later, I discovered something I could do to help resolve my financial crisis and generate some extra money throughout my graduate study—babysitting. Stella asked me to assist with Helena Katherine for two days because she had to go for a conference in Orlando. I wanted to do it for free because she had done a lot to help me, but she insisted on paying me. Soon, I got other offers and I babysat both Ghanaian and non-Ghanaian children. Sometimes when parents were on the night shift at their jobs, I would spend the night with the children. My pay rate ranged from $6-$10 per hour. For six weeks, I took any babysitting job I was offered. It was very exhausting dealing with children round the clock, especially, when my Summer A class began. I quickly learned that American children were less docile than Ghanaian kids. However, by the middle of June, I had regained the money I had "borrowed" for Maxi's calls, and I had begun saving. Fortunately, I got hired for an assistant managerial position at the Diamond Village office. It paid only a minimum wage of $5.15/hour and I could only work 20 hours a week, but the job was not stressful at all, and I got to interact more with the village residents.

I created "The Maxi Fund" (in a jar), into which each week I deposited some money toward expenses for his trip to America.

****

Saturday 12:15p.m.saw me at the Diamond Village parking lot waiting for Brad. Five minutes later, a battered gray Toyota

Camry drew up by my side. I was in very high spirits and Brad's infectious smile made me feel as if we were on our way to an exciting adventure. The drive to Regal Cinema took under 10 minutes. Just as I had anticipated, we each paid for our tickets. Then, we entered the lobby and I was immediately assailed by the seductive warm scent of fresh popcorn. I wanted some very badly.

"Would you like some popcorn?" Brad asked.

"Yes," I responded. We joined the shortest line to the confectionary stand. A couple of minutes later, it was his turn to be served. I began digging into the pocket of my shorts to have my cash handy.

"Don't. I will get a large popcorn and we can split it," Brad said. So, did that mean that he was paying or would I have to give him my share of the money?

"Do you mind if we have it with butter?"

"No, that's good," I responded. *My mother and Esther Benjamin would be horrified!* The server went to the popcorn stand and began to heap the popcorn into a paper bag. Half way through the process, he stopped and then added some oil before filling the bag, after which more oil was used to garnish the popcorn.

"Anything else?" the bored-looking white server asked.

"Two medium drinks. I want a coke… and you Jibordi?"

"Erm…," I said, wanting to protest, but feeling I was wasting time dilly-dallying. "I will have a coke as well."

"No ice, right?" he asked, and I nodded. It was sweet of him to remember that I didn't like ice in my drinks. Brad paid for the snacks, handed me the popcorn and one of the drinks, and got some straws and napkins.

It was packed inside the theatre. Most of the back seats were taken, and so we had to sit closer to the front row. While we waited for the movie and watched the advertisements, we began eating the popcorn. My fingers became buttery, and the popcorn felt warm and tasted salty and delicious. Brad placed the bag in between his thighs and every now and then, I would lean over and dip my hand in for the popcorn. There were times we reached in at the same time and our hands brushed against each other's. The first time it happened, I jerked my hand away as if it had gotten in contact with a hot stove, but after the first couple of times, it was not a big deal, and we even laughed when it happened. The movie was hilarious, and reminded me of the MGM musicals I watched years ago when people burst into song in the middle of conversations. By the end of the movie I was feeling slightly sick from the amount of buttery popcorn and coke I had consumed. We spent the time on the drive back to my apartment complex discussing the movie. All too soon, we were back in Diamond Village. "Thank you so much, Brad. I had a great time. Thanks for the popcorn and drink," I said.

"Great! By the way, would you like to come over to dinner at my parents' next Friday? My mom would love to meet you." I wondered what Maxi would think of my platonic relationship with Brad. I didn't want to refuse Brad's invitation. I had enjoyed my time with him. I was curious to meet his parents and I was eager to make some ties outside the Ghanaian community.

"I would love that very much. Thank you for inviting me."

"Awesome! I will pick you up. Five thirty okay with you?"

"Yes, thank you. See you then."

I spent that evening babysitting the two-year old fraternal twins of a Portuguese student couple. All the while, I kept thinking about whether I was going to tell Maxi about my meetings with Brad, and his invitation to dine with his family the following week. By Sunday evening, I still hadn't made a final decision. When I telephoned Maxi he spent a few minutes telling me about Nii Q and Lia's traditional marriage ceremony.

"It was very nice, and gave me ideas about our traditional marriage ceremony. It made me think of how much planning is involved if we intend to do it this year," he said casually as if we were only discussing the weather.

"Traditional ceremony this year?" I echoed in shock.

"Well, or next year... definitely before I come over... if I still come," he said.

"Why wouldn't you want to come?" My tone rose.

"I don't know...I just want us to consider other options. We can have it before I leave for America. From what you told me earlier, I have already missed the deadline for this year. By the time I am ready to come over, you would have finished your programme. However, it might be cheaper for you to return home immediately you complete your programme next year so that we get married. We can always return to America later for my graduate studies. By that time, I am sure it would be time for Trixie-Ann and co," he ended on a jocular note.

In March, I had visited the Chemistry Department and learned that the admission deadline had been back in January.

That had been so disappointing but we had tried to take the news in stride and work toward a spring or latest, a fall 1998 admission for Maxi. Perhaps, as Maxi suggested, it would be cheaper to return home immediately I graduated, but I had heard about the optional practical training (OPT) programme where international students were permitted to work in America for a year for experience. The OPT would give me the opportunity to save some money to take back to Ghana. I hated the idea of being dependent on my parents once again when I returned home, and at this point, Maxi himself was struggling to keep his head above water. Besides, I was of the opinion that once I was here, it was best to take advantage of all opportunities rather than put things off in the hope of coming back to America in the future. Was that the only reason why the thought of returning home immediately made me feel very unsettled?

"Are you still there?" Maxi asked.

"Yes, I am."

"Perhaps we should think it over and discuss it in a few weeks?"

"Yes, that's a good idea," I eagerly grasped at the opportunity to postpone that discussion.

"So… anything interesting at your end?" Maxi asked.

I took a deep breath. "Kind of interesting… I saw Brad this week. It was such a surprise!" I began, ready to remind him of Brad.

"Oh, he's the white guy who helped you on your first day in your college, right?" Maxi stated without hesitation.

I was surprised, "How did you remember?"

"I was impressed he was so helpful. I included his name in the prayer requests at church and we prayed for him for about a month. I wanted him to be blessed for being such a good Samaritan to you."

I was touched, "Thank you, Maxi."

"Don't mention it. So, what happened with Brad?"

"We talked. He wanted to know how things are going with me, and he advised me about school. He knows all the professors in the college, so he was able to warn me about pitfalls," I said.

"That's very good! It is easy to avoid making mistakes when you learn from the experiences of others," Maxi returned in a warm voice.

I summoned courage and then went on. "His family— parents and sisters, live in Gainesville. He said his parents are very interested in meeting international students. He wanted to know if I could join them sometime."

Maxi didn't say anything for a moment. "Hmm... that sounds like a good idea. You will get to meet people of different cultures. So far, your interactions have mostly been with Ghanaians," he said.

I felt a smile break out across my face. "You're right. I still find it difficult interacting with people here. It is hard sometimes to even pick up a phone and make a call," I confessed.

"The best way to overcome fear is to face it. I am sure after going to a few of those sessions at Brad's parents' home, you will be more comfortable."

I grimaced at the irony of how I had presented the situation in such a way that Maxi felt it would be to my benefit to continue my interaction with Brad. When had I become so conniving?

I put down the telephone, quite amazed and a bit horrified at my audacity. I hadn't told Maxi about the lunch and the movie outing with Brad, and I had described the visit to Brad's home as if it was a big meeting of international people instead of a family dinner. Worst of all, although the visit the following week was a fait accompli, I had presented it as if I was asking for Maxi's opinion as to whether I should go or not. It seemed to me that the way I handled the Brad situation was reminiscent of how I had dealt with my parents in the past. Why could I not deal with Maxi in an adult fashion and be truthful and straightforward? Was it because I was trying to prevent a quarrel and/or because I knew I was doing something wrong? Either way, I felt uncomfortable. I thought leaving home and living on my own would automatically make me independent, but obviously, I still had some growing up to do. Another thorn in my flesh was Maxi's talk about our traditional marriage ceremony and the idea of discussing it with my parents this year. I had a sneaking suspicion that it was not going to be as clear cut a situation as Maxi was painting it out to be. I felt the beginnings of a migraine and rapidly filed both topics in my mental to-do list.

Chapter Twenty-Four

Brad's family lived in a huge brownstone house in the northwest part of Gainesville. Dr. Bradley Goldstein IV was in his late fifties or early sixties. He had similar physical features as his son, but had graying brown hair and light blue eyes. He greeted me in a jocular brisk fashion, clasping my hand tightly in his large paw. His wife, Linda Goldstein, was a few inches taller than her husband and slim. She had obviously passed on her blonde hair and vivid blue eyes to her son. As I shook her hand, I noticed a smudge of green paint across her thumb. Brad and I stepped into the house. I could hear loud voices and barking noises. My heart sank like a stone. I was not comfortable around dogs. Just then, I heard the thumping sounds of a running animal, and moments later, a huge golden brown dog raced up and started jumping on Brad, then me. I instinctively stepped back behind Brad and stifled a scream. I almost dropped the bottle of wine I had brought as a gift. I had read in the International Students' Handbook that it was appropriate to bring along a small gift when invited for dinner in an American home.

"Down, Stallone, down!" yelled Brad. It took him a few moments to get the dog under control. "He is harmless, just very friendly," he assured me. I swallowed a shuddering breath.

I didn't know how I would survive the evening with Stallone the dog. All I could think of were scenes from Stephen King's movie *Cujo*. I controlled my overactive imagination with great difficulty. It was unlikely that the exuberant Stallone was riddled with rabies. He was obviously part of the family, and the last thing I wanted to do was to offend the Goldsteins; some Americans cherished their pets like they were humans. I stepped out from behind Brad and stood still as Stallone began sniffing my feet.

"Leave Stallone outside while Jibordi is here," Linda Goldstein told her son. "We will give her time to gradually get used to his playful ways."

"I am so sorry," I said, feeling mortified. "I am not very used to dogs."

"That's okay. Let's join the others, shall we?"

The door was shut in poor Stallone's face. It was a delightful evening. Ten of us sat behind a large oval dining table. Linda and her daughter Janice served the food which began with salad and bean soup. Everyone oohed and ahhed over the soup Linda Goldstein had prepared, and although I murmured politely, it tasted like beans boiled in water, and was not in the least spicy. We had tangy pork with grilled potatoes and a pasta salad. For dessert, there was strawberry cheesecake and coffee. All through dinner, people asked me questions about Ghana, everything from the politics, the food, the languages, and education. When I discussed life in Ghana: the clothes, music, art, and the various foods, I felt myself become more animated, and found myself gesturing rapidly with my hands as I tried to describe things. I even talked about my family and Maxi. They all listened to me intently, even the children.

"What about the animals?" piped Celeste, Janice's six year old daughter, "Do you have lions, tigers, and giraffes?"

I looked into her earnest elfin face and wished I didn't have to disappoint her. "Eh, I haven't come across any lions, tigers, or giraffes," I admitted. "All I have seen are animals like goats, chicken, sheep, antelopes, peacocks, and guinea fowls."

"No lions?" she looked like she was about to cry. "I thought Africa is full of lions! I read about it in school!"

"Certain parts of Africa, such as East Africa," I said. "Perhaps there are lions in parts of Ghana, but they are not common."

"Oh… what is a genie fowl? Is it a magic fowl? Does it give you three wishes?" In an attempt to redeem myself, I spent some minutes describing how a guinea fowl looked, the kind of eggs it laid, and how the meat tasted. The adults watched the scene with amused looks on their faces. Everyone had something to talk about; a funny story to narrate, and when we realised it was past 10 o'clock, the dinner party broke up. I wanted to help with the dishes, but Linda Goldstein refused. "No, that's Bradley's job. It is late and Brad will give you a ride home. Thank you for joining us. I hope you come again soon. Don't be a stranger, okay? You are welcome on Friday nights."

"Thank you so much, Mrs. Goldstein," I said fervently. "I had a wonderful time."

"Call me Linda," she said.

The talk during the drive back to campus was rather desultory. Brad seemed lost in his thoughts, and I was mentally exhausted. I did have a wonderful time, but it was a strain being in a social setting with a group of people I was just getting to know.

"Did you have a good time?" Brad asked as we neared to campus.

"Yes!" I said at once. "Your family is so wonderful. I haven't talked this much since I left Ghana," I said.

"They love you too. You were very good with the kids. They thought you were awesome," he said. I glowed at his praise.

"I am sorry about Stallone… that he had to stay outdoors because of me," I said.

"Stallone is fine. It is not the first time we have kept him outside. We have some friends who are allergic to dogs or whose children are scared of them," he said dismissively. He pulled into the parking lot and turned off the engine.

"Thank you so much!" I said.

"You have already thanked me," he teased. I opened the passenger door and picked my handbag from the floor. Brad also stepped out of the car.

"I will walk you to your door," he announced.

"You don't have to do that. I will be fine," I protested.

"My mother will have my neck if she gets to know that I left you in the parking lot so late at night," Brad insisted.

"Well, then we won't tell her. It will be our secret," I teased back. Brad locked the car doors and checked the windows to ensure that they were properly rolled up. We walked through one of the little gates into the compound of the complex. As we climbed, the stairs I began searching my handbag for the keys to the apartment.

"Here are the keys," I said triumphantly as I lifted them out of the bag with a jiggling sound. I shoved the apartment key into the lock and hesitated. What was the polite thing to do? Do I say goodbye and go in? If I invited him in, would he think it is an invitation for something more? If I didn't invite him in, would that be rude? I looked up. Brad was leaning against the entrance of the apartment. He seemed relaxed and in no hurry to leave.

"Would you like to come in?" I asked.

"Sure, for a short while, if you are not sleepy," he answered promptly. With my heart thumping in my chest, I turned the key and opened the door. The light switch was by the door so I turned it on. I stepped in, giving a sigh of relief that I had tidied up that morning.

"Please have a seat," I gestured to the couch by the window and deposited my bag on the desk. "Would you like anything to drink? I have Coca-Cola, Gatorade, tea…"

"Gatorade is fine," Brad said as he sat on the couch. I bustled about in the kitchen for a while and returned carrying a tray with a jug of cold lemon-lime Gatorade, two glasses, and a plate of gingersnap biscuits. I placed the tray on the table by the couch and poured the drinks.

"The apartment is quite large for one person," Brad said thoughtfully as he picked up a biscuit.

"Yes, it is. I will furnish it gradually. I didn't want to spend money doing that now," I said.

"Yeah, no need to do that in a hurry. There are always deals on cheap furniture. If I get the job with CNN, I can give you some of my furniture from my apartment. I don't plan to take them with me."

"Thank you. But I shall buy them from you," I said.

"And I will give them to you," he returned firmly. "I was planning to dump it." I could hear his teeth crunching the biscuits. "You do miss your country, don't you?" Brad suddenly asked in a soft voice.

"Yes…" I said, wondering where he was going with that.

"I could see it when you were talking at dinner. You were…" he stopped, as if trying to search for the right words. "You were vivacious as you spoke about Ghana, and yet, there was this depth of yearning with a trace of sadness that held us mesmerised. We were all enthralled."

"Oh…" I said inadequately. I hadn't meant to put my emotions on display. I felt embarrassed, as if I had stood naked in front of strangers.

"There's nothing wrong with that, Jibordi," Brad said, his blue eyes looking deep into my brown ones. He reached down and picked up one of my hands from my lap and held it. "Don't be ashamed of showing your feelings, especially if it is love," he added gently.

I felt something indescribable but which I identified as a dangerous leap between us as his grip on my hand tightened. I couldn't move. His blue eyes kept me hypnotised. I was afraid if I spoke I would say the wrong thing. He used his other hand to gently trace a finger up my arm, and then moved it over my skin in small whorls. His fingers felt light, smooth, sensual, and warm.

"You have such beautiful skin, Jibordi," he murmured deeply. "It is so smooth, and rich, and lovely. It is like a mug of warm, thick, luscious cocoa. I wish I could paint you." I sat still, rather mesmerised and speechless.

My mind was spinning so fast that I couldn't pin down any thoughts in a coherent fashion. Oh blimey, was the only rational thought I could identify within the whirlwind of emotion. Brad caressed my arm, and it was hard to describe the feel of his skin and the emotions it evoked, and the aphrodisiac whiff of his aftershave. Looking in his deep eyes was like drowning in an ocean.

A finger moved over my skin in circles, and then, all fingers were making light sweeping movements up and down the length of my arm, igniting it in the process so that I felt as if a fire was being stoked. Then, Brad stopped and looked at me, as if he was trying to figure out what I was feeling. He tilted up my chin slightly, and now his lips were descending upon mine. His kiss tasted of sugar and spice. His lips were thinner than Maxi's. He kissed me lightly and when I didn't draw back, his lips became firmer, more assertive, teasing, playful, and demanding. I found myself kissing him back. His kisses felt pleasant and somewhat thrilling, yet safe and experimental. As if Brad read my thought, he pulled me so that I was resting on him. His hands were around me and he now began to run his tongue along the line where my two lips met. My lips parted ever so slightly so that his tongue slipped in and touched mine. We were now deep kissing, our tongues like two fishes chasing after each other playfully. I felt my detachment dissipate like a fog in the early morning sun. My fingers were now entangled in his soft golden locks. The hair on his head was so unbelievably silky and soft; it was like running my hands through the hair of those dolls my parents used to buy me from their trips abroad.

His hands had slipped under my blouse and were caressing my bare back. I heard us breathing heavily. Brad moaned out my name. I also felt a name on my lips, but it wasn't his. I was saying Maxi's name soundlessly. Brad raised his head and looked at me. He seemed fascinated by my skin. He kept running his fingers up and down my face. His fingers traced my lips.

"You taste so sweet," he whispered.

"It is the gingersnap biscuits," I returned. It seemed funny and I began to giggle. He smiled back. For some reason, the laughter stabilised my senses, and I felt some degree of control return. I pushed against his shoulders.

"What is wrong?" Brad asked me. His eyes were dark with passion and when he lifted an arm to pull me back, I could see it trembling slightly. I bit my lower lip. My mouth felt so dry. Things had gotten out of control. I had been so sanguine that I could manage the situation long before it got to this stage.

"I am sorry…I can't," I said softly, feeling almost frightened. I had been a willing participant. I couldn't blame Brad for being upset. He sat up abruptly, reached for his glass of Gatorade and tossed it off in a gulp. He set the glass back on the tray. "Is it because of your boyfriend?"

"Partly," I answered, feeling like I was literally in the wrong position at that moment to preach about Christian principles.

"He's lucky." Brad said impassively.

I stole a glance at his face, wishing I knew him well enough to read his facial expression. "Are you upset with me?" the words were uttered in a despondent note, and popped out of my mouth before I was aware I had uttered them out aloud.

"Upset?" he looked at me genuinely perplexed. "Why should I be upset?"

"Because we… because I…" I stuttered, finding it hard to articulate that I thought he would be angry because we hadn't slept together. Brad gave me a stern look.

"Of course not! Look, Jibordi, I didn't come upstairs with you because I wanted us to have sex. I did want to spend more time with you. And then, I wondered how it would be to kiss you, so I did. I just got carried away."

I believed him. "I also got carried away. I'm sorry," I admitted. We smiled at each other. I could feel the magic begin to weave a spell over us once more.

"Do you have a girlfriend?" I asked.

"Not at the moment. I did have one, but Alice and I broke up over the Christmas break," he said. He didn't sound distraught over it.

"How old are you?" I asked him.

"I will be 26 next month. And you?"

"I am 27½ years…I cannot believe I kissed a younger man!" The horror stricken note in my voice set us both laughing once more and then looked at each other smiling. I knew we were still friends, and that our friendship had reached another level.

"It's late," Brad said with a look at his watch. He rose to his feet. "As you know, I will be driving to Atlanta tomorrow afternoon. My interview with CNN is Monday morning. I'll return Tuesday. Perhaps we can do something together this week?"

"Okay. I wish you all the best with your interview. I hope you have a safe trip," I said. "Good night, Jibordi," Brad said. He bent slightly and planted a kiss on my lips. Once more, I found myself kissing him back. For one long minute, he put his arms around me, pushing me back slightly so that my back was against the glass window in the door, and pressed himself against me. Then he let go of me abruptly.

"I have to be going," he muttered. I stepped aside and opened the door.

"Bye, Brad… thank you," I said.

He lifted a hand in a gesture and hurried to the stairway. I waited till I heard his footsteps thump down the stairs before I shut the door, locked and chained it. I leaned against the door for a moment and then went to the bathroom. For a long while, I stared at the face in the mirror. I didn't know who she was anymore.

****

I was up at dawn. As I normally did each morning, I instinctively reached for the black leather-bound Bible from under my pillow, but I didn't open it. I lay down thinking; replaying the events from the previous evening. I was unnerved by a number of things.

At 27 years, I thought I pretty much knew myself; strengths, weaknesses, and values. I liked to know the rules, even if I was going to break them, but now, my rules no longer seemed to apply. Just as I had accepted the fact that the sun rose in the east and set in the west, I had known for years that I loved Maxi. It would have been easier to accept if I had fallen in love with Brad, but I had not. It was such a bewildering new experience how with all our cultural differences we had been able to connect so quickly. I had focused so much on Brad's "whiteness" that our friendship and chemistry had taken me by surprise. I remembered Maxi's fervent voice some weeks before I left admonishing, "Don't change, DD, promise me you will never let America change you." Had I altered as Maxi had feared might happen? Or was it that America presented me with circumstances I had never gone through in Ghana that revealed facets of my character I had been unaware of?

I wished there was someone I could discuss my feelings with. It then hit me that my emotional and spiritual support system was very far away. I attended church in Gainesville but hadn't developed strong ties with any of the church members. Although people were generally friendly, I still felt a cultural divide. I didn't also feel that close enough to do so with the Ghanaians in Gainesville. It was rather ironical that the one person I actually felt close to in America was a non-Christian, younger, white American male. I thought of Maxi, back home, believing in me, trusting me, and thinking of me. I remembered our last conversation, when he surprised me with the information that he had prayed for Brad just because Brad had been kind to me when I needed help. That was what finally broke me down. I began to cry, and then, at last, I was able to pray.

Fortunately, it wasn't in the plan that I call Maxi that weekend. He knew me so well that he would have sensed that there was something wrong. The following Monday, I wrote him an email narrating everything up till the time Brad and I arrived at my apartment complex.

My experience with Brad had left me shaken, and my way of handling it was to push for progress in getting Maxi over to join me. Before ending my letter, I informed him that I had saved enough to pay for the GRE fees and the UF application. I asked about his plans regarding the GRE.

Maxi wrote back the following day. He wasn't ready for the GRE because he hadn't studied for it. There was so much going on at home: his mother hadn't been feeling very well lately, his older brother Alex was in Kumasi most of the time, and as their father's income still supported his two families, Maxi contributed a lot toward the household. Although teaching had its advantages, because he had the long vacation off, it didn't bring in much money, so he was thinking of finding another job or starting a business. If we chose the option to get married at home and return to America afterward, then the money would be best spent purchasing items for the traditional marriage ceremony.

"You need to find out the list of items that are required as it differs from tribe to tribe as well as among families," he wrote. "It may be a good idea to ask your parents."

I had no clue what my parents' response would be. Even though my father had said Maxi and I could marry if we were still so inclined after I had completed the programme, would the UG be willing to start planning the traditional ceremony this soon?

And what processes would mine entail, I wondered, being half Ga, half Ewe? I remembered a casual discussion I had with my grandma on traditional marriages, during one of my visits. She had explained that the traditional processes of asking for a woman's hand in marriage could differ depending on which part of the country one was from. "But generally," she said, "The process follows a common pattern. Just as when you are entering somebody's abode you knock on the door, you go knocking, seeking permission to enter." She went on, "While it differs slightly among ethnic groups, this first part of the marriage ceremony is the time when a delegation from the prospective groom's family formally visits the woman's paternal family and asks permission to be allowed to come and ask for the hand of the daughter."

"Ah, what a long process," I said.

Grandma ignored my whining and continued, "They go 'knocking' on the door with drinks and sometimes, money. The father's family accepts the gifts and arranges a time for the groom's party to return for an answer."

"Why do the family members of the father have to be involved? Can't the father alone negotiate, after all it is his daughter?"

"Dzigbordi, in our part of the world, marriage is never about the individuals alone; it is between families. Thus it has been and will continue to be," she said with self-satisfied finality.

"Where was I? Ah yes, during the interval between the two visits, the prospective bride's family investigates the other family to ensure their suitability. When the groom's family returns and the answer is positive, the bride's family presents the groom's family with a list of items (dowry, if you will), comprising clothing and other household items for the bride and token compensatory gifts for her parents and her brothers."

I had read about the dowry being brought by a woman to her husband in marriage in other societies. When I mentioned this, my grandma said, "Well, in our part of the world, it is taken that the man is the one who goes to marry the woman. And these things he provides are to show her people that he can take good care of their daughter."

"What about the gifts to her parents?" I asked.

"You know, no one can adequately compensate for the worth of any human being or for how much the parents have expended on their daughter. But the gifts are given in recognition and appreciation to the parents, for having nurtured their daughter to be a suitable wife to the prospective groom."

"And the gift for the brothers?"

"Oh that," Grandma laughed. "You know, the brothers make a show of bravado, that they have protected their sister from harm and predators so they deserve compensation."

I smiled at the recollection. The intricacies of cultures! I decided to postpone sharing my thoughts in the return email about approaching the UG until we spoke the following week.

Brad phoned Tuesday afternoon to let me know that CNN had made him a job offer. Although he wasn't graduating until the fall, they needed someone immediately and he would begin work on August 1. He wanted to know if I was interested in lunch the following day. I accepted his invitation for Bahn Thai, a popular Thai restaurant on 13th Street. Brad picked me up at noon the following day. Our reunion was quite relaxed and casual. On the way to the restaurant, he gave a summary of his interview with CNN. He would be working in the fairly new online news division, CNN.com. The pay he mentioned seemed very substantial, and the job came with benefits. We arrived at the restaurant about five minutes later. Soon after, an efficient looking waitress named Michelle settled us down in a booth, presented us with glasses of water and informed us that we were welcome to start the buffet. We sat for a while at the table chatting.

"When are you leaving Gainesville?" I asked.

"In about three weeks' time. Some friends are helping me look for an apartment. I'll return in two weeks and finalise accommodation and sign the lease. But it is not the last you are going to see of me; I will be home some weekends, and I will still come down for meetings with Tanaka and to write the examination in November. Before I forget, we have to arrange a time for you to come over to my apartment to select whatever furniture you want."

"Brad, please do let me pay you for the furniture. You will need to furnish your new apartment," I pleaded.

"No way Jose!" he retorted. I laughed. The first time I heard the expression, I thought the speaker was referring to a person named Jose, only to be told it meant "absolutely not!"

Brad was still speaking, "I have had that furniture all through graduate school. Some of them were passed down from friends. I am not accepting any money for it, so let's not spend the time arguing about it. I was going to dump them, anyway." He reached down and took my hand which was resting on top of the Formica table. "You're one stubborn lady, aren't you, Jibordi?"

I smiled, and then sighed. "Brad...I am sorry for what happened the other night," I began, looking down at our hands as I felt unable to look into his face.

"Why? What happened? Oh, you mean the kissing!" Brad's voice was slightly amused. I glanced around furtively to make sure there wasn't anyone close by.

"Yes," I returned simply. Brad was shaking with laughter.

"Perhaps, we should discuss this as we eat?" he suggested and let go of my hand. So we went to the steam tables. The names of the various dishes were displayed: spring rolls, coconut milk soup, pad thai, Thai curry chicken, spicy beef, plain rice, fried rice, cut watermelons and oranges... the food seemed endless. I selected the spicy beef with rice and added some hot spring rolls. Brad heaped his plate with pad thai, rice, spring rolls and curry beef. I took a tentative mouthful of the spicy beef. It tasted delicious, but not in the least spicy to me. I took in a second mouthful along with some rice.

"How is it?" Brad asked.

"Hmm... great!" I said, after hurriedly swallowing the mouthful.

"Tell me about the boyfriend," Brad asked me suddenly.

"Maxi?" I asked surprised.

"Yep. That's his name, isn't it?" he responded.

"What do you want to know?" I asked.

"Anything… how did you meet him? How long have you known him, etcetera…?"

"We met at the University of Ghana during our first year. We were in the same chemistry class. He was my lab partner…" I leaned back and continued speaking, giving him an edited version of my relationship with Maxi. He listened attentively as I spoke, as if what I was talking about was of supreme importance. The parts I left out had to do with my parents' feelings toward Maxi. I told Brad how active we were in church, how we worked together on projects, and so on. I added that Maxi was planning to come over for a Master's in Chemistry next year.

"It sounds quite serious," Brad observed thoughtfully. "Five years is such a long time. You must care a great deal for each other."

"Yes… it is… we do," I agreed, attempting to address both statements. I felt I had to include an addendum. "As Christians, Maxi and I believe in abstaining from premarital sex," my words were all tangled up. I took a deep breath and went on. "I am sorry, Brad. I shouldn't have… I mean last week was unfair to Maxi and to you. I don't know what happened. I don't usually do that. I am not like that… I mean…" My voice broke. Brad was looking at me curiously, as if he found me an enigma.

"Wow, Jibordi calm down," he said gently. It was when he tried to pull the fork out of my right hand that I realised that I had been clenching it as I spoke.

"I am sorry," I said inadequately. I relaxed my hand so that the fork fell in my plate and leaned back in the seat feeling overwhelmed. I had been thinking and praying over what had happened nonstop since Saturday morning. Our interaction today confirmed that on some level, there was a strong connection between us that made me especially susceptible where Brad was concerned. We communicated very easily, and there was also was his lethal combination of attractiveness, friendliness, open-mindedness, and evident interest in me.

"Don't sweat it, Jibordi. There was no harm done. I must say that I am very impressed. I have a lot of Christian friends and I haven't heard them agonise over premarital sex. Some of them even cohabit," he said thoughtfully, then went on in a lighter note. "Putting religious principles aside, I think I do appreciate how you feel about Maxi. I wouldn't like the idea of my girlfriend kissing another guy the way we did last week. Apart from your principles and guilt, we were very good together, weren't we? I mean, it wasn't all that bad?" his tone was as a matter of fact, but I detected an underlying amusement.

"It is not funny!" I protested.

"No, it is not," he agreed. "But, I must say, Jibordi, for someone who never engaged in such practices with her boyfriend, you sure are a good kisser!" his bright blue eyes twinkled at me. I couldn't help laughing back, and the atmosphere lightened considerably.

"You are incorrigible!" I exclaimed, and then added, "Besides, I never said I didn't kiss Maxi. We just haven't slept together. All my kisses and other related activities are reserved for him," I said trying to sound stern.

Just then, the waitress who had seated us down earlier came to the table with a water pitcher and refilled our glasses. We didn't speak while she was there. I could hear the chatter of other lunch customers, the clink of silverware against emptying plates, and the sound of loud voices in a foreign language from the kitchen area. The lunch crowd seemed to have increased in the last 45 minutes.

"Let's go for round two," Brad suggested, so we returned to the buffet. This time, I had some grilled pork and chicken satey with more rice, while Brad focused on more of the curry chicken and egg plant delight. I was already full, but the food tasted delicious.

"I have something to say," Brad began in a rather serious tone soon after we had started on the second round. I looked at him with a raised eyebrow.

"I promise that I will not breathe a word to your Maxi when he arrives, cross my heart. I also give you my word that as irresistible as I find you, I wouldn't kiss you again except perhaps on birthdays and holidays. The most I'd give you on normal occasions are brief hugs and pecks on the cheek," he solemnly declared with a hand on his chest.

"But a peck is a kiss!" I argued.

"Well, take it or leave it! Hugs and kisses are standard greetings in my family, as you should have noticed by now. We are a very demonstrative lot, you know. Now, tell me more about the indomitable Maxi!"

Now that I had been able to express my feelings, I felt more relaxed and enjoyed the rest of our time together. We had been sitting in the restaurant for over an hour and half. The lunch crowd had peaked and now people were trickling in. "Let's go for one more round," Brad suggested, "Perhaps some of the watermelon?"

I nodded eagerly. We returned to our table with our plates piled with chunks of watermelons and slices of oranges. The oranges were cool, seedless and very sweet. Eventually, my overloaded tummy refused to receive another morsel of food and I leaned back in my seat in defeat. Our waitress appeared carrying the check in a small basket.

"How was everything?" she asked us.

Simultaneously, Brad said "Great as usual!" and I "Delicious!"

Immediately she set down the basket, I grabbed it. "Give it to me!" said Brad, trying to wrestle it from me.

"No!" I exclaimed, pulling it back. We were both laughing. His hand was covering my hand that was holding onto part of the check. The waitress was also laughing with us.

"I will leave you two to sort it out," she said finally as she moved away from our table.

"Let go of it, Jibordi!" Brad said sternly.

"No... I will pay this time... to congratulate you on your job," I said spluttering with laughter.

"Well, at least, let me pay my share," he beseeched.

"No!" I said.

"Then the tip?" he pleaded with a very disarming smile.

"No!" I don't know what was funny about the situation, but we were both finding it amusing. From the corner of my eye, I noticed a group of people approach us on their way to the door, but I didn't look up.

"Okay… you win. I give up," Brad said, but still didn't let go. Neither did. A shadow fell over our table. I looked up from the basket I was clutching to see Danny Commey looking down at our joined hands with a smirk on his face.

Chapter Twenty-Five

"Dzigbordi?"

I was laden with a basket of clothes and a bottle of detergent bound for the laundry room. I looked up sharply to find Danny Commey hurrying toward me. I gave an inward groan. It was the day after the lunch at Bahn Thai. I had introduced him and Brad. Danny had nodded but hadn't said much to him. After he had left, Brad raised an eyebrow and asked who he was, and I explained that he was one of the Ghanaians I had met in Gainesville.

Danny reached my side and said, "I went to see Stella and was just about to pass your place when I saw you descend with your laundry,"

"Hmm…" I was glad that I had gotten out of my apartment before he had arrived.

"Doing laundry?"

Obviously! "Yes, I have to work in the office in about half an hour. I thought there would be enough time to get the clothes into the washer," I said.

He fell into step and we walked toward the laundry room which was in the same building as the office.

"So, Dzigbordi… Hmmm! Oh my! That was very interesting, eh?"

"What was interesting?" I asked obtusely.

"Well, well, well! You are one dark horse!"

"What are you talking about?" I demanded hotly.

"For months, you've being playing hard-to-get, going on and on and on about your boyfriend and faithfulness and values and not being the sort of person to mess around and so on. I actually came to believe you. Not knowing…" his voice trailed off and he stretched out his hands as if his message was pertinently clear.

"Not knowing what?" Feeling needled, I stopped walking and turned to glare at him.

"Not knowing, you were saving your pussy for a white boy!" he stated coarsely with a leer as his eyes wandered slowly down my body. The crudeness of his speech took my breath away.

"How dare you talk to me like that?" I asked in a low shaky voice. "My relationship with Brad is none of your business!"

His eyes widened and he stepped back instinctively. But he wasn't ready to give up yet.

"So, what do you think your dear boyfriend would say when he gets to know what you and your white friend are up to?" he asked, looking at me with a sneer. "I was there in the back corner booth all along, you know. I was with classmates working on a presentation over lunch. I saw you when you came in. I watched you holding hands together several times, talking, laughing and looking into each other's eyes…"

What a slimy creature he was! Several times he had asked me to come over for Scrabble or to go see a movie with him, but I had rejected his invitations because he hadn't included anyone else.

"You are just being dirty-minded and spiteful!" I could feel specks of saliva fly out of my mouth and onto his face. I saw him flinch. "Brad has been a gentleman, very kind, and respectful to me; more than you have been. My relationship with my boyfriend is none of your business, and I will appreciate it if you keep your nose out of my affairs in the future!" I spun away from him, and in my rage, forgot about the laundry basket which dropped from my hands. My clothes—shirts, panties, bras and other items flew across the patch of grass. I picked up the basket and rushed to gather them. Danny also hurried forth and began helping to pick up items. I cringed inwardly when I saw him handle the pair of big comfortable cotton panties I liked wearing while having my period, as well as a pair of my more fashionable lacy purple underwear. He hastened over and dropped the handful of items in the basket.

"Come on, Dzigbordi," he began contritely. "It was only a joke. Why are you so upset?"

I said nothing.

"I thought we were friends. I was just teasing you because I saw you with that guy and you looked like you were very…. eh… comfortable with him. I was surprised because I wasn't aware that you socialised outside the Ghanaian circle," he said, looking sincerely into my eyes.

Ha! That was an old trick that used to take me in; people would make the most horrible of statements, and when you reacted negatively, they would say it was a joke. It was as if once they labelled their utterances a "joke", it excused all forms of obnoxious behaviours.

"I am sorry," he said, looking at me helplessly.

"Humph!" I resumed my walk to the laundry room.

"Are we cool?" he asked anxiously.

No, we aren't "cool". I wanted to talk to him about his attitude, but frankly, I didn't have the energy.

"Yes," I said shortly. "I have to hurry and start the laundry so that I won't be late for my shift."

"Okay. Talk to you later, okay?"

"Yeah, sure," I returned.   Unfortunately, that was another incident I would have to keep from telling Maxi about. Maxi could describe my professors and outline my daily routine and class schedule for each day of the week. He knew the names of all the Ghanaians I interacted with, as well as their peculiar characteristics. Yet there were a few key things that I was keeping from him, and the Brad situation was one of them. As close as Maxi and I were, holding some of this information in reserve did create a barrier in our relationship, even if I was the only one who could feel it. I couldn't help but ask myself whether Maxi was going through his own struggles.

*****

The summer seemed to race by very fast. I celebrated America's Independence Day for the first time. The day before Independence Day, the Richters and Odonkors were going to view the Gainesville annual firework show from Flavet Field at UF, where people from the city gathered annually to celebrate Independence Day. The place was packed, and people brought along chairs, blankets, and food. When darkness fell around

9:30p.m., the main attraction began; it lasted for about 20 minutes. The Gainesville fireworks were spectacular! I watched the show entranced, oohing and aahing along with the children. Then on July 4, in the afternoon, I joined the Goldsteins for my first barbecue party. It was held outdoors in their courtyard and the place was swarming with relatives and friends who were hugging, laughing, and shouting across the yard to each other. Brad picked me up and dropped me off, but did not stay. The festivities continued through the evening when the Ghanaian community in Gainesville had a party in the Diamond Village Common Room.

The party was supposed to have begun at 7:00p.m., but people started trickling in after 8:00p.m. Almost the entire Ghanaian community turned up. There were a few other Africans and Americans present as well. Most people brought along dishes, savouries or drinks. By 9:00p.m., the place was jamming with music—soca music, Ghanaian highlife, music from the eighties onward. I loved it! I hadn't danced in months and the rhythm warmed my blood and feet.

A week before Brad left for Atlanta, he took me to his apartment so I could select the furniture I needed. I got a bookcase, a lamp, a bedside drawer, a relatively clean mattress which came along with a frame and headrest, an armchair and a table. I also took an entertainment center even though I wasn't sure I was ever going to buy a television set. Brad's roommate, Conrad, who had a truck, was generous enough to help us cart the things to Diamond Village, and carry them upstairs. After consulting with Brad, I gave Conrad $40 for his labor and transportation. Brad stayed behind and helped me arrange the furniture. He stayed for about an hour later and we sipped lemonade, played UNO and talked. It was so easy to converse with Brad and we segued seamlessly from one topic to the next. I felt the magic creeping up upon us once more. Although his moving away would make my life simpler, a part of me wished he was still going to be in Gainesville.

"I am going to keep my promise not to kiss you," Brad said with a twinkle in his eye when it was time for us to part.

"Thank you, kind sir," I said pertly.

"Unless you have changed your mind?" he asked, smiling at me as we stood by the door leading outside.

"Nope!" I retorted. Brad laughed. He kept his word and gave me a hug and a deep kiss on either cheek.

"Promise you will keep in touch with me and with my parents. Mom says she is going to invite you to Friday dinner and some other events. Don't be a stranger," Brad said.

"No, I won't, I promise," I said. "I will be in touch by phone and email. I can't wait to hear all about your job at CNN!"

"And you also have a standing invitation to visit anytime you are in the Atlanta area," Brad added.

"Sure, thank you," I said, and then he left.

****

Now, my apartment was furnished, albeit with mismatched old furniture, but that was good enough for me. Saving money was paramount. I was still trying to find more ways of making money. The babysitting brought in a steady income. As the number of notes increased in the "savings jar" I opened a bank account with the Campus Credit Union. I had been informed about the importance of building up credit, so I used some of that money to get a secured credit card with a limit of $500.

Soon, I was registering for the fall semester. It also meant another budget for the UG. I didn't tell them I was working and I felt guilty about that. Although they would like me to get an assistantship to help with the tuition, they wouldn't approve of me spending all my spare time babysitting instead of studying.

Maxi and I had our discussion about the future but did not come to any consensus. I insisted he apply to UF and take the GRE. The examination results were valid for five years, and so it would not be a waste. He completed the UF application and mailed it to me and I submitted it with the fee. I also sent him money to register for the GRE, but he said he wasn't ready, and there was a note of finality in his voice that kept me from pressing on with the subject. I wanted to ask him to make sure he put that money aside for the exam, even if he was not yet ready to take it at that point in time, but something warned me not to be so blunt, so I held back.

At first, Maxi was upset with me because I refused to ask the UG for the list of items needed for my dowry. He asked that we undertake a one-week prayer and fasting so that the chains of uncertainty and despair would be broken and I would get the needed courage to approach the UG. We fasted from 6 a.m. to 6 p.m., drinking only water, for a week. It was a tough process, but I did my best to stick to it, and to find time to pray in the library during my spare time. Even though the purpose of these sessions was to pray about discussing our marriage plans with the UG, I found myself praying for strength for both of us to survive this long-distance relationship so that we would be truthful with each other and be as close as we used to be when I was in Ghana. I also prayed about Brad and asked forgiveness for how I had acted with him the first night he came up to my apartment.

After the week's activity was over, Maxi and I found that the prayer sessions had not brought us to any consensus, we were still polarised. I still felt convinced that it was not the right time to approach the UG, while Maxi felt we should take the bull by the horns and present our plan of action. He asked if he could write my father a letter or arrange a meeting with him, and I gave an emphatic "NO!" I wondered how he could even think of the possibility of writing Papa another letter or asking him for a meeting. Had he forgotten the repercussions of the first letter he had written? Why did Maxi think that he could force Papa into a decision through his missives?

"I wish you would have more faith in the power of God," Maxi said sadly during our conversation the day after the fast had ended.

"I have faith in the power of God," I answered, "But I also believe that timing is important. Faith does not mean that we should plough blindly into everything."

"We will never know till we try, would we?" he said rather sadly. I believed the problem was that we both had different fixes to our situation. I felt that Maxi coming over to school would solve a lot of our problems; however the plan that had seemed simple and straightforward at home had now changed because he really did not want to come to America. On the other hand, he wanted a clear indication that my parents would accept our marrying and soon, and that meant that he expected me to make the necessary moves to elicit that response.

In the end, we agreed that saving money was the priority and that in my final year, I would approach my parents with the idea of marriage and that perhaps the preliminary process of "knocking" could be done just before I graduated. If Maxi was coming over next fall, we would do the traditional ceremony before he came to join me.

****

A lot was happening in Ghana. Mawuli and Gifty were expecting the baby early October. Lia and Nii Q were getting married on November 22. JD, Frannie, and Mickey were graduating from medical school that year and were talking about going abroad to train within the next few years. Frannie was going to Britain for her residency because she was a British citizen. JD and Mickey were applying to schools in the US.

I knew that Shands Hospital was one of Mickey's choices and hoped it would work out. JD's choices did not include Gainesville, but once she was in the US, it would be easy for us to arrange visits to each other. I missed my best friend so much, and writing letters and emails was not the same as talking face to face with her. I also hadn't told her about Brad. A part of me was afraid that she would express disappointment in me.

It was a good thing that Brad had finally moved to Atlanta. I don't know whether I would have been able to resist his mix of chemistry and caring. Brad soon settled down in his new environment and before long, had made a lot of friends. Even then, he found time to check on me every other week and ask how I was doing in school. His mother would sometimes invite me to dinner on Friday and would arrange for me to be picked up and dropped off. As time went on, I became slightly more comfortable with Stallone the dog and would no longer scream anytime he came close to me. It even got to the stage where I could stroke his fur for a few seconds and have him give me a couple of licks (though I would shower immediately I returned home if that happened).

The Benjamins also kept in constant contact with me, and once a month, I would go over to Tallahassee and spend the weekend with them. I now considered them family. I was comfortable enough to joke with Uncle Pip. I also had enough knowledge about the rivalry between the football teams to initiate some of the joshing. It was not the end of the world if Auntie Esther caught me adding additional salt or sugar to my food; she would give her usual lecture about the importance of moderating salt and sugar in one's diet, but it was not something to stress over.

Although I kept busy and I had friends and family around, there were days I felt unsettled. Those were the days I would spend several hours lost in a grey cloud. It was a feeling of acute loneliness even in the midst of company. Sometimes such feelings could be so extreme that they would leave me with a feeling of emptiness and yearning that could linger for days. I prayed about it, but it never completely went away.

Because I did not feel I could discuss how I felt with anyone, I found myself reading the Bible and spending more time in prayer than I had done since I left home. I prayed and prayed about the Brad situation until I felt I could put it behind me and move on. I bought a radio and tape combo system from Wal-Mart to play my gospel cassette tapes and listen to the radio. I discovered BNN, a conservative Christian radio station. What I enjoyed most was their radio dramas, especially Adventure in Odyssey, which was broadcast late afternoon. I always made sure I was at home to catch it whenever I could. I attended Sunday school and my area's cell meetings and got to know more of the church members.

Things improved between Maxi and I, especially after I had let go of my guilt where Brad was concerned. Maxi was impressed with my immersion in church and the Bible, and I always had something new to share with him.

Most importantly, I began questioning my own spiritual growth in the light of the Bible studies we were doing. We had started a discussion on the topic of lust— lust of the eye, lust of the flesh etc. One day as I took my Bible to have my quiet time, I decided to use one of the passages we were yet to treat, Matthew 5: 27-30. I read the passage, and as I proceeded to meditate on it, I remembered Brad saying some of his Christian friends were cohabiting. Now that is fornication, which the Bible frowns upon as much as adultery. The verse 28 caught my attention, "But I say unto you, that whosoever looks on a woman to lust after her has committed adultery with her already in his heart…" Whoa! Wasn't I being self-righteous here? If Maxi and I believed that fornication was wrong, what about the heavy petting, what about the phone sex? Is that not lust? I felt a sense of revulsion in my inner being. Who were we deceiving? Come to think of it, how Brad must have laughed silently at my vehement denial. He obviously did not want to judge me so he did kept quiet. Oh God! Who had we been deceiving all this while? I couldn't continue with the meditation but fell on my knees, weeping my heart out, and crying unto God for forgiveness— for myself and for Maxi. I resolved that we had to put a stop to it. I knew it was not going to be easy but it had to be done.

"It seems so long until we can be together," Maxi said during our Sunday chat.

"Yeah, I know… time seems to go slowly, but in some respects, it is moving so fast," I said.

"I cannot wait till I can hold you in my arms again DD," he said.

"Eh… Maxi, I need to tell you something…"

"What is wrong, DD?" he asked in a breathless voice.

I proceeded to tell him the epiphany I had had.

He was quiet for a long time, then he said, "DD, I don't know what to say. Ermm… it is something to think about. I promise you I will take a look at the scripture and also go to the Lord in prayer and let you know the outcome."

When we ended the chat I felt so relieved. I prayed we set things right.

I didn't bring up the subject with Maxi for the next two

weeks, wishing to give him some space as he did his own research. When he still hadn't said or written anything on the subject, I brought it up once more.

"What did you decide about the phone sex issue?" I asked him one Sunday just as we were rounding up our conversation.

"I don't know, DD. Honestly, I think you are taking those scriptures a little too literally. I am not disagreeing with you per se, but I think it warrants additional analysis," he said.

"What additional analysis?" I patiently asked. I was aware that Maxi enjoyed our "romantic" sessions; our time apart was very hard on him, and it made him feel connected, so I was prepared to have a drawn out discussion before he came to the same conclusion I had.

"Matthew 5:28 is about lust; and you know how easy it is for a man to look at a beautiful woman and think of her in a sexual way? That is the sort of thing the verse is referring to. You know that you do not have to be in love with someone to feel lust toward that person. Our situation is different; we love each other and are wholly committed. We plan to get married as soon as we can. Our attraction toward each other is an attribute of that love. Is it wrong to express that feeling we have, as long as we do not actually act on it?" Maxi's tone was almost imploring.

He sounded so convincing that I was almost swayed by his "analysis." Was I being unfair to Maxi? Would refraining from our romantic sessions make us feel more disconnected because of our long-distance relationship? I hesitated, remembering how bad I sometimes felt after one of those sessions.

"DD? Are you there?" Maxi's voice interrupted my reverie.

"Yes, I am."

"What are you thinking?" he asked.

"You are making sense, but I am still not convinced," I blurted out.

"Hmm…" he said noncommittally.

"Maxi, you may be right about it, but I do not feel comfortable after these sessions. Is it alright with you if we take a break from them for a while? At least, hold off till I feel otherwise?" The silent stretched between us for a long minute.

"Sure… I understand," he finally said.

"Are you upset?" I tentatively asked. I wasn't going to go back on my decision, but preferred it if Maxi was on board with me.

Maxi's response was instant. "Of course not! I am disappointed, but I also know that it is important that we are on the same page where this issue is concerned. I love you, DD, regardless of whatever the final decision we take. So, no more phone sex unless something changes, and hopefully, before long, we will be married, and we can have phone sex all day and come home at night and enact all our fantasies!"

"Hmm, we can't spend all day having phone sex instead of working!" I returned, pleased that Maxi was prepared to go along with my decision even if he didn't quite feel the same.

"Who says we cannot multitask?" he chuckled, with that wicked note in his voice that usually preceded one of our sessions. He must have realised what was happening, because he changed the topic abruptly and ended the conversation soon afterwards.

The decision allowed us to focus more on our relationship as a whole, rather than just the physical aspect. As the weeks went by, we continued to write and talk and share, and eventually became as close as we had been before I left home. Brad had been an adventure, a novelty, but Maxi knew me inside out. We were from the same culture, and we had shared experiences—good and bad. He was the one I imagined spending the rest of my life with. I had a feeling all would work out as planned; Maxi would join me in America and we would get married, start our lives here and end up back home. If for some reason he was not able to make it, I would initiate discussions with my parents in my final year of study and set the ball rolling.

Maxi now channelled the time we used to engage in phone sex to discussing plans about our future; the wedding, careers, children and so on. His excitement about the future was rather infectious, and made me feel better about our relationship than I had in a long time. I had dwelled on the hurdles we had to overcome with my parents for so long without focusing much on the rewards of following through. Maxi reminded me that if he seemed to be overdoing it at times, it was because he was a doer and believed in taking action, while I had a more cautious approach.

"You are right, Maxi," I said, after one of numerous discussions of our rosy future together. "There is a lot to look forward to. Thank you so much for reminding me of that. I want you to know that I love you so much, and I am looking forward to the wedding night and beyond," I recklessly added with so much fervour that he laughed.

"DD, I refuse to dwell any more on the wedding night and beyond, in this phone call. I am sure you are going feel the pinch when you receive your next phone bill," he cautioned.

"Who cares?" I said cheekily.

"Good night, DD. I love you."

"Night, Maxi. Ditto!"

That night, it took me quite a while to fall asleep. I kept replaying my conversation with Maxi. I was entering my third semester of study, and after that, my first year in America would come to a close. It had been a long first year (and counting). I thought of the loneliness and heartsickness of the first few months in the country, my fight with Maxi over Charity and Daniel Commey, and my friendship with Brad. A lot had happened, both good and bad, but I had learned a great deal about myself; I had grown up and was now in a stronger place both spiritually and with Maxi, than I had ever been. I did not know what would happen over the next year, but what I did know was that whatever happened, Maxi and I would go through it together.

Excerpt from the Second Book...

"I don't want to go home... not yet. I don't want to go home... not yet." The litany played over and over in my mind as I scanned through my mail. Today's offering was a JC Penney coupon for a sale the coming weekend, a utility bill, and an invitation to apply to American Express for a credit card with a limit up to $50,000.

No letters from organisations. Fifty-two job applications in six months and all I had to show for it were twenty letters acknowledging receipt of my applications, four rejections, two phone interviews, and one on-site interview. Every day, before I fully woke up, I was conscious of a feeling of dread, my stomach clenching and a hot tightness in my throat. The uncertainty of my future was driving me mad.

The US economy was bad, and each day there was more ghastly news. People in seemingly secure jobs were being laid off every day, and there were hiring freezes across the country. This was definitely not the time to be on the job market; especially for someone who needed additional commitment from an employer to process a work visa so that I could remain in the US legally.

I lay down on the couch and began channel surfing in an attempt to escape my thoughts. I settled on *Casablanca* on Turner Classic Movies. I could quote all the lines, but I could never resist watching parts of it whenever it was shown on TV. After the movie ended, I noticed I had not checked my phone for messages since afternoon. That evening, my best friends, JD Tamakloe and Celia Yu and I spent time together at the Golden Corral and we had stuffed ourselves till we could eat no more. The occasion had been full of laughter and the swapping of stories, and for a few hours, I had been able to put my anxieties in the background. We had a rule that we would turn off our cell phones or put them on "silent" or "vibrate" whenever we had one of our girls' night outs. I extracted the phone from my bag, turned up the volume and started scanning the call history. I had four missed calls and one voicemail notification; three "unknown" and the fourth from my cousin Gladys in Canada. I dialed my password as I walked into the kitchen. I placed the phone to my ear and bent my head to the left so that it was being supported by my shoulder and cheek. I started putting away dishes that I had left to drain on the rack.

"Hi Dzigbordi!" said my cousin Gladys, thrilled. I could hear her son Ezekiel babbling away in the background. "No! Stop that! Zeke!" she shouted. "Oh sorry, DziDzi, Zeke is on the rampage…I haven't heard from you since you returned from your conference. Just calling to find out how you are doing. How did the presentation go? Did they get your name right this time? Give me a call this weekend and we'll catch up. Can you believe the weather's already cold over here? You Floridians are so lucky! Anyway, call me! Love ya!"

I laughed. JD was my oldest friend but Gladys was both friend and family. I made a mental note to buy a phone card and return her call the next morning.

"To delete, press '7', to save, press '9'…" the automated voice prompted. I pressed '7'. "Next message… received at 7:59 p.m.…" That was the unknown number. It was perhaps my mother calling to check on me; the calls from Ghana sometimes showed up as unknown. But it wasn't my mother.

"Hi Dzigbordi!" said a voice I hadn't heard in years. "This is Maxwell Owusu. I am calling to let you know that I will be coming to the States next weekend. I will be living in Boston for nine months. Please call me back. I hope we can meet during my stay. I really need to talk to you. Dzigbordi, it is very, very important, and it will be better if we talk in person. Goodbye and God bless."

I stood in the kitchen, frozen, unable to move. My heart thumped, and it felt like a heavy pebble had dropped to the pit of my stomach. I started to straighten my head. The phone shifted out of my grasp, but I was able to grab it back in the nick of time.

"To delete, press '7', to save, press '9', to repeat this message, press '4'… for more options, press '0'," the automated voice said, uncaring of my emotional discomfort. I pressed '4' and listened to Maxi's voice again… and again. Maxi, whom I hadn't seen or spoken to for several years. Maxi, the man I had planned to marry and live with forever. Why did he need to speak with me now? What did we have left to say to each other? We had said everything that needed to be said, and more.

I saved his message, and then pressed "2" on my speed dial, and then "TALK". It went straight to voicemail.

"JD, call me when you get this message. It is very important!" I said. My voice sounded rather sharp. I flipped the cell phone shut. I abandoned the dishes and returned to the sitting room. I needed someone I could talk to about this, and apart from JD, the only other person was Gladys. However, the call to Gladys also went to voicemail.

I sat on the couch and tried to focus on a storybook I had started the day before, but it was useless; my mind was thousands of miles away, my thoughts more than a decade back, into another millennium and another world. I returned to a time when I was much younger and idealistic, when I believed in happily ever after; a period when I thought I knew all there was to know about life and about myself.

By midnight, neither Gladys nor JD had returned my call. At one o'clock, I turned off all the lights and huddled under a comforter on the couch in the sitting room, instead of sleeping in the bedroom. I watched TV until the drone of voices and music sounded far away; I transitioned into dreamland. I travelled all the way back to a land and a time when I was so innocent and so much in love; a time when I spent several hours out of my day dreaming about a young man named Maxwell Kofi Owusu. We had come a long, long way since then. What on earth had gone so wrong between us?

Printed in the United States
By Bookmasters